Praise for Book One

Dawn of Fire: Avenging Son

by Guy Haley

'The beginning of an essential new epic: heroic, cataclysmic and vast in scope. Guy has delivered exactly what 40K readers crave, and lit the fuse on the Dark Millennium. This far future's about to detonate...'

Dan Abnett, author of Horus Rising

'With all the thunderous scope of The Horus Heresy, a magnificent new saga begins.'

Peter McLean, author of Priest of Bones

'A perfect blending of themes – characters that are raw, real and wonderfully human, set against a backdrop of battle and mythology'.

Danie Ware, author of Ecko Rising

THE MARTYR'S TOMB

A DAWN OF FIRE NOVEL

THE MARTYR'S TOMB

A DAWN OF FIRE NOVEL

MARC COLLINS

BLACK LIBRARY

A BLACK LIBRARY PUBLICATION

First published in 2023.
This edition published in Great Britain in 2023 by
Black Library, Games Workshop Ltd., Willow Road,
Nottingham, NG7 2WS, UK.

Represented by: Games Workshop Limited – Irish branch,
Unit 3, Lower Liffey Street, Dublin 1,
D01 K199, Ireland.

10 9 8 7 6 5 4 3 2 1

Produced by Games Workshop in Nottingham.
Cover illustration by Johan Grenier.

See Black Library on the internet at

blacklibrary.com

Find out more about Games Workshop
and the worlds of Warhammer at

games-workshop.com

Printed and bound in the UK.

---

*Dedicated to the memory of Julie Langdale and Ciaran
John Gregor Reid. Forever in our thoughts and hearts.*

For more than a hundred centuries the Emperor has sat immobile on the Golden Throne of Earth. He is the Master of Mankind. By the might of His inexhaustible armies a million worlds stand against the dark.

Yet, He is a rotting carcass, the Carrion Lord of the Imperium held in life by marvels from the Dark Age of Technology and the thousand souls sacrificed each day so that His may continue to burn.

To be a man in such times is to be one amongst untold billions. It is to live in the cruellest and most bloody regime imaginable. It is to suffer an eternity of carnage and slaughter. It is to have cries of anguish and sorrow drowned by the thirsting laughter of dark gods.

This is a dark and terrible era where you will find little comfort or hope. Forget the power of technology and science. Forget the promise of progress and advancement. Forget any notion of common humanity or compassion.

There is no peace amongst the stars, for in the grim darkness of the far future,
there is only war.

DRAMATIS PERSONAE

OF TERRA

Roboute Guilliman	The Avenging Son, Lord Regent of the Imperium
Morvenn Vahl	Abbess Sanctorum of the Adepta Sororitas, High Lord of Terra

ORDER OF OUR MARTYRED LADY

Irinya Sarael	Canoness
Josefine	Battle Sister
Agata	Battle Sister
Sybele	Battle Sister
Beatrice	Battle Sister
Oxanna	Battle Sister
Selene	Battle Sister
Eloise	Sister Superior, Conductor of the Artillery Choir
Angharad	Novitiate

BLACK TEMPLARS

Gaheris	The Emperor's Champion
Urtrix	Marshal
Barisan	Sword Brother, Squad Fidelitas
Aneirin	Neophyte, Squad Fidelitas
Arvin	Initiate, Squad Fidelitas
Fenek	Initiate, Squad Fidelitas
Partus	Initiate, Squad Fidelitas
Havdan	Initiate, Squad Fidelitas
Tavric	Sword Brother
Micael	Initiate
Ranulf	Initiate
Eralicus	Neophyte

| Hargus | Techmarine |
| Toron | Venerable Dreadnought |

HOUSE HELVINTR AND TASK FORCE SATURNINE

Katla Helvintr	Jarl Paramount of House Helvintr, captain of the *Wyrmslayer Queen*
Tyra	Huscarl
Calder	Huscarl
Bodil	Gothi
Yazran	Magos astrocartographic
Ana	Master of Auspex
Arkadys Solvarg	Navigator
Augustus	Custodian
Astrid Helvintr	Daughter and heir to Katla, lost beyond the Rift

VELUAN HOPLITES, THE SHRINESWORN

Maxim Draszen	Colonel
Yitrov	Colonel
Joachim	Trooper

LEGIO ARCONIS

Melpomene	Princeps,
Takravasian	Warlord Titan *Vengeance of Sareme*
Valtin	Moderatus
Tovrel	Sensorus
Skell	Steersman
Bertolt	Princeps, Warhound Titan *Dune Hound*
Lares	Princeps, Warhound Titan *Nightbeast*

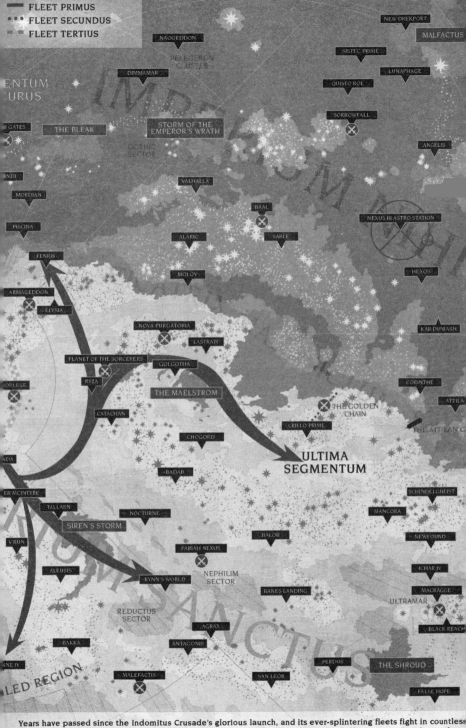

Years have passed since the Indomitus Crusade's glorious launch, and its ever-splintering fleets fight in countless warzones across the galaxy. No cartograph, even this one, should be considered all-encompassing due to the immeasurable scale and fluidity of the crusade as it battles to save the Imperium of Man from total annihilation.

Prologue

He had long since realised that a journey of a thousand miles, or of ten thousand years, began with a single trudging step.

The lesson had been hard taught but it remained as true now as it was at the beginning. One foot in front of the other. Across battlefields beyond count, through wars whose number and name had become dull smears in the memory. Ever forward on the pilgrims' path, until the bitter end when Death finally claimed him. He relished the inevitability of the moment. That time and place when all would be resolved; for was Grandfather Death not also Greatfather Time? The galaxy's myriad mythologies all danced to the same tune. Behind the masks of divinities, of mortality, Assassin orders, death cults, they were all of them striving towards the same godhead. Serving the same master.

There was an irony there, the Pilgrim was certain. Imperial scholars and xenos philosophers could debate it until their own time ran short. Minds struggling to accept it; to simply chew the gristly fodder they had been offered and *accept*. He had accepted his place in the great confusion of life and death – though his role had changed many times. Now he knew his path and his duty.

It had led him here.

The Pilgrim crested the low rise of what had once been an ornamental garden and passed beneath the statues of saints who hid their faces as though in shame. A ripple of dulled pleasure passed through him as he noticed them. Perhaps he would preserve them, bring them up to the ship. Add them to his galleries. He dismissed the thought. It could wait.

The bombing of the southern continent had cast up so much debris that it had begun to fall as a gentle ashen snow. Everything was slowly being shrouded in a grey pall – the remnants of planetary populations, atomised macro-masonry, the billionsfold cremation of the living and the dead. The great mausoleums of heroes and martyrs had not even had time to truly burn. Precision strikes had shattered them utterly on the molecular level and reduced them to this. The ashes of memory. He could taste them on his tongue, through failing helm respirators, and he found it good.

He looked down across the waste that he had made.

Tandria had been a beautiful world, once. Even he could appreciate that. There was no point in idle, empty hatred for what the Imperium built. Not without an appreciation of what it meant and reverence for what it had been. What land had existed between the shrine cities had been pleasant and arable. A paradise, slowly strangled by the incursion of hollow artifice. He shook his head. He heard the bones of his spine creak and realign, and he removed his helmet.

Even in true-life, before the gifts of the god had made him as he was, he had not been an icon of beauty. Never would his rough features have graced a remembrancer's canvas in the way of one of Fulgrim's breed, or the propaganda picts as a scion of Guilliman might have. No... He had ever been an ugly but functional weapon.

Weapons such as he were made to do this. To end worlds and break civilisations. To drown paradise, brick by brick, beneath the same utilitarian craftsmanship and then to daub those works with the icons of compliance and rule. Of slavish devotion to a dead ideal.

'They called it Unity,' he breathed, from between rotten teeth, 'and we believed them at their word.' Pale lips drew back into a sneer, gums black with long-clotted blood. Air hissed up from atrophied lungs with a sepulchral sigh and portions of his armour wheezed in sympathy – acting with systems grown, evolved and cultivated rather than engineered. He was massive. Vaster than he had been in true-life, and yet so many of the organs that had made him what he had been – that had made him Astartes – had withered on the vine.

False gifts... Those who still considered themselves Unbroken called them false gifts. Carved out from the trickery of the Pretender Upon Terra. The Pilgrim turned to once again regard the statues and their hidden faces. They loomed over him from their plinths, but in every way that mattered he dwarfed them. He reached out and drummed his fingers against the base of one, almost without being aware of it. Seven taps of his fingers and then he moved on to the next. Presenting it like an offering.

'I reject you. Renounce and denounce you. I have exceeded your grasp. Once, twice, three and sixfold. These are the wounds I make against you. The cuts in the skin. The eyes plucked out. I shall break and blind you, one and all.'

'My lord?' a voice simpered from behind him.

He ignored it. It was as rough as his, another one of his brothers come to chastise him for his languid pace. He did not turn, even when it came again.

'My lord Tuul?'

Grommulus Tuul turned with a graceless motion and stared down at his compatriot. The warrior was a shrunken thing by comparison, by no means unblessed but merely differently gifted, and it brought a smile to Grommulus' lips to note the disparity. The Pilgrim's own armour was ancient Terminator plate overgrown like rotten coral or dead bone. Fungal growths and slicks of wet gangrene had worked their way through the armour with a terrible inevitability, and parts of it were pockmarked with strange gaps – honeycombed like an insect's hive. Things moved eyelessly in those dark crevices.

'You disturb my meditations, brother.' Tuul intoned the words carefully as he watched the world's ongoing collapse. 'Our task nearly done, and you disturb me...'

'Forgive me. I merely...' The voice trailed off, uncertain of how to proceed. 'It is not yet complete. Not yet sacred. I only wish us to move swiftly.'

'Of course you do, brother.' Tuul chuckled dryly and scooped up his axe from where it had rested against a nearby votive bench. The mechanisms of it clicked and chittered, as had become their custom, in the manner of an insect's mandibles. It was a hungry thing, from the edges of its teeth to the deepest recesses of its gears. It had grown with him – turned strange and twisted in the long sojourn from the defeat at Terra. It had been *consecrated*, just as he had, in the sight of the god. 'Fear not. Matters proceed apace.' He turned, testing the weapon's weight in his gauntleted hands, and then swung it round in a perfect arc. Stone hissed against stone and half of one of the graven saints slid away, bleeding dust. 'They have their crusade, brother, and we have ours. We simply have the advantage of serving a more honest master.'

He took one last deep breath and drank in the dying world.

'Ready our ships. Send word to the cult echelons. Soon our Sevenfold children shall exalt in the presence of their betters, and the final sanction can begin at last.'

ACT ONE

SOULS OF STONE

Chapter One

THE HANGING GARDENS BURN

WAY OF SIGISMUND

HEART OF FAITH

The Hanging Gardens burned.

The fires had swept the shrine city's outer precincts ahead of the cult advance, lit in fits of pique and petulant deviance as befitted unruly children. Irinya Sarael gazed out across the once verdant gardens and felt the bitter pangs of loss – old and new. Her grip tightened upon her bolter as the burning blossoms spiced the air with strange smoke. She could smell it even through the seals and filters of her helm – a cloying too-sweet stench clawed its way up behind the smoke, speaking of new rot and atrocity.

'With me!' she barked over the vox, and her Sisters moved to answer. Across the defensive line hewn through the Hanging Gardens, the Order of Our Martyred Lady flowed into place, like shadows from the smoke. Battle Sisters wore their armour with silent pride, while alongside them fought the lightly armoured novitiates of the Order. Once they might have tended these gardens in placid repose, but now they were called to action.

Irinya looked about her, bolter raised as she advanced. Josefine was with her, muttering quiet prayers as they marched down the marble sweep of a stairway. Down and onto the sodden earth, soaked with the blood of countless souls. Loyalists and traitors. Visionaries and madmen. It had been kept sacred and it had been profaned, day after day, for the span of months. The months of the siege. She gritted her teeth inside the confines of her helm. The stench of rot was stronger now, just as it was with every incursion.

'By the glory of the Throne we shall hold, and by the light of His will we shall endure!' she bellowed. Banners snapped with the sudden rush of wind, flapping on the archways to the rear of the Sisters, as the bodies shook and swayed between the great crimson spills of fabric.

The Hanging Gardens were not named idly.

Once, in happier times, the faithless and heretical would have been hanged from the white marble walls – their throats crushed slowly by chains or strong hempen ropes – so that their last sights would be of the mortal paradise beyond. They would die in shame, with only the fleeting glimpse of beauty to haunt them to their torments, denied forever the grace of the God-Emperor's light.

Once it had felt just. Now, though, so many hooks hung empty and the bodies that lingered were crow-eaten things of dry flesh and dusty bones. The war had stolen everything that the crusade had made righteous.

The instruments of that despoliation stalked through the smog and murk, wrapped in sackcloth and stolen flak armour. She knew they were not the architects of the ruin that had befallen them, not in truth. Puppets. Deluded fools who had traded lives of sanctity for the hollow horror of obedience to dark gods. The flesh of the enemy was rimed with dried pus and etched with ritual scars. They had carved weeping eyes into their skin, over and over again. Barbed with eight points or weeping seven tears – it mattered not, only that they wore their infamy proudly.

'Disgusting,' Josefine intoned. Irinya could hear the angry tremor in her voice. She wanted nothing more than to burn them from the earth. Though her Sister was helmed, Irinya knew that her pale features would be twisted into a glare behind its lenses. If she could, Josefine would have smote the enemy with a look alone.

It was hard to disagree with her. The enemy stank, revelling as they did in their own filth. They wore soiled bandages, not to staunch their wounds, but to cultivate the corruption of their flesh and souls. These were the Children of the Sevenfold Revelation, who had sprung up like a contagion across the seven sacred worlds of the Golden Chain.

And who now came for the last of those worlds.

'Not here,' she whispered. 'Not this world. Not her world.'

Behind the Sisters the wall guns had begun their thunderous refrain, staining the ashen skies with trails of fire. In response the enemy's crude artillery returned fire, alongside rains of plague-ridden corpses hurled by makeshift trebuchets. Flesh spattered wetly as it landed, casting up caustic showers of acidic blood and bile. Everything they did was an atrocity.

'They are near enough now, surely.' Agata spoke from Irinya's left. The Sister hefted her flamer and patted it appreciatively, savouring the weight of the sacred weapon. It was called Last Light and Agata was not the first, merely the latest stalwart soul to bear it into sacred war. She would not be the last.

Irinya nodded. 'Near enough. We shall render His wrath unto them, and they shall regret the day heresy took root in their hearts. Whether they came from other ravaged worlds or betrayed their oaths to this one, they shall know punishment.'

The wall guns fired again. Behind them, within the Bastion

Sanctus, she knew Colonel Draszen of the Veluan Hoplites, the 'Shrinesworn', would be watching the contracting lines through his magnoculars and directing the fury of the cannons. Within the hallowed courtyards of the Presidium Imperator Gloria Sister Superior Eloise would be raising the Hymn of Right-eous Obliteration and coaxing the Exorcist missile launchers to furious heights of castigation.

Combined, their fire would break the enemy. Canoness Irinya and her Sisters were the bulwark that would hold the foetid ranks of the foe in place – pinned like insects under glass.

Irinya raised her hand and the line of Battle Sisters raised their weapons. They were unified in the moment, oath-sworn to the defence of Velua and the undertaking of the Indomitus Crusade.

'In the name of the God-Emperor and His Reborn Son, cleanse them all!'

There was a thrill to holy war that the endless tribal skirmishes of his home world could never match.

Aneirin, once a son of the jungles of the death world of Dakaram, now a Neophyte of the Black Templars, plunged into righteous battle, forcing his way through a heaving mass of diseased bodies. He passed under an archway whose pillars held the glowering skulls of martyrs entombed within them, moving through the outer gardens, away from the Battle Sisters and the unseeing eyes of the hanging dead, and swung his chainsword round and through two of the enemy cultists. Soiled robes tore, sprayed with the sudden gout of thick syrupy blood. They fell away in silence, and Aneirin scowled to see it.

Silence, in the face of a warrior such as himself, was a con-demnation. It was not enough to see the enemy bleed; he would see them driven before him in lament.

'Filth!' he bellowed. Knives scraped against his plate and autogun fire deflected pitifully. He could already hear the guns of the Battle Sisters nearby, further to the west, deeper into the Hanging Gardens, committing at last in the sacred song of war. There was a beauty upon Velua. He had grown up on Dakaram, far from here, amidst the chants of the Forever Hunt and devotion to the Walking-Sun-Who-Scars-The-Heavens. It was only later he had been told by the sages of the Chaplaincy that their august deity was merely a veiled face of the God-Emperor.

How many faces does He wear? Across time and space, and the galaxy's span?

It was nigh impossible to consider. In an empire of a million worlds, the god they served could wear so many more faces than that. The God-Emperor that tended to the souls of the privileged was not the same as the one who swept His scythe about the boundless poor. Nor was the God-Emperor who ruled over worlds of steel and stone simply the mirror of the master of plain and forest.

He wore His great burdens as a panoply of might and majesty. Only a god could guide the fate of a species, of an empire, and turn the very stars themselves.

'Praise be!' Aneirin bellowed. All these thoughts had passed through his mind in the time it had taken to break the back of the enemy squad which had been advancing through the Marbled Grottos. Statues, the ones which had not already been toppled and defaced, stared at him with mute acceptance of their fate and his presence. Blood streaked their pale countenances, and the foetor of the enemy lingered about them like a vile mockery of incense. He could see his battle-brothers moving between the mouldering statues and through the smoke, firing as they moved. The flash of a power weapon split the gloom and one of the mutilated idols fell, impacting the mud with a heavy wet slap.

Aneirin's breathing steadied and he lowered his blade at last, shaking free yet more of the enemy's flesh from its whirring teeth. The vox clicked in his helm, like the echo of the weapon's machine spirit's hunger. Special dispensation had been sought and granted by the Chaplaincy, that Neophytes such as himself would be allowed to wear their helms – the better to fend off the foe's toxic miasma. Aneirin honoured the sacred machine spirit of the helmet, whispering a prayer as he listened to the message.

'*The youngblood has promise, Barisan, though I think if you do not leash him then he may plunge into the very heart of the foe alone. As though he were Sigismund himself!*' Laughter followed the declaration across the squad's vox, though there was little mockery in it. A mirth born of camaraderie and growing respect. Brother Arvin was something of a trickster, though none would doubt his zeal or commitment to the crusade. As wry in his humour as he was exacting in his wrath.

'*You might learn something from his boldness, brother,*' was Sword Brother Barisan's measured reply. Aneirin's master knew when to indulge the passions of the Crusader squad and when to rein them in. '*There is no shame in untempered wrath – for that is the fuel of the Eternal Crusade.*'

Aneirin turned as the other members of the squad strode into the square, occupied now only by the Neophyte and his slaughtered prey. Bodies were strewn about, limbs severed and torsos gouged open as though by the passage of some great beast. It was only as the other warriors drew closer that Aneirin realised that the open space was carpeted in tiny bodies. The foul vapours and plague clades cast up by the enemy had devastated the local wildlife. The corpses and bones of birds lay everywhere, crunching under the boots of the Astartes warriors. Here and there lay dead cherubs, their aquiline pinions bent and broken.

'So too shall the passage of the unclean scar the earth, and leave in their wake a desolation,' Aneirin quoted from memory.

Barisan, at the head of the small band, shook his head with a smile hidden behind his helm. 'Indeed, Aneirin. Well learned. The touch of the Archenemy is ruin and despoliation. Spreading from the Rift, and all the unbarred hells of mortal fear.'

Arvin hefted his pyreblaster with an arsonist's relish, its long barrel already greasy with the ash of cremated bodies. He turned from the rest of his brothers and began to incinerate the cultists with the cleansing, sacred flames. Smoke once again stained the already sullied white marble of the walls that encircled them, rendering the stylised images of saints and the God-Emperor all the dourer.

'Thus ever to heathens,' Arvin said with a nod. 'May they burn forever in their own sins.'

'Such is the God-Emperor's will,' Aneirin finished. He turned to face Barisan, impressed as always with the simple potency of the man's authority. He wore the armour of a full battle-brother, Mark X plate sanctified by the Chapter's Techmarines and consecrated by the Chaplaincy. Beneath that armour Aneirin knew there dwelt a stern but patrician face, so different from his own unformed youth. Barisan was dark of hair, his pale skin marked by the passage of time and the creeping scars of service. An exemplar, as Aneirin hoped one day to be.

A sudden realisation flooded into the Neophyte's mind.

'Brother... The Champion. Is he near? Does he honour us with his guidance in sacred warfare?'

Barisan was silent for a moment. Aneirin wondered if he was contemplating the answer, or simply assessing the urgency which had flooded the Neophyte's voice.

'Where else would he be, brother? He is at the heart of the conflict.'

He fought at the heart of the conflict and existed as the heart of faith.

Even on a world barnacled with sacred things and holy relics, Gaheris was singular in his purity. The Armour of Faith turned aside all the weakling blows of the enemy, even as the Black Sword hewed through them in a sweep of blinding light. He moved through the ranks of the foe with swift economical motions, his every action exact and considered. He could hear the vox cries of his brothers, and of the Sisterhood who supported them. Calls for reinforcement, for support, for clarity. He was elevated beyond such things. As much as he was a leader of men, he was also the bearer of the God-Emperor's holy wrath.

'For He upon Terra!' he bellowed as he swept through them. Leprous flesh parted. Sluggish blood barely flowed from their wounds. Vermin fled from the corpses in tides of worms, lice and maggots. Even the parasites knew the end was upon them. Gaheris had led his warriors out in force, to cleanse the enemy while the Sisterhood and the Hoplites held the walls. They would strike out into the core of the enemy's strength and break them. That was their sacred oath.

They stood now in the way of the war. It was both the Eternal War and the End War. The conflict which had been kindled so long ago upon Terra and which had ended and began anew there. The God-Emperor's war. Sigismund's great undertaking, and now the regent's renewed crusade.

As though it ever ended. As though we would allow it to end. The thought was a comfort as much as it was a goad to greater deeds.

A shambling cultist, already looking half-dead, turned at Gaheris' sudden motion, before the back of a gauntleted fist drove it into the muck. Bubbles rose from the filth before Gaheris brought his foot down to complete the execution. Its skull shattered under his tread.

Not one of the animate dead then, he mused. Merely another

soul waylaid by darkness. Gaheris shook his head and drove the blade down and through the corpse's heart, to be certain.

'The wiles of the enemy are deceit, trickery and malice,' he whispered to himself. 'They mislead and corrupt. I will not be deceived.' He looked up again, seeking the light of the Emperor's guidance.

Golden light coiled around a knot of darkness, somewhere beyond the ornamental gardens and garlanded tombs. Where the makeshift siege weapons of the enemy fired and thundered, there lay his prize. The one who directed the foe's poisonous efforts. When their false prophet was dead then the enemy would falter and break – not simply on this front but across all Velua. All that remained was to trust in the God-Emperor's grace and follow His sacred light.

There he would find his reckoning.

Chapter Two

DAMNATION'S GAZE

SACRED SHADOWS

VOICE OF THE DEAD

Colonel Draszen watched from the walls as the enemy's push faltered against their lines of defence. The Bastion Sanctus remained inviolate, straddling the great walls of the shrine in brutish defiance, engraved with gilded prayers and the beatific faces of saints. He reached up with one trembling hand and wiped the sweat from his brow. His other hand rested on the bronze-and-crimson helm which sat upon the battlements. He had only just removed it, but already he regretted it. The sudden rank rush of claustrophobia was now locked in conflict with the constant thunder of the guns at close range and without the audio-dampeners threaded into his helmet.

Thank the Throne for the Sisters, and for the Angels who walk with them. He allowed himself the luxury of the thought. *The grace of the Emperor shields this world, where all others have...*

He exhaled shakily and dabbed again at his forehead. He felt as though he were drowning in his armour, weighed down by sheer despair. Despite the efforts of the crusade forces which had arrived to shore up their defences, Velua was still imperilled. Marshals, captains and lord generals had all turned from the defence of this one world to attempt to save others. Even now they were out there, in the void, fighting with all the Emperor's fury. All the while, the other worlds of the Golden Chain had suffered and broken. Six of the seven great shrine worlds now lay in ashes and ruin.

Draszen had wept and he had raged. Now all that was left to him was the ceaseless anger of the guns, and the vain hope of directing them in glorious purpose. Their defiance was all that remained. All across the world the enemy abounded, their numbers beyond count. Lesser shrines and cities had fallen. Candrus. Selstia. Guvrel. The defenders had been driven back, bit by bit, sacrifices made to buy time. Now the Black Templars were unleashed and the Legio Arconis waited. The Sisterhood fought and suffered, while the Veluans held the line. Like the plates of a great suit of armour, encircling the last vestige of hope.

He reached again for the magnoculars and gazed out at the battlefield. Knots of black and red resisted the tide of soiled white. Holding like rocks amidst the waves. That image, again, that clawing cloying dream of a sea. Of drowning. Hemmed in by walls of his own armour. His own flesh. Drowning, until the despair swallowed him whole.

He swallowed hard. He wondered just how long they could hold out. Six worlds had fallen. *Six!* And still the enemy came on. Rapacious in their hunger. They would tear everything down, given enough time. As relentless as any xenos fleet.

'How do we endure?' he whispered to himself. His free hand gripped the worn stone of the walls now, kneading at it as though it were ready to crumble in his fingertips and fall away beneath him.

It was only then that he saw it. It stood atop a parapet of its own and gazed out across the battlefield, surveying the war as surely as he did. Yet that was not all. As the magnoculars found it and focused, details emerged that both horrified and fascinated him. The figure's flesh was mottled with rashes and lesions, its robes stained. The cloth, once white, was now so heavily coated in spilled blood, pus and bile as to seem a riot of competing colours. It wore its corruption like a mark of rank. The eyes, though. The eyes were the worst part. Haunting, corpse-grey orbs, leaking rheumy tears and yet teeming with power just beneath the surface. He could see, even from this distance, the greenish light which danced beneath the cataracts like algal blooms in the deep oceans. Like rot below the surface of flesh.

It raised a thin hand and pointed, directly at him.

Draszen felt his heart convulse in his chest and for one terrible moment he thought he had been smitten by the enemy's own hand. Death, though, did not claim him. Witchfire did not burst through his skin. He did not collapse into a pile of maggots and viscera. Instead, in that moment, he understood. He finally saw with absolute clarity exactly what they faced and what was coming. These savage and undisciplined things had not been the instrument of ruin. No. Such things were coming. They were coming, heralded by the eyes of the mad prophet upon the parapet. He would have laughed had it not been so pointless. So hollow.

He thought of throwing himself from the walls. He thought of reaching for his sidearm and raising it to his own mouth. That, at the very least, would be mercifully swift.

He looked back out across the wasteland and saw that the thin, staring figure was gone. Nothing remained to even indicate that it had been there. He swallowed again. His throat was very dry, and he could feel the beginnings of a cough scratching its way up from the depths. Like knives against the inside of his lungs. Like claws against the marble of a sepulchre.

Colonel Draszen let the magnoculars fall against the stone and turned away from the vantage, his helm forgotten. He kept walking, without looking back, until he was far enough into the support tunnels and alone enough that he could finally begin to run.

The enemy had breached the network of feeder tunnels and maintenance alcoves which threaded beneath the Hanging Gardens, and so the Sisters had been forced to violate their sanctity as well, in pursuit. Irinya's squad moved into the tunnels with caution, cut off from their reinforcements by baleful necessity.

In the darkness beneath the earth, where only those deemed holy enough to tend the gardens were allowed to dwell, the Children of the Sevenfold Revelation had committed themselves to wholesale and wanton vandalism. Everything was smeared with soil and blood, the desecration coiling into unholy sigils that hurt to look upon. Irinya kept her eyes down and her bolter raised. Though she found even keeping her gaze low did not spare her pain. The bodies of the blessed lifetenders lay piecemeal – torn apart by the fury of the enemy to wallow in the now brackish water which spilled from cut conduits.

'By their deeds shall they be judged,' Irinya hissed. Her Sisters paused and those able made the sign of the aquila across their chestplates in remembrance of the fallen. 'And by their righteousness shall they be remembered.'

There were seven of them now. Seven warriors of the Order of Our Martyred Lady, alone and unsupported by the preceptory's forces. Canoness Irinya took the lead and the others followed behind – two abreast in the tight confines of the stone corridors.

Josefine and Agata were at her back, bolter and flamer raised in defiance of the darkness. They were the longest-serving of her Sisters, wearing the ravages of time beneath their helms just as she did. Behind them there came Sybele and Beatrice, young and made vigorous by the call to crusade. They whispered prayers in the cloying dark, as though words would repel the shadows better than Last Light's pilot light as it sputtered and snapped. At the rear were Oxanna and Selene, both grim and silent. Selene swept her heavy bolter from side to side as though anticipating the enemy at any moment. Oxanna did the same with her meltagun. Its spirit thrummed with the urgent need to do violence.

The chamber shook with the ceaseless thunder of the wall guns above, with the screaming detonations of the Exorcist missiles, and with the solid, oddly wet impacts of the enemy artillery. Dust trickled down over their armour, rendering them into statues in the cold dark – like monuments in a barrow. Irinya thought of the graven visages which haunted the world. The blank eyes of saints, rendered in marble, so unlike the individuals they were raised to honour.

Somewhere above, the symphony of war shifted.

Irinya paused and raised her fist, stopping their advance. 'Something is wrong,' she whispered. 'Our guns have fallen out of synchronous fire with the Exorcists. *Listen.*' The other Sisters craned their heads upwards. 'The walls are compromised.'

'Or perhaps they have run out of ammunition?' Josefine ventured.

'Or new orders. We cannot know that it is the hand of the enemy.' Agata nodded in agreement. 'It could be many things.'

The rhythm of fire did not alter, and Irinya cursed the simple hopefulness that so many still evinced. Despite their losses, and the other dead worlds that preceded this grinding, hateful war.

'Regardless,' she continued, 'we have our duty. Once we're above ground again, then we can take stock of the situation.' She paused, weighing her words. 'And render as much hurt upon the enemy as we are capable of.'

Something moved in the shadows and Irinya spun on reflex, bolter up. A small sound drifted from the darkness, like the sigh of gas from a corpse. They advanced upon the source in one motion, their every movement in perfect lockstep, until the light of the flamer caught it within the firelight. A survivor...

Irinya paused and then realised her error. The blood- and filth-soaked figure before her, nursing his wound, was not one of the attendants. He was of the enemy. He looked up at her with dull, cattle-like eyes. The look of one who knew that his death was upon him, but was too much of a puppet to truly care. Her lip curled back in a snarl and she stepped forward.

'Traitor,' she stated bluntly.

'What...' the dying man wheezed. 'What was there to betray?'

'Enough,' Agata snapped. She stalked forward, flamer raised. 'Let me end the wretch.'

'The enemies of man are wretched things,' Irinya said, but did not nod her assent. 'Yet from the throats of the enemy, truth can still be wrung.' She placed her hand on her sword but did not draw it. She did not enjoy bearing the weapon aloft, casting its pale light. The action inevitably returned her thoughts to the past, and to loss. It was a mournful thing to wield, even in the savage joy of holy war. The threat of it might be enough, though. 'Your dispositions,' she said. 'You come in force, but you must know you do not have the numbers to carry the day. You are a base and ragged horde, so there must be something else. There is a trickery or scheme behind your actions. I offer you one chance, before you burn forever. Repent. Offer up this information and it may lessen the suffering that awaits you beyond.'

The traitor laughed at that, heading lolling back to bang against the stone wall of the catacomb. 'So sure in your knowledge of what comes after. A seat at the right hand for the faithful...' He trailed off into a wet cough. Blood stained his lips. 'Damnation and fire for those who dare to resist. Yet I know what waits beyond. A garden glorious. My god waits there, enthroned in living death. Where is your god? Why does He not protect you?'

'Let me end him,' Agata said, pleading now. 'His hollow blasphemies sully us all.'

Irinya drew her sword. It was light and beautiful in her hands, a master-crafted weapon. The hilt was silver, the handle wound with real leather and reinforcing coils of steel. Its blade was a smooth span of polished metal, its substance was banded, dark on light, mottled like water caught in the sunset and flash-frozen. A thing of sacred beauty that had carried the name Truth's Kiss for as long as she had known of it. The power field went live with a hiss and cast a silver-white illumination into the close chamber, like the touch of moonlight.

Underlit by the blade's light, the cultist seemed even more drawn and ghoulish. In some ways, the purity of the light revealed the enemy's true face. Pallid flesh marked only by the random constellations of a rash, which even now seemed to shift and change at the behest of mad biological whims.

'Thus will all the enemies of man be ended,' she said. 'In the sight of the God-Emperor and His saints.'

'She will not protect you.' The cultist laughed, and Irinya almost flinched back at the pronouncement. 'You have all been so busy building high walls and tall towers... never planting seeds.' He exhaled in a sickly rasp of curdled air. 'Never pausing to savour the gardens your flesh will become.'

Something sparked behind the man's eyes, green and lurid. Irinya's blade was already falling, but too slowly. He unwound, coming apart in a spreading cloud of fungal light and abhorrent psychic power. Her blade passed through momentarily empty air and embedded itself in the wall behind. The unlight boiled and bubbled out from his failing flesh, a coiling and writhing miasma that blossomed with colours that should not exist, a layer of greasy light upon the surface of the world.

It passed them over, whether by design or the strength of their faith, and undulated into the corridors beyond. The man had been nothing more than a conduit for whatever fell power he was sworn to, and now its influence was loose once more.

'Throne!' Sybele cursed as she made the sign of the aquila. 'God-Emperor, who reigns eternal, deliver us from the evils of the immaterial and–'

'Hush,' Irinya cautioned, and the girl's prayer became a muffled refrain. 'Prayer in the face of the enemy is wisdom, but defiance by strength of arms is truth.' She drew the blade back up and held it before her face, inspecting it for any damage or weakness. It remained as it had ever been. Flawless and heavy with memory. 'What remains to us is to find what the enemy has wrought and bring it to ruin.' She had erred, she realised suddenly. She should have heeded them and left him to die.

A new sound joined the tumult of war, now. It rose about them in a slow, soft moan and yet was more damnably audible than the howl and thunder of artillery.

The dead men were stirring, roused by whatever sorcerous contagion had boiled forth from the cultist. The corpses spasmed and shook as the unnatural affliction washed over them. Skin withered to the bone like dried leather, until tendons and sinews snapped and strained under the sudden pressure. Eyes burst in their sockets and wept blood and humour down their cheeks. Teeth gnashed in drawn-back gums even as fingers hooked like claws, scrabbling at the cold stone and tearing at their own vestments and flesh.

They hated the mortal forms they occupied. Despised, with every fibre of their unholy being, the confines of human perfection. They turned, almost as one, and saw the Sisters.

Agata was already firing, raising her voice in a savage shout as the flamer's breath cut through the darkness – a darkness that now felt deeper and more malignant than it had mere minutes

before, the shadows no longer sacred. Bolt-shells joined her
exuberant defiance with wrathful shouts of their own.

Irinya turned, blade ready, and plunged once more into battle.

Prophet Weryn stepped back into the makeshift bunker, the
ersatz temple that formed the heart of their new defiance. It
lay far ahead of their own lines, carved out from the enemy's
holdings and made holy.

The Sevenfold faithful brought their worship with them in every
way. The temple had once been a storehouse, a squat rectangle of
stone and rockcrete tucked away to the rear of the gardens. Out
of sight, out of mind, and shielded against the elements which
were allowed to play over the verdant growth. Now it had been
adorned and sanctified with their worship. Disarticulated human
skeletons had been used to transform the close space into an
ossuary – hung from cords of dried muscle, scattered about on
the floor, or crudely mounted upon ledges and shelves. Spread
between the skeletal remains were more intact bodies, bloodless
and pale where they were not riven by plague or mortal wounds.

It was a sacred place. In its confines Weryn felt almost at
peace. Within the bunker the war might as well not exist, though
he was still close enough to hear the thunder of artillery and the
screams of the dying. They were closer to the walls than they had
ever been, carving their path through the outer gardens. Here
he knew a truer divinity amongst the leavings of battle than ever
he had as a servant lurking in the shadows of the great cathedrals. Before the Sevenfold Revelation had shown him the way
and awakened the potential within his blood.

He crouched before a makeshift altar and looked up into the
cataracted eyes of a withered corpse. One of seven, folded across
the flat surface of the fane.

'I offer myself again to you and your wisdom,' he whispered
and pressed his head to the stained floor. 'Give me your grace,

lord. Speak with the voice of the Grandfather and anoint us in your light.'

The prayers stung upon his tongue, burning words that scrabbled across the world's skin to burrow beneath and blossom within the sacred immaterium. They were vital, living things. Not the calcified and dead rote recitations to an uncaring corpse-lord. When Weryn spoke, these masters listened... and answered.

One of the corpses jerked suddenly. Its head snapped around on a broken neck, eyes fierce with green flame, tongue lolling from its distended jaws. Teeth had rotted and loosened in its withered gums, and so it slobbered and chattered when it spoke with a voice that was not its own.

'My dear friend, my chosen disciple and acolyte. How goes the war?'

Weryn suppressed a shiver at the Pilgrim's voice. The air had grown close and electric with psychic resonance. Witchfire danced around the corners of the room and the shadows it cast were warped and misshapen. They seemed horned and distorted, swollen with unnatural rot, yearning to ooze their way onto the material stage. Waiting in the wings for the appointed moment. Weryn could feel it, drawing nearer.

'We advance,' he allowed carefully. 'The gardens are burning and their shrines are toppled. We have killed many of their lesser holdings. Selstia burns. Guvrel drowned in its own blood in a single night. They resist, of course. Quite sternly. We push for the gates at the Bastion Sanctus now. The crusade reinforcements were...' Weryn swallowed. 'Unanticipated, and have put greater steel in their spine. Angels walk with them.'

'Oh of course they do,' burbled his patron's voice from between the splayed lips. *'There are always demigods walking, where their false faith is challenged. Soon, though, you will have angels of your own. Already the outriders should be reaching the system's edge.'*

'You will grace us yourself, lord?'

'In due course, should the omens ring true...' The corpse's

expression changed in that moment, becoming distant and slightly vacant, before returning its attention to Weryn. *'There is much yet to be done, and more to be prepared for. You have been good and loyal servants, all. The Children of the Sevenfold Revelation shall know their reward. The Grandfather shall bequeath it from his bounteous garden and it shall embrace every last soul who wears your mark. This I promise. We are all his grandchildren, all part of the great and woeful universal family of humanity.'* The corpse burbled with laughter. Maggots and other crawling vermin squirmed from the gaps between its teeth, falling to the floor and skittering away into the darkness.

There was beauty, Weryn had to remind himself, in the horror. The galaxy was cold and cruel, turned malicious by the unending spite of the Imperium. Only by embracing the deeper darknesses that cloaked the Grandfather's infinite love could there be any hope of salvation, now that the skies had split and the stars were drowning in the universe's own blood.

'Their faithful are many,' Weryn said suddenly, his words a mad babbling rush. 'Sometimes I doubt if we can carry the day, but if you are with us, my lord, then no enemy can overcome us.'

'We shall drink the wine of heroes together, amidst the ruins of their high spires. And if not with you, then some other organ of resistance. That is the joy of our service, Prophet Weryn. There are always other souls to carry on the work.' It laughed again. Colder, this time. More distant. Weryn felt the joy seep from the room like pus from a lanced boil. *'There is nothing more noble than death in service to an ideal. Sacrifice for the sake of something greater than ourselves. Knowing that we represent–'*

'The seed of something purer,' Weryn finished. 'I know. I know. Paradise only comes to us through suffering. We can die in the cages they have made for us, or we can build a garden over their bones.'

'And that hour is fast approaching. One way or another. Have

faith, my servant. Hold the course and endure the barbs of angels. Soon they will have no power over you.'

The corpse's head fell back against the cold stone and then the entire body spasmed at the expenditure of sorcerous power. Black fire and rot bubbled up and out through it, until nothing remained but the withered and cracked bones.

Weryn rose on unsteady feet and padded to the door. He opened it carefully and gazed out. He did not have the strength yet to cast another baleful glance at the walls – to weaken the resolve of the foe – nor could he cast forth his animating will through lesser conduits. Instead he merely surveyed.

His mind expanded and his vision soared. He could see the distant spires of the cathedral city and the great temple-fortress of the High Sacristy, shimmering behind their void shields, grasping at the heavens like the avaricious fingers of the corpse-lord Himself. Weryn had long since learned that the gilding of the Imperium was merely there to hide its sins, from the Golden Throne all the way down to the gutter.

He lowered his gaze from the hateful bulwarks of the enemy and instead took in the worship which was taking place outside the temple space. The dirt square, now a muster field, had once held only agri-haulers and chem-trucks. Now it seethed with the faithful. The luminors of the Sevenfold Revelation stalked along a line of captured soldiery. Behind them stood the liberators, the common warriors of the cult, watching with their pale faces, daubed in grave-ash and marked with black ink in the semblance of skulls. The luminors, by contrast, bore only the acid-etched marks of false tears down their cheeks. One of them, armoured in appropriated flak-plate, was touching a long-bladed machete to each of the prisoners' foreheads, and then walking on. When she reached the end of the row she turned and repeated it, before stopping at the centre of the kneeling line. Fourteen men, in all.

'Repent your blasphemies. Turn from the false light and embrace the true. Be god-marked and glorious. This is my offer to you. A final offer, before the end.'

The first in line, a grizzled veteran, raised his scarred head and spat in the luminor's face. She smiled beatifically, lips creasing around pox-scars, and let the blade slip across the man's throat. Gently. Like a kiss. He fell back gasping, unable even to claw at his throat with his bound hands. A bad death, Weryn judged. It was not how he would wish for his service to end.

Weryn cleared his throat and stepped forward to stand beside the luminor. He recognised her now. 'Luminor Ceren,' he said, and bowed lightly to her. 'If I may?'

'Please, prophet.' Her smile did not fade. 'Perhaps the book will trump the blade.'

He smiled back and turned to survey the broken men and women before him. Grovelling on their knees. Still convinced that a merciful god would save them. They still believed in *Him* and yet...

'Where is your Emperor?' Weryn asked simply. 'The galaxy is broken. Burning. Everything is flux, and the ruin of the established order. He was supposed to brace up the heavens and ensure that your spires never toppled. That your indulgence never ended. Where is He now?'

Silence reigned for a beautiful moment. He could almost taste the doubt as it metastasised in the air. Doubts would become truth, truth would become acceptance, and they would find their place in the fold. It had happened many times before. For every gutter-veteran of the cult there were dozens of Astra Militarum defectors who had brought their skill and arms to the side of righteousness.

'He is with us.'

The voice was quiet, almost lost in the storm that yet surrounded them, but a quiet defiance was more than enough. Weryn's features curdled as he turned, and he stalked forward towards the one who had spoken. Weryn smiled indulgently, almost mockingly, as he looked down at the one brave soul. Young. Not yet calcified into shape by the Imperium's relentless weight, nor a green and unskilled conscript. He shone with belief, wrong-headed and banal as it was, and Weryn smiled to see it. The youth spoke again.

'His Reborn Son walks with us. The crusade is with us. Anything you've gained will be swept away.' He spat onto the ground, and hung his head again.

'Perhaps that is so. When we send you to Him, you can see if that is true.' Weryn shook his head and then turned to Ceren. He nodded, once.

She raised the blade, licking her lips as she did so, and prepared to bring it down squarely between the youth's eyes. Weryn was already picturing how the boy's face would split. Where the blood would run. How the eyes would fare. Whether the bone was strong, or weak and crumbling.

He was imagining just how the boy would die and rot when the first explosions sounded from nearby, from far too close, from inside the meagre barricades they had raised. Weryn looked up sadly from the line of soldiers and sighed. Ceren was already running, whooping at the head of the liberators who were now following. Banners snapped and fluttered in the wind, emblazoned with the weeping eye.

For a moment Weryn felt cold well within his bones, passing through him like a shadow across the sun. The Grandfather's sacred love retracted for a fraction of a second, and he shivered. Something was coming. Burning with dark fury and murderous light. He could taste the passage of it upon the ether.

'A brief respite,' he muttered, more to convince himself than the abandoned sacrifices. 'Soon there shall be far more martyrs on both sides.'

Chapter Three

HOLY WARRIORS

DEATH AND DARKNESS

FALSE PROPHETS

They charged through the dust and ash of battle, bellowing hymns to the God-Emperor.

Even years after his ascension they still felt strange to Aneirin. They were hard-edged and certain things, not like the invocations he had made to the Walking Sun. Life upon his home world had been harsh and hot, urgent and fierce, where death had lurked behind every shadow.

There was a comfort in knowing that some things did not change, entirely.

I am no longer a child of the Forever Hunt. I am a son of the Eternal Crusade. I do not seek for tribal glory, now. I fight for the dominions of humanity and His sacred realm.

It had not been an easy thing to leave behind the beliefs that had shaped his young life. Even now, with the memories becoming nothing more than a smear of struggle, he could not entirely set them aside. The God-Emperor was the light he had chased his entire life, desperate for the attention of a distant godhead, and now he had been raised up to His side as an Angel of Death. He had learned of Rogal Dorn and Sigismund, and though they had no place in the pantheon of his birth, he had made space for them. He honoured them now in every word and deed.

Deeds such as these: sacred undertakings at the hands of holy warriors.

His sword was a crimson blur as it passed through the ranks of the enemy. None could stand against them. He wondered, not for the first time, how these cultists – so rag-tag and under-supplied – could have posed such a threat to the sanctity of a holy and civilised world such as Velua.

'*And yet,*' Barisan's voice answered in his memory, as it had any other time he had raised the boastful concern, '*how many other shrine worlds lie burning in the void, with the enemy's mark upon them? We gain nothing by underestimating this foe. We do not need to understand them to destroy them, but we must have the measure of them.*'

Aneirin scoffed again as he turned on his heel and raised his bolt pistol. He fired three times, each shot precisely aimed at the centre mass. They burst in quick, gory succession. Where once three flak-armour-clad figures had stood there were now only detonated torsos and detached limbs, splayed across the sullied marble of the floor.

They moved and fought as a unit, as did the other squads engaged around them. Pushing onwards between the statuary and the fronds of perfumed ferns. Above them the watching saints had been made strange and cruel. Dried flaps of human skin had been crudely belted to the faces of the statues, the lips worked obscenely wide by blade and chisel. Branches had been jammed into the sides of their heads, to rise as makeshift horns or antlers. Wherever possible Aneirin shot them or swiped them aside with his sword, but many were out of his reach.

'We will undo all this,' he whispered to himself. 'The light of this place shall shine once more, when the filth has been cleansed from its steps.'

The enemy died in droves before the Black Templars. Arvin laughed as he burned them to ash, his pyreblaster sweeping in wide arcs until the cultists were nothing more than shadowy silhouettes burned against the white stone. Bones cracked under his boots as he moved. Barisan was with him and his blade sang with every motion. Heads flew free. Blood arced heavenwards. He punched and kicked and drove the enemy before him, every movement an economical execution of martial violence. Fenek and Partus fought side by side, joined by their bonds of devotion. Chainswords swept around as they guarded each other's flanks. Havdan brought up the rear, firing again and again. Each shot found its mark, chosen for the maximum infliction of harm.

'Into them! For the glory of the God-Emperor! Return them to the gutters they have crawled from!' Barisan cried.

The enemy roared their petulant defiance; gnats biting in futility against the flank of a great beast. The Black Templars bellowed in response, their voices a vox-amplified wave of sound that drove the enemy back. The lesser cultists, compelled by their own weakness more than their daemonic masters, staggered in their charge.

Even had they not, it would have done them no good.

The Black Templars were a storm surge of black and white, gold and crimson. Sword Brethren with their heavier armour and red shoulder trim pushed ahead. Swords, axes and maces were drummed against shields. Power field against power field. The air was filled with fitful lightning, seeking grounding. It stank of ozone and spilled blood, even above the unwashed rot of the cultists.

A wall shattered to Aneirin's right and the hulking profile

of Venerable Toron loomed through the dust and shadows. His rotator cannon opened up with a resounding boom, and a cluster of cultists exploded before they could even raise their heavy weapons platform.

'For the glory of Him on Terra! For His Reborn Son! For the Praetorian, who shall return to us!'

The machine-voice of the Dreadnought growled over them as it stalked forwards, swinging the great blade held aloft in its right manipulator arm. Even the bravest of the enemy turned and fled then. Aneirin broke into a run, following behind the hulking armoured profile of the Dreadnought. Their squad, Squad Fidelitas, fought now as part of the wider war. The full wrath of the remaining Black Templars upon Velua was being loosed against the foe.

He felt righteous. Here in the heart of the conflict, with his sworn brothers about him, and the notables of the Chapter at their head, Aneirin knew that their victory was assured.

'Where is he?' he asked, as he drew level with Barisan. The older warrior turned his head by an increment to regard Aneirin as he parried another weakling blow.

'He is at the head of it, as you well know. Focus upon the moment, Aneirin.'

'The Champion should be supported,' he pressed. 'He may not need our aid, but our swords will end the conflict all the quicker. Cut to the heart of them and gouge it out. That is our way. The Eternal Crusade. The blade thrust to the core, and the cleansing flame. That is our creed.'

Barisan shook his head and sighed. 'I have seen many warriors blinded by glory, though it is usually their own. The Champion walks his own path, a path blessed by the God-Emperor in His infinite might and majesty. Your path is that of the Neophyte, to one day stand as an Initiate in your own right. To train others as I have mentored you, and perhaps to rise beyond that. Every warrior – be they Chaplain, Marshal or High Marshal, every Champion – began as a mere Neophyte.'

Aneirin nodded but Barisan seized him by one pauldron.

'You nod, brother, but do you understand? The Champion is a comet. He pursues his own course, as the God-Emperor wills. We follow too closely at our peril. He is inspiration, but he is not the absolute. Honour him, venerate him, but remember your duty to your brothers.'

Aneirin was silent for a long moment. The blade dropped to his side and idled, teeth whirring and biting at the air. 'I understand,' he said. He let his gaze lower, head bowed in shame. 'I will not lose myself to a hunt for glory. I will abide. I will learn.'

A great crash arose as Toron felled another barricade, his greatsword splitting a wall of toppled columns and casting them to one side. Explosions burst around the Dreadnought as the enemy artillery finally resighted, no longer caring whether they killed their own so long as they hurt the relentless enemy.

Aneirin watched the great Dreadnought as he weathered the storm of fire and thrust his blade up and into the tormented sky, as though he could pull the very heavens down upon them by will alone. He had been told, many times now, that the venerable Ancient had once been a Marshal in his own right. He had fought and bled and died for the Imperium in the times before the Rift's opening and the call to this new crusade. On perceiving his new form, he had immediately demanded a sword. The Techmarines of the Chapter had tried to soothe his new and bellicose spirit, but his wrath had been unbound.

'In life I was a brother of the sword. You tell me that in death I cannot perform my duty? I will not be denied. Forge me a blade, or give me to the darkness!' had been his declaration.

High Marshal Kordhel himself had intervened, and the forges of the *Eternal Crusader* had rung with the effort. The sword that Toron wielded was a mighty thing, as tall again as a battle-brother and cannon-wide. They had wound chains around his arm, great black links binding him to the weapon, to his duty once again and to war in the God-Emperor's name.

Aneirin did not yearn for the living death that Toron had embraced, but for that surety of purpose. It was not enough to merely do his duty when others such as Toron or Champion Gaheris *lived* it. As a warrior of the Adeptus Astartes he was beyond fear, but doubt remained.

'I will abide. I will learn. I will do my duty,' he repeated, to himself alone.

The Sisters fought as they moved through the darkness, illuminating it with blade, bolter and flame.

The dead hounded their every step. They reared up from the shadows, all snapping jaws and hands knotted into claws. Their skin had begun to run like wax, or to weep blood in sanguine trails, or to bulge with mould and rot. They droned on and on in one voice. It was the buzzing of flies and the tolling of bells, and the laughter of daemonkind.

'I renounce you!' Irinya spat. 'The enemy shall put falsehoods in my way and I shall see them brought to ruin!'

'Ruin is the gift of the Throne!' her Sisters bellowed, their own voices raised as one against the cacophony. They were righteous before the impure, and they would not be found wanting.

Agata growled as she fought. Holy fire vomited forth from the nozzle of the flamer and reduced the shambling dead ahead of them to ashes. Bodies tumbled back, wreathed in fire, and were crushed underfoot. Their armour was smeared with the greasy residue of broiled human fat, stained with soot and weapon discharge. They seemed more sepulchral, more like the unfeeling statues that surrounded them in these tunnels. Heavy weapons fire howled back down the corridor in a storm of bolt-shells and melta-blasts as Oxanna and Selene discharged their weapons. The fusion light rendered the catacombs hellish and bright for one glorious moment and then faded, leaving only the after-images of their surroundings.

Faces stared at them from the walls in impassive judgement. The visages of saints and martyrs, old and new. Irinya almost started back as she regarded one. Teneu's face looked at her, made strange by the flawless carving of the marble, so much so that she almost had not recognised her. Old shame bubbled up within her as she looked for too long a moment at the graven image.

I failed you once. Do not mock me now.

She brought her blade up, the light of it haloing the immortalised visage of its former owner, and swung it through another ravening corpse in the robes of a gardener. She pushed on, past the dead, and past the weighty gaze of memory.

The Lady of Woes, they had called Teneu, when she had been borne back to Velua as a martyr and a hero. Irinya still could not reconcile the symbol with the girl she had known. The quiet and reserved girl who had become a stern but just commander. The kind of warrior who would be followed to whatever end.

To whatever end.

Irinya turned aside another enemy and its face split at the edge of her blade. She pushed it onwards and drove it back against the wall hard enough to crack bone and shatter teeth. It dropped, robbed of the pestilent anima which had motivated its ruined flesh. They had fought through the reanimated husks of attendants and cultists alike, and none had been pleasant kills. They had taken utter physical destruction or sufficient trauma to the head and heart before they would stop. They had chattered and screamed and laughed every step of the way, spewing invective and bile.

Finally, the Sisters emerged out into a larger circular chamber, a stairwell winding upwards and towards the surface. The centre of the chamber had been dominated by a pool of water, long since grown brackish and clogged with algae. Strange colours writhed and glistened in the pool, reflecting off the brass discs and bowls, watering implements and beakers which had been sat around it in waiting. Water still trickled into it from subtle culverts set into the walls, carried by small aqueducts to dribble lazily into the well.

Something else moved within its depths now. As they drew near they saw where the bodies had been deposited. The torn vestiges of robes marked them as cultists and they had all died by ritual violence. Irinya could not tell whether it had been by their own hands or those of their brothers. Their water-logged flesh had begun to run and flow, rotting together into a gestalt mass of ruinous meat. Limbs waved gently in the strange currents. Things pulsed and shifted with unnatural life and eyes opened wetly in the distended flesh. Too many eyes, yellow and rheumy, stared back at her. She thought momentarily of some deep-sea animal – boneless, strange and grasping.

'By the Throne,' Josefine breathed. Her bolter's sight wavered for a moment as they spread out around it.

'Burn it,' Irinya declared simply. 'Burn it all.'

The Black Sword plunged through the base of a great cannon, hewing open its control mechanisms and forcing the entire assembly to slump in mid-fire. The shells fell short, instead detonating an ammunition dump which had sprawled along the base of an ornamental wall.

Trees and masonry blew apart in showers of shards and splinters. The Armour of Faith was proof against such destructive by-blows. To Gaheris the debris that rained down upon him was nothing more troubling than a light drizzle. He was armoured in faith, armed with purity, and blazed with the righteousness of their cause. Even now the enemy shrank from him, more afraid of his glory than of any other of his brothers. He could hear the chanted hymns and war cries rising around him as more and more of the Black Templars joined the fray, jostling for the honour of being near to the Champion at the moment of assured triumph.

'The faithful are a multitude, where the impure are but few! Before us they falter! As shall all the servants of false gods!'

Enemies were bisected where they stood or cut down as they turned to flee. He let himself loom over them like the God-Emperor's wrath incarnate while las-fire and autogun rounds pattered fruitlessly against his armour. He reached out and seized one of the attackers by the skull, crushing it to bloody slurry between his fingers. He let it fall and cast his eyes around again.

The God-Emperor's golden light was moving and shifting as the Champion drew nearer to his prey. The heart of the enemy. Always he was guided to the most important of foes, the better to deliver the wrath of the divine.

'I do not fear you!' he bellowed aloud. 'I am His instrument! I stand clad in His holy armour and bear the Black Sword of heroes! Who are you to stand against me? You have sold yourselves to denizens of the warp and their empty promises, and you will die knowing that you are nothing!'

Did I ever know such righteousness as a member of the Chaplaincy?

It was not a new thought. It had dogged his steps since he had been chosen. This elevation, a process he had always viewed from the outside, was such a different beast when he lived it. He had thought himself a learned man, a being shaped by the mysteries of the Chapter's catechism, and now he bore it upon his shoulders as he bestrode the warfront. Numinous and terrible. Exalted.

And I will wield this power well and wisely, as He wills it. I shall stand as example and exemplar, till death claims me and the mantle passes.

Gaheris strode past cracked-open tombs, their occupants decanted across the sullied stones. Some had been mutilated further, others hung like totems. Everything here was marked with the symbol of a weeping eye and Gaheris brought his sword across the profane symbol at every opportunity. By martial force the taint could be excised and the enemy driven back. They would reclaim this, bit by bit, and redeem what could be saved.

And if not then no matter the sanctity of what lay beneath, no matter what he destroyed, it was better that it be ended than defiled.

The light shifted and contracted. Ahead of him he could see the outline of a wizened figure, small and insignificant, but marked by the God-Emperor's sight as a target. Gaheris pushed himself forward, breaking into a run as he drew closer to the wall behind which the figure cowered.

The wall ceased to exist. Gaheris came through it in a storm of masonry and bone fragments, swinging the Black Sword. It passed through empty air, and he spun on his heel to confront his prey.

The man was old, withered and worn, but brimming with psychic power. It was coiled around his tired bones, writhing beneath his skin like the vermin that teemed through his soiled robes. He looked up at Gaheris as though he could break the Champion with a look.

Gaheris shook his head. 'You? Truly? You are the enemy's heart and vigour?'

The man's throat worked as he swallowed hard. 'We all play the parts that the Grandfather gifts us with. I am his creature, as you are your god's.'

'All this.' Gaheris gestured about himself with the crackling edge of the blade. 'All done at the urging of false gods and daemons. Heresy, cast forth by false prophets.'

'I am but one of many. You cannot stop the phage in its cycle. It grows, spreads, unstoppable and–'

Gaheris brought the sword down, tip-first, towards the prophet's skull.

As he did the man's hand shot up and the air frothed with discharged witchery. His eyes bulged and flashed a sickly, jaundiced yellow. The air became turbid, stolid, and the blade moved through it as though through deep water. Gaheris could feel the energy pulsing against his armour, clawing at him as it sought to burrow through the sacred ceramite. Against any other warrior it might have found purchase, but instead it skittered across the plate.

'Suffer...'

Gaheris gritted his teeth and pushed forward. The blade moved, near imperceptibly, but it was enough. The crackling energy field of the sacred blade burned bright amidst the sorcerous fug. Insects boiled into existence from behind reality's skin, snapping and biting at his armoured gauntlets. They sought to drown the light of the blade beneath a tide of filth.

'Not...'

The insects were flooding across his eye-lenses now, blinding him, yet still he forced the blade onwards, inch by inch. Each movement surer than the last, as though the bubble of corroded, toxic air were losing its power. It spasmed as the blade passed through it, a boil ready to be burst.

'The witch...'

A thunderclap roared out as the bubble of tortured reality finally detonated. The cloud of insects blew away, caught in the sudden hurricane wind.

'To live!' Gaheris finished the oath as the blade speared down and impaled the stone beneath.

Past where the prophet had once stood.

Gaheris rose and dragged the blade up, roaring with fury as he stalked after the prophet. The man's gait was swifter than it had any right to be and he fumbled with something at his cuff. As he passed through an archway, two figures lumbered through to replace him, standing as a line of flesh and steel. They had been agricultural servitors, but now their mechanisms ran with rust and tainted oil. Sigils had been carved into the plates of their reinforced chassis, smeared with human blood, and crowned with bones. Their flails and scythes rose and fell as they toddled forward with unsteady gait, determined to slay the prophet's enemies.

Gaheris glowered at them as they came forwards, his eye-lenses burning crimson as he raised the sword.

Chapter Four

INTO THE LIGHT

GODS OF IRON

ANTHROPOMANCY

They came up and into the light, through smoke and steam and the stink of spoiled meat.

'The works of the enemy are abhorrent and inhumane,' Irinya breathed. 'Where the foolish are deceived to service, the faithful can see the horror they wear plainly. It is the same with all pretender cults. Be they of the warp or born of the xenos.'

Sybele stepped forward, her bolter raised. She pointed with the barrel and they all turned to follow her gaze. 'And yet, out of dark places, we are led to where we must be.'

Earthworks stretched out to either side of them, trenches hiding the strength of the enemy's artillery. They could see the spotters, scurrying here and there like ants, as they range-found and directed the ruinous fury of the guns. So close that they could note the Veluan Hoplite heraldry where it had been defaced or outright excised. Rust wept and bled from where there had once been brass edging and gold plate. The tears of the abused machine spirits, perhaps, though Irinya was no tech-priest to judge such things as a matter of faith.

'He guides our hand and our wrath.' Irinya nodded approvingly. She sheathed the blade, breathed a small sigh of relief, and then unshouldered her bolter. 'In His name.'

'In His name!' Their chant rose a fraction of a second before the bolters began to fire. Shells caught the spotters and knocked them from their perches in bursts of blood and bone. They tumbled like dolls, even as other cult soldiery were turning and returning fire.

Las-fire sizzled past the Sisters' heads, searing lines of light across their eyeline. The shots seemed to linger longer than those of the loyalists, like scars cut into the skin of the world, infected and raw. The very soul of Velua was in pain, crying out and weeping pus like the Throne-damned sigil of the Sevenfold Revelation. It flapped on banners, glared out from the hull plates of the artillery, and sat with a strange mongrel pride on the breastplates and robes of the cultists.

Irinya did not pity them. Perhaps she would have pitied the men and women they had once been, just as she pitied the foolish girl she had once been in the schola. Beyond a certain point there was no longer the excuse of ignorance, merely the truth of spite. Heresy was a disease, as the cultists well demonstrated. A blight upon the body and soul of the Imperium.

'They will not succeed,' she declared.

'They will not prevail,' Josefine echoed. 'We will not let them.'

'Still,' Agata growled, 'the struggle should be worth it.' She was striding before her Sisters now, holy fire spraying from Last Light. A migraine-bright smear of light lanced out as Oxanna fired her melta, gouging a great glowing chasm through the side of one of the enemy tanks. Ammunition cooked off and the tank shuddered, swelled, and then exploded outwards and upwards in a column of flame. More cultists were moving now, turning from their gun-lines and doubling back against the Sisters. Bolt-shells tore the heretics from their feet. Limbs flew in welters of gore where others were seared to death by flamer and melta. Corrupted bodies burst to ash, their taint cleansed by the purifying fires. Their wounded souls would never be redeemed, but the Sisters simply did not care.

'Those who have turned from His sight are the enemies of humanity. Less than the xenos, that is born bereft of human purity, for the heretic chooses to forsake their one true liege lord. The God-Emperor protects only the faithful!' Josefine shouted the declaration as the enemy lurched into their gunsights. Their own droning hymns answered her, even as the cultists were cut down. They sang and prayed, chanted and laughed, tolled bells and waved their banners. Smeared with filth, crawling with vermin, their flesh marked with lesions and rashes, they threw themselves at the knot of Sisters. They knew, on some soul-deep level, that these interlopers were weak and isolated. That soon enough they would run out of ammunition, and be easy meat for the flock.

Bolters began to click dry. Irinya drew her blade again and stepped forward.

'If I am to die here then it will be at the cost of a hundred of your mongrel breed. Come! Try and end me! He is with me, and if I fall He shall gather me up to His right hand, to fight His wars forever more. I am exalted. I am already saved!'

She did not fear death. She was willing, even eager, to die in service to the Throne. The fear that had haunted her down the years had been the idea of a soft death. A bureaucrat's death, an administrator's end, surrounded only by mounting missives and the burden of some schola. Her fear was unworthiness. It was failure.

For a moment her swing almost faltered. She nearly hesitated. Her blade turned aside a rusty cleaver and then spun about to slam through the meat and bone of the wielder's neck. Hot blood misted across her faceplate, and she drove the enemy back.

There were more of them now. An unwashed tide of the mad and the depraved. Their chanting did not alter, did not fail, even as they died. It rose, stronger if anything, as they pushed onwards to die. Bells rang until they fell from the twisted claws of hands. Throats worked until staved in, shot, or strangled. The Sisters fought even as the hands clawed at them and the blades rose and fell. Some broke against the plates while others quested for gaps in the armour. The enemy wanted them prised open and torn apart.

Then the bells and chants were drowned out. A horn blared across the melee of the gardens, and even the artillery quieted at the sound. They stuttered in their barrage as the crew working it panicked, gaping at the sight that lumbered inexorably towards them across the marble-and-foliage choked expanse. At the shadow that reached out to envelop them all.

An iron god strode forth to face them down.

She sat, enthroned in iron and armoured in adamant, staring down at the world through the auspex-senses of a god of war.

Princeps Melpomene Takravasian watched the cultists break and run in their multitudes, fleeing before the coming of the Warlord Titan *Vengeance of Sareme*. It had not always had that name, but had adopted it willingly in the years since the coming of the Rift and the loss of the home world. The forge which had birthed it, which it had defended for centuries, was gone. The forge world had drowned in madness and outrage, swarmed by hereteks who had torn down the sacred places and gouged out the implants of the priesthood.

Even now, to think of it sent a spasm of pain and rage up from the core of her gut – echoed by the Titan's war-hungry machine spirit. Melpomene looked out upon Velua and saw echoes of her own loss as the filthy tide rose to consume them. There had been no oceans upon Sareme, the water long since boiled away by relentless industry-as-worship, but she thought again and again of a poison sea drowning the land, consuming the cliffs by degrees.

That is how they dream of breaking us. Grinding us down beneath their lice-bodies, until there is nothing left but bones.

'I refuse you,' she said aloud, simply, from her throne. Implants and communion points ached and pulsed with the engine's fury, and she gritted her teeth.

'Princeps?' Moderatus Valtin turned to regard her, the cables laced into his scalp shaking like braids with the motion. They both shared the pallor common to those who had grown to adulthood beneath the smog-stained skies of Sareme, but where Valtin's scalp was shaved close to his angular skull, Melpomene's hair was black and rich, cascading down her back like spilling oil. She looked as a queen ought. Here and now she was the ranking princeps of what remained of the Legio Arconis; a proud war-leader whose laurels were well earned from count-less campaigns. Valtin respected that rank, yet was not so dumbstruck as to ignore any concerns that arose.

'A momentary lapse. Forgive me.' She inclined her head and returned her full attention to the manifold. Light blos-somed behind her eyes as she shared her senses with the Titan, drinking in the cognitive inload through the mechanisms of the Mind Impulse Unit. Targets alighted in runes of burning crimson, while the Sisters, Black Templars and Veluan Hoplites were picked out in vibrant green.

Viewed from above, the Hanging Gardens were a long rectan-gular sprawl away from the walls, divided into tiers by a series of ornamental rivers and canals. The complex used more water than an entire hab-block on any other world would consume in a full year, a testament to the wastefully inefficient extrava-gance that this world's masters indulged in. The enemy, their red signifiers bleeding light, were advancing along one of the main thoroughfares – the Via Aristereon – while uncounted guerrilla actions raged amidst the foliage. Stiff resistance greeted them at every turn. The Sisters and Veluans were accounting well for themselves, while the Black Templars surged on ahead through the enemy's lines, seeking command points and disrupting the cult's initiative.

The tactical perspective pivoted and shifted, contextualising the limited progress of the defenders. Sweeping red inroads were layered over the gardens where the cultists were moving in force. They had surged across the other cities of the world in a tide, yet they were taking their time in assaulting the High Sacristy. Even this path of attack had been chosen more for symbolic reasons than tactical ones: to humiliate the elders of Velua and demonstrate their contempt for the Imperium's grandeur.

She felt the pressure building in her forearms as the great Titan yearned for weapons discharge. 'Sensorus Tovrel, I want an optimal firing solution calculated. Mass enemy casualties, the majority of their artillery silenced, and the pressure relieved upon the Sisterhood. I note priority rank designations in the active operational area. Clarify them.'

'Clarifying, princeps!' called Tovrel. She was the youngest of the crew, perpetually channelling her rawness into diligent practice. Her bionic eyes darted and clicked as she tracked signal returns and parsed sensor feedback. 'The command squad of Canoness Irinya Sarael are amidst the artillery, and Champion Gaheris is advancing into that area as well. I have singled out their location runes and incorporated their present locations into the firing solutions.' The girl nodded, almost to herself.

'You have my thanks, sensorus,' Melpomene replied and then gestured to her opposite side. 'Steersman, take us forward.'

The Titan shook reassuringly as it lurched forward and into

new motion. The enemy's artillery was firing, concentrating that fire upon the *Vengeance* in futility. The shells burst against the active voids in flares of rainbow light and the Titan strode on through the fusillade without pain or care.

'Voids are holding, my princeps!' Valtin called. 'Reactor output is steady, by the Omnissiah's grace. All systems hold.'

'Establish communion with the others,' she growled and within a moment there were two other presences joining her. She saw them as blurs of grey-green and silver, marked with the Legio's colours. Lesser lights, drawn to her own radiance, the two Warhound princeps were flickering representations, their presence distorted by distance and the stone structures which wound through the gardens.

<Sister,> growled Princeps Bertolt, his teeth drawn back like the dune hounds that shared his engine's name. *Dune Hound*'s princeps was lean, drawn, all hard edges extrapolated through the manifold. <Give the word. We are ready to strike.>

<Ready and willing,> said Princeps Lares. By contrast she bore a quiet intensity that befitted the mistress of *Nightbeast*. <We have the flank. We have speed and strength. They waste their shells against you, and will find no purchase.> There was a growl like stalling servos. <One day we shall reclaim the home world just the same. The heathens of corroded iron will suffer just as readily as these weak disciples of the flesh.>

<The flesh is weak,> Bertolt agreed. <We cannot trust in it when there is cold iron to rely upon.> The projection shook its head, sputtering with static. <They may be the Emperor's Angels, and His chosen warriors, but they are not of the Credo Omnissiah.>

<Enough,> Melpomene said, cutting across the charged chatter. <We will draw their fire and break their lines. You will sweep from the flank and grind their guns to ashes. Support the canoness and the Champion. Break the encirclement

and allow the greater strengths of their forces to come to bear.>
She drew a deep breath as the Titan's machine spirit surged up
once again. <Show the enemy that this push is folly. Make them
quake before they ever try to threaten these shrines again.>

She cut the link and urged the Titan onwards. She raised her
arm from the throne and *Vengeance* echoed her movements.
Energy built within the great engine's forearm as the volcano
cannon charged. She could feel her flesh burning with false
fire, her veins ablaze with the echo of pure energy. The reactor
pulsed and her entire body seized. The ignition became everything, her entire world, as the fire and the rage consumed her.

The volcano cannon lashed out in a beam of pure energy.
Swathes of sweetgrass and blossoms of saint's tears were atomised immediately. Buildings held for a few seconds longer before
slumping like drunkards and succumbing to the energy blast.
They ran like candle wax in a furnace, or blew away like ash.
The Titan swept the blast over the central knot of artillery
pieces, burning away their defiled hulls even as the machine
spirits crooned in the thankfulness of release. Scrapcode spiced
the air as the engines died, breaking apart under the relentless
onslaught, collapsing in rivers of molten metal, or detonating
as shells cooked off.

Secondary explosions flickered across the trench-line. Cultists were silhouetted in the glare before they were swept away.
Melpomene's lips curled into a sneer of triumph as the detonations rocked the enemy emplacements.

'Now,' she breathed.

The two Warhounds swept in from either side of the artillery emplacements, mega-bolters howling as they raked the
enemy with fire. More artillery engines began to die. Cultists staggered and fell in the rain of shells, their bodies torn
apart to leave nothing more than carrion scraps. The two
engines were twins in green-grey and bronze, their hulls slick

with sacred oils and powdered with the drifting ashes of the engagement.

Melpomene nodded to herself and then opened a vox-link.

'Canoness Sarael. Champion Gaheris. The Legio Arconis brings you deliverance.'

The ship's interior was a mosaic of other places and other times.

He had added to it over the subjective millennia, layering history over the ship's ancient iron bones and letting it blossom through the structure. Statues gazed down with their dead eyes, books were piled at the bases of them, and glassaic had been sealed into place as though it were a terrestrial chapel. Over time every last square inch of metal had been slowly colonised, covered over with rough stone and dedicated to the Pilgrim's craft.

Grommulus Tuul stood in the centre of the chamber he liked to think of as his refectory and reached up to brush his gauntleted fingers across the face of a corpse. Weryn no longer replied to his summons and he wondered idly whether or not the prophet still lived.

'A shame, if not,' he mused.

Slaves moved around the uneven perimeter of the chamber, slowly marking out circles of grave-dirt and the ashes of martyrs. Through one gap in the circle two robed and masked serfs dragged a naked corpse, stripped of whatever finery had once adorned it. Fingers had been severed or broken where they could not be robbed of their rings, silks had been ripped from the limbs and the body was left completely exposed to the Pilgrim's gaze.

He reached out with one great hand and stroked the bare cheek with an avaricious smile. 'Fear not, little cardinal,' he muttered, laughter bubbling up behind it. 'We shall not let you go to waste.'

They had found the man staggering through the ashes and ruins of one of Tandria's murdered cities, half-blinded, and delirious from hunger and thirst. Yet another bounty of the Golden Chain's slow demise. He had required very little encouragement to die; they had not even laid blade or shot upon him. He had died quite readily of fear alone.

Grommulus dropped his hand to his belt and drew a barbed knife, its edges lined with rust. He braced one gauntlet upon the man's birdlike chest and then began to carefully incise beneath the ribcage. There was little blood. Most of it had pooled or coagulated elsewhere in the body, with the wonderfully predictable cascade of rot and biological failure. Grommulus had watched it erupt through countless subjects, and had experienced it himself during the agonies of the becalming. Where once he might have known horror, now it generated a sympathetic calm within him.

He tilted his head, and then reached into the cavity he had created, slowly seeking his goal with a methodical precision that spoke to many attempts. He began to hum lightly as he worked. Around him, in the flesh-apiaries strung between the statuary and glass, the carrion-bees stirred at last. They spread great wings, gleaming like oil upon water, warped into the patterns of death's heads and the questing strands of phages, and took flight. Where some were content to crawl over and within the dried husks of corpses that had been strung up as hives, others found the cardinal's corpse a much more appetising prospect. They congregated in swollen black masses around the eyes and mouth, or scuttled into the new wound and around Grommulus' seeking digits. He waved them away with his knife hand, and began to cut, until the liver finally slipped free.

He winced as he hefted the organ and looked down. Bees were crawling into the holes of his old wounds, chewing at his own plague-ridden flesh, and then flying back towards their nests. He smiled at the thought of being a part of the next harvest, when their produce was taken and fermented to produce the wine of heroes that the warband had always honoured. Perhaps he would imbibe when the ritual was done; or perhaps he would wait until the undertaking was complete in truth. Six worlds were dead, but his master would not be satisfied until the seventh followed them to the grave, and the False Emperor's light was at last snuffed out.

'I have made my oath, to this place and this moment,' he whispered thoughtfully. 'I am not one to fail in my most sacred duty.' He looked down at the silent corpse again. 'Am I, cardinal? Shall you be my confessor?'

The cardinal did not answer and Grommulus laughed, deep and lyrical.

'I did not think you would, my friend, but you will play your part in this drama nonetheless.'

He turned from the corpse and deposited the liver onto a copper dish, its surface crawling with verdigris. Grommulus reached out and began to palpate the mass of flesh slowly and deliberately. He towered over it, crouched like a cathedral gargoyle, his ulcerated tongue tucked into his cheek as he focused. His immense Terminator plate whirred with the sound of stuttering servos as failing mechanisms caught and realigned before the armour systems shifted again to compensate. It was in a constant state of adaptation, much as he was.

There were some who considered that the disciples of the Grandfather were stolid and unmoving individuals, so opposed to change that they could not adapt or evolve. Nothing could be further from the truth. Rot was necessary for other things to flourish and grow. That was what the followers of the Changer could not countenance, and what the ossified dogma of the Imperium would never accept.

'Even He must moulder upon His Throne if we are ever to

birth a greater empire,' Grommulus muttered absently. He scratched at his cheek with his free hand, where a new lesion had begun to spread. Even now, so long after the first revelation, he was still finding ways to be surprised.

The liver was not cooperating, not as others had in previous days. It felt to him as though there were so many fates in flux since the Rift had opened. Since Guilliman had returned to walk amongst the living and launched his little crusade. What was the primarch's paltry effort next to wars that had raged for ten thousand years? The Long War. The only war which still truly mattered, and he, Grommulus Tuul, had been *chosen* to be one of its standard bearers.

'Hmm...' he mused as he manipulated the tissue. 'Yes, here we are. A little morsel of the future to be teased out.' The signs were as clear as they could be. This was a man who had been so intimately tied to this clutch of worlds and systems, who had been a cardinal-king of one of the vaunted Golden Chain. Shrine systems, singing into the forever dark, shining like beacons in the cold void. His soul would have shone with knowledge and revelations, and his flesh contained the echoes of that spiritual trauma. Like bruises spreading across skin.

Then he felt something. A gnarl of resistance like old scar tissue. It was a knot of growing uncertainty and it brought a scowl to his face as he traced it out. His fingers moved more urgently now. He leant closer. There was an art to anthropomancy, and he had practised it many times before when guidance and clarity were required. He could have summoned psykers, sorcerers and plague-seers to plunge into the future's tides. The domains of the Traitor Legions crawled with such beings, and he could even have unseated the mind of a Tzeentchian mystic with the correct pox or parasite, the better to make it vomit forth secrets and revelations.

Yet Grommulus Tuul trusted only the work of his own hands

and the execution of his own will. War could be trusted to subordinates, but divination was a personal undertaking. To hold the threads of fate, woven through the cosmos like so many veins and arteries, tracing them back to their core so you could *squeeze*. That was a thing of beauty. It was intimate. It was perfect. Or, at the least, it should be.

'No,' he whispered as he interpreted. Ideas became certainties behind his eyes. They became truth. Sureties could be pernicious in times such as these. Especially when they were... 'No,' he repeated. 'That can't be. It shall not be.'

Doors opened and broke his frustrated reverie. He turned from the bowl and wiped his gauntlets on his thigh plates. A sigh bubbled up from within him.

The warriors who strode into the chamber had served him through countless campaigns and undertakings. Veterans, one and all. All had followed him to his new purpose and embraced it as their own. Ulgrath, with his cruel sneer nestled amidst the burn-scars and rad-marks of his shrunken head – his armour blackened by his old commitment to the Destroyer cadres. Dakren, hung with so many philtres and phials that he clattered when he walked. He shone with the lambent light contained within each, the brewing contagions and poison mixes lending him an alchymical air. Others lingered behind them, waiting in the wings for the good news that they anticipated he would deliver.

Nema, Tandria, Asininia, St Jowet, Beneficia, and Palrec. Six glorious victories, six dead worlds, had granted them a sense of invulnerability. These were days of plenty, and the harvest of flesh had been more than expected. Slaves, vectors and raw materials flooded the holds, and the carrion-bees were feasting. To say nothing of the warband.

'There will have to be,' Grommulus began, chewing over the words as though he could work the distaste away through effort alone, 'alterations to our plans.'

Chapter Five

HEALING WATERS
SCIONS OF THE FAITH
BEARING THE STORM

They had passed through shadow and smoke, and into the embrace of healing waters.

After the coming of the Titans the battle had been all but over. The cultists had broken and fled, dragging what materiel they could salvage back into the undergrowth. Running battles had persisted, dogging their heels as they headed out of the gardens and into the wastes their war had created. To scuttle under whatever rocks would hide them.

The loyalists had pursued as far as they could before the order to withdraw had come and all of them – Sisters, Astartes, Veluans and even the Titans – had begun the journey back to the safety of the walls. The Titans were the God-Emperor's grace upon the world, yet a limited resource. Without resupply or direct support they were deployed sparingly. Three Titans were not enough to pacify a world in upheaval, no matter who marched with them.

Irinya and her warriors finally took the opportunity to

breathe, to set aside their armour and to have their wounds attended by the Sisters Hospitaller and the cardinal's chosen apothecaries. Scrapes, cuts and bruises were all meticulously checked for signs of infection. Their mouths and noses were examined for parasites, and blood was taken in gurgling vials by a needle-equipped servitor unit. They brushed off each indignity as it arose and prepared themselves for the next. Duty was a matter of overcoming those trials in the service of the Imperium. Had they been found wanting, or impure, then they would have accepted their fates readily with bared necks. Yet all of them passed through the cordons and quarantine measures, waved on by rebreather-wearing clerics and medicae personnel.

Now they took the time to recline amidst the healing waters and the steam which rose from them. The springs bubbled deep from beneath the High Sacristy, far from the front and the walls, close to the heart of the world's faith. Above them sprawled the inner precincts of the cardinal's palace, layer upon layer of sacred stone and holy sites.

Irinya was not certain whether they were natural hot springs or warmed by hidden heat exchangers beneath the smooth white marble. For other deployments she had studied every detail and immersed herself within the spiritual history of their surroundings, but Velua was a cold comfort and an unsettled posting. The past was best left undisturbed, when the fires of the present still burned and drew her eye.

'Better than the tunnels, at the least,' Agata grunted. 'I would happily fight the rest of this war out in the open, as we did at the end, if it meant never venturing below ground again. Give me the open plains and the enemy face to face, and I will die contented.'

'You should not be so eager to die, nor reckless with your life,' Beatrice put in. Agata shook her head in response and turned away from the other woman.

'There's joy to be had in smiting the enemy,' Agata replied with a snort. 'It's as much an act of worship as prayer.'

Beatrice sniffed. 'I know that as well as you do,' she said. 'I am no coward, and I won't be accused of such by you merely because your choler outstrips your virtue.'

'Enough,' Irinya put in wearily. 'Battle is behind us, and it is ahead of us, but in this moment we are Sisters. We have our calm, and we have our duty. We must take the opportunity to rest and rearm while we can.'

All eyes were on her now and one by one the others nodded. Apologies were muttered even as Agata and Beatrice turned from each other and busied themselves dressing wounds, or bathing.

Irinya stood, clad in a simple white supplicant's robe. The others were similarly attired, but now she could appreciate their differences. Without their armour they lacked that cold uniformity. Irinya's skin was dark save where it was marked by old scars. The wounds crept up her neck, up across her close-cut hair and the scalp beneath it. Her eyes gazed out from that tired face, the weight of years that even rejuvenat could not entirely erase, pale blue and weary.

She could not have been more different from Agata, whose youth burned as intensely as her flamer, and whose skin was pockmarked by burn scars. She wore her brands with a cocksure pride, never allowing them to truly tarnish her strength. They shone amidst her pale skin, upon her cheeks, and just below the white of her hair. Beatrice and Sybele shared the same tanned complexion, where Oxanna was ruddy and dour. Selene, by contrast, affected an austerely shaved head – the better to demonstrate her own interpretation of piety.

All so different, Irinya thought, *and yet shaped for singular purpose. All threads in the same great tapestry.* In many ways that was the strength and joy of the Schola Progenia. So many aspects and examples of humanity spun together until they emerged, fully formed, as those who would serve most true and fight the hardest.

Her time in the schola had been fraught, but had also included some of the most contented moments of her life.

'You knew her, did you not?'

Irinya looked up. Beatrice had turned to speak to her, her eyes wide and bright. She was a newer addition to the squad, drafted in to replace other fallen Sisters. So many had flocked to the call to crusade and the words of Morvenn Vahl, when the abbess had added her own voice to that of Primarch Guilliman.

'What did you say?' Irinya asked.

'The saint, the Lady of Woes. They say you knew her. Fought at her side, before her martyrdom and elevation.'

The air had grown close, warm even beyond the rising steam and the wafting scent of the aromatic herbs which burned in low braziers around the chamber's edge. Irinya coughed, clearing her throat. She remembered Teneu; her end, her sacrifice, and all that had come to pass as a result of it. She collected herself and then continued.

'I knew her, yes. She was my comrade, my commander and my friend.' She swallowed hard. Thoughts of Teneu, of the *Lady of Woes* – and Throne how she hated that title – sat ill in her heart and mind. This world was cloaked in the memories of her, elevated almost to a form of artisanal worship.

'What was she like?'

Irinya was silent for a long moment.

'She was...' Irinya found herself struggling to find the words. Feelings and memories bubbled up through her, evoking thoughts she had long considered banished. This world, this conflict, was dragging them out one by one and making them face the light. 'She was singular. Of all the warriors I have served with, she was the most driven and the most... gifted.'

'I have heard it said that she carried the Emperor's grace,' Josefine put in. 'That she lived and died wielding His light. That is why they made her a saint, is it not?'

His light. Irinya forced a smile even as the thought drove her close to tears. 'She bore light close to her heart, yes,' Irinya said.

The others fell silent, sensing her reticence. The close air of the chamber seemed stifling now. The rising steam and incense felt like the whip of ashen winds, and the water felt like the burning slag of buildings or the molten lifeblood of a dying world. She turned and looked across the chamber, seeing only questing columns of basalt, broken and carved with ruinous symbols.

Teneu lay at the base of one. Her armour was ragged and sword-scarred, red with her spilled blood. She raised her head, her eyes cataracted and unseeing, yet fixed upon Irinya.

'Why?' the spectre asked, voice cracking. Blood ran from her lips as she spoke and her whole body tremored. She rose unsteadily, armour servos juddering, limbs spasming erratically as she moved. The ghost image shuddered with the hell-light behind it, the charnel illumination of burning cities and a world gone mad. Teneu's lips peeled back from bloody teeth, and Irinya felt her own eyes close. She willed herself to remain calm, to remain unmoving. Panic rose in her breast, hot, urgent, and electric.

'Canoness?'

She opened her eyes again. Selene laid a hand on her shoulder, leaning forward in concern.

'Are you well?'

'I will be fine,' Irinya said as she swallowed back bile and forced a smile to her lips. 'I have to be. Besides...' She paused. 'We have done well this day. We have fought hard and bled the enemy. It will be a time before they can assault our walls in such force again. We reflect and we take heart, for the war rages on.

Soon the war council will convene, and we will face the other luminaries of the crusade and of this world.' She laughed bitterly. 'In all things, from the heart of battle to the centre of bureaucracy, one thing holds true. The Emperor protects.'

'The Emperor protects,' said Cardinal Erikos, bowing his grey-haired head in the direction of the warriors who had already gathered beneath his perch of marble and gold.

The Hall of Heroes was one of the centrepieces of Velua's High Sacristy. Every inch of the chamber was gilded or ornamented with precious gemstones, and the stonework crawled with murals the way a convict was marked by ink. Above them the God-Emperor gazed down, hands outstretched as though to cup the galaxy between His fingers. Saints and warrior-hosts spilled outwards from Him like the folds of a great cloak, and nestled amidst the multitudes were renditions of the blessed Nine Primarchs, Sebastian Thor, and Alicia Dominica.

Gaheris looked around the group of disparate fighters, drawn from so many branches of the Imperium, while they all looked back at him with barely disguised awe. He stood to the cardinal's right, evoking the image of the Emperor's wrathful right hand, with his helm mag-locked at his belt.

He had pale features, sharp and determined, crested by close-cropped blond hair. He was like a statue come to life. When he moved, even outside of combat, it unnerved those around him. A being such as Gaheris, both stolidly physical and yet spiritually numinous, was almost fundamentally *wrong* and yet it was to him that they turned. He had understood this as a Chaplain: the disconnect from the mortals they had been made to protect, and the importance of cleaving to the Chapter cult. He had still been a symbol then, but for the benefit of his brothers. Now the weight of the laurels rested upon his head, and he stood as one of the worthies here, amidst these scions of the faith.

He watched from across the chamber as Canoness Sarael made herself known. She strode into the great hall clad merely in a supplicant's robes, and yet the authority exuded from her in a wave. He knew that she had forged ahead of other lines of advance, even fighting amidst the weapon pits of the enemy. She had stood against the cultists even as the Titans had marched to her aid, as they had fired into her very midst, and continued to fight. That spoke to a resourcefulness and tenacity that he could not help but admire in a mortal.

'Canoness,' he said simply as she drew up opposite him. The woman bowed her head, and he found himself noting the myriad scars upon her scalp, dating them as best he could by eye. They spoke of a long legacy of sacred warfare. 'You honour us with your presence.'

'The honour is mine, Champion Gaheris,' she replied, and then turned to kneel before the cardinal. 'I thank you, Cardinal Erikos, for including me in this council of war.'

'There are no servants of the Emperor whom we would turn away in this time of need,' the cardinal declared with a sage nod. He looked from Irinya to the others who stood before him. Princeps Melpomene of the Legio Arconis looked up at the cardinal with an easy defiance, her back ramrod straight. She turned her head to return Gaheris' gaze and smiled, broadly and unnaturally. It took him a moment to realise that she was not smiling at all, but instead baring her teeth – an attempt to establish some sort of dominance with the chamber's apex predator.

Gaheris followed the cardinal's gaze as it moved to where a black-coated figure stood, sipping tea from a simple metal cup. He was an older man, perhaps not as biologically aged as the cardinal, but one who wore it honestly. His left arm, the one raising the cup to his lips, was a stuttering augmetic – all tarnished steel and rubbery plastek – almost the definition of a scavenged limb.

Commissar Ignatio Rugrenz was a man of quietly forceful power. One had to be when they were one of the many political officers who held the leash of the Savlar Chem-Dogs. Even now Gaheris was unsure how they had come to serve with Fleet Sextus. The defenders who had been left behind had occupied Velua while members of Battle Group Thor, led by Marshal Urtrix, sought to save other precious worlds deep in Ultima Segmentum. They were rag-tag and badly matched, and discipline amongst the penal soldiery fluctuated more than that of even the beleaguered Veluan Hoplites.

Gaheris shook his head as he watched the commissar nonchalantly enjoying his refreshment, as though he lacked a care in the world. For what it was worth, Gaheris had never seen the man even look perturbed by the circumstances of the war – but nor could he doubt the ferocity that the chem-boosted soldiers had displayed above and below ground.

To the right of the commissar stood a man who looked utterly uncomfortable. He was not used to command, Gaheris noted at once, and held his bronze helmet in his hands, turning it over and over again as though it would soothe his ailing nerves.

'Acting Colonel Yitrov,' Gaheris said with a nod to the man's new rank insignia. 'You honour us with your presence.'

The man's ruddy jowls ceased quivering through pure shock alone, and he nodded back, his bristly black moustache jittering above his lip as he tried to force the words out. He wheezed as he spoke.

'Thank you, esteemed Champion. I must confess, I don't feel worthy, here amongst such notables. Yet circumstances being what they are, it is my pleasure to represent the regiment at this, uh, august council.' He swallowed hard and raised a hand to wipe at his mouth, before falling silent once again. The desertion of Colonel Draszen, who remained at large, was clearly weighing heavily on the man who had been chosen to assume his position.

'Now that we are all gathered,' the cardinal put in, 'we can begin to discuss the matters at hand.' He drummed his long, thin fingers against the arms of his throne. His white robes pooled around him, making him look more fragile and small to Gaheris' eyes. Like a child's doll dressed up in its owner's clothes. Despite his physical frailty and slender build, the cardinal was ablaze. His eyes were bright and strong, clear and cognisant of the fact that lives depended upon his every decision – not merely as a leader, but as a shepherd of men.

Erikos stretched out one hand and a hololithic cartograph flickered into being in the air between them. Servo-skulls flitted through the light-beams of the hidden generators and began to broadcast their own representations onto the map. Runic marks flared up to indicate the disposition of their forces, while red sigils pulsed with the locations – confirmed or suspected – of enemy or insurgent elements.

'The outermost of the shrineholds and monastic holdings are, as of now, considered lost to us,' Yitrov put in as he leant closer to survey the disposition of cult forces. 'A concerted push could, of course, recover those areas, but knowing the enemy they are also already defiled and likely to be laced with traps. We proceed, though, in our reclamation. The push into the Hanging Gardens has disrupted some of the enemy's might and bought us further time to fortify. We will, in due course, extend our cordons out past the gardens themselves to reclaim our lost shrines and take stock of what has been lost. I would advise–'

'Caution, I am sure, and in other circumstances perhaps that would be wisdom,' Irinya put in. Gaheris watched her without expression as she moved to the map and swept her hand through it, from the immaterial spires of the High Sacristy, down to where the once orderly avenues of shrines and devotional infrastructure had collapsed to a stylised depiction of ruin and trench networks. 'This is our holy ground. These are our places of worship. Where the bones of saints, martyrs and heroes are entombed for the greater glory of the Imperium. What cost do we measure their loss in? In mere ground? Bone by bone? Or do we mark them in the wounds done to the very soul of the Imperium? Do you not think that these blasphemies hurt Him yet further, in His eternal agonies?'

'If there is gutter work to be done then the Savlar will sink to it,' Rugrenz put in placidly. 'I'm told they think that there will be spoils in the sullied places, and will exceed their remit regarding...' The man trailed off, waving his augmetic hand in the air with an audible clicking. 'Regarding legitimate salvage.'

'I will have no looting of the sacred places,' Erikos put in with a sniff.

'Nor will I,' Gaheris said. He drew the Black Sword and pointed it across the chamber. The tip of it grazed the hololith, distorting it momentarily as he held the man's gaze. 'I do not doubt that you, a commissar with experience in herding the penal troops, know how best to corral your soldiers. I will tolerate no blasphemy from them, and will not hesitate to execute any who break faith with the defenders of this world. Or who expose themselves to heretical artefacts.'

The commissar, to his credit, stared down the blade and then looked up to Gaheris with a smile. He sipped his tea and then stooped to place the cup on the floor.

'But of course, Champion. Believe me when I say that there are none less reticent than myself to exact punishment on the Savlar. Whether that's a bolt to the skull or simply sending them back to the pit they despise. Rest assured, we will ensure they do their part.' He patted the bolt pistol holstered at his hip. 'One way or another.'

'Perhaps this is an opportunity,' Irinya volunteered. 'A chance for your soldiers to earn the God-Emperor's favour and forgiveness in the cause of holy war. Redemption, or at the very least a measure of grace, bought in blood and suffering.'

'I will certainly be happy to volunteer that viewpoint to them, canoness,' Rugrenz said with a low chuckle.

'All very well and good,' Melpomene said from the sidelines. 'We'll happily quibble over who goes where and who is not allowed to touch what, but you will still not give my engines full leave to walk in strength. We had to take the initiative ourselves, when the guns drew too close to your pretty walls.'

'A slight which I am willing to forgive, in the God-Emperor's sight, despite the wounds done to the sacred gardens and the architectural losses beneath the feet of your machines, princeps.' Erikos leant forward on his throne, looming over the princeps, who returned his gaze evenly.

'The Machine God is bounteous to those who serve. The Omnissiah protects those who protect themselves. Your little parks can be landscaped again. Your buildings can be rebuilt. It is harder, far harder, to reconsecrate what has been made unclean. I am of Sareme, do not forget. We know well the ravages of the Archenemy and the taint they carry as sure as breath. Do not hide my guns when they may yet burn the enemy from their unholy places!'

'No weapon is beyond our consideration,' Gaheris said. Despite himself, he found that he liked the princeps. She had a straightforward manner. Aggressive, eager, unflinching. She reminded him, in many ways, of his own brothers.

'None,' Irinya agreed. 'The Champion and I speak with one voice. As crucial as it is to preserve the religious infrastructure of this world, its survival is the more pressing issue.' She swallowed, collected herself, and then continued. 'Six other worlds already lie despoiled at the enemy's hands. That is without considering the disparate calls for aid which have drawn the other crusade elements away. These are harsh times. Lean seasons.'

She turned and regarded Gaheris. 'Has there been any word from Marshal Urtrix?'

Gaheris shook his head and began to pace around the hololith, distracting himself by checking and rechecking tactical details and dispositions. 'Nothing, canoness. The astropaths have sent missives and sung their hymns into the dark, and still there is no answer. All that comes back are the wails of despair, the mortis cries of dying worlds, and talk of a kingdom of iron brought to ruin.'

'An ill omen.' Erikos shook his head wearily. 'As though there are any other kinds in these darkening nights. I thank you all for your insight and your counsel. We shall reconvene in the morning and there we shall more properly consecrate our plans for a renewed offensive. I have prayed to the God-Emperor...' He paused and knotted his hands in front of him, as though to demonstrate to the assembled notables what prayer entailed. 'And He will guide us to victory. All storms end. All wounds inevitably heal. We will endure this and we will emerge stronger. That is my vow.'

'Fine words,' the canoness said with a bow. 'By morning we will ready our forces and sally out, securing what we can and ensuring that no enemy agents remain close to our walls. Sappers and saboteurs will abound in the enemy's arsenal.' She cut across the air with one hand. 'In His name they shall be driven back and purged.'

'Praise be,' Gaheris responded simply. He made the sign of the aquila across his chest. 'The canoness has the right of it. Until that time I shall take my place upon the walls and hold the night's vigil.'

With that, Gaheris turned with a bow of his head to leave the great chamber, out from the riot of grandeur and spectacle and back towards the waiting war.

* * *

The Champion walked the battlements alone and watched the day die.

He was not truly alone, of course. No wall would remain unmanned in a time of war. He passed by common line troopers as they gazed out from the parapets, and watched as they clutched their lasguns that little bit tighter. They stood taller in his shadow, as though the very presence of one of the Emperor's Angels could strengthen their resolve and protect them from the encroaching darkness. Some offered up prayers or made the sign of the aquila as he passed.

Little gestures. *Human* gestures.

Gaheris could hear the beating of every individual heart, could move and kill them faster than they could blink, and still they were mysteries and miracles to him. The Adeptus Astartes were forged to be blades in an eternal war, shields for worlds and populations such as these, and yet all too often the common men and women of the Imperium stood by their own strength. Fought until they could fight no more and the blood poured from them, and death finally raised them up to the God-Emperor's side. They did not have the luxury of the sacred gene-seed carrying on their legacy, but they had the lives they had built, the places they protected, and the children they had sired.

Cities such as this, worlds like Velua, were built of the people and their stories. Humanity would endure here long after the stones of this place were dust. The stories of these times would outlast the marks on the map where they had once transpired.

He admired them, but he did not envy them.

From what he knew of his own recruitment, he had been liberated from a world of lush forests which had risen through the foundations of ancient, ruined mega-cities. The world had reclaimed so much of what humanity had built in a bygone era, and the people of his home world had lived simple lives before the coming of the Imperium.

The Ecclesiarchy had built chapels from the bricks of the old cities, and consecrated them to the true faith. Gaheris had served in one of those churches when he had been a youth, as an acolyte of the temple and as a defender of the faith. When the Black Templars had descended from on high, he had been one of the few to pass the trials. A world of simple folk; of scriveners and supplicants, amongst whom there had been few true warriors. He remembered...

The skull-masked figure loomed over him as he knelt, clad in sacred black, taking him by the chin. The roughness of the ceramite gauntlets, the strength of their simplest gestures before they spoke.

'This one will do. A crusader if ever I saw one.'

And he had become more than that. More now than ever before. He had risen into the ranks of the Chaplaincy, trusted and honoured beyond the common warriors. Now he stood as Champion, blessed by the God-Emperor's incarnate grace. He served just as Sigismund had once served. An indefatigable instrument, burning in the firmament.

'I shall not fail you. That is the only thing anathema to my soul,' he said, addressing the empty air.

Out beyond the void shields the sky was a riot of gold and crimson. The setting of Velua's sun cast waves of burnished light across the heavens, till the entire world seemed crowned in fire. It pleased him to see the beauty of the place shine through, unscored by artillery or missile trails, untouched by rising smoke. For a moment it seemed the war was far away – out beyond the skies and across the stars, where his brothers yet fought.

'And yet I told them my place was here,' he breathed, confessing to the cold and deepening dark, as the sun continued its descent. 'This world burned with His light, and I imagined that He had a plan for me. To stand as His sentinel. His Champion. To fight before the walls and take the heads of the enemy's vaunted. As Sigismund once did.'

It is not enough to emulate, he thought. *I must be the example now.*

Movement caught his eye further along the wall and he moved to follow it. Even without wearing his helm, his sight was more than sufficient to trace the source of the disturbance, but he did not need it. It was not a subtle thing that moved through the world, like a sign, like an omen.

The wolf was crafted of golden fire and ashen grey. It nosed at the air and continued onwards, snuffling at the ground or raising its head to growl at the fleeing dawn. At times its passage would stutter, like a vid-screen wracked by bad signal, where other times it shone with absolute clarity. He could tell, from its bearing, that it was a she-wolf. She turned and regarded him, blue eyes gleaming in the shadows. She was criss-crossed with old scars, as though she had fought and struggled for so very long before her trials had brought her here.

Then she was gone. Lost to the darkness, with only the hint of firelight to have marked her passage.

Gaheris blinked and moved forwards as though to follow. For a moment he feared he would vanish too, swept away into the immaterium by the devices of the enemy. He reached for empty air and then allowed himself to kneel, to consider the vision.

'What does it mean?' he asked, as though the heavens would finally answer. 'My lord, my God-Emperor, what do you intend for me?'

Alone, Gaheris carried the weight of the oncoming storm, and let its omens pass over him.

Chapter Six

REMEMBRANCE

DAUGHTERS OF THE EAGLE

WISDOM OF AGES

With the council disbanded Irinya chose, at last, to walk the sacred precincts of the High Sacristy.

She ignored the walls, where patrols would only serve to disturb her, and the distant presence of the retreating enemy would only infuriate her. To drive them back was a victory but to have them beyond her wrath felt almost sinful. Instead she descended, down through the levels and along the sweeping marble staircases which threaded into the darkness. Banners billowed in the incense-breeze, fluttering around the silent statues of heroes. The movement gave them the curious illusion of life, as though the saints and martyrs yet walked amongst them. They also concealed sallyports and hidden kill-alcoves, if these sacred places were ever violated.

Worship was inextricable from violence. That was the universal truth which the Cult of the Saviour Emperor had carried forth from Terra ten thousand years ago. It was the singular revelation which had been nurtured upon San Leor, transplanted to

Ophelia and Terra, tainted by association and purified in blood. Battle and bloodshed were sacred things. They were ritual tools which had fuelled mankind's dominion of the galaxy.

Even now, with that great realm sundered, the holy violence of their faith was the greatest tool available to them.

What lies beyond the Rift? she wondered, as she had wondered countless times before. *What remains of our brothers and sisters? The great holy places of the galactic north?* She did not know. Perhaps she would never know. The regent, perhaps, had some idea. A demigod would know such things and so restructure the very universe to serve that understanding. Perhaps they were all mere pawns to such a being, waiting to be moved into place. Waiting for the perfect moment to reclaim what had been sundered.

She thought again of what had been lost, as she pressed her hands to the great gilded doors of the Sanctum.

Before her, surrounded by ornamental pools of clear water, sat the sarcophagus. She did not recognise the woman whose face graced the statuary upon it, just as it had seemed a stranger in the tunnels beneath the Hanging Gardens. This was not Teneu as she had known her in life, but a strangeling simulacrum. All the hopes and dreams and fears of Velua's populace had annealed to it like the accumulation of silt, leaving a visage warped by expectation and the enthusiasm of sculptors. The figure of the saint lay as though in state, dominating the white marble and gold sarcophagus, but she did not keep her vigil alone. It was bedecked with martial renditions – warriors of the Sisterhood stood shoulder to shoulder with stylised carvings of the Adeptus Astartes. Heroes and angels defended her sacred resting place with bared weapons and exposed hearts. Golden flames surrounded them, dancing across the marble fields like the aftermath of an artillery barrage.

It spoke in a single voice: that this was the grave of a warrior

and a hero, a woman who had given her life dearly to deny the
Archenemy of mankind.

And who had been blessed. Exalted. *Gifted.*

Irinya bit back the words that threatened to spill from her. Choked by doubt and fear, rage and pain, she merely slumped resignedly to her knees. She felt pain as they hit the cold stone, a reminder of her age.

Age catches up with us all, does it not? I pray that I die well, before infirmity robs me of the chance. Only then, perhaps, will I be worthy enough to stand at His side and fight with you again, forever.

Her thoughts roiled. This was a place of sanctity – a truly sacred space within a city-complex of shrines and graves and holy places – and yet all that she felt was uncertainty.

'O, God-Emperor, who reigns above, and guides the galaxy's turn, hear me. I am but a humble servant and supplicant. I come before you shriven of sin and free of the ravages of heresy. Where others have succumbed, I have been steadfast. Where others have broken, I have endured. I remain where...' She let her eyes rise from the floor to the sarcophagus. Lit by the flickering light of a hundred candle flames it seemed to burn with its own supernal radiance: in wrath, and in judgement.

'Canoness Irinya?'

She rose and turned at the interruption. Irinya's motions were too quick, motivated by a sudden shame, the sense of being caught. She looked into the pale green eyes of a novitiate of the Order. The girl, no more than nineteen years Terran standard, seemed almost as shocked as Irinya was. She stammered and looked away, perhaps expecting punishment to manifest from thin air at her having interrupted the canoness' meditations.

'Forgive me, canoness. It was not my intention to–'

'Hush, child,' Irinya soothed and raised her hands. 'This is no sanctioned affair of state. Simply an old woman taking an opportunity to...' She trailed off. 'To pay her respects.'

'Those who pray at the martyr's tomb shall be shielded from harm. That is what they say.' She swallowed. 'Do you seek her aegis before returning to the war?'

Irinya laughed. 'No, child,' she said as she shook her head. 'He will protect me from harm without troubling the saint's rest. I merely came to see it once again. In truth I have not been here since she was interred.'

The novitiate's entire manner changed then. Excitement surged through her. 'You were here then? You knew her? In life?'

'I did.' She paused. 'What is your name, child?'

'Angharad, canoness, Novitiate Angharad.'

'Do you know the history of the saint, Angharad? Do you know what shaped her and set her upon her path, and kept her safe before the end?'

The girl hesitated. 'I... We have been taught of her life and her martyrdom. She was of your Order, the Order of Our Martyred Lady. She died upon Navmire, in the face of the blood cults and their warp-spawned masters.' She tilted her head, as though considering. She gestured to one of the murals that adorned the walls, a station of the martyrdom where a stylised rendition of Teneu faced down horned shadows. She had a sword raised in defiance of that darkness.

A chainsword.

'She eschewed finer weapons,' Angharad volunteered eagerly. 'She wielded a simple chainsword, as a mark of her piety and dedication.'

Irinya blinked. Her hand fell to the hilt of Truth's Kiss. 'Is that so?' She could feel her knuckles tighten to whiteness around the handle. She gritted her teeth, unsure whether to laugh or weep. 'Thank you for the lesson, child. If you'll excuse me, I wish to meditate upon the wisdom of the saint.'

Angharad nodded eagerly and turned to leave. 'God-Emperor bless you, canoness.'

'May He watch over you as well, Angharad.'

She knelt again before the sarcophagus, closed her eyes, and embraced the prayer of remembrance.

Rytask was a dry world, moisture-starved and sun-scorched.

Why it had been settled at all in mankind's storied past was a mystery, but there were uses it could be put to. The faithful adored the places in the universe defined by suffering; the better to sharpen their zeal and wear in their piety.

Irinya barely remembered the world that had birthed her. There were impressions sometimes. Grey towers climbing the cliffs, with the green lichen coiling between them. Light refracted through glassaic windows that made the entire world glow, burn and sing. She had been orphaned young, as all who found their way to the schola were, and had been chosen for holy service. She had disembarked with countless others, boys and girls, none of them older than twelve. They had been told by grim-faced instructors that salvation lay ahead, that they would be tended to in their weakness, and raised up in the sight of the God-Emperor.

First, though, there had been the climb.

If there were some other way to the top, a proper road or the use of a lifter or shuttle, then it had been kept from them. They had been given simple Militarum-issue packs, a day's supply of water and rations, and expected to make the ascent alone.

Of the dozens released from the landing fields, it was Irinya and Teneu who had made it to the top first. Irinya by sheer force of will, and Teneu by a determined canniness. Their joint ascent had sealed their friendship.

Years had passed together, their fates intertwined, each vying for recognition amidst the isolated mountain halls of the schola. Teneu, coming from a more privileged upbringing, had been singled out for advancement, while Irinya was ever at her heels – motivated by nothing short of pure spiritual momentum. She did not resent the other girl, not truly. Their competition only ever spurred both of them on to greater heights.

Irinya strode out onto one of the great observation balconies which ringed the schola, breathing in the chill air of the mountain's heights, and gazed out over the sun-baked plateaus below. The mountain, she had learned, was known to the local populace as the Emperor's Eye, eternally watching over them and shielding them from deviance. She had heard it said that the Imperial Palace had replaced what had once been Terra's greatest mountain range, incorporating the peaks into its bones. From here she understood, in some small sense, the raw dominance of the Imperium. Even the greatest of nature's wonders were but playthings for humanity's relentless, rapacious ingenuity.

Her senses finally acclimated to being outside, to the roar of the wind and the blistering sunlight, and she meandered from one end of the vast terrace to the other. One rim of it, now bathed in sunlight, was set aside for the local species of avian – an aquiline breed which evoked the proud symbol of the Imperium, and whose nesting had been encouraged, earning it the name of the Eyrie.

It was only then that Irinya heard the weeping.

Teneu sat, her robes pooled around her, cradling something in her hands. Irinya drew nearer, peering over the other girl's shoulder. She gasped. One of the eaglets lay in her hands, tiny and featherless, and completely still. Her hand fell to Teneu's shoulder without even meaning to and the other girl looked around, still sniffling.

'I don't know what to do,' she whimpered plaintively. 'I came out to tend to them and found this one. I don't know how it could have happened. I've been so careful.'

She wondered if it had been simple jealousy from their fellows. Envious of the position Teneu had achieved and the responsibility lavished upon her. So many of their instructors whispered *of the girl's promise, her diligence augmented by her more noble background.*

Irinya sighed and stooped down beside the other girl. She reached out and gently took the corpse from her hands, nestling it in her own. She looked down at the poor scrawny thing, its eyes barely even capable of sight. To die so young, with an entire life denied to you, was a thing of cruelty. She prayed every night to the God-Emperor that her life would be long, filled with meaning and true service. She did not know if He heard her. There were wars burning in the firmament and millions, billions perhaps, of more worthy souls spread across His Imperium.

What were a child's dreams next to those?

She prayed now. She leant her head forward and intoned the words, the Valediction Against Death and the mortuary prayers of the Sisters Hospitaller. She let them hiss between her teeth even as tears stung her own eyes.

She felt warmth blossom between her fingers, the tingling sensation of skin caught in bright sunlight. Her body hid her hands from the sun's glare, but even if it had not the sensation was different. It was a light balm, a warm rush of vitality.

Something stirred.

She sat back sharply, almost dropping her charge. The eaglet raised its head and looked around without sight. It cawed softly, and then found its strength and began to chatter wildly.

'What...?' Teneu blinked away tears, her brown eyes wide, and looked down at the eaglet. No longer dead. No longer cold. She reached out and took it back into her arms. 'How?'

Irinya looked at her, dumbstruck. 'I don't know.'

'A miracle,' Teneu breathed.

'Hush, sister, it is not–'

But Teneu was already up and moving, running out across the balcony and into the schola proper. Shouting of miracles.

* * *

Irinya shook herself, as though from a dream, and looked up. The familiar stranger of Teneu's transfigured visage gazed down at her from the sides of the sarcophagus, her passion and her rapture etched there, without a single morsel of her humanity.

Irinya rose silently, wiped the tears from her cheeks, and stalked off into the shadows.

'Training,' Barisan had said, 'is the soul of duty. You must be ever ready for battle. You are beyond human, yes, and superior in so many ways – but that gift will only endure if its edge is kept keen.'

Aneirin's mentor said many things. He found he did not yet understand all of them, but when he spoke of the need to keep himself prepared for war, Aneirin understood that as the plain wisdom it was. That was why he moved, alone, below the spot-lumens in the plaza. Cradled by the palace's interior walls it had been a place of personal reflection and self-castigation once, as he understood it, but the demands of the war had seized and changed it, as so many things upon Velua were changing.

There was always this, though. The purity of the moment. Not true and honest combat, but allowing his body to surrender to the reflexes of battle. He moved organically through the open space, turning and pivoting. His sword rose and fell, not yet engaged, cutting through the empty air as he allowed his mind to flow through combat routines.

The correct angle to successfully decapitate a greenskin.
The physical weak points of the constructs of the necrons.
The best way to engage with the aeldari devil-breeds.

Such knowledge had been imparted to him by the gift of hypnogogic programming, and reinforced by the lessons of Barisan. He was still young in the ways of the Chapter, and yet he took to the art of war with all the vigour that had carried him through the jungles of his home world.

'I serve,' he hissed through his teeth, 'the will of the Walking Sun. The God-Emperor of Mankind. I shall not be found wanting.'

'A fine statement, youngblood,' a voice growled from the shadows. 'And fine form. Barisan has trained you well.'

The bass rumble of the Dreadnought's reactor was as sudden as his voice; so lost had Aneirin been in his training, swept up in his thoughts, that he had almost not realised that the honourable warrior had been standing sentinel in the darkness. Venerable Toron loomed out of the shadows and strode towards him, tilting forward to regard the Neophyte. Aneirin lowered his blade and returned the Ancient's gaze. He was sweat-sheened, stripped to the waist, even in the night's cold. He chuckled to himself, imagining how vulnerable he must appear to the living weapon. 'You honour me, Venerable Toron.'

'I merely state what is obvious. There have been many Neophytes through the years of this crusade. Some have lived, others have died. You, I like. You have promise. Spirit. I have seen it in others before.'

'I strive only to do what the God-Emperor wills, Ancient. If that pleases you, then I am pleased in turn.'

'Such humility from one so young.' Toron laughed, a staccato machine-rasp that grated against Aneirin's spine. 'I thought I had grown beyond the grasp of miracles.'

Aneirin took the opportunity to study the Ancient's iron skin, pitted and scarred by centuries of war. He was not of the new pattern, the Redemptor tomb which would be the fate of those Primaris brothers both wounded and honoured enough to endure the living death. Looking upon Toron, considering the iron tomb and the knightly sleep to which the Dreadnoughts were confined, Aneirin wondered if his own faith and his duty would survive such a crucible as they clearly had in the old warrior.

'A primarch walks. There are miracles aplenty, some would say, in these nights.'

'Ha,' the Dreadnought growled. 'A true miracle would be the Praetorian returning to us. Still, a demigod is a demigod. The Avenging Son strides the stars and conducts his great war. And here we are, at the heart of it. Crusaders, all. Led by Champions and Marshals. Standing side by side with the saint-sworn.'

'And a regiment of thieves and murderers,' Aneirin volunteered.

'The Savlar, yes. All the more reason to lead by example. Let them see the heathen put to the sword, and see what their hearts say then.'

At that pronouncement the great sword that Toron bore crackled into life and bathed the corner of the square in light. Aneirin watched as the power field flickered and danced along the massive blade, alighting on words of devotion, oaths of moment, and prayers to the God-Emperor. The blade crawled with script, the way a tattooed devotee's skin might, or the pages of an immense book.

'We are the lesson, and the wisdom of ages, youngblood. It is our duty to pass it on to those who will heed it.'

Chapter Seven

WALLS OF FAITH

SACRIFICE

UNCLEAN GODS

Gaheris knelt upon the wall as a supplicant, but when he rose to stand it was as a symbol.

He had passed the night in fitful patrol, haunted by the echoes of the vision. Still he had not grasped its meaning – the wolf, stalking alone across these battlefields. What did the God-Emperor intend by it? What path was it meant to set him upon? He had considered that it might be an omen of the sons of Fenris, and yet there were none active in this battle group. The Space Wolves yet fought their own wars.

'As we all must,' Gaheris muttered.

Others had gathered to greet the dawn. Soldiers in the red and gold of the Hoplites worked uneasily beside the ragged Savlar. All toiled under the shadow of Gaheris and his brothers. He stood like a sentinel, a statue crafted of black iron and zeal. The others stood spaced out evenly along the wall. There were two hundred of his brothers still in active deployment upon Velua. An obscene commitment to any other Chapter. Not to the Black Templars. Now they held the walls and waited to see what storm would next break. Mortals were being rotated from the defence lest they break as their wayward colonel had. Gaheris and his brothers would be the iron of their defence – never fatiguing.

For ten thousand years they had fought and bled as the vanguard of the Eternal Crusade, vowing never to rest until mankind's dominion was restored. The traitors would finally be held to account and the xenos would be swept away, leaving a galaxy worthy of the God-Emperor.

'Perhaps the vermin have learned their lesson,' Barisan growled over the vox. Gaheris shook his head. He was not sure where the other warrior stood in the line, or if he would even notice the gesture.

'No,' he said. 'They have no restraint left. We have seen it in their attacks of late, and it is clear that something has incensed them. Their false prophets lead their assaults and invoke the warp more often. It is the weakness of their spirits.'

'As you say, Champion.'

Behind them the dawn bells were beginning to toll. They split the air with their clamour, calling the faithful out to their many duties. Scribes flowed from their blockhouses in a grey tide, eager to transcribe and illuminate their sacred texts. Behind them came the more drab and subdued archivists whose job it was to sort through proscribed texts or forgotten archives in search of books to burn. Novitiates of the Sororitas Orders moved amongst them, ever vigilant, even as they turned their hands to the mundanely important task of taking rubbings of the carvings upon the wall. Protection against the threat of losing the sacred knowledge and remembrances there inscribed. A necessary measure; not an admission of defeat, or even the fear of it. Simply what had to be done in the circumstances. The same way the lesser functionaries of the Ecclesiarchy would be desperately moving their money and resources, in a futile attempt to outlast the coming storm.

It had been Gaheris' experience, even as a Chaplain, even as a line warrior, that the further down you went into any mortal organisation, the more riven it was with doubt and sedition. On worlds such as Velua and her sibling shrine worlds, this had manifested as a seething, crawling heresy, worming its way into the souls of the populace. How many of them were Militarum deserters, or minor clerks forced to take up arms by the rot in their hearts? Who amongst the false prophets had once been clergy or pious men and women? All of them lost to the body of humanity now; shed like old skin, while something new and venal slithered off and into the world. Spreading poison.

He drew his sword and rested its tip upon the solid stones of the outermost wall. The earliest settlers here had named it as the Emperor's Wall, for it marked the outermost boundary of the first township they had established. They had trusted in Him to protect them from the horrors of a galaxy still reeling from apocalyptic civil war. The Cult of the Saviour Emperor, for all their lack of imagination, had possessed a rugged determinism that had seen their settlement flourish, built around the temples of the High Sacristy.

They had girded the settlement with walls of faith and those walls endured even now. It was more than the bricks and mortar, more than the defenders who stood upon them. It was formed of the hopes of the people, their faith in deliverance, and the Emperor's grand dream. Humanity, bounded by faith, united by singular purpose. By His will.

Gaheris let his fingers tighten around the blade's handle, and then drew it up.

Whatever was coming, they would face it down. With fire and faith.

* * *

The undercroft was filthy, but that suited them well. It was far back from the garden-girdled walls, beneath the ruins of an old church, where the Imperial dogs could not find them. Driven so far and with such spite that all the progress of the Sevenfold Revelation felt as though it were ashes, they had fled through the undergrowth and whatever tunnels they could find, till their feet ached and bled. The Children had gathered once more, licking their wounds and retreating across the once verdant plains with murder in their hearts and blood on their teeth. In truth they had never expected to win, but to hurt the enemy, to wound them, that was enough.

The Indomitus Crusade could not be weathered by open confrontation – not until the appointed moment. The warp whispered of other failures, tinged with success. It spoke of the blood spilled at Machorta, and the shrieking aftermath of Gath-alamor. It cajoled them with tales of counter-crusades launched by masters of the dark faith, and the Imperium turning upon itself in its desperation. That warmed them in their cold hovels and halls of the dead. It brought joy to atrophied hearts and smiles to sore-covered lips.

Weryn smiled himself, to hear it. The warp spoke with the voice of the Plague God, the voice that the Pilgrim's words had opened him to. It spoke in the wheeze of lung-rot, and the bursting sores of black-pox. It whispered through septicaemia and ague, gout and goitre, and spoke of the infirm purity of what it meant to be human.

That voice, that sacred guidance, had saved him in the end. It had allowed his gifts to addle the great Champion of the enemy, to distract and mislead him, so that Weryn could escape.

He was not sad, not truly. To falter, fail, and degrade. That was the joy of life. A joy that Weryn, in his desperation, was now extinguishing.

The blades were rusted and decrepit, pried from the sealed

tombs of Imperial heroes, but they did the job as well as any other. Their edges opened throats, their pommels staved in skulls. Death in all its ugly glory roiled out from the hands of the faithful to embrace the sacrificial masses.

Seven had died first. Then fourteen. Next twenty-eight. Then fifty-six.

They died in sevens, and groups of sevens. They embraced it willingly and with resolute silence even as the blood flowed and curdled upon the old stone of the tombs and sewers. Luminor Ceren, her sallow features scarred and bruised from the combat, stepped up and cut another throat, watching the blood run black down the front of the man's smock and flak armour.

They were, all of them, infected. The origin or strain of the pestilence did not matter, only that they had given themselves over to it. Allowed it to worm through every part of them. They were the truest disciples of the god and his ways. Angels of disease, allowing themselves to die so that others might triumph.

'This is our gift,' Weryn said. Voices raised behind his in agreement and affirmation, chanted prayers and praises. 'We offer up life to the great cycle, so that death may be averted. We let it pass us over, and instead we deliver it unto our enemies.'

The air was thick with the stink of spilled blood, and flies had begun to swarm in the close underground spaces. Lichen and mould crawled from the cracks, forced from between the stone as though squeezed through the fingers of an obscene hand. Reality curdled. The very skin of existence was writhing, palsied, as something moved beneath it. Shapes pushed at the fabric of the world, stretching it out, distending the natural order. Lumens sputtered and dimmed, flames flickered in their braziers, and Weryn felt his heartbeat hitch.

A blade, ancient and weathered, like the sacrificial blades writ large, forced its way through the empty air, wriggling like a maggot as it sought purchase. It tilted, slipped, and then caught against the flagstones. The blade screeched as it cut into the stone, anchoring itself into the floor. Something sighed, a corpse exhalation, as the first of the minor gods began to force itself into being.

It stood taller than a man, at once withered by decay, and yet also engorged with wet rot. One eye glistened in its misshapen forehead and when its mouth opened it was to reveal a mass of uneven peg teeth, around which an ulcerated tongue coiled.

Weryn fell to his knees and Ceren followed suit. Soon all the cultists were kneeling, praying, offering up thanks to the gods-who-walked.

'All we have to do,' Weryn whispered, 'is hold but a little longer. Soon he will be amongst us and we shall be redeemed.'

The daemon laughed and spread its arms. The blade had begun to flake with rust.

'*Be not afraid,*' it sneered. '*We shall deliver you.*'

The bells began to toll oddly, their ringing distorted as though the metal had suddenly warped and shifted. Aneirin looked up at the sound, the strange timbre resonating in his enhanced hearing. He growled, bared his teeth, and tried to shake it away.

His squad mates felt it too. He could sense their unease, the sudden wave of fundamental wrongness which swept the walls. The bells were the least of it, an omen ringing in his ears, but the world itself had grown sickly. The air was thicker, somehow, and looked to be bulging unevenly. Strange changes in colour flitted across the stuff of reality like a poorly developed pict, like deep-sea bioluminescence. Obscene and unnatural. Aneirin raised his sword, even as his brothers readied their own weapons.

The storm broke.

Things forced their way into the materium, writhing and wriggling as they defied the laws of mortal physics. They were swollen with decay and riddled with disease, their every exposed surface alive with unnatural vermin and phage. They laughed as they materialised, as the wall stones cracked beneath their feet, as the disciplined Veluans and the ragged Savlar both reacted with screams of horror and retches of disgust.

'Hold!' Gaheris' voice echoed across the wall, vox-amplified so that all who yet fought could hear him. 'The enemy are amongst you but they are figments! Echoes of unclean gods! False, base, and weak before your righteousness! Brothers! Bring them illumination!'

The air caught fire. Sacred flamer oil ignited as it was hurled forth. Plasma lit the wall as its pure light dispelled the curdling dawn. Inhuman bodies burst apart, detonating in rains of viscera and seared flesh which dissipated almost as soon as it was blown apart, fading back into the sea of souls.

One of the daemons had appeared directly in front of Aneirin, its mouth split in a toothy grin vertically down the centre of its face, right under the pus-weeping eye that crowned its distorted skull. He hurled himself forward, roaring in rage, sweeping his chainsword for the thing's swollen throat. It moved faster than he had expected, jerking back with a serpent's swiftness, and already its blade was sweeping up to return the favour.

'Bastard!' Aneirin snapped. This was not a mortal foe, this was one of the Neverborn. The warp given flesh and arrayed against them, as the stories said they had been in ages past.

The false gods of Chaos hungered for the galaxy. They thirsted for the souls of humanity, and wished to tear down and defile all the sacred places of the Imperium. Their every step was ruin and taint. He felt things squirm over his boots and almost lost his footing.

The heavens opened. It began to rain: a thick, heavy and unnatural rain. Great droplets spattered against the walls and burst apart into gobbets of maggots, great buzzing flies and glistening fungus. Where it struck the common soldiery they were suddenly wrestling with swarms of unclean things, weighed down by burrowing insects or assailed by biting flies. Helmets and armour held for a moment, before being overwhelmed, and the occupants died screaming. Some of the mortals were acquitting themselves well, despite the odds. Aneirin watched the Veluans firing into the twisted figures, or gouging at them with their shock bayonets. The Savlar fought madly, lashing out with simple punch knives and trench weapons, their eyes wide and mad with inhaled combat stimms. The air was thick with the stench of rot, hyper-adrenaline and burnt flesh.

Aneirin took this all in in the time it took his enemy to lunge for him again. It raised its blade in trembling, near-skeletal hands and staggered forward to swing.

Aneirin sidestepped and brought his sword round in another sweeping blow. It struck the corroded blade and drove it back. He pushed, driving transhuman strength into every blow as he forced the Neverborn to retreat, step by step, towards the edge of the wall.

'*Sons of Dorn!*' the daemon laughed, its voice a migraine scratch behind his eyes.

Aneirin blinked back tears, and kept slashing and hacking. Slivers of metal spiralled up from the sword, flesh came free in sloughing tatters of skin and rancid meat.

'*How long do you think your defiance can last? Ten millennia? More? You are young, next to the infinite enmity, but we wait for you, fleshling! Succumb! Submit!*'

Its mockery broke into outright laughter and Aneirin growled. He ducked beneath its swipe and drove his whirring chainblade through its already cracked and weeping sternum. The teeth caught and snarled against distended bone, clogging with unnatural flesh. He held it there for a moment, transfixed, pinned like an insect, before he drew back his leg and kicked it from the walls.

He turned, triumphant, exuberant, to face his brothers. To rush to their aid.

It was then that the first of them began to die.

Chapter Eight

THE HELL BENEATH

ANGELS AND DAEMONS

WAY OF WOLVES

They were dying.

Trooper Evran fired blind from around the corner of one of the subterranean tunnels, lashing the oncoming horde with bright blasts of las-fire. Cultists died by the dozen as she and her squad mates hosed the approach with fire. Las vied with solid-shot auto-fire and the throaty gasp of stubbers, but still the cultists came on. Again and again they threw themselves forward only to die, even as their fellows crushed their bodies beneath their boots, joining them moments later.

Evran had to laugh. The cultists were horribly provisioned, most of their arms and armour scavenged from the dead and apportioned to men and women who had never intended to be soldiers. There was a madness in them that passed in some sense for bravery, and that drove them on despite their ineptitude.

Her own kit was ramshackle and makeshift, scavenged from a dozen other units, but she kept it in good condition. The last thing she wanted to do was to die.

'No gakking way am I dying down here!' she shouted over the din of gunfire. Tygan turned to look at her and Evran could see his smile, even with the bulky nitro-chem injector in the way.

'Killing enough of 'em that we won't have to!' Tygan laughed. 'Stupid bastards! They just run at the shots. They've lost it!'

They had both seen it before in the deep prison sinks. Men who gave up, who walked into the toxic wastes of Savlar, or who tried to goad the guards. Enough hell could break anyone's mind. That was why they had volunteered, dredged up from the madness of Savlar to fight the Emperor's wars. To live and die by His mercy.

She had always thought that was a madness of its own. The Imperium was a monster made of men and madness. She did not have to be a gene-fixed behemoth like the Black Templars or one of the dour-faced Sisters loaded with their sense of moral piety to endure it, though. She had lived this long, under the guns of the enemy and the looming shadows of commissars. Little men in robes and borrowed armour wouldn't–

She paused. Something was moving out in the gloom, slowly and deliberately, pausing over every corpse like a patient reaper. Gnarled arthritic hands lowered to tap at the heads of cultists, where they remained, or to brush along a shoulder. It chortled noisily as it walked, danced, jigged through the rows of bodies, savouring the stench of death and the myriad faces it wore.

The thing paused and looked up with one rheumy eye, as though only now noticing the Savlar. It grinned and sped up its pace, loping forward, giggling impishly. Every now and then it would flicker and fade, only to leap forward as though by tele-portation. Hoar-frost crackled along the walls of the chamber as it moved. The air behind it shimmered with gossamer projections, like the suggestion of insectoid wings. It reached up and a great rusted blade was conjured into being, slicing through the suddenly turbid air.

'*Rejoice, brothers and sisters!*' the thing said. '*There are places enough for all of you!*'

The Savlar were already firing as it finally drew level, as the cultists flooded in behind it, and as they all began to die.

Irinya looked up as the bells tolled and the storm broke above them.

The shrine city was screaming, roaring its pain towards the heavens, even as the thunderheads clamoured like the laughter of mocking gods. She could hear the resounding report of bolter fire. The fury of competing godheads howled down from the walls as angels and monsters clashed.

Irinya and her Sisters had been holding a rear support position, down and off the walls, seeing to refugees, but they could see the corpulent light which danced and flickered there now. The vox was alive with the screams of dying men and the static-crackle of inhuman things, broken only by the stalwart prayers of the Black Templars. Rocks in a storm, pillars holding against the filthy tide.

Irinya heard the screech of rockets and watched as the iconic missiles of the Exorcists scraped the dome of the sky, hurtling over the embattled walls and out towards the plains.

'Report!' she barked, and the vox spasmed again before Sister Eloise spoke.

'*Enemy advance in force! We have auspex returns of looted Militarum vehicles and the screams of their machine spirits. I am committing all of our available artillery while the wall guns are imperilled. God-Emperor willing, they will be stymied if not outright destroyed.*'

'His grace go with you, Sister, and guide your aim true,' Irinya sent and then closed the link. She gestured to her squad. 'We move to the walls. We hold the gates. Nothing gets through. The enemy cannot breach them. They cannot be allowed into the city proper. Those gates are all that stands between the populace and annihilation.'

The stink of the warp was in the air, carried upon the thick rain, dragged up with the buzzing swarms of fat black-green flies. The sacred precincts of the city's defence were running with filth, flowing from the tormented skies to sully the marble. It spattered against their armour, squirmed underfoot, and soaked their red cloaks to their backs. Irinya wiped foetid water from the lenses of her helm with the back of her hand and broke into a run, her Sisters moving with her with well-disciplined cohesion.

Around them the civilians were breaking. Old women hobbled into shelter, screaming from the welts already rising on their skin. Mothers shielded children with their own bodies. Merchants dashed for cover, their wares forgotten. The semi-ordered life of the shrine was collapsing under the weight of the unholy deluge, washing away whatever hope had remained of peaceful existence in the shadow of the war.

It was weakness to think that conflict would never touch you. The galaxy did not allow for such luxury. Not even here, in the heart of sanctity. There was only war and those bold enough, strong enough, faithful enough to fight it. To wade through the pain and fire of a thousand battles. Her Order understood that: the need to fight until a righteous death claimed them. The Black Templars knew it, with their doctrine of the Eternal Crusade. The Astra Militarum understood, else regiments would never be raised for the forever wars of the Imperium. Worlds tithed. Souls offered up as heroes, angels and saints.

She thought of Teneu again. She thought of the duty she had embraced and the sacrifice that this world, these people, allowed to define her. The people of the Imperium did not think of saints as the people they had been, only as the symbols they had become. Transmuted, base to gold. Flawed to perfect. The way the Astartes were transfigured from mortal clay.

She could see the fire of the Black Templars' fury atop the walls as she advanced through the civilian precincts towards the battlements. She could hear their war cries even over the howl of the wind and the bellowing of unholy things. Witch-light danced along the battlements, catching upon the parapets until it seemed as though the entire length of the shrine's walls was ablaze. Men and ashes tumbled down from the sky, impacting the ground with wet thuds.

Irinya raised her weapon, ready to shoot anything that came from the walls or that tried to force the gates. Her squad followed suit. Other squads of Sisters moved with them, their own weapons and voices lifted. Squads Halcyon and Profundis swept round to the right of Irinya.

New thunder broke the day. The gates at Penitent's Way bulged at any unseen impact and then burst inwards. The first of the stolen Militarum vehicles to reach it had been wrought into a makeshift battering ram, filled with explosives and toxic effluent, and allowed to detonate. Cultists poured through the gap, already aflame, already dying, even before the Sisters opened fire.

The enemy were singing and laughing, dancing through the carnage in mimicry of their unholy masters. They died more easily, though. Bolter shells detonated in their flesh, showering their comrades with meat and bone. Melta blasts and flamer fire snapped out, and set more of them to burning. Robes atomised. Plate melted, reshaped, and boiled away. The squads of Sisters took up their own hymns as they pressed on, and the bells of the Sacristy tolled with greater vigour and truer timbre. The enemy flailed at them, driving forward into their fire, and ducking under the withering arcs, sleek as serpents, vermin-quick, as they sought to close the gap for their own crude weapons and rusted blades. The Sororitas' shots were precise. Skulls burst. Spines detonated. Arms were torn off at the elbow or shoulder. Weapons flew through the air to clatter impotently against the ground.

Black lightning earthed itself amidst the corpses and the waves of biting flies, crackling over the bodies as they crisped and burned. The smoke rose, thick and acrid, and things moved through the smog, laughing as they did. The offerings of death stained the earth and the air, and the Neverborn called by the slaughter slid into reality with a sickly pop like detonating void shields.

'Abominations!' Irinya bellowed, and her Sisters joined her in their righteous hatred. The daemons roared back, throwing spittle from rotten-toothed mouths, shaking heads crowned with pus-slick horns and broken antlers. Single eyes glared out at them, as the things raised their swords or swung bells or censers, like a mockery of an Ecclesiarchal parade. Battle and death, sickness and decay, these were the rites of the daemons. This battleground was their church.

Above them the statues of the saints watched and wept black tears from holes in their eyes or vomited it from their open mouths, like cathedral gargoyles. The world shook with the savage thunder of artillery and the detonations of more bomb trucks as they sought to breach the walls. Cultists staggered from behind the half-formed daemons, their cheeks marked with lye and gunpowder burns, wrapped in diseased rags, barefoot and bleeding.

A volley of bullets caught Beatrice and bore her to the ground, screaming into her helm as the rounds cracked ribs and buckled armour. Where they struck a gleaming residue crawled over the plates, hissing as acid and taint tried to eat into the sacred armour. Engravings and words of prayer vanished in a gasp of vapour as the metal pitted and warped. Oxanna and Sybele moved to support her, even as Irinya stepped forward, Josefine and Agata at her side. Selene fired her heavy bolter,

standing firm as she reaped a harvest of men. Shells burst
amidst the enemy in a shower of blood and limbs.

Irinya drew her blade. Pale light spilled out from its shaft
and the pall of smoke lessened but a little beneath its radiance.

'Come, then,' she said simply. 'Come and face His wrath!'

Gaheris bisected another gurning face and pushed the daemon
back, even as maggots burst forth from the wound and then
spread, consuming the entirety of the thing's unnatural form.
He turned and fired his bolt pistol until another skull detonated
and the headless creature blew away to ashes and lies.

Runes were appearing across his vision with disturbing
inconsistency as the enemy blinked in and out of reality, their
very presence distorting his optical read-outs. The life signs of
his brothers flickered with painful regularity, even as the first
signals started to die outright.

He gritted his teeth and forged on. Gaheris was fighting his
way along the wall, inch by bloody inch. Daemons died by blade
and bolt around him, and he saw it through the haze of golden
light as the Emperor guided his hand. He spun, ducked, wove,
and forged on through the flood of enemy bodies and seeking
blades. The Armour of Faith turned each blow aside.

'I am His Champion!' he roared. Even the daemons faltered
before such holy rage. He stood upon the walls, burning with
the Emperor's light, his sword's edge blazing with radiance.
The Neverborn screeched and snarled, their jovial demeanour
fleeing before the Champion's enkindled wrath. 'Ten thousand
years we have stood against you! Across all of space and time
we have fought you and hounded you to your lairs. You are
nothing! The dreams of false gods! Puppets and figments. I
renounce you. Now and forever. Till the stars burn out, we
shall fight and resist you!'

You are Sigismund as he was before the walls. You are the

guardian at the gates to hell. You are anointed in the sight of the God-Emperor of Mankind, who speaks through the deeds of stalwart men and the strength of their sword-arms.

He remembered the words of the Chaplains as they had anointed him, as they had readied him for the truest battles of the Eternal Crusade, armed with black steel and armoured in faith. Though he himself had once been of their number, he had never forgotten the lessons he had learned as a Neophyte and an Initiate. Though he had been called to wield the sacred crozius mace of a Chaplain, he had been a brother of the Black Templars. Each and every one of them knew the way of the sword.

Could I have imagined that this would be my fate? To be called to this solemn duty? To these battles? To raise the Black Sword where another Champion might have done in my stead? Would I have been the one to anoint him, and sanctify his efforts?

Gaheris heard the blare of war-horns and watched as the Legio Arconis stirred in the city beyond the walls, marching down the main thoroughfare of the Saint's Parade. Guardsmen and civilians were running amidst the feet of the three engines – the Guardsmen towards the walls and the civilians away from it. The guns of the Titans would not help the melee upon the walls but would stem whatever forces were able to break through the gates.

The enemy's wanton destruction had been their own greatest foe. Now the doors were obstructed by burning wrecks and dying men where they had rushed too eagerly for their prize. He could see the enemy massing below as he drew closer to the edge of the wall. A flood of cultists, spilling from their transports, boiling up from vents and subterranean passageways. Intent on defiling what belonged by right to the God-Emperor.

All this he absorbed in mere glances. Daemons continued to fight and die around him, just as his brothers died, mauled by the touch of the immaterial and the insane. He fought on, driven by zealous fury, his reactions instinctual.

He shot out the knees of a gibbering, pus-weeping daemon and then turned the Black Sword one-handed, driving it down and through the constantly flexing maw of the beast. It laughed and cooed around the blade even as its material form bled away. He could feel the fire of the daemon's death burning against his armour, the crawling contagion of its existence setting the false nerves of the plate ablaze.

This was what he had been forged for. Shaped by conflict, taken by the hands of the Chapter's Apothecaries and made into a warrior of the Adeptus Astartes. A Space Marine. He had been a hero before he had become a Champion. Bearing the God-Emperor's wrath and His purity.

Gaheris fought as he had never fought before, even as the cloying fire of the enemy bit at the sacred stonework. His blade rose and fell, his bolt pistol barked, and he moved inexorably through the battle. Towards those brothers who needed him most, to the daemons in whom the might of the Archenemy was most entrenched. Heralds and champions of daemonkind died beneath his blade, sent back to the hells of the warp with nothing but the most keenly sharpened contempt.

Time stopped.

Gaheris halted in his tracks, watching the tableau of battle as it froze in place. Reality held still, its breath caught in its throat. Daemons reared back, forever poised to strike. Brothers were set in grim perpetual defiance. Ashes, flames, blood drops, all unmoving. Everything had come to a single, shuddering stop.

Fire rose again upon the walls, in two great roaring arcs of golden light. A gate formed between them, birthed from incarnate madness. The doorway held, but the flames flickered – gold and ochre warring with the unholy fire of the warp. He watched the gateway spasm and flare, the light that held it seeming to

struggle to survive, wavering amidst the darkness. He acknowledged it for what it was, this waking dream, and embraced the
sign from the God-Emperor as it blazed across his sight and
mind.

'What do you want from me?' Gaheris asked plaintively. 'What
do you need?'

The golden flames roared up, screaming into the sky. The light
was absolute, all-consuming. He could see something nestled at
its heart, like an ember waiting to blaze once more.

Black in the midst of the conflagration, its surface darkened by
the relentless flame, rendered down to a tarnished and reduced
thing, was a throne. He could see it now, clearly, burning with
its own dark light. A throne – *the* Throne – and upon it, with
the golden light crawling over it, a corpse-lord, a skeletal king,
draped in silence and wrought from ancient wonder.

The gateway lived and died by His agonies.

Gaheris fought the urge to sink to his knees, to bury his sword
into the stonework and rest his head upon the hilt, even as every
fibre of his being demanded to do just that. His armour snarled
and whirred with contradictory feedback as he struggled against
every natural instinct.

Something pushed past him, moving towards the gate, and he
saw again the she-wolf that had haunted his past waking vision.
Advancing towards the portal without fear, the wolf's passage
dispelled the weakness of the gate. The fires howled and rose,
untrammelled and unrestrained, yet with the enthroned figure
at the centre of it. The Throne burned brighter, stronger, its
light blinding as the gateway yawned wider.

And Gaheris finally, absolutely, understood.

Chapter Nine

MORTAL FOES

DIVINITY'S EYES

FAITH'S FURY

Aneirin rejoiced in the combat, even as the waves of daemon-kind came and faded, breaking and surging against the walls in a constant cycle of unholy life and death.

On the world of his birth they had been ruled by the turning of the seasons, torn between the fitful joy of their meagre harvests and the crushing surges of the barren times. Predators had crowded around the villages then, seeking to prey upon their flesh. Now the Neverborn came to reap their own tally and to pluck lives from the worlds of men.

'Aneirin – hold fast, protect the mortals!' Barisan's voice rasped in his ear, the Sword Brother clearly wrestling with his own battles. He couldn't see his mentor, nor any of the rest of his squad. The enemy was everywhere, a tide of filthy bodies – river-swollen and malformed. He had seen men drowned through accident and misadventure as a child. Seen their fish-pale skin and the bloating that came with it. These daemons had those marks, as though in mockery. They were

every nightmare of death and suffering dredged up from mortal minds and given form. Existential dread wrought into the semblance of flesh and set loose against the defenders of humanity.

This is the true test. The war we were made to fight. The battles we were meant to endure.

He did his duty. He heeded his mentor. Where he strode, where his brothers stood, hope endured. Mortal soldiers fought with greater resolve, holding the lines against the impossible. His sword snarled as he put himself between the daemons and their prey. Whirring adamantium teeth turned aside the blows of rusted longswords and weeping blades.

He could feel the shaking of the earth as the great Titan war engines advanced upon the cultists silhouetted against the enormous holy reservoirs nestled within the walls, near to the High Sacristy itself. The walls there were the purest white, their immense surfaces inlaid with golden aquilas. He caught only glimpses of the Titans, like tribal totems come to life, gods of iron and woe bestriding the world, alight with the dawn's radiance.

The rattle of metal on stone drew his eye back and out towards the wall's exterior. Ladders clattered against the edge, and the enemy were already beginning the long climb. He heard it again: more of them, more bridgeheads wearing against the bulwarks.

The first of the cultists surmounted the lip of the wall, clambering up with verminous eagerness. The man's eyes were running with thick rheumy tears, and his skin writhed with internal motion. Insects bubbled up from open, untreated wounds and his head snapped this way and that, lips flecked with foam.

Aneirin slammed his chainsword through the first cultist's skull and sent him tumbling back down the ladder, showering the others in skull fragments, brain matter and gore. A ragged cheer went up from behind him and the Savlar and Veluans rushed to the edge, firing down as Aneirin turned about to protect their rear and flank. The very possibility of fighting back had galvanised the soldiers. Mortal foes could be felled by mortal hands. They were not nightmares and phantasms which only heroes and demigods could slay or defy.

They were brave, no doubt. Weaklings by any measure of transhuman skill, but determined nonetheless. The Savlar did not want to die, and the Veluans did not wish to see their home stolen away. Such things were fuel to human fires – the light of the God-Emperor kindled within them to *resist* and to fight at all costs.

'Hold!' he bellowed. They would not know that he was the least of his squad, a mere Neophyte within their brotherhood. They saw a warrior of the Adeptus Astartes, an Angel of Death. A statue come to life and set in their midst for their protection and defence. How could the walls falter with such warriors upon it? It could not. It would not. He had to take that dream and shape it into certainty.

'You are warriors of the Imperium! You are blessed in the sight of the shrines of the saints! Hold this wall! Hold this line!'

The intensity of autogun and las-fire ratcheted up once more. Solid shot lanced down from the walls, even as las seared across skin or bit at armour plating. Robes caught fire. Blood fell down upon the waiting cultists like rain, rendering them crimson like the devotees of a charnel lord of slaughter.

Aneirin opened a vox-link. 'Brother Barisan, this section of the wall is holding.' He looked up as runes spooled across his vision and gritted his teeth. 'I am observing losses across our force disposition.'

'*We hold, Neophyte. That is what matters. To die in service–*'

The signal cut out for a moment, broken by a burble of roiling static that sounded like inhuman laughter. When Barisan re-established the link Aneirin could hear the pain in his voice.

'*Support is coming. Our brothers are redeploying. The Sisters are coming. The Legio walks. We are the rocks around which this storm breaks. We hold until we cannot. We endure and we defend this world. That is our duty.*'

'As you will,' Aneirin said, and bowed his head. He raised his blade, seeking out the enemy, already moving to relieve his brothers.

He would fight by the will of his Initiate and the example of the Champion.

'Give me tactical overlay,' Melpomene growled.

Everything was confusion and madness, claws of unreality scoring their way across the manifold. She could see the walls, and she could visualise the enemy, but the very stuff of their existence offended the noble machine spirit of *Vengeance of Sareme*. This close to the engagement – such a limited thing by their scale, and focused upon the walls – the engine's mighty weapons could not be brought to bear.

'Interface with the local auspex returns and the wall's sensors. We shall provide long-range fire support by eradicating the enemy at the base. Their transports, their breaching mechanisms, their ladders. I want it all to burn.'

'Omnissiah willing we shall have tactical cohesion in three minutes, princeps!' Tovrel called, hunched over her sensorium array, hands in constant motion as she made the necessary calculations. New data blossomed across Melpomene's sight and she blink-clicked it into place. Crimson runes painted themselves in a swathe of unit placements and threat assessments, just beyond the walls.

They had walked from their berths and out into the storm, almost unbidden. Now they came down one of the main devotional avenues towards the gates. They saw with the eyes of divinity. Through the innumerable machine-senses of the god-engine, they perceived the cut and thrust of the enemy, the labour of the defenders, and the agony of reality as it was mauled by the daemonic incursion.

'We are relief, wrought from iron. We are vengeance, formed of fire. We are the doom that faces the enemies of Mars and the heathens who would defy the Machine God.'

'Glory be to the Deus Mechanicus,' the crew chorused. Flesh voices melded with binharic exultation as the engine strode forth. Melpomene embraced the Titan's senses and let their co-mingled perception soar, seeking the other engines of her deployment.

Dune Hound and *Nightbeast* had loped ahead along the devotional way, crushing ornamental gardens to stone splinters beneath their feet. The lesser Titans were far smaller than the encircling curtain walls, dwarfed by their majesty in a way that *Vengeance* was not. Mega-bolters spat and howled, raking the enemy's ranks as they tried again and again to advance into the city. Crashed vehicles were atomised, blown to splinters and shards of burning metal.

Melpomene breathed out, a long and envious sigh, as she relaxed back into the embrace of the machine spirit. It hungered and snapped like a chained beast, desperate to do violence. The restraint that she enforced upon it chafed worse than inaction. It could fire, if it so desired. The volcano cannon would unleash such glorious destruction – sacred conflagration in the sight of the Omnissiah-as-Unmaker.

'Fire,' she growled, her voice twinned with the noospheric cast of the god-engine. 'Bring them to ruin.'

The engine shuddered and sang as the missiles flew free and *Vengeance of Sareme* finally committed itself to the battle.

The spell broke.

Gaheris moved with new strength and surety. The Black

Sword was an extension of his movements, the chains that bound him to it cinched a little tighter, biting against his armour as he strained the blade to its furthest extent. Limbs tumbled free, their claws still flexing and twitching though separated from their bodies. The daemons screamed as he came for them, their laughter dispelled like the passing of rain.

He was past them, through them in a blur of sword and powered plate. Everything was reduced to the moment as he moved and dodged, parried and slew. He lost track of his brothers save for impressions of their positions. Toron was somewhere, his artificial voice raised in a constant bellow of hate. Black Templars joined him with their own cries.

The Black Sword rose and fell with a relentless rhythm, primal and guided only by his skill and his faith. The God-Emperor was with him. In every strike. In every thrust. The hand of humanity's master strengthened his own. More than ever he felt the touch of the divine and let it fuel him. He was all of faith's fury given form. He was the Emperor's Champion. Where he strode the fire of the warp withered and died, flickering back down to nothingness. Mould receded, unclean blooms died in his shadow, and the vermin that had scuttled and crawled with the enemy advance hurled themselves from the wall rather than stand against holiness incarnate.

The daemons recoiled from him, or threw themselves forwards in desperation, seeking killing blows. Ancient barrow blades shattered and unclean flesh parted. His black armour was stained and smeared with coagulated black blood, thrown in thick gobbets by the sheer violence.

Still they came. A knot of seven advanced along the battlements, their blades lashing out indiscriminately against mortals and transhumans alike. Their eyes alighted upon Gaheris and they began to jabber excitedly, hefting up their blades as they scampered forward to meet him. It was almost comical, here upon the walls, to see them bound like excited children – yammering and laughing, counting in the droning monotone of buzzing flies before once again beginning to babble. They were the names of diseases, he realised, pouring from the mouths of the daemons as though they were prayers. Lungrot and Beggar's Palsy. Scaleflesh and Black Ague. On and on the words tumbled, seeking to find purchase in reality, seeds cast into a mortal garden and awaiting the chance to take root and thrive.

The noose of lumbering swollen bodies closed around him. Blades scraped across his armour, scoring the perfect black with scars that already crawled with rust. One of the blades hooked under his arm, seeking to work through the joints and hew the limb away.

Gaheris lashed out with sword and fist. He drove the armoured cliff of his helm into the ragged faces of the daemons, driving them back. He felt unnatural bones break, blood crawling and screaming against his armour, felt flesh snag against the joints of his gauntlets and his vambraces. Every part of the daemons fought him, every part of their being was forked and barbed against him. He drove his fist through the laughing, snorting visage of one and felt its teeth gnaw at his knuckles, even as he reduced its skull to pulp.

'In the God-Emperor's name!' he roared, and the daemons jerked back at the utterance. The radiance spilling off his armour burned brighter, and he forced them back and away. One dived for his back again but the sweep of a blade cut it from crown to groin, and it fell apart in a wet unravelling of intestines.

Toron had come at last, moving to the Champion's defence with stolid inevitability. The Dreadnought's great sword rose again and the barrels of his rotator cannon spoke once more with fire and wrath.

'Fear not, Champion,' the venerable Ancient intoned, 'there

are more than enough of the enemy for all of us.' He turned, tilted his chassis and swept the lip of the wall with cannon fire. The iron hooks of their ladders exploded to shrapnel and chunks of rotting wood spun free with them, sending the entire ramshackle contraption sliding back down into the abyss below. Screams echoed up before being swallowed by the greater tumult of battle.

'Well met, Ancient,' Gaheris shouted, still locked in combat with the steadily decreasing circle of daemons. Only two now remained, jabbering and whimpering, bravado gone as surely as their allies had faded.

'*Anathema!*' the daemons whispered and muttered. '*Anathema! Anathema!*' And it made Gaheris smile to hear it. Perhaps the primal fear had always been with them and only now did he hear it given voice. He ducked low under one wavering strike and swept his sword round, hewing the daemon apart at the knees. As it fell he rose and brought the sword round again and again, taking it to pieces as though he were cutting cordwood. He spun at the last stroke and impaled the last of the daemons through the eye, eliciting an inhuman shriek. Reality shuddered and undulated once more as the remains of the daemons began to disintegrate.

'Such shall be the fate of all falsehoods and lies made flesh. So shall we end the enemies of man.'

'Praise be unto Him who puts swords in the hands of the faithful and delivers fire to the unrighteous!'

The Dreadnought turned back towards Gaheris with a whine of servos. His bulk was enormous, towering over the Champion and blocking the wall like a barricade. Gaheris could hear shots pinging in futility against Toron's rear armour.

'You fight well, Champion. A little recklessly, perhaps, but that is your calling. Nevertheless, you should not overextend. We gain nothing from your early martyrdom.'

'You honour me, Ancient Toron.'

'It is not my place to honour you, Champion. The God-Emperor in His wisdom has chosen to do so. I do not question His judgement, nor the interpretations of the Chaplaincy. Long has it been since I have sat in any such capacity. Should I be honoured because of age? Some primacy of endurance? No. This is a new galaxy. Primarchs walk again. The Imperium embraces our crusading fervour. All things sharpened to their true keenness. That is the dream. A galaxy burned clean. A realm made pure.'

Gaheris held his silence for a long moment as he looked up at the Dreadnought. For a rare moment the battle had stilled. The enemy was dispelled.

He nodded once. 'That is His will. An Imperium cleansed. An empire made whole once more.' He went down on one knee, deactivated his sword, and held it to his forehead. 'And He, in His glory, has shown me how that dream shall be realised.'

Chapter Ten

GUIDANCE

CONCLAVE

LAST RITES

Irinya knelt before the throne and slowly raised her head to gaze at its occupant, a poor mimicry of the Emperor's living entombment if ever there was one. Cardinal Erikos looked down with a wan smile and tilted his ring-bedecked hand upwards. She rose to her feet and nodded.

'Thank you, your grace. I am honoured to have been selected to deliver my report.'

'You were there, at the gates, even as angels graced the walls.'

'I was,' she said, remembering the smoke and fire. The blood of the unreal upon her blade. Her Sisters fighting and falling. Beatrice had been among the casualties of the preceptory, a loss which would not easily mend within the squad. 'We did what was expected of us, no less than the Astartes would have done. The line held. The High Sacristy's sanctity was preserved. The war engines of the Legio Arconis were, as ever, invaluable. They held the enemy at the gates at our side and were more than the match of the cultist's armour. It was the Champion who rallied the men upon the walls and drove back the warp's denizens. Without him and his men there would have been no victory.'

Erikos gave an almost distracted nod. Irinya wondered just how versed he was in military matters.

'It pleases me to have you here,' he carried on, and gestured off to one side. A serf began the long ascent to the raised throne, clasping a jug of wine to their chest with one arm while balancing a goblet in their other hand. A boy, no older than twelve years Terran standard, wrestling with a vintage worth more than his entire lineage. 'It is so refreshing to have good human intelligence from faithful and trusted souls.' He looked around conspiratorially, and then returned his gaze to Irinya. 'The Astartes... They are a breed apart, are they not? We are blessed indeed to have them here, and the Black Templars are at least of the faith proper... But they...' He trailed off.

'They frighten you,' she finished, and shame flickered across his features. 'It is an understandable thing. They are fearsome and ferocious, without quarter or mercy. They are the Imperium as it should be. Without fear. Without doubt. Without sin.'

'Have you spoken with them at any great length?' Erikos asked. 'I have made my overtures. I have led the Champion and his trusted lieutenants in prayer, on occasion, but they keep their distance.'

'I have had the pleasure of speaking with Champion Gaheris. He was most flattering in his assessment of our "tactical worth", but he also offered sincere blessing in the God-Emperor's name. It is my understanding that he was of the Chaplaincy.'

'Faithful through and through then,' Erikos said with a nod. He seemed overbalanced, in that moment, like a child's toy set to exaggerated motion. 'Do you know where he is?'

'The Black Templars came off the walls, after ensuring they were secured, and spoke of a tactical conclave amongst their

brotherhood. Perhaps they seek the guidance of the God-
Emperor?'

'As we all must, upon occasion.'

'The God-Emperor speaks to the Champion.' Irinya paused. 'If He would speak to anyone with His true voice then it would surely be one of His Angels. They have the strength to bear its weight.'

'It has long been my assertion, canoness, that He places His burdens upon us to test the strength of our character.' Erikos sipped thoughtfully at his wine. 'I have given this some thought, down the years, from the days when I was simply another preacher at the firing line. Dedication and devotion elevated me till I stood where I stand now. It is not a responsibility that I take lightly.'

Irinya knew that was true, but that it had not been dedication and devotion alone which had helped Erikos' ascent. His family connections, and a degree of ruthless politicking, had seen his rise to Velua's synod, and he had used that power to vie against other entrenched factions within the religious government of the seven sacred worlds of the Golden Chain. Irinya had taken no pleasure in sifting through the files relating to the man; she could even respect that he had always acted as he believed the Emperor demanded, but this performative modesty sat ill with her.

Candles flickered about the edges of the great chamber, casting a ring of light which encircled the cardinal and the canoness, conveniently hiding many of the guards and functionaries who waited in the wings. The flickering lights and the gentle drip of melting wax filled the silence which she had allowed to grow.

'I did not think it was,' she said. 'You strike me, your grace, as an able servant of the God-Emperor whose rule has been blighted by circumstance. Yet all of your old foes and rivals are gone, and you remain. Demigods rise to your defence. The support of this world is essential to the crusade and so it is important to the lord regent.' She paused. 'It has value. It is built around the bones of saints, and we will not allow our hallowed dead to be profaned.'

'You speak with great respect and wisdom.' He smiled. 'I would expect nothing less from one who had walked with Saint Teneu. Who served at her side and was witness to her martyrdom.'

Irinya's jaw set. She looked at the cardinal and tried to suppress her surprise. Clearly Erikos had done his research as well. 'You are well informed, your grace. My service is a matter of minor note to most. A footnote in a greater story.'

'Perhaps one day you will do me the honour of telling me it, eh?' He laughed gently and sipped his wine. 'It would warm my heart to hear tales of the saint in her youth, rising through the ranks and undertaking her first miracles.'

Miracles. The word caught in Irinya's throat, too painful even to give voice to. *She bore light close to her heart.* She had told Josefine that before, and it was true. The girl who would one day be a saint had borne love and light in her heart. The God-Emperor's love had enfolded her.

The eaglet, stirring again in Irinya's hands, feathers against skin, drawing in a new and shuddering breath. Life and light moving through it by His will and her desire to help.

'She was a miracle,' Irinya said. She took a step back, but her eyes never left the cardinal in his voluminous robes. 'Blessed and beautiful, and she held the love of all those fortunate enough to stand with her. I had that honour, and I treasured it, but in the end we failed her when she needed us most.'

'Such things are outside the control of mere humans,' the cardinal said evenly. 'By definition, martyrdom is an extension of His will. He did not wish her to die, for the God-Emperor is a merciful god to those who serve Him, but it was necessary for His great design. The galaxy turns on the blood of martyrs and the Imperium is refreshed, rejuvenated and made stronger by their noble sacrifice. Such acts inspire the multitudes to greater acts of service and we can rejoice in that passing, knowing that it has served Him so.'

'I–' Irinya began but faltered. She was aware of her breathing, of the pounding of her heart, and the sweat beading her palms. 'I understand. It is not for me to question His wisdom or His intent.'

'Quite so, quite so,' Erikos mused. 'We cannot question what unfolds for us. Not when the galaxy is burning end to end and His beloved son returns to stitch it back together with armies and new wonders.' He smiled a little. 'Even almost a decade on there is still a sense of awe at what has been accomplished.'

'And what will be accomplished in the years to come,' Irinya finished. 'The primarch is the regent. The Emperor's great administrator. A being who shaped the Imperium as it is, to shield it from the weakness of lesser men. He is returned to us now at the hour of our greatest need. Worlds have been liberated, the alien and the heretic driven back, so that we can stand here now, and look forward, across the Rift, to Imperium Nihilus.'

'You believe that is his plan?' Erikos asked. It struck her that the cardinal did not doubt that it could be done, merely that it was on the primarch's agenda. She smiled. Perhaps the man was more savvy than she'd presumed.

'I believe so,' she said with a nod. 'It isn't enough to shore up what we can here in the light of Sanctus. The Imperium cannot, will not, remain divided.'

'I agree utterly. And by the strength of angels, it shall be done.'

'Brothers,' the Champion said breathlessly. 'I have been blessed with a vision from the God-Emperor once again.'

The brothers of the Black Templars met in the city's heart, in a mighty amphitheatre, an open space beneath a mural-painted dome, where once the scholarly luminaries of the seven worlds would have gathered to discuss the depths of the God-Emperor's divinity or to debate treatises for their philosophical worth. The war had left it empty and abandoned; everything maintained a thin layer of dust and the dull weight of neglect. The lumen globes which ringed the great space had been allowed to burn low, their glass casements rimed with dirt and chemical residue, and cast a dull greasy light over the assembled warriors. Fewer than two hundred of them remained now, Aneirin noted grimly. There were gaps in the lines and groupings of brothers, where squads gathered in mourning yet with grim resolve.

Gaheris stood at the centre of the open space and there the shadows seemed to part, wreathing him in a numinous and ethereal light. Aneirin was in awe every time he saw the Champion, but in this moment he truly seemed blessed. Singled out by the hand of the stellar radiance that was the God-Emperor of Mankind.

Aneirin stood with the other members of Crusader Squad Fidelitas. Barisan had stepped forward from the throng of brothers, representing their interests in the informal conclave. Others had gathered, squads Iram and Excelsis foremost amongst them, eager for recognition and glory. They too were buoyed up by battle-lust and eager to hear the Champion's words.

Aneirin stood beside Arvin, and with them were the others – grim Havdan with his scarred visage, his mouth twisted into a perpetual sneer. Fenek, his hair and beard allowed to grow unkempt as a monastic devotion, stood shoulder to shoulder with Partus, who near compulsively let his fingers play over a small beaded aquila chain, mouthing prayers.

'Be silent,' Fenek grunted under his breath, and Partus shot him a look of zealous frustration. 'The Champion is speaking, brother – even prayers must be stilled for that.'

Aneirin was inclined to agree. He watched the Champion as he gestured about the circle of brothers, rapt at the warrior's oration.

'He has spoken in words of fire and glory. He has shown me the Imperium as it should be, once again made whole, shored up by the hands of the faithful!'

There were cheers, unbidden, and Aneirin realised that he himself was amongst those caught up in the fervour.

'I have seen the way to the Imperium Nihilus! A stable gate by which the Imperium might reclaim what has been lost these last years! With faith, we can prise it wide and deliver unto Lord Guilliman a revelation! One which will shape the future! One which shall set free those who suffer beneath the lash of the Archenemy and the ravages of the xenos!'

'Praise be!' Even Barisan was envigored now, lending his voice to the chorus. Only Toron stood silent, the Dreadnought's chassis unmoving as he processed what he was hearing.

'To do this, though...' Gaheris trailed off for a moment, wrestling with something momentous. His armoured form quivered, near imperceptibly, before he continued. 'To do this great thing, we must abandon the defence here.'

Silence reigned for a long moment. Every last warrior held their peace and their breath. The great open space of the auditorium suddenly felt claustrophobic, the air close around them. Barisan's features had twisted into a scowl. Aneirin could see the displeasure radiating from him. Other brothers held their silence, their stances suddenly strained.

'I know that this is a hard thing to hear. A burden that would crush lesser men. Yet He has spoken, and we must heed His words. Is it not the way of our order to cleave to His word? His guidance? Do the Chaplains not interpret His voice as it speaks through our material universe? A universe shaped and secured by His will?'

'And yet...' The Dreadnought's artificial drone cut across the silence that followed Gaheris' pronouncement. 'We are servants of our duty and our faith, entwined. Without one, we lose the other.'

'This is the God-Emperor's vision. His words. His will. Would you deny that, Ancient?' Gaheris seemed incredulous. He was the light around which the entire chamber seemed to revolve, and he stood opposite the stark black bulk of the Dreadnought.

'I do not deny the God-Emperor's divine will. He has a plan for you, Champion. All can see that. I question whether that plan means abandoning the defence now. We are the iron of this world's resistance. Its backbone. What would they have without us? The Hoplites? The *Savlar*? The Sisterhood would hold, true enough. There is strength and honour in their preceptory.' The Dreadnought fell silent. 'There is no honour in abandoning them.'

'Oftentimes the path of faith is paved with distasteful actions. We must walk through darkness to serve the light.'

'We must rise above the darkness, in order to bear the fire of civilisation,' Toron intoned grimly. 'If we are not the example, if we are not stalwart and true, then how can mortals follow in our footsteps? The Imperium follows our example. They are, all of them, crusaders now. Whether they walk the martial path or not, all work towards that common goal. All serve Guilliman's crusade, and toil to ensure it will succeed.'

'It is for philosophers to quibble over what it means to serve,' Gaheris said bluntly. 'Perhaps in the salons of Terra or invested spaces such as this one – but those are matters for scholarly souls and brighter times. Here and now we have only the moment. Our service is measured in ground reclaimed and worlds liberated. The Great Crusade never ended for us. It never ended for Sigismund, but that duty is based upon always forging forwards. Whatever the cost may be.'

'The cost shall not be my honour. You may debate, vote, decide what you will...'

The old Dreadnought stepped forward and his arm rotated, bringing the great sword down and burying it in the stone. Cracks spiralled out from the impact, splitting the pristine floor which lay between him and the Champion. Aneirin's breath caught as he watched. It took everything in his power not to rush forward, to declare for one side or the other. Escalation seemed inevitable. He could see from the corner of his eye that countless others were likewise straining, fighting their every instinct to intervene.

'If you return to the stars and seek this false glory then you will do it without me, Champion. I will not abandon them to their fate. I will fight at their side, as the Emperor wills. When the forces of the crusade return I shall greet them as brothers or they shall bear me into the records of the Chapter. I will be remembered as one who did his duty, even unto death.'

Gaheris looked upon the Dreadnought and sighed. For a moment, to Aneirin's eye, it was as though the aura of potency surrounding the Champion flickered. He was hurt or perhaps simply disappointed.

'If that is your wish, then so be it. You will convey my words to Marshal Urtrix, if we cannot reach him astrotelepathically?'

'You have my word, Champion. Now speak. Tell us of this revelation that wars with reason.'

Gaheris held his peace for a moment, as he contemplated his next move.

'What do we do?' Aneirin asked quietly.

'We wait,' Barisan growled. 'Whatever happens, we wait until all is revealed.'

The Champion exhaled and the light which had gilded him

burned anew, brighter, like a caged inferno. His every sinew was taut, and his armoured suit echoed his motions with its artificial muscles.

'I speak with the voice of the God-Emperor when I tell you that He has set out a path for us, a way across the stars, and a wolf shall lead the way.'

'A wolf?' someone called. 'The Wolves of Fenris fight their own battles! There are none in our fleet and none with the local battle groups. How will we find this wolf?'

'It is not a Space Wolf who will lead us,' Gaheris said, with a weary sigh. 'I have seen the road we must walk, and it is in the footsteps of a she-wolf.' More clamour and confusion rose, and the Champion cut the air with his outstretched hand. 'Be it heraldry or some other sign, we shall find it. We shall seek out the omens that have been placed before us, through the sacred guiding sight of the Navigators and astropaths.'

'The God-Emperor shall deliver us! He lights our path through the darkness!' Brother Tavric, the leader of one of the other Crusader squads shouted. 'If the Champion declares a path then surely it must be the path of the righteous? Shall we quail before His calling or shall we rise, triumphant, to the challenge? That is the question put before us – the interrogation of every last loyal soul. Will you serve His word, or falter with doubt?'

'We must be cautious,' Barisan said and stepped forward. 'The Champion bears the God-Emperor's favour and His intervention upon this mortal field. None doubt that. Such disputes are for the Chaplaincy to determine. I would stand before the Black Sword and declare myself as a stalwart son of Dorn, a Black Templar who has never shirked from his duty. I bear the red of a Sword Brother for my dedication to our Marshal and the High Marshal beyond him.' Barisan paused, collecting himself. 'Yet Ancient Toron also speaks with the wisdom of his august position and the years of his devotion. He has passed beyond death and returned to us, to fight the God-Emperor's wars. He bears the mantle of the Eternal Crusade, just as keenly as any other of us.'

'I will not ask you to follow me without question,' Gaheris said softly. 'I lay the path before you, but I cannot make you walk it. Discuss it amongst your squads and let the leaders declare their decisions. Stand with me or stand with the Ancient. Whichever way the blade falls, you will serve the crusade with honour.'

They laid Beatrice to rest amidst an ornamental garden of remembrance, where the biers of long-dead heroes sat surrounded by marble statuary and carefully cultivated splendour. It was positioned along the innermost walls of the cardinal's palace, at the High Sacristy's heart. While the city's great gardens swept out and into the spaces beyond the outer curtain walls, this was one of many more intimate horticultural areas that nestled between the shrines, perfuming the air with its sweet blossoms.

She had not deserved her end, but there was some comfort to be had in the place chosen for her interment. Irinya led the procession of Sisters, both from their squad and from the wider preceptory, out into a ring of low stone walls surmounted by rearing ouslite cherubs. Braziers burned, shrouding the area in a fine misting of smoke and incense, flickers of flame leaping from between the coals. The light caught upon their armour, even where it had been blackened in mourning. Their red cloaks fluttered in the breeze, and all thoughts turned inexorably to the blood spilled by their Sisterhood, time and again.

San Leor. Terra. Ophelia. Armageddon. On and on marched the toll of time. The battles they had fought and the foes they had faced, even before the Great Rift had split the heavens, had been a trial – an eternal test of their human resolve.

'We bear our Sister to her final rest, freed from the mortal weight of war and released to fight forever at the Emperor's side,' Irinya began.

'To serve beyond the veil of death, their duty unended, their vows unblemished.' The others joined her as she spoke the words, a sacred refrain for the glorious dead. All of them were heroes, all of them martyrs.

Irinya looked up from Beatrice's bier, across the great open space of the garden, at the other Sisters lost to them. A hundred bodies, arranged in ten rows of ten, lay before her. Cleaved open by the blades of daemons or the ravages of more mortal foes, they were all armoured and shrouded. Even now the artificers of the great shrineholds were working feverishly, to provide marble tombs for each of them.

A fool's errand, Irinya thought. *There will be many more graves and martyrs to fill them before the end.*

'By the example of saints,' she began, and faltered. She paused, collecting herself, as every eye rose to watch her. 'By the example of saints are our Sisters led, for peace is a gift unearned. We strive and we suffer in His name. We endure through the tide and the tempest, so that the galaxy might be once again made whole. It is our place to suffer. Our place to serve. In death, we find our reward.'

She looked out again across the sea of bodies. The area had previously held the graves of menials of note, those souls who had redeemed their low blood through dutiful service to the shrine world's masters. They had been hastily disinterred, buried elsewhere or not at all. Irinya had never thought to find out. She bowed her head.

'We commit their bodies to the earth and commend their souls to the God-Emperor.'

As one the gathered congregation went to their knees, silently and grimly marking the losses of their Sisters. Incense drifted across the gathering in fine clouds, dispensed from censers carried by cherubs. The biomechanical constructs paused now and then, perching on statues or arches. Stubby fingers clung to the stonework, knotted around the chains that bound them to the censers. Irinya found herself reminded of the Black Templars and their habit of binding their weapons to themselves – a martial custom, steeped in tradition. She felt the weight of her own chains, constricting about her, as surely as they bound the cherubs and the Black Templars.

She looked up to one of the archways that ringed the open space and saw a massive silhouette standing, watching their rites. Burning braziers lit the figure from behind, only succeeding in emphasising its martial bulk. It was as though the very thought had summoned him.

Champion Gaheris looked out across the field of the dead, and then went down on one knee. She nodded her thanks for the gesture of solidarity, though she had no idea what might have provoked it.

'We give our Sisters to the earth,' Irinya said quietly, 'and we trust that the flame kindled by their passing shall burn the enemy to ash. We shall avenge them, though it takes every last drop of blood. We shall wash this world clean of the enemy's taint. We shall endure.' She paused again and turned from the rows of bodies. 'We shall survive this.'

Chapter Eleven

BURDENS LIFTED
THE DEAD'S VIGIL
OUTRAGE

They carried their burdens forth and lifted them towards the stars.

St Jude's Port was a squat and functional conurbation which skirted around the north of the High Sacristy's interior, bearing more of the hallmarks of the Mechanicus than the sacred trappings of the Ecclesiarchy. From the port's landing fields supplies had once flowed inexorably from orbit to feed Velua's ravenous need. Now it was quiet and intended only for purely military matters.

For the guards of St Jude's Port the procession was a surprise; not merely because it had not been recorded upon the manifests, but because of the beings who made it up. The Astartes of the Black Templars marched in rows of four, bearing their honoured dead upon marble slabs. Hefted upon the shoulders of the two central brothers, while two stood guard at their side. They came armed and armoured, bearing weapons of such destructive might that it made even the hardened Hoplites quail from the sight of them.

'Move aside,' Aneirin said plainly. Squad Fidelitas were amongst those at the fore. He had been selected to bear the Chapter's standard, with the heraldry of the Champion and the honours of Battle Group Thor.

'My lord,' one of the guards murmured and bowed in awe, stepping from their path. Aneirin stood a little taller and did as he had been bidden, announcing the Champion's intentions.

'We return to our ships with our honoured dead. We who bear the God-Emperor's light and who weather the storms of war so that men such as you may do your meagre duties.'

'Of course, noble lord.'

Aneirin was about to move on when Barisan moved past him and knelt down, coming face to face with the young soldier on guard.

'What is your name, boy?' the Sword Brother asked.

'Joachim, lord,' the man whispered, faltering at the very presence of the Space Marines.

'My brothers have bled for this world, Joachim. They wish to...' Barisan paused, collected himself. 'They wish to return to their ships and inter their dead. I wish that also. I wish to lay my brothers to rest where they might be honoured by our Chapter – the rites observed, their legacy secured. You will not understand this. You will not understand much of what is to come, but what I can tell you is this. What we do is sacred, and it is necessary.'

'I–' Joachim trembled and began to babble, unable to force the words out. It was more than mere nerves. The man's entire being recoiled at being so close to the gathered warriors of the Chapter. For him it was as though a host of statues had come to life and now marched before him in impossibility.

'I know, I know.' Barisan smiled.

Aneirin watched the gesture, watched it wash over the human, and comfort him in some small way. He frowned, no longer remembering when such emotions had held sway over him. As a child, perhaps. A babe in arms, dependent on a mother or father. A simpler creature. Barisan's words broke him from his thoughts.

'Know that you are, all of you, true servants of the Imperium. You have done the God-Emperor's work and seen to His defence.'

The boy and his fellows finished their withdrawal. Barricades rose, and the procession continued on towards the waiting Thunderhawks and Overlords. The newer and larger Overlords sat alongside the traditional lines of the Thunderhawks, their weapons and reactors quiescent. The soldiers watched on in awe as the procession of the Black Templars made its way towards the ships. Some made the sign of the aquila. Aneirin could see a few weeping openly.

Aneirin was silent for a moment and then turned, fixing Barisan with his gaze.

'They are strange things. Weak and overawed. It amazes me that they endure without us.'

'Aye, but you must remember the lessons of the Chaplains,' Barisan said, and lowered his head. 'It is not the swift path which leads to salvation. It is the long journey. That is the essence of our Eternal Crusade, but we must also remember why we do it.' He gestured back. 'It is for them. It is for the masses of humanity who cleave to Him and who bear Him up in their prayers. They whose souls go to Him when their duty is done. Without that, there is nothing. We are nothing. There is no Imperium without humanity and no humanity without the faith.'

'I understand,' Aneirin said.

'Good,' Barisan replied with a nod, as the first gunships began to lift off. 'Then hold it close to your hearts and *live* it.'

* * *

Toron had not chosen to linger and watch his brothers leave in shame and deceit. Instead he returned to his patrols.

He was not sure why he had chosen the gardens, but he walked amongst them beyond the walls, servos whining as he pushed on over uneven terrain. Clinging blossoms and lurid fungi were crushed beneath his iron tread, casting up clouds of dust, pollen and spores. His artificial senses kissed the air, tasting the various types of biological detritus in circulation, though ultimately they meant nothing. Perhaps there were other members of other Chapters who would have seen a delightful irony in that, mused upon the philosophical nuance of standing amidst beauty and being unable to appreciate it. A scion of Sanguinius, perhaps, or one of Guilliman's myriad sons.

He was beyond such things. As a Black Templar he had never aspired to the Chaplaincy, or considered himself a great thinker. He had wielded his blade with no small skill. He had fought the wars that the God-Emperor demanded. As a Dreadnought, mortal concerns and conceits had faded from him – as atrophied as his flesh and bone. The sarcophagus gave him life and motive function. It allowed him to continue to fight and strive, to endure. He was a thing of iron and wrath.

Even before his interment anything soft or gentle had been pared away by the knife of his apotheosis. Yet he still had his honour, even if others felt it convenient to put it aside.

There were others out here, beyond the walls. Pioneers and pathfinders. Snipers and scouts. He saw hidden eyes turn towards his bulk, taking in his martial bearing, and his lack of fear before the enemy. He did not cower. He did not hide. He wore the cross of his Chapter proudly and stood as an example to all those who remained to fight.

'Fear not, brothers!' he declared. 'I stand with you.'

* * *

The Champion stood before Cardinal Erikos, statue-still in the silence that had filled the audience chamber. From where he stood Gaheris could see the little man quivering, his drawn features contorting from one emotion to another in quick succession. Shock, anger, fear, despair. An entire cavalcade paraded across his face in mere seconds. Gaheris remained impassive. He had made his announcement, and would weather the consequences far better than this mortal man would weather the announcement itself.

How weak they are, who sit enthroned in false gold and piety, he thought idly. *Give me the preachers of the Astra Militarum any day over those who would rule from a distant pulpit.*

'This is an outrage!' Erikos repeated. 'You cannot– I will not... How can you do this?'

The cardinal leant forward from his throne, so far that he almost overbalanced. Aides and guards hesitated at their posts, poised to rush forward and relieve the man, but at the same time cowed by the Champion's presence. He had come armed and armoured, and even the cardinal's guards seemed puny before his might.

The only figure who did not move was Irinya. The canoness stood sentinel, not quite at the cardinal's right hand, but at enough of a remove not to compromise her own authority. Gaheris noted her bearing. Every part of her was tensed and coiled by deeply simmering anger. She shared the man's outrage, but she would not march in support of it. Not yet.

'I have made plain to you the circumstances, cardinal. The God-Emperor in His glory has spoken to me.'

Gaheris stepped forward and the guards flinched at their posts. One of them moved towards him, gun raised. Gaheris turned his withering gaze upon the man, and the guard's stride faltered. He stepped back into his place and lowered his weapon.

'He speaks to me, cardinal. I do not have to pretend to hear His words as some itinerant charlatan. I am not the mad prophet upon the street corner who screams of the world's end. When worlds are ending, He has deigned it so. He has stretched out His hand from His Throne and He has chosen me to lead in His stead, to be the light in the darkness. I will not turn from that duty, cardinal. I will hold it close and embrace it to my core. When the wars are done, then there may be an accounting, but I have done as my Emperor demands, and obeyed the will of the divine.' He turned his gaze from Erikos to Irinya. 'Will any of you stand in my way?'

The canoness kept her silence for a long moment. He had known the news would be a blow, to so many of them, and yet of all of them it was Irinya whose judgement would bear the most weight. He did not know why he had gone to watch the funerary rites and offered his silent solidarity. Had he sought, in some way, to obtain her blessing? Or had he known that only anger could spring from this, and held his tongue?

Gaheris waited to see if her hand would go to her sword and she would step forward to challenge him. If there were any here who would do such a thing, she was the only true candidate. He was ready for any contest of arms. He had already determined the optimal strategy for disarming and disabling every last opponent within the audience chamber.

This was not uncommon for him. A warrior of the Adeptus Astartes would habitually combat-assess everyone in any given space in the time it took others to breathe a single breath. In a heartbeat he knew their capabilities. A moment later he knew how he would take them apart. That was the gift and curse of a mind shaped for the God-Emperor's wars. He had wondered, in his youth and folly, what life he might have had if he had not ascended.

Would I have remained in the ruin-temples and never strayed from that narrow path? To live and die a life of shallow service, 145

in the shadows of Old Night's grasping ambition?

He had long since realised that none of it mattered. He had served. He would continue to serve. To whatever end.

'We cannot stop you, Champion. We would not know where to begin,' Irinya said with a dry laugh. Gaheris could not help but smile. 'Yet know this...' She paused, gathered her courage. 'Before the birth of our Order there were others who claimed to know the God-Emperor's mind, and who acted as they decreed fit His design. Both my Order and yours were the instruments which helped to end such a man. We learn from the past so as to avoid its mistakes and its crimes.'

'A bold comparison, if nothing else.' Gaheris paused. 'I am not Goge Vandire. Nor am I the rumours and fears that others would lay at Guilliman's feet. It does not please me to leave this place, yet I trust in the hearts of its defenders. The Order of Our Martyred Lady should look to their own history, as you say, and you should note that death in the defence of the sacred is the greatest honour that a true believer can receive. The blood of martyrs is the seed of the Imperium. From sacrifice and struggle comes victory. Did the God-Emperor Himself not lay down His mortal existence so that His Imperium could endure and continue to endure as mankind's aegis?'

'Yet you walk from the battle. You turn away from sacrifice. You chase vainglory!'

Erikos' blood was clearly up now. The little man had turned a shade of purple, his ringed hands clattered against the arms of his throne, and his lips had peeled back into a snarl. Fear had made him bold, bold enough to spit invective at the Champion. Gaheris weathered this storm as he had so many others. Words were poor weapons against faith.

'You would abandon us! You would abandon your duty.'

'There is no point to this.' Gaheris sighed. 'Have the marshal return and chastise me. Beseech crusade command, if you must. Yet do not think that you can bar my path.' He drew his sword and turned, arms spread. 'I bear a relic of the Chapter. The Black Sword, in emulation of holy Sigismund. Do not make me sully its purity by using it to defeat your men, all of them, from here to the landing fields.' He fixed the cardinal with a furious glare, his pale features contorted with the first signs of genuine rage. 'Rest assured, it will be done. Nothing will keep me from my path.'

He turned and walked from the chamber then. All that could be said had been said. He would not let their narrow mortal viewpoints hold him back, nor restrain him from his duty. Let them hate, let them fear, let them struggle and suffer. If they survived then it was by the grace of the God-Emperor alone.

Chapter Twelve

CONTAGION OF FEAR

SIGNS AND OMENS

JUSTICE

Irinya did not know how the word first broke free of their cordons of silence.

Perhaps there had been too many present to see how the Black Templars transports had screamed into the heavens, their wings trailing blazing promethium. Or others had noticed the false stars of the Black Templars voidships shift from their constellations. Somewhere, someone had talked, and now the truth was out, spreading as surely as plague, and carrying its own contagion of fear. Panic was inevitable. Already there had been riots amidst even the most faithful. Irinya and her Sisters had been forced to take to the streets, bearing the brunt of the pathetic attack. Rubbish and rocks had clattered impotently against their armour, but they had managed to dispel the mob without resorting to lethal violence.

'This is what the enemy want,' she had told her squad. 'For us to turn upon each other within the safety of our walls. To despair, and then to falter.'

'Where are they?' the crowd screamed. 'Where are the Angels?' More missiles hurtled down at the Sisters and they held their ground. The cardinal's decree was still for non-lethal force. Swords were yet sheathed, bolters hung at their shoulders. They trusted in their armour and their training to see them through to safety. The Hoplites were moving to join them, to fortify the approaches to the palace and to hold back the seething crowd.

A man, wild-eyed and gibbering, broke the cordon and hurled himself at the line of Sisters, as though he could surmount them in a bound and find some long-sought answers beyond them. Irinya caught him, near effortlessly, by the throat, and held him in mid-air. His legs kicked impotently, like one of the hanging victims in the gardens beyond the walls.

'Is this how true servants of the Emperor act?' she bellowed, shaking the man like a marionette. 'You shame yourselves! You shame Him!' Laud-hailers screamed behind her words, hammering the rioters with a wall of sound and fury.

The entire crowd recoiled in a single animal motion, staggering in blind panic even as their voices rose again in a dull cattle-whine. Irinya bared her teeth in a snarl as she hurled the man back into the arms of his fellows. His ankles bent awkwardly as his lower body hit the ground, and the crowd seemed to groan and mewl with one voice. Their pain was a singular pain, shared and spread out through the masses of humanity.

'Return to your habs and to your duties!' Irinya bellowed. She drew her sword and clattered the unpowered blade against her armour, advancing as she did. The rest of the Sisters, a line of twenty, fell in with her, rattling their own weapons against their plate. The savage drumbeat rose and fell, and with it came yet more panic and fear. The crowd turned and ran, makeshift weapons forgotten in their wake, to be crushed beneath the boots of the faithful.

Josefine stopped and picked up the crude club one of them had been swinging, letting it drift idly through the air as she moved it in imitation.

'Desperation is a dangerous thing,' she whispered. 'They would have achieved nothing with these weapons, and yet still they came – in their multitudes. Sticks and stones against powered armour.'

'Sometimes the masses are moved simply to do something, anything, so that they do not have to face down their fear,' Irinya said. 'They think it better that they come here and demand answers, shoulder to shoulder with others, than sit in their habs or kneel in prayer – simply fearing that what they have heard is true. We have shown them resolve here, and that will last a while. They are not criminals, not yet, not by any means, but the day is coming when they will look at us and see weakness, not strength.'

'And when that happens?' Josefine asked, though she already knew the answer.

'Then we will be forced to treat them as the heretics they will have become, and they will be no different from the enemy outside the walls.'

The world spoke anew in signs and omens, in dark wonders and miracles.

Weryn knelt in the darkness beneath the earth and knew peace. He had rolled up his robes so that his bare flesh could press against the mouldering stone, feeling every barb and bite of the world as it intruded against his flesh. His feet, unshod for so long now, were scarred and bleeding, the wounds bright with infection and red with inflammation. He no longer cared. Every welt, every wound, was a gift from the Grandfather of All.

Bodies had been piled around him, culled from the faithful this time as the cult desperately sought new communion with their patron. Instead all that poured from the mouths of the corpses was a bubbling tide of constant laughter as the Neverborn danced from vessel to vessel, occluding any hope of contact.

Weryn did not fear. Suffering was part of the plan – a necessary undertaking for the paradise that would blossom through the cracks once the Imperium was ashes and ruins. He thought again of the great crack that had already torn the foundations of reality. That wound in space and time that men called the Great Rift. He was sure it had always been there. Waiting to be born. Waiting for the winds of calamity to shift just so, and for the meat of the galaxy to rot away. The universe was crumbling to its bones, and yet the vermin that was Imperial man thought he could thrive amidst the entrails.

'I can pity a man for his blindness, as much as I might envy him,' Weryn whispered, and the chattering laughter of the daemonic shifted with his words, casting back mangled echoes like distorted vox-leavings.

Envy. Envy. Envy.

The mocking babble of tongues rolled over him in a wave, and he embraced it close. These were not the times to fear or doubt. These were the ages of revelation and the promised victory. Even now there were signs above. Fire roaring towards the heavens, trails of black smog cutting across the skies and obscuring the false stars. At first Weryn had thought that perhaps the enemy were withdrawing their whole strength and surrendering Velua to the Children, but in truth the ships were a symptom of a keener sickness.

The first of the new defectors had let them know, as they slowly made their way across the muck of the ravaged no-man's-lands around the great shrine city. Weeping as they told it, tears that would soon be acid-etched into their cheeks as a sign of service.

More sweetness in that single sentence than existed in the entire war.

The faith-ridden heathens in their black armour, bound by the chains of their dead duty, had finally quit the field. He trembled when he had first heard the words, as he trembled now, prostrated upon the ground, desperate for the sacred judgement of his betters. Even without their guiding voices he could sense their presence, coiling about him in the frigid air like tendrils of black smoke. Soon they would come, from out of the void and the ether. Not the Grandfather's lesser daemons, but the Guard of Death itself. Called to task and set to purpose.

'Prophet?'

Luminor Ceren stood behind him, flanked by others of her rank. They were hung with trophies – some fresh from the enemy and others gouged out of the earth or liberated from tombs and reliquaries. Finger bones seemed common, nailed to the flesh or strung along chains or wires in simple necklaces. The war was transforming them, one and all, into something stronger. Wrought of iron and bone, made transcendent by plague and suffering. The poisons they ingested and the scarification they undertook were transformative acts, cutting away at the human chrysalis until only the divinely inspired remained.

'My friends,' Weryn said as he rose unsteadily. Drool and bile trickled down his chin, and he wiped it away absently. 'Grandfather Time wears away all obstacles, and reveals all paths. This is our hour now. Our time to rise and triumph.'

'So you have said before.' Ceren sighed. The luminor was battered and bloodied, the entire right-hand side of her face reduced to one elongated bruise. Blood had dried in cracked brown formations down the side of her neck, and Weryn noted where a bullet had torn through her shoulder. The resultant wound had already scabbed over, black and glossy like the exoskeleton of an insect, the surrounding pale flesh threaded with the red of inflammation and the grey-black of creeping necrosis. 'We fight them,' she went on. 'We go again and again to the walls. We go forwards and we go under. We stand alongside daemons and still we are thrown back.'

'That will not always be the case,' Weryn insisted.

He rose and walked past Ceren and her men, up a flight of rough stone stairs marked by faded warning glyphs, and out into the open air. Outside the confines of the temple space, the world was alive with sound. Engines roared and bucked as they readied for service. The tanks and artillery pieces which had been taken from the Veluans had been altered, fitted with curved and spiked plates – inspired, the artisans insisted, by ever more pressing dreams. He breathed in the thick fug of promethium fumes and sighed as though it were sweet perfume.

'We will rise, and when we do it shall not be with daemons at our beck and call.' His eyes glimmered with a wet, sickly light. 'When we stand before the enemy it shall be with angels of our own.'

He had run, and he had never stopped running. Fear and sweat clung to him, and he feared that his scent would betray him to the hounds of the Ecclesiarchy and the vengeance of the Angels.

Everything had passed in a blur at first. He was not sure where he was once he had left the walls, out of the doors of the Bastion Sanctus. The streets were unfamiliar to him, so long having been spent at the defensive line. He had continued to run, peeling off the signs of rank and armour, his cloak cast to the winds.

Colonel Maxim Draszen, though he no longer thought of himself by rank, regretted losing the cloak now as he shivered in the abandoned Munitorum depot at Faith's Reprieve, still within the city's walls. He had laughed bitterly when he had found it, the area designation like a mocking blow. Yet it

had walls, for the moment, and though it was abandoned and
empty it allowed a perfect vantage-point for him to creep out
in search of food. That had been days ago, weeks perhaps. Time
had become elastic under the lashes of pain, hunger, frustration and desperation. He had already had to chase off other
scavengers and stragglers, to keep his patch clear and his space
free. Hands knotted into fists or stretched out like claws, his
teeth bared like an animal. There was very little remaining of
the proud man he had been.

*And yet what choice did I have? When the enemy came? What
choice remained to me?*

There had been wailing and screams in the night, as bad
dreams circulated through the shrine's flesh. Daemons, it was
whispered, had walked abroad and danced upon the ashes of
Velua's holiness. The sacred soil was profaned, and nothing
would save them now. He wept to think of it. He did not sleep,
just curled into a ball in a corner, and rocked.

Spot-lumens swept out across the city and alarums sounded.
All the fury and thunder of a siege, of a city riven by desperation, of the faith of a people dying. He scrunched his eyes closed
again, dispelling the light that burned brighter than the day, and
felt the tears cut through the grime upon his cheeks. He had
not bathed himself since his desperate flight, had barely even
thought to. He looked across to one of the shattered windows
and caught a glimpse of himself in the warped reflection. His
skin filthy, his hair bedraggled and his chin marred with stubble.
His eyes were narrowed, bloodshot slits in a face that seemed
to have aged years in days.

Has it been days? Weeks? Months?

He rose unsteadily, sniffling and shuffling towards the doors.
If everyone was at the walls again then perhaps he would be
able to slip out, find some food, or perhaps better shelter. There
were other groups of scavengers and criminals, perhaps it was

time to join up with one of them, scrounge enough to buy protection or join up with one gang or another. He could–

The sirens came again, closer now. He heard the clatter and roar of armoured personnel carriers as they screamed around a corner. Barked orders, distorted by the boom of vox-amplifiers and laud-hailers. Warnings faded away and were swiftly replaced by the sound of singing, of prayer, of women's voices raised in the eternal refrain of sacred hymns.

'Oh, Throne,' Draszen breathed. 'No.'

The door to the depot burst in, reduced to splinters by one sharp power-armoured kick. A figure strode in through the gloom, lit only by the crackling edge of a shock maul. The actinic glare of it caught on her features, wreathing them in an unearthly light. He recognised her, though. He recognised the burn scars winding up her neck, even as her face twisted with an ugly glee. He had seen her in the canoness' entourage, bearing a flamer. Even armed with only a shock maul, she seemed to burn with righteous indignation and holy fury.

'By the Throne,' she breathed, almost in imitation of his own panicked invocation. 'The God-Emperor does deliver, when He has a mind to.' She stalked forward and raised the weapon.

'Please,' Draszen began, 'please, don't–'

The maul swung and cracked him in the side of the head. He tasted blood and felt the dance of energy through his reeling nerves. His face seized and spasmed, muscles contorting and jaw clenching at the blow. He hit the ground with a solid thump of impact, and gazed up at her, gulping like a beached fish.

'Canoness,' he heard her vox, the last words he understood before unconsciousness finally took him. 'You won't believe who we've found.'

ACT TWO

THE HUNTER'S PATH

Chapter Thirteen

UNDERVERSE QUEEN

SHIPS OF FOOLS

ETERNITY'S VISTAS

The ship slid from the warp like an echo of grander times, a regal vessel of war at the head of an armada.

In times such as these, a fleet like this was a blessing. A wonder. They had set out, at the crusade's inception, as torch-bearer fleets and carried the secrets of the new age to those Chapters who had required them most. With those duties done they had been broken apart, remade, redistributed to active crusade fleets, and otherwise made use of. The men and materiel of Task Force Saturnine had found themselves seconded to a mission which bore the seal of the regent himself, though the auspices of which were yet shrouded in secrecy. All they knew was that they served the will of the fleet's new mistress.

Katla Helvintr was that mistress.

She stood upon the bridge of the *Wyrmslayer Queen* and felt the wounds of her past weigh upon her, just as surely as the wounds done to the vessel. They had both come through the wars of exploration, and the betrayal that had followed. They both wore their scars with a robust pride.

Hers were the white lines of blades and claws, weaving between the older scars of her bio-acid burns. Those burns had been tattooed over, wound with knotwork and runes, inked by hand without machine artifice in the old ways of Fenris. The visage of a skeletal wolf stared out from the ruined side of her face, and its bones were etched down her entire left side, wherever the acid had kissed. The old wounds and the new failed to diminish her strength. Her eyes still burned, the blue of Fenrisian skies, with that same primal energy – tempered though it was by grief and pain.

'Where are we?' she asked, weariness creeping into her tone. Every time she looked about her she felt that same ache. So many of the faces were new, their place amidst the crew not yet alloyed together. Too few of her Fenrisian kin had survived the battles and butchery at Draedes. Instead they were the regent's creatures – all starched uniforms and starkly Terran sensibilities. She did not hate them. She resented their presence, she mourned that her kinsmen had died in such droves that these interlopers were required, but she could not bring herself to truly hate them.

'Unclear,' called her new Master of Auspex. The woman, Ana, was capable, certainly, and lacked a little of the formality that Katla railed against. That went a long way towards Katla tolerating her. 'Attempting to match with astrocartographic records. This close to Rift-space, things are not always as they were. God-Emperor willing we'll have precise details soon.'

'All is shaped by the Allfather's design,' she muttered, almost to herself. It had become a mantra since the betrayal. Why else would these things have happened if not by some great design, carved into the heavens like runes into bone?

She was part of that design, as was great Guilliman, the Avenging Son, who had set her upon this task.

Others failed. Perhaps you will prove true, where they could not be trusted.

She hated the accusation in his words, and yet he was not wrong. It was Katla alone who had limped back from the battles of Draedes and Endymica. Bereft of success, of allies and of family.

That last one bit deepest. She was a jarl, though few amongst this new mongrel crew called her such any longer, and she had intended to pass that title on to Astrid. The fullest part of her joy. Her pride and her glory. The girl had been the promise of a better future for the dynasty. One who could make the necessary compromises with the other houses of the once great Compact. The elders, herself, the late Davos Lamertine – hells, even the betrayer, Gunther Radrexxus – they had all been, in their own way, inflexible. A new generation could have cut through that and embraced the new age. The age of change and upheaval, and *opportunity*.

All lost, now. All gone. Beyond a wall of fire and spite. Beyond the Rift.

'I will cross it, this time,' she hissed from between her teeth. 'If you endure, girl, I shall drag you back from whatever hell has been made of Nihilus.'

'Captain?' Another young ensign, too tan and too formal to be of the world of Winter and War, turned to regard her. Too quick to serve, these ones. Duty was baked into them, like stamped steel. They lacked the honesty of the forge, devoid of the marks of their testing. Perhaps she did hate them, a little, for that.

'Nothing. Simply wondering aloud.' She sighed, scratched at her brow, and then rose to her feet. She stepped off the command dais and down towards the great bulwark doors of her command bridge. She could still see the places where claws had scored the metal, though they had been repaired by masters of their craft, and could remember where the blood – her own amongst it – had spattered the decking. She shook the vertigo of memory away.

Amongst the Fenrisian crew who remained there were some who considered the ship cursed, a wight-vessel dredged up from beneath the galaxy's ice. They called it, and her, in whispered tones, the *Underverse Queen*.

Katla was not sure she could disagree with them. The ship felt strange, changed and liminal. As though it no longer truly belonged to her or to the world of the living. They had passed through fire and they had frozen, near to death. In the face of such things it was no surprise that she had changed with it.

'I will go and speak with the star-seer, see if there is any progress,' she said with a sigh, and stalked from the dais, out towards the great arterial corridors of the ship. 'Until then I do not wish to be disturbed. Hold course, keep faith, and the All-father will deliver us.'

Alone, she felt the pressure of command fade, and she could breathe once more. Outside the confines of the bridge she felt free, able to quicken her step and enjoy the ancient halls of the vessel. The *Queen* had served at the will of her dynasty for generations, since the gift of the Warrant had raised up the first of her ancestors from the ice. They had been trusted crew, yes, but she was still a savage daughter of a savage world. A woman who had never expected to leave her home world, let alone to ply the void in the Allfather's name, and scar their family name into the annals of legend.

What were they now? A vagabond dynasty, their holdings likely in the hands of their enemies, kept afloat only by the curt kindness of a primarch. She had ceased to be a free entity and existed now only on sufferance, only so long as she had a duty to perform.

Katla walked past the windows of an observation deck and lingered, taking the time to study what lay beyond. Space itself had grown elastic and tormented, riven through with the flickering light of the warp and the madness which it brought. Systems such as this, not quite in the grasp of the storms, were infected with a primordial uncanniness. In the months and years of her long quest she had seen worlds that ran like wax, shaped by uncaring hands as easily as a child's putty. Planetary bodies which had been warped into colossal symbols of the unreal and the holy, worlds that burned in the dark while their suns sat cold, asteroids made of teeth and blood, rings shaped of suffering.

This place still held to the physical parameters of a stellar system, but she could already see the edges of it where the warp's kiss had twisted it with maleficarum. Clouds of ice and dust writhed as though alive, their colours distorted and malevolent this far from the star's distant light.

She shook her head, turning to look at the things she could trust. The fleet which had once been Task Force Saturnine was a motley assortment of Imperial Navy vessels and their attendants, ships that had been pressed into service to deliver precious secrets to Astartes Chapters across the Imperium. Katla did not pretend to understand what they had done, only clung to the certainty of what they would do at her hand.

'Captain,' a voice broke in from the shadows, and she spun about. Her hands went to the axes hung at her hips, and gripped the handles, before she realised who had spoken.

'Augustus,' she breathed. '*Skitja*, but don't scare me like that.'

Custodian Augustus moved with surprising stealth for so monumental a being, taller than even the Astartes that Katla had met in her lifetime. The Custodian Guard were a breed apart, shaped by unknowable gene-craft into something truly alien to her understanding. Before they had broken their long stewardship of the Palace they had seemed almost things of pure myth. Now true demigods stalked the stars, and brought His gold and glory to the darkest of places.

If Augustus was bothered by a little swearing it did not show in his posture, or on the impassive faceplate of his gilded helm.

'Forgive me, captain.' He looked around. 'Though I would suggest that your operational security requires work. If I had been an assassin then you would, more than likely, be dead.'

'I wouldn't count on it, Custodian. Many things in this galaxy have tried to kill me.' She gestured to her scarred and tattooed side. 'And yet I endure. Perhaps I have the Allfather's grace, to be so lucky, eh?'

The featureless helm tilted at that. 'Careful, captain. I will tolerate many things out here upon the frontier of Sanctus, but not idle attributions to His will.'

'I am always amazed, Augustus, that one such as you can have so many names and yet so little character!' She laughed and bared her teeth in a flare of white. 'And as I have told you before, I detest being called captain. Like some freighter mistress. I have been a queen before, and those close to my side call me jarl. I would extend that courtesy to you.'

'As I have told you before, captain, I will not use titles of rule for others. Only He has dominion over men. Only He is fit to sit atop a throne.'

'Undoubtedly,' she said cautiously. 'But I was lauded as such, in my time. That should be worth something, should it not?'

'You are a sanctioned rogue trader. You are the captain of this vessel. Nothing more.'

She laughed. 'Oh, Augustus. One day you must tell me how they excised the sense of humour from you.' She went to move past him, to continue on towards the seer's oubliette.

His guardian spear swept out, barring her path. 'You have a duty, captain. I lingered with these ships of fools in order to ensure that you uphold it.'

'Do not think that I don't know my duty, Custodian. I received it from the regent himself. Not once, but twice.'

'And it is my duty to ensure that you do not fail twice, captain.'

She scowled at his words. 'What happened before was–'

'Unforeseeable, yes. Perhaps.' The Custodian moved forward, only a fraction, but with such speed and surety that something animal behind Katla's eyes screamed at her to run, to retreat, to make herself safe from the thing that was no longer truly a man. 'There have been many events in the Imperium's history that others might declare as unforeseeable. Yet somewhere, inevitably, there were those who were forewarned. It has been the same with every other sentient species to claw its way up from the muck.'

'And you think I do not have the sight to see? That I will blunder into folly?'

'I fear that you are being ill-used in this endeavour, captain.' Augustus drew his spear back and gestured with its tip. 'I am here to observe your progress, nothing more. Pray that it never comes to more than that.'

She drew herself up and strode past him, past the tormented views of the system, and towards the seer's sanctum.

The sanctum was crowded with machinery and equipment that was eldritch even to Katla's keen eye. The mechanisms had been taken, haphazardly, from the seer's previous observatory above the Navigator's moon of Vandium.

Still, it had been swift, and that in itself had been a kindness. She had not sought his services, so much as she had taken him wholesale. He and all his works. That was, as the Warrant declared, her right.

Katla strode through the chamber, beneath arcs of electricity and spiralling hololithic star charts. Light and sound warred for dominance in a room whose purpose could only truly be understood and interpreted by one of the Mechanicus' tech-priests. That was the manner of being she had plucked from his observatory and pressed into service.

Magos Yazran stood in the centre of the room, his arms spread and his mechadendrites extruded, parsing the noospheric data from the air. His red robes billowed in the artificial atmosphere of the ship, coiling about his iron limbs, swathing him in blood. At the edges of the meditative dais, two skitarii kept vigil, still and silent.

Katla stood and observed for a moment, hands folded behind her back, and then coughed to draw his attention.

Yazran's head snapped round and he saw her. He blurted something in binharic and the skitarii stepped back from the edge of the dais, turning to face the huntress.

'Helvintr,' he said coldly. The magos astrocartographic had not yet truly forgiven Katla for his abduction, nor the damage done to his observatory. 'Come to check on our progress, have you?' He used his flesh-voice in their interactions, purely so he could gripe about her in binharic to his guards. 'If I have any greater clarity on our objective then I will let you know, on my own conditions.'

'Where are we?' Katla asked, utterly without preamble. The trail was waning, and this close to the Rift it was harder to keep their bearings. Reality was slowly rebelling against their progress, turning the void strange.

He scoffed, his binharic-emitters squawking with a whine of bemusement. He raised a finger to the air, like a tribesman testing the direction of the wind, and then lowered it.

'Still on course galactic east, Ultima Segmentum. Near-Rift space. Empyreal saturation accounts for forty-seven point five per cent, averaged, of this system's complete material-immaterial mass interactions. It is...' He paused. 'Perhaps not dying, but certainly it lives in an entirely contrary way.'

'Not presently, though I'm sure it will be determined through cartographic cross-examination of what is and what was. Astronavigation and the vagaries of warp-materium overlap are my specialities, Helvintr, but that does not mean that every star and system in the void is known to me. The important thing is that we are drawing close to the anomalous fluctuation.'

'The Gate.'

That was what mattered, in the end. The very idea of a gate, a new passage across the Rift. Of all their leads this had been the strongest, and yet the most tenuous. Yazran's best calculations shifted with each passing day as monumental empyreal flux buffeted their best auguries.

Yet it remained the prize. The Gate. To know they were drawing nearer was enough.

'If you insist upon calling it that. If your guesswork, and mine, is well founded, then perhaps in ages to come it will be referred to as a gate, lauded alongside other stable passages. You understand such things, of course. You are a rogue trader. You go where others dare not, as it has always been. Operational records are laden with examples of such daring. From the realms carved by the Winterscale Dynasty to the excesses of your own Davamir Compact. If there were any who would dare the Rift then you are amongst them...' He paused. 'And yet it is more than that, is it not?'

'You would not understand,' she said, and bared her teeth. 'There is no common humanity left in you. You are an iron priest, served by wights and hollow men. What would you know of love or kinship?'

'Little,' Yazran said, without complaint. 'I have not engaged in genic procreation. My priority has been, as always, to leave my mark upon the fabric of the Imperium itself. To become enmeshed as part of the Omnissiah's great design. I do not doubt that you have cast your eye over the dominions of humanity and considered, "Why should I not make them mine? Why should my mark not grace the maps and charts of a thousand void-sailors?"'

Katla laughed. 'Why not indeed? Ask yourself, then, how many explorators and rogue traders, down the annals of the Great Crusade and beyond, thought the same as you? How many fought and bled to leave their scrawl across the galaxy's skin?

'Few of those who did were primarchs,' the magos offered, again in his flat diction. 'Why should we restrain ourselves when our orders flow from one such as they?'

'Skitja, but do not let the Custodian hear you utter such blasphemy,' she muttered and shook her head. 'These are the ages when legacies are built, true enough, but that is not what drives me. No longer. I have lost too much to the ways of traitors and their hidden blades, but if there is a chance... even the smallest of chances that my daughter yet lives, then I would walk through hell to see her delivered safely.'

'Sentiment is an inefficient fuel for such undertakings,' he said, and the slightest flicker of humanity danced across his words, 'but in this instance it is clearly the optimal personal motivation. The genetors would claim the hand of the Omnissiah in even that, base-wired into the human condition.'

'I suppose,' she said with a laugh, 'I should find that comforting?'

'It is immaterial how you find it, Helvintr. You took me from my place of contentment, from my duties, and stole me out to these hostile stars. I have adapted. I have amended my data. You have amended it further with your words here, today. Perhaps if you had prioritised that information then our circumstances would have been different. Yet here we are, facing down the vistas of eternity, and attempting to find common ground. You lead a war-fleet, sanctified in the Omnissiah's name. You

bear the mark of the Regent of Terra, and you seek dangerous
passage – all for the sake of love. That in itself is a duty worth
undertaking.'

'No matter the cost?'

The priest was silent for a long moment as his mechadendrites
moved into new configurations, like constellations realigning.
His optical lenses whirred and clicked, and she was put in mind
of a cogitator as it strove to complete a particularly gruelling
calculation.

'No matter the cost, Helvintr. If it is the state of the universe
that has driven you to these ends, then that disorder must be set
right. Sometimes the greatest recorded wisdom of the ancients
lay with a single grand stroke of genius.' He turned from her, leaving her silhouetted amongst the duelling equations and stellar
interpretations which drifted through the air. 'Seek your own.'

Chapter Fourteen

HIS JUDGEMENT
THOSE WITHOUT SIN
FALSE FAITH

He was not sure how long he had been in the cell.

Time had become elastic for Draszen since his capture. They had starved and beaten him, deprived him of water and sleep. The chamber was constantly illuminated, so he could see every cracked brick and worn flagstone. He could see where blood had been spilled and where lone teeth nestled between the rocks, not forgotten but intentionally left as a message. A reminder. This was a place of pain and suffering and there was no escape, not truly, save through death.

He had not thought of the penitent cells since the last time he had consigned a soul to their depths below the palace. Crime was not unknown upon Velua, as it was not upon any world of the Imperium, but they had been minor offences – punishable by a maiming, or a sacrifice of flesh. Men and women had accepted indentured servitude as well, in kinder times, working their sin away through sweat and toil.

These cells were for those intended to hang or burn or be

drowned, and left to moulder amidst the vistas of paradise. That was their fate. That was his fate. He was prepared for it, he realised. He would take responsibility for his sins and he would accept the punishment, and for that it would be swift. The Emperor's justice, His judgement, would be absolute and rightly so.

They had left him naked, stripped even of the rags that had once been his uniform, and he shivered against the flagstones, with no bedroll or blanket to rely upon. There had been weeping at first, drifting from the other cells, but bit by bit that had ceased, until the only sound of crying was his own. He had soiled himself at some point in the last night, his bowels and bladder finally giving out after the relentless and unceasing torture. The Sisters who administered his punishment did not even seem to properly regard him. Certainly not as a man. He wondered when one of the Space Marines would come for him. He had not seen any prowling the halls, eager to render judgement, and for that he was glad.

He was lying, shivering and weeping and filthy, on the floor of the cell as the locks finally creaked and the door slid open. Two Sisters strode in without looking at him, and then lifted him bodily out and into the corridor. They each took one arm, carrying him between them like an invalid through the cell blocks and into an empty room.

He sat there for what felt like hours, slowly sticking to a cold steel chair, his manacled hands resting on the equally oppressive table. He could feel his breath hammering in his chest, alongside his racing heart.

Is this it? Am I going to swing now? Am I truly ready to die?

The door opened and a woman entered, taking her own seat opposite him, placing a sheaf of papers before him as she did so. Unlike Draszen she was armed and armoured. All the potential for peace, slim as it had been, had been drained and gouged from her, rendering her as something iron-hard, cold and cruel.

'I–' he began, but she shook her head and her gauntlet cut the air abruptly.

'No,' Canoness Sarael said firmly. 'You will not speak unless first addressed.' She looked at him and her cold eyes narrowed, contorted by pure disgust. His silence held and she continued. 'You were found amongst beggars, whores and thieves at the lowest ebb of our great city. Not standing proudly in its defence. Not upon the walls, where you were meant to be. Where you were *needed*.' Her lip curled as she spoke the words. 'You deserted your post, your duty and your Emperor. How do you plead?'

He let out a ragged sigh and hung his head. 'I have... no excuse. I saw the face of the enemy, and it was horror and despair and death. I couldn't... I didn't want to face it.'

'And now all you shall face is the Emperor's justice.'

'I wish to make amends. To die and be shriven of my sins. I failed. I broke and ran where others stayed and fought. I will never make amends for that, save in death.'

'Only in death does duty end,' she said. 'A lesson you would have done well to commit to heart earlier.' She reached out and tapped the pile of parchment before her. 'These are your records. Every award and commendation. All of your accomplishments and achievements. I will commit them to the flame forthwith, I only wished you to see what you once possessed before we take it from you forever.'

He swallowed and looked down at his feet again. 'Will I be hanged?'

'It was considered,' she said bluntly. Her gauntleted hands rested upon the table now, arched as though poised to claw through the metal. Her revulsion at his very existence was palpable. 'There have, however, been changes of circumstance that would render such a symbolic act hollow.'

'I don't understand.'

'And never will.' She sighed. He could sense the weariness drifting from her now, the cloying smoke as her inner fire slowly dwindled. He was going to die, of that he had no doubt, but he wondered if the canoness was not, in some way, already dead. Defeated without the final blow ever coming. Something had broken her, and what remained was a thing of sharp edges and deep wounds.

'You do not deserve to know what has come to pass and what desperation has come upon us. All that remains is for you to serve as best you are able. That is my gift to you. That is His judgement. Service, even unto death.' She rose and scooped up the papers, turning from him for perhaps the last time. He felt the tears rising to his eyes again and the ragged sobs about to burst from his throat.

They stopped a moment later when the red-robed figures slid into the chamber, their augmetic eyes focused upon him with inhuman scrutiny. He did not even have a chance to scream as they seized him, dragged him to his feet, and pulled him into the deeper darkness beneath the cells.

Irinya emerged from the cell as though a weight had been lifted from her.

To have seen the deserter, the once great man, and been able to pass the Emperor's judgement upon him felt like righteousness. All the pain of the recent nights bled away, and even the wounds of the Black Templars' withdrawal seemed to leave her. However wearied her physical body was, her spirit exalted at the undertaking.

The gaoler of the forbidden place, the deepest cells, was a shrunken old man – dwarfed by his sombre black robes – who

was named Brother Martinus, and he smiled at her as she
emerged. Avuncular, personable, and utterly without conscience.

'A fine choice, canoness. It is so infrequently that the old rites
are allowed to be indulged.'

'And with good reason,' she growled. 'This is not done idly.
Not to him, nor to any of the rest of them.'

'Desperation is a powerful agitator,' the old man said, with
a disconcerting chortle. 'None of the prisoners here will ever
know the circumstances which led to their...' He paused and
waved his hand in the empty air. Each finger was bedecked
by rings of dark metal, their edges and inner surfaces subtly
barbed to elicit pain from the wearer. 'Elevation, shall we say?'

'A craven euphemism for what will be done to them.'

'From a certain point of view, perhaps. They shall be made,
in their own way, without sin.'

'Those of us without sin are rare,' she said, with a bitter laugh.
'This is expurgation by the most direct means. The most useful
of avenues left available to us, without...'

She trailed off, unwilling to put the loss into words. Gaheris
and his brothers, paragons and champions, had failed them.
What are we to do, when the strength of angels proves false?
she wondered. They had turned away when they were needed
most.

'The enemy's strength grows. The False Angels are amongst
them, and we cannot resist them by common strength of arms
alone. These prisoners will buy us time. They will earn us our
place amidst the Emperor's chosen, and by their sacrifice shall
all who resist yet be exalted in His sight.'

'Yes,' Martinus hissed, and his lips peeled back with undis-
guised glee. 'Oh how I wish I could be there personally to watch
their holy transfiguration. I have dedicated my entire life, my
entire life, to the study of human anatomy and its weaknesses.'
He beamed proudly and ignored the curling of Irinya's lip. 'To

see it extended to its most logical of conclusions. The very apotheosis of spiritual suffering.'

'Yet it will not be by your hand. They all go to the hands of the Machine Cult in accordance with their pacts with the Ecclesiarchy. They will invoke their own rites, as we do now.' She sighed. 'God-Emperor, grant me the serenity to accept what must be done.'

'There is nothing to fear, canoness,' Martinus said, his hands clasped before him. 'The God-Emperor, in His infinite bounty and promise, shall provide.'

Striding out of the dungeons, Irinya felt her vindication fleeing. Righteousness died beneath the weight of absolute necessity. Consumed in the fire of defiance; of the things that must be done in order to survive. She hated it as much as she knew how essential it was. When she had passed her judgement upon Draszen and condemned him to his fate, it had felt pure. Now, with Martinus' intervention, it felt tainted.

She felt old.

Weariness was creeping into her bones, compounded by the weight of the world that she defended. Velua, with its bright soul and its songs. With all of its dreams and delusions. The galaxy was changed and a demigod walked amongst them, and yet they could not embrace the bright future that awaited them. The Veluan Hoplites might never muster in service of the crusade or earn new honours – instead they would cower, assailed by their own doubts as much as the enemy.

'And there is so much doubt,' she whispered to herself. 'So much uncertainty.'

Before it had been the presence of Teneu's body upon this world, the place of her interment rather than that of her martyrdom. Irinya had been present at both, but it made it no easier.

She moved slowly through the winding passageways beneath the High Sacristy, armour clattering with the strain of every step. She would not shed it. Not ever again. The days of ruin and infamy were upon them and she would face down her duty as a warrior, even if it meant her death.

A martyr's death... She almost laughed at the thought. Had she not begged for such a thing, once? She had asked to return to the front, to stand sentinel amidst the crusade fleets with demigods and Titans precisely so that she would find meaning amidst the outrage. To serve Him as best she could. The abbess had supported that dream, and encouraged it.

'Take to the stars. Serve at the front. That is what we were made for. His chosen servants, His daughters, shaped by circumstance to hold the fate of the galaxy in our hands. Bear up the blade and defend His realm.'

Those words had been a comfort and a guide down the long years of the crusade. She had fought through the blood-warrens that remained of the Cicoran orbital-hives, and she had descended into the mine-pits of Sancram, where the pallid, eyeless workers had risen up against Imperial rule. She had torn down their temples of black crystal and spite; cast them into the depths to burn forever.

Yet here in the light of faith she knew pain and fear. She understood doubt.

Velua was the truest battlefield of her long career. It was the crucible that would test her, within and without.

'And if I must face it alone, with only your memory, then I will do it,' she said to the empty air, as though those long lost to her could yet hear. 'I will do as I have always done. What is needful.'

Chapter Fifteen

THE SILENT DEAD

PILGRIMS' END

GHOSTS IN THE MACHINE

'Contact, captain!'

The utterance grated and yet Katla smiled and gestured from her brazen throne, hand clawing at the empty air.

'What is it? More detritus and flotsam cast up by the warp's tides?' She had taken her spear, Fimbulgeir, down from the gilded mounting behind the throne and sat with it laid across her lap. Her axes nestled beside it, ready to do harm. Wrath-spitter, the ancient volkite pistol, sat along the arm of the throne, forever within reach. The betrayals of the past had made her wary, and the Custodian's words had stung her. Now she sat, enthroned, armed and armoured, epitomising the warrior queen that the Emperor's watcher so disdained.

'Returns are spotty, captain, but it looks to be a becalmed flotilla. Bulk carriers, mass-transports. They're broadcasting pilgrims' signum codes. Engines and reactor are both cold.'

'Ships of the dead,' she breathed. 'Underverse leavings.'

On the ice- and storm-tossed seas of Fenris, it was ever a bad omen to find a ship becalmed. To sink and be dragged down beneath the ice, to falter on the rocks or to make red snow when raiders came, there was at least honour in that. To be left adrift, to succumb to hunger or to simply give yourself to the sea... It was a dishonourable death. It was worse in the void. A ship was a city unto itself, a crew of thousands. Each and every one of them at the mercy of the vagaries of interstellar travel.

If they were lucky then they died in the materium, slow and painful but without the fear for the soul that the warp generated. Ships that were lost to warp-madness, which were vomited back into the real with their forms corrupted and twisted – or worse, their souls and spirits *changed* – they were the truly damned.

'Immaterial assessment? Are they fresh from the warp? Or did they die upon hard reality?'

'I will petition the Navigator for their assessment, captain.'

She tapped her fingers along the rune-marked haft of the spear, seeking comfort where none was forthcoming. She knew that all eyes were upon her. She could see their hooded looks out of the corner of her eye, feel their breath held, waiting for the blade to fall. For a decision to be made.

She was queen. She was jarl. She was, Allfather damn them, *captain*.

'Have we established any wider astrocartographic sense of where we actually are?' she growled.

The crew looked away from her, upwards, as though they could coax an answer from the absent Magos Yazran by will alone. She scowled and spat.

'Ready a boarding party. We'll go aboard the lead ship,' she said as she consulted a chart, 'the... *Flag of Faith*, and ascertain what has become of the crew, then we'll empty their data-vaults for their logs and maps. Throne willing that will steer us back onto a clement course.' She sighed. 'Damn you and your vagueness, star-seer. Allfather give me surety and steel.'

* * *

Fire cut the eternal night as the boarding charges detonated, blowing in the exterior airlock in a shower of shrapnel and a rush of correcting air pressures. The void suits that clad them were newer marks, symbols of the regent's favour, and they let her boarding party move out from the shuttle and into the ship with a sinuous grace. She felt like a wolf again, a reaver alive only in the hunt. She could have entrusted the honour to any of her huscarls or armsmen, yet she had ever led from the front. The void held no fear for her.

The pack she led was a mixed affair. Those at the fore, intent on the correct rites of breaching and the attendant equipment, were newbloods. Regent's men, all. With her, in a loose circle, poised to strike from the rear of the gathering, were those warriors blooded to her cause. All bore the blood of Fenris in their veins, whether pure from the source or carried down by generations in the void. They were the warriors who had stood with her as the cultists and their inhuman masters had ravaged her ship and wounded her to her core. She still wore the scars – body and soul.

'Standard boarding protocols,' she said, loud enough for the newbloods to hear her. 'I want control of the ship's systems as soon as possible. Core out the data, find evidence of the crew. If none remain then we give it a death of fire. If there are any useful souls... well, they will help the cause. The maps are paramount. Command deck and Navigator's eyrie as a matter of priority.'

'Aye,' came the chorused response.

Discipline was holding. That, at the very least, was something. Perhaps something of quality and strength could yet be alloyed together from the Terran and Fenrisian elements.

Katla's axes were sheathed at her hips and Fimbulgeir was braced along her spine by mag-locks. She already had Wrathspitter in her hands, though she acknowledged that the volkite was more than likely overkill. It would do unnecessary damage to the ship if it fired, even as it burned the enemy into ashes. But there were things in the dark of the void, in the bowels of old ships, trapped beneath the ice of reality – clawing like wights as they sought to find purchase. Alien monsters, parasite kings wearing the faces of men, daemons from beyond. She gritted her teeth within the confines of her helm and then forged on, into the dark.

The ship was as dead as the auspex had claimed. Everything was still, with no sign of even the most rudimentary of ship-board motion. The suit's spot-lumens cut narrow beams through the stygian dark, illuminating silent cogitator banks and unre-sponsive panels. Servitors hung in their support cradles, even their cyborg bodies devoid of life. It was a ship of the dead in truth, a lifeless husk spat out by the uncaring galaxy. It had set out with hope, no doubt, and it had found only slow death and disappointment amongst the stars.

'This is a cursed place,' murmured Calder. He was one of her oathsworn, her trusted, and her heart was warmed by the presence of him. He was not as reliable as Eirik had been, but the trials of their shared past had tested and strengthened the man. He had risen to the occasion, and now stood as one of her chief huscarls. 'We should have burned it from the stars,' he went on. 'It is touched by maleficarum.'

'Are you a *gothi* now, Calder?' asked Tyra from Katla's other side. She was a more playful soul. She had a kernel of joy within her soul and delighted in keeping it well fed and burning.

'I do not claim to be a gothi,' Calder said, slowly and deli-berately. 'This place simply feels foul. It has a taint to it. I do not have to walk with spirits like the old woman to know that!'

'Enough,' Katla said. 'Don't humiliate us in front of the Terrans.'

That brought grim laughter from the two. Dishonour was still worse than death.

Is it? Katla thought. She had passed through both in recent memory. Both had left their scars, and had bitten deep into her soul – warded though it was by the finest of a gothi's art. She brushed a hand along her left side, aware of the wards and marks inked upon her skin even through the protection of the void suit, and the armour she wore beneath that.

My skin is my final armour. The cage for my soul, protecting it from the ravages of the Underverse and the hunger of its denizens. I will not fail or falter here. I will prove myself true, and rise to this new challenge. For beyond that lies my reward.

She cursed herself for cleaving to mortal glories and material prizes. Those distractions had ensnared her before, when the other dynasties had joined together for profit at the regent's behest. The galaxy could have been theirs, then. New routes of trade opened up – opportunities spiralling out from the crusade and the promise of reclamation. Imperium Nihilus would have been returned to the bosom of the Imperium, and the fractured dominions made whole.

They could have been heroes, in those days. They could have redrawn the maps and rewritten history. The name of Helvintr would have been adulated across the entirety of the stars. But it was not to be. Instead everything had been taken from her. Even the fullest part of her joy.

'I want this vessel's heart in my hands,' she growled.

'Aye, jarl!' Calder and Tyra chorused in rare unison, brought to heel by their queen's command.

They moved as a single unit, guided by her intrinsic understanding of the ship's dimensions. The *Flag of Faith* was a standard, overweight and ailing Jericho-class vessel which had been intended to move the pilgrim and penitent masses of humanity in their endless flitting from sacred place to sacred place. She had known entire rogue trader houses, the itinerant Torvander sprang to mind, who had made their fortunes off this cattle-like procession.

Katla was no stranger to faith. She held her own beliefs and cleaved to the Allfather's will, but she would not allow herself to be a passive vessel of it. To bear a Warrant of Trade, to work beneath the primarch's eye, that demanded an active participation. There were no spectators in her work. There were no idle souls when the Emperor's work was to be done.

They advanced down withered districts – whole ship-sections run wild. Strange growths coiled and moved along the pipeworks and conduits, furred with fungal corrosion and an oily sheen which made her think of sickbeds. If Calder and Tyra were affected by the ship's condition they did not voice it. Calder focused on the door systems which had uniformly seized, working to mollify whatever machine spirits yet remained, while muttering prayers of the iron priests. Tyra paced between him and Katla, turning her eye ever backwards, ready for any attack. She had shouldered her autogun and instead hefted a boarding sword. It was a brutally direct weapon, the edge hooked to better enable it to drag the foe beneath the waves and drown them in the ice sea. A sentiment it carried eagerly to the void. Tyra's face was a pale smear behind her faceplate, split by the wideness of her grin.

'You'll get your chance, soon enough,' Katla cautioned.

Tyra just shrugged. 'I'm in no rush, jarl. Just watching your back.'

'And I'm forever grateful,' Katla said, smiling. 'I'm eager for battle too, but a wise queen does not seek it out without cause. This ship may be dead or it may be a trap, but we do not spring it without cause. We secure the ship, we claim its heart and brain. We hold them in our hands and we squeeze if necessary.'

'One step closer to that,' Calder grunted. The door began to slide open and he gleefully offered up another prayer. 'Soul of the machine, thank you for your kindness.'

They moved on deeper into the *Flag of Faith*. Here the

vessel's structure and systems seemed more weathered, more worn. Corrosion had wormed its way into the bulkheads and floors, stagnant water pooled underfoot or dribbled down the walls, and the air was thin, barely oxygenated. Her suit's systems were compensating for the environmental failings, but she noted tics and catches in its operation. The air filters clicked and hissed in her ears, straining and struggling, and she feared that she would know a slow death. The creeping threat of suffocation, dying with her hands curled into claws, beating against the walls.

Was that how they died? Was that these pilgrims' end? Faith drowned in the darkness?

She shook aside the thoughts. Melancholy and malaise haunted places such as this, becoming little more than yet another cautionary tale for voidfarers. Whatever evils had occurred within the walls of the vessel, whatever tragedy had taken place, they had been trapped within the ship's iron skin, till the entire thing reeked of it – wreathed in the stench of death and madness. She had seen it before, faced it down with axe and spear. Ships burning in the fires of failed translation, of immaterial intrusion, or the more mundane deaths that could find you amidst the stars. Systems failure. Environmental collapse. Holed through in the underdecks. Fire in zero gravity, the crawling horror of it. She had weathered all storms, and there was nothing yet in the void that could unseat her or steal her bravery.

Not even this. Not even the cold and dead corpse of a ship, at the head of a flotilla of the damned.

Eventually their wanderings brought them to the vessel's quiescent heart. The reactor decks sprawled, layered through with conduits which fed precious power to all other parts of the ship, their bulk intruding into the central wards of the enginarium. Coolant stacks loomed taller than hab-blocks, rising up into the coiled darkness of the interior. They passed beneath great sweeps of coiled wire, vast as triumphal arches, and into the heart of reactor control.

There were no tech-priests or enginseers. She had expected at least a few. If there were to be any bodies then surely they would be here, knelt in obeisance to the machine, hitched to dormant systems. Yet here there were none. Not even the remains of the attendants of the ship's systems lingered.

'Odd,' Calder said, giving voice to her misgivings. 'None of this makes sense. Where would they have gone? The entire crew? Even the most devoted of their iron priests?'

'Ghost ships,' Tyra breathed. 'Wights came for them and dragged them all away into the Underverse. That is what this is. We should burn them all from the void, jarl. We should end this farce now and not root around amidst the bones of dead ships. You would not do it upon the ice and we sure as skitja should not do it here and now. I would rather we be safely aboard the *Queen* with every gun in the fleet turned against these ill omens. They stink of maleficarum. The warp has its claws in them.'

'These are yet good and noble machines,' Calder said. He had begun to fuss at one of the control consoles, turning his meagre understanding towards the task. 'They can be roused and inter-rogated. Same as any other.'

'Enough, both of you,' Katla cut in. She turned to Calder. 'Keep working. Bring it to partial yield. I want enough power to make this quick and easy.' She shook her head and patted her axes. 'And if the worst should come to pass then we will face it in the oldest way. Blade to blade, with fire and hate.'

'Aye,' Tyra said, nodding. 'I can abide by that.'

Calder's hands worked at the controls with a cautious speed. He had never truly mastered a system such as this, only gleaned the rudiments from his apprenticeships in the bowels of the *Wyrmslayer Queen*. Now he was forced to bring that borrowed understanding to bear, or else the entire venture was doomed.

Systems flickered around them as the reactor slowly began to kindle, lights blinked in the heights and something rumbled beneath their feet, like the shuddering breathing of a fitful god. Other sounds drifted in amidst the rousing machines. From above, from the shadow-shrouded arches and walkways, came a gentle clattering – like old bones in a sack, stirring in the wind.

As the systems re-engaged and the light returned, all three looked skywards and beheld what had become of the crew.

There were ghosts in the machine.

Not good and sacred spirits, but unclean things that had whispered in through the protective bubble of the Geller fields. Those who tended the systems had heard the voices in their dreams, drifting through the immaterial tides clothed in the lies of inspiration and revelation.

Just a small change and everything will be better. One little alteration and the nightmares will stop, the screaming will finally quieten, the torment will end. I'll save us all.

By such delusions were ships killed and crews slaughtered, and if not slaughtered then *changed* to something other than human perfection.

The things that scuttled and crawled and oozed down from the shadows had been men and women once. They had been enginseers, ship's crew and pilgrims. They wore their old identities now only as tattered rags and remnants, strung across warped muscle and borrowed metal. They had twisted and altered, their forms as malleable as wax under the flame.

Katla and her crew could only raise their weapons in half-ready futility, as the children of atrocity descended with murder in their hearts and mad laughter upon their lips.

Chapter Sixteen

NATURE OF SACRIFICE
OF LOVE AND DUTY
FRAGILE FAITH

Irinya allowed herself, momentarily, the indulgence of restful prayer.

She was not sure why her wanderings had brought her here. Velua did not lack for temples, shrines or fanes. She could have taken the knee in any one of them, yet she had found herself drawn inexorably to the Basilica Sigilitarum, dedicated as it was to Malcador the Hero and his glorious sacrifice. A sacrifice that had ensured that both Emperor and Imperium lived undying to fight against the alien, the mutant and the heretic.

She had always had faith in that sacrifice, in the very nature of sacrifice. Malcador was often claimed as one of the first martyrs, though other minor cults and their temples afforded that honour to others. There were shrines aplenty to the Great Angel, who put himself between the Emperor and utter annihilation. Other, more shrouded, congregations spoke of the Sacrifice of the Nameless Thousand, and some great deed they had done in the Emperor's name.

The altar of the Martyred Hero was surmounted by a statue of an aged figure, arms braced as though seated upon a throne, with a great eagle rearing up behind him, wreathed in flames. Braziers burned behind the eagle, rendering the golden flames yet more lifelike. Of all the temples on Velua that she had visited, this one seemed the most ostentatious. She wondered, idly, if this place had borne some significance for those who honoured Malcador the Hero. What had driven them to honour him so? Other figures, she knew, had been venerated by the other sacred worlds of the Chain. Talvet, for example, had honoured the Great Angel above all others.

It did not do to play favourites when it came to saints and martyrs, she had long since learned. She bowed her head and prayed, intoning words that came not from catechism but from her own simple faith.

'Holy Malcador, great hero who guided the Imperium and gave up his life for it, I ask for your guidance in these times of struggle and trial.' She paused, as though waiting for a reply. The golden statue kept its counsel, and the God-Emperor did not speak.

She thought of Gaheris and the surety with which he had heard and interpreted the Emperor's voice, even if it had led him away from what she was sure in her heart was their true duty.

'You should be here,' she breathed.

She was alone, accompanied only by the distant serfs and priests who attended the shrine. They moved in absolute silence, heads bowed beneath robes of white, grey or black, depending on their station. They had simply nodded to her and ushered her deeper into the sanctum. A visit by a canoness, she knew, was an honour for them – despite the circumstances.

Offerings were burning, ceaselessly burning, before the altar. Incense and candle-smoke rose up in trailing fingers. Others had left fruit or bread, or small tokens of brass and silver. Desperation had made the populace generous. What little they had was being offered up to the cavernous maw of the temple and to the limitless need of the God-Emperor.

'When they pray to you, they think only of your necessity. They cry out for miracles in an age where they have been abundant. Your son walks the galaxy. I have stood in his very presence. We march at the forefront of the mightiest war since your Great Crusade. Bless us, my Emperor, reach down from your Throne and guide us. Send unto us your light.'

A sudden breeze stirred the great chamber and she looked up sharply. The golden visage of Malcador had not altered. No revelation burned in the air before her, just the candles, whose flames shuddered but a little. She laughed gently, despite herself. Irinya lowered her head to her clasped hands, and returned to her prayers.

Just as she had been taught.

The training was relentless, shaping them from the raw ore of girls into tempered young women. Beneath the burning sun of Rytask and the stern gaze and keen whips of the Dogmata, they learned every form of sacred combat and holy prayer available to the Adepta Sororitas. They were kept cloistered away from the boys, now men, who were undertaking their own training. For the Astra Militarum as Tempestus Scions, or perhaps to join the ranks of the Commissariat. Just as some of the women would, for the great organisations of the Imperium took all who would serve them. All save the Sisterhood, bound by the Decree Passive.

'Lesser duties,' Sister Mathilde had always said. 'Less sacred and less important than those which will be bequeathed unto you.' Both Irinya and Teneu had believed it. To stand with the Sisterhood was to stand amongst the elect; only the Emperor's Angels were more blessed in His sight.

'And to be so,' Mathilde had continued, 'they are transmuted from mortal lead to divine-touched gold. That is their strength and their nobility, but we stand as mere mortals – elevated only by skill and by peerless faith. Of all who walk in His shadow and serve His will, only we are anointed in His light. For who amongst the regiments of the Militarum have stood before Him and accepted His judgement and instruction? Only the truly faithful.'

'Praise the faithful, for they see the universe as it is and endeavour to make it as it must be,' Teneu put in, ever with a quote upon her lips. Irinya looked at her in awe, amazed as always at the girl's limitless recall. Mathilde's features creased into an indulgent smile as she watched the girl.

'Very good, Novitiate Teneu.' She turned her gaze towards Irinya and her mirth subtly curdled. 'And you, Novitiate Irinya, do you have anything to add?'

Irinya's tongue felt leaden in her mouth. 'It... It is the Emperor's fire that burns brightest in the hearts of humanity, driving out the darkness and ensuring the supremacy of the species.'

The older woman at least seemed surprised, if not outright impressed. 'Sufficient,' she rasped.

Mathilde would have seemed ancient, her leather skin wedded too tight to her bones, her hair turned iron-grey and corpse-white, save for the vitality that burned through her. She moved with a singular passion, the kind of mobility in agedness that only true faith and strength of will could bring. She wielded a cane, not for any aid to her bearing, but to rap the knuckles or the lower back or the backs of the knees of inattentive novitiates. Irinya had known its bite many times in the past.

'It is not enough to memorise what you are taught,' Mathilde said, archly. She turned away from the two novitiates and stalked around to her side of the desk, settling into her hard wooden chair. 'It is a living faith which must be embodied with your every breath, till death in service to the Throne finally claims you. You must *embody the attitudes of our founders, of the first who rose to His defence and heeded His will.' She paused and smiled, nodding in the direction of Teneu. 'You must be miracles, if you are to serve Him.'*

Irinya scowled. Teneu reddened and looked down, away from the older woman and her misplaced pride. The news of the miracle with the eaglet had spread quickly through the halls of the schola, becoming an air of myth which had dogged Teneu. For despite the girl's most ardent protests there had been few who would believe that a lower-born specimen such as Irinya could have been responsible.

The tests had begun shortly afterwards. Tests of purity from Sisters Superior and assessments from an endless parade of Ecclesiarchy priests, and Teneu had suffered through them with nary a complaint. It did not matter how much either girl attempted to correct them, it was for naught.

'Is that all, Sister?' Teneu asked. She struggled to keep the pleading from her voice and released a small sigh of relief when Mathilde nodded.

'That is all. Other duties call me.' She paused, and her piteous gaze returned to Irinya. 'Learn from your peer, Irinya. Perhaps some of her grace might rub off on you, eh?' The old woman rose and stretched, before stalking from the room.

Irinya sat at the desk, fingers drumming against the wood, fuming silently at the indignity of her own treatment. Her eyes were closed and only opened when she felt a hand nestle atop hers.

'I'm sorry,' Teneu offered quietly. She was looking down again, eyes brimming with tears. 'I don't want to be a weapon against you, no matter how much they try to wield me.'

'I know.' Irinya sighed. 'I know.' She shook her head and her white hair shuddered and moved with the effort. 'You've done nothing wrong. You never do anything wrong.' She laughed a little. 'That's half the problem. You're already half a saint in action.'

'Oh, hush,' Teneu said, and laughed with her. Her fingers squeezed Irinya's in reassurance. 'You may struggle with scripture but you fight with the best of them in the training halls. And you...' She trailed off. 'You were the one who saved the eaglet. I borrow your grace and your glory.'

'It doesn't matter,' Irinya said. She raised her hand and took Teneu's, palm to palm, fingers interlaced. 'You are what they want to see. I'm not. I do the best I can but if they want to lionise you, then let them. Prove yourself worthy of their praise and their adoration. Be true to the saint. I will always be at your side, sharing in your light.'

Irinya felt the bond in her very soul. The auguries had promised that their fates were twinned – steeped in omens of glory and martyrdom. Those who read the stellar signs and the tarot had spoken often of the light of the God-Emperor's grace entwined around both of them. Each of them bearing His radiance and yet only one of them passing a torch onwards into the future.

The expectations of the Sisterhood, so bound up in notions of sacrifice and suffering, might have crushed the spirits of weaker women, but Irinya and Teneu had found it in themselves to rise. To defy those presumptions and to give themselves over to duty.

Teneu was silent for a long moment. She looked at Irinya, her brown eyes wide and almost pleading. 'Do you promise? We will rise together or not at all.'

'We made the climb once. How hard can it be to rise through the ranks?' Irinya laughed a little and rose, stretching her back as she did, rolling her muscles. 'You have a good heart and a strong soul, Teneu. If that can't carry us through, then nothing can.'

Irinya felt the tears running down her cheeks and opened her eyes, rising unsteadily from the pits of memory. She looked around the great hall of the basilica and then moved off down the central aisle.

Candles stirred in her wake, their flames flickering violently as she hurried from the chamber and out into the cold of the night. Other votive offerings had been laid out, candles adorning every windowsill and door stoop, beside lines of salt and icons of silver and cold iron. The populace, those of them allowed a break in the perpetual shift patterns, slept in the secure knowledge that the God-Emperor would protect them. That their simple rituals towards sanctity would be enough to dispel the encroaching darkness and the taint of the Archenemy.

Irinya shook her head and made the sign of the aquila across her breastplate. The armour was more reassuring than ever in these turbulent times, both for herself and those around her. When the people of the shrine city looked upon her they saw hope and steadfast service. Even when they stood in opposition to the rioters and the desperate, they were showing the steel of Imperial resolve.

An unbowed humanity, standing strong in the face of adversity and their myriad foes.

She marched on. Out of the basilica, up the many stairs which wormed through the body of the shrine city like arteries, across the great bridges that spanned the gaps between tiers like ancient ivory. She walked the bones of the city, under arches lined with skulls, past guards in the red and bronze of the Hoplites, and onwards through security cordons and guarded doors.

Everything was at high alert, as much to curb the knowledge of the Black Templars' exodus as it was to safeguard the shrine's sanctity. She could see the tension in the lower halfs of the guard's faces, the nervous way they toyed with their weapons, the catch of their breath at her approach. Everything stood upon the edge of a knife now. The pressures would soon overwhelm them without a strong hand, a vision of leadership to replace the near-euphoric power of faith which had auraed

Gaheris and his brothers. Only by standing shoulder to shoulder and speaking with one voice could they anneal the defenders together – the pilgrim masses, the civilian populace, the Hoplites, the Savlar, and her own Sisters. Without it they would crumble, fall apart and perish. She knew this in her soul. She had no doubt that Erikos knew it as well.

Knew it enough to be in seclusion, fending off her summons with rerouted messages and placeholder vocal simulacra which stated, incessantly, that the cardinal was 'deeply enmeshed in communion with the God-Emperor, in sacred prayer', and that she should 'please attempt to seek the cardinal's guidance at some other time'. She scowled as she walked, sending a gaggle of robed scribes scattering in myriad different directions to escape her ire.

Even a man of power could only hide behind excuses and platitudes for so long.

So she ascended, up through the tiers of power, as unbothered by the finery and pretences as she was by bolter fire. Her sword was sheathed at her hip, reassuring in its weight. She touched it as she walked, thinking of the girl Teneu had been and the martyr she had died as. Her visage gazed down from amidst the saints, still mired in the familiar strangeness of the rendition. Here, so close to the seat of power, Teneu's image was dappled with gold and inset with precious jewels. Chains of silver and platinum coiled about the necks of the busts, dripping with rubies and emeralds. Her face vied with other saints, warring for dominance in great coils of marble and metal, winding their way down towards the doors of the cardinal's chambers with a crawling inevitability.

Two guards stood outside the room, wearing a heavier variant of the Hoplites' ceremonial armour. They wielded long double-handed halberds, ornamented to resemble the Master of Mankind's own Custodian Guard's guardian spears. She scoffed audibly at the affectation and stepped forward into their range.

'Move aside,' she said evenly. 'I would speak with the cardinal.'

'The cardinal,' said the one on the left, drawing himself up, 'is indisposed. We are here to protect his vigil.'

'You will move, or I will move you,' Irinya stated simply. Her hand was now locked around the handle of her sword, a breath from drawing it free. 'You've idled too long in the shadow of great and powerful men, begging for scraps. Perhaps the war will find you in due course, but for now if you seek battle it is with me, and me alone.' She let go of her sword and spread her arms. 'I'll even allow you the first strike. Those blades look fine enough, but they're unpowered. I doubt they'll even scratch the lacquer upon my plate. And when you're done with that then I'll take my turn.'

She patted the pommel of her sword, drawing their eyes down to the elegant lines of the blade.

'Powered steel,' she went on. 'A holy weapon that has held firm against traitors, mutants, and heretics beyond number. She is called Truth's Kiss, and whoever knows the edge of that blade understands the light of illumination that He upon Terra casts out into the universe. They feel it burn before the blade ever even touches them.' She laughed, then, indulgently. 'Would you stand against it? Would you be unscathed by its fire?'

They were silent.

'Then let me pass.'

They stepped aside sheepishly. One of them turned to enter the access codes and the lock bolts thundered back, one after another. Irinya strode forward, placed her armoured gauntlets against the thick dark wood of the doors, and threw them open.

The chamber was impressive. Even her own spacious accommodations within the convent upon Terra could have fitted into the room twice over. Desks and tables dominated the entrance hall, covered with papers, missives and data-slates. Before the war it had been mountainous but now it had grown, a bureaucratic infestation which sprawled across more and more surfaces. Files and petitions had slipped onto the floor, like miniature avalanches, casting a pall of disarray over the normally ordered and composed workspace. Plates and glasses had accrued alongside them, piling up, their contents neglected and half-eaten, or already mouldering. The entire room stank, rife with the odours of rotting food and human excretion. If the man had been maintaining a solemn prayer vigil then it was one so zealous that he had neglected even his own most basic care.

She noted now the other stench beneath the mundane rot. A smell she knew all too well. She tasted death on the air.

Irinya moved around the table, her movements suddenly swift. The guards moved in behind her. She heard one curse. The other raised a hand to his mouth. She ignored them. She was moving around the piles of papers, to where Erikos sat in one of the high-backed chairs, folded into himself, as though he had finally drifted off to sleep while at his work. That would have been forgivable. Understandable, even.

What she saw was not.

'Oh, Throne,' she breathed. 'Oh, Throne, no.'

Erikos was slumped down so far that he was almost kneeling upon the floor. Pale, bloodless, he stared straight ahead, unseeing. In one hand he held a simple silver blade, the kind which might be used to open letters, now stained crimson with his own life's blood.

Irinya stepped up to the cardinal's corpse, reached out, and closed his eyes with suddenly trembling fingers.

'Emperor protect us all,' she breathed.

Chapter Seventeen

POXTIDE

TO DIE IN FIRE

WOLF'S FLIGHT

A tide of the insane and the broken dogged their escape, clawing at the decking with too many fingers, dragging themselves along the walls and ceilings with misshapen hooks, oozing like slugs or scuttling on many-jointed legs. The dead and diseased of the great pilgrim ship chased them with the passion only the inhumanly insane could muster, giggling and jabbering with a profusion of tortured voices – as though the words were being dredged from other minds and throats and souls.

The victims and disciples and vessels of the warp-spawned disease boiled through the corridors surrounding the reactor core, and all Katla could do was stop and fire. Her current rate wasn't enough. Wrathspitter was a fine weapon, ancient and venerable as all volkite weapons were, but even its deflagrating bursts weren't enough to stem the tide of horrors. For every swollen hybrid of flesh and metal that exploded or collapsed aflame, there were always more. Hundreds of crew. Thousands of pilgrims. All of them transfigured into ghoulish mockeries of the human form. She had never seen their like before, and prayed she never would again.

You were not meant to come here, their forms said. *You were never meant for the void or the stars. We were waiting for you.*

Katla feared no thing in the void. She had stared into the Rift and spat in the face of cultists and madmen and alien gods. Even so, she knew when the odds were against her. When to cut her losses and run.

'Move!' she screamed. 'Gods and spirits damn you, move!' She fired again. The air filled with crimson light as the beam of the volkite lanced down the corridor, atomising a lumbering brute with cleaver arms and a flame-gouting grille where its face should have been. Other faces gurned out from its remaining torso, veering between childish giggles and petulant mewling before falling silent forever as the motivating animus finally died, or fled.

Impish things waddled in the wake of the larger monsters, chortling wetly as they dragged tiny blades or wickedly sharp claws along the ground. The screeching of metal upon metal cut through the din of the pursuit, setting Katla's teeth on edge.

'Throne damn these monsters,' she spat. 'You think you can put me down, vermin? I've outlasted greater beasts than you! You do not end me!'

The wyrm, Bodil's voice hissed from out of memory. *The wyrm will be your fate and your end.* Often the old woman's words, the gothi's words, had haunted her. An omen. A bad star. Yet she knew well enough that prophecy was as much shield as blade.

'You are not the ones that end me,' she hissed.

'Back to the Underverse with you!' Tyra spat. She had turned on her heel to lend her own covering fire to Katla's. Her autogun barked in the close confines, staining the air with gunsmoke. Her sword was sheathed, waiting for its moment, and yet Katla could tell from the woman's movements that she dreaded it too. For the enemy to be that close would mean they were desperate or they were dead. Katla's own axes hungered, so much that she almost felt them stirring at her hips, just as Fimbulgeir's weight had grown oppressive along her spine.

She was a warrior, by the Throne. She should not be running through the dark like a chastened cur – and yet, there were so many. Too many. Sprinting at her on stilt legs, slithering on their bellies, hanging from the vents and the pipes like morbid chiropterans. Cloaked in their ruined humanity and their dead dreams, the infected came ever onwards, forever hungry for the flesh and souls of the faithful.

To reduce them to yet more fuel for atrocity, to stitch them across the iron skin of the ship until it was a writhing nightmare in its own right.

The ship shuddered as though in understanding, rejoicing in sympathetic horror as it woke – or perhaps as it remembered what it was becoming. The metal walls of the corridor flexed, like an intestine contracting.

They had to get back to the airlock. Back onto their ship. It could be done. Even with the unholy things behind them. It could be done.

'They're in the walls?' Calder asked, fear creeping into his voice as he forced the systems of another door, the thick metal of the bulkhead hissing as it slid away to the side. 'If they're in the Throne-damned walls then what hope do we have?'

The constant motion of the corridor stilled and then resumed with wild abandon, so terrible that Katla feared the ship was shaking itself apart. Or perhaps, dreadfully, *awake*.

'They're not in the walls,' Katla said. 'Or if they are then it doesn't matter. It's not just them, it's the ship.'

'The ship?' Tyra yelled. 'What the hells do you mean?'

'The ship is infected. Warp-kissed. Maleficarum is in its

bones. The ship is alive. They are it and it is them, and it is going to swallow us whole if we don't get out.' She triggered the vox-link in her suit. 'Augustus. Can you hear me?'

'Captain,' came his reply. Like ice. Like purest indifference given voice. He seemed, even now, as he so often did, like a statue given life. Marble clad in gold, colder than either. That was the surety, frustrating and inhuman as it was, that she needed right in this moment.

'I need you,' she began, through gasps and heaving breaths. She fired again and the vox-link sparked with static feedback. 'I need you to signal the fleet. I want target locks on every last pilgrim ship. Kill them. One and all. Burn them from the stars before they can turn against us. You will wait for my signal, and if it doesn't come then you consider me lost, and you kill this ship as well. Is that clear?'

'Perfectly, captain.'

She heard him give orders, calmly and crisply. She could hear them filling the bridge, spoken with an absolute authority that even she had never commanded in that space. He would not be sitting in her throne. He would not be pacing the space of the bridge, spear readied. He would be standing before the main viewports, poised and waiting, as still as a sentinel upon distant walls.

A being of absolute, divinely mandated patience and precision. Crafted, painstakingly, for what had been determined to be the greatest duty in the Imperium.

'Excellent,' she breathed. 'Good.'

They were moving as she spoke. On and on through the rebelling innards of the great ship. Heaving systems were wheezing to life, vox-panels were jabbering in the voices of the dead and the insane. Laughing. Mocking. It was not enough for them to die. They would die knowing that the warp rejoiced in their deaths and that there was a place in the great tapestry of flesh and steel waiting for them. Then Augustus' voice was gone, drowned in the discordant din as her own vox-unit began to scream. She tried to clear the frequencies, but as she did she realised whose voices they were. The open broadcast channels of the Terran members of her crew. Dead, dying, or transfigured.

They pushed on, the three of them, truly alone now. Firing and moving. Moving and firing. Holding a tiny line of fire and fury until Calder had worked the next set of controls. Increasingly he was having to waste time – rewiring and subverting – to the extent that Tyra had needed to use her sword to help force the door. Soon they would have to gouge and cut their way through the door systems, push them open by hand. By then the enemy would be upon them.

Katla fired again. The sweeping beam bisected another row of the enemy and gouged into the walls of the corridor, leaving a red-hot wound in the ship which bled smoke. The air stank suddenly of cooked flesh and burning metal, of misfiring electronics and unclean blood. The ship groaned and the decking bucked beneath their feet. Even now the ship's titanic wrath was growing, kindled by their defiance. Monstrous things flooded every corridor and walkway as though they were veins and arteries, through which the perverse creations gambolled in mockery of an immune system.

'When the door is open,' Katla said, 'you will both run for the next.'

'My queen, I–' Tyra began, but Katla's hand cut across the air. She fired again and then spoke, her command cutting through any defiance remaining in Tyra.

'Get Calder to the shuttle. Get it ready to fly.' She holstered Wrathspitter and drew her axes. A squeeze activated the runic studs along their grip and the blades sparked to life. Compact, like the hand-axes common to her home world, they were nameless extensions of their queen. She tightened her grip and strode forth. The spear could wait. For now all she needed was the moment, raw and bleeding, where steel met steel.

Augustus' command rippled through the fleet, dancing across the vox from ship to ship. The *Wyrmslayer Queen* was a monstrous thing, scar-hulled and bellicose. Its machine spirit had come through fire and borne the taint of the enemy within its corridors. It had been mauled and abandoned, left to limp away from the Rift's edge and the predations of the xenos-tainted. Whatever it had lost, whatever wounds it had suffered, the great vessel had not diminished. If anything the repair work done to her in Guilliman's shipyards had added to her character, adorning her warlike soul with the wounds to match it.

She was not simply a hunter any more. Nothing in the void was what it had been since the Rift had opened and the crusade had come. She was a warrior now. A queen in truth, ready to stand against the darkest of odds and the mightiest of foes.

She was not, however, alone.

The ships which had once formed Task Force Saturnine had been painstakingly gathered for service. Nothing done by the hand of Roboute Guilliman was idle or in error. Even those actions born of desperation were considered and reasoned. Task Force Saturnine had been formed to bear the Primaris gene-technology and essential reinforcements to those in direst need. A detachment intended to relieve fleet-pressures upon the Lion Warriors had accompanied them, in the earliest days, led by gold-armoured warriors of the Custodian Guard, whose very presence would show that this was a true gift and not a deception of the Archenemy.

Augustus was the last of that undertaking. The remainder of his brothers had dispersed amongst other crusade fleets, the better to serve the will of the Emperor and the direction of Trajann Valoris. He did not regret it; duty was duty, after all, and there was no greater duty than service to, and the defence of, the Throne. Now he stood, armed and armoured, upon the bridge of a ship at war, watching that duty poised upon a blade's edge.

'Have all vessels confirmed orders?' he asked.

'Aye, lord,' croaked a member of the bridge crew. He did not dignify them with a look in response. He did not enjoy the confines of the bridge, nor its trappings of superstition. The old woman, Bodil, Katla's gothi, was not here and that was a mercy for her. Even the suggestion of witchery sat ill with Augustus, no matter what laxity had been permitted on Fenris these ten millennia.

It is not for me to question Him, yet He allowed such things. Permitted by His decree, and He rewarded them with authority and responsibility. A hunting pack, called to heel by their master's voice. Are we so different?

He dismissed the thought as the pointless nonsense it was and returned his focus to the task at hand. 'Attack pattern gamma sigma, purgation variant, locked in. On my order all ships will burn the enemy craft from the void. Precision strikes to drives and reactors. Bridge-kill secondary. All but the *Flag of Faith*. We hold fire upon that ship until the captain's signal.'

'Aye, lord,' the bridge chorused. He raised his spear and pointed it out across the space of the bridge, towards the great viewports and the open void beyond.

'Fire.'

The other ships in the flotilla obeyed in the same instant. Lance batteries committed themselves wholesale, searing across the void to open the bellies of the pilgrim hulks. Hull plates split and burst, disgorging great streams of materiel and bodies out into space. Too far away for any but Augustus to observe the details, the mangled and malformed bodies spinning through the void, burning and freezing in equal measure. Twisted faces writhed and gurned, even as the void sought to leech the life from them. Limbs still flailed, as though they could grasp the abyss itself and swim free of its deathly embrace.

Things squirmed and moved in the ships' titanic wounds, planes of flesh undulating beneath the riven metal like an insect in its cocoon. Spasming motions drove the hull plates apart and away, cast out into the void where even the weapons of the fleet had yet to touch them – coming apart in their own internal struggle.

Some of the enemy ships, and they were undoubtedly now the enemy, were already turning even as their engines were holed through, as fire and metal careened out and away from their bodies. Momentum kept them moving and turning, even as they pared themselves apart to compensate. Whole sections of the ships unfolded and unfurled, coiling away from the main bodies with an organic grace, like flowers blossoming. They moved and changed in the way that rot emerges from a mouldering corpse, and with it came all the attendant vermin. Yet what tumbled out towards the loyal vessels were not maggots and lice. They were the transmuted and transformed victims of the plague, the bodies which had been burned and frozen and cracked, still moving, still swimming through the void towards them.

'Contact the *Woe of Ages* and the *Hunter of the Black Sea*,' Augustus stated simply. Unfazed, he turned back towards the crew, fixing Terran and Fenrisian alike with his even gaze. 'Have them deploy fighter wings in defensive pattern. I want a clear corridor to the *Flag* at a moment's notice.'

His lip curled.

'We shall not lose her.'

All was screaming and the screech of metal upon metal.

Even powered blades did not fully cut the warp-infused steel and twisted bone of the creatures. A thing reared at her, its skull grown wild and tree-like, to gore her on the metal-tipped spurs of its false antlers. She caught it across the throat and hurled it back into the boiling throng of bodies. They laughed even as they tore their fellow apart, pushing on past him and through him in pursuit of their prey. Jaws snapped and clattered like steel traps, ribcages yawned wide around madly pulsing organs and blinking mechanisms.

She fought with all the fury she had carried to the stars from the ice. She split skulls and opened up throats, even as they spurted oil in place of blood. Some wounds wept with less identifiable fluids, pumped from obscene perversions of human organs. She carved out those aberrant glands and cast them to the decking.

The enemy crowded in. They dropped from the ceiling and scampered along the ground, clambering along the walls, or loping into melee range on elephantine legs or exaggerated metal stilts. They were made from ruined skin and rotted meat, wrapped around deck-plate bones and the ruins of uniforms and void suits and simple robes. Half-ruined aquila pendants had been garlanded about the neck of one huge specimen, its stocky girth seemingly the result of several armsmen melded together. Arms reached for her, muscular and running with distorted tattoos. Fingers flew free as soon as they came into axe range, hewn off in precise strikes as she ducked and danced through the encroaching melee.

This was what it meant to serve. To ply the void in the Emperor's name, facing down the mad and the broken. Stalwart where others were cowardly. Forthright where others deceived.

Blade-fingers clawed at her suit. She drove them back, forcing the monsters away, spitting her hate into their faces. Her voice became a low rush of prayers and curses, wards against maleficarum, and oaths to the Emperor.

The door slid open behind her. She didn't move for a moment, so intent upon her stand – her final stand. A hand grasped at her shoulder and Katla edged back, turning to join Tyra and Calder as they ran. Tainted blood was smeared across her, hissing with acidic rapidity as it ate at her suit. Katla cursed.

Tyra's boarding sword lashed out at Katla's side as they fought their retreat. Katla took a moment, sheathed her axes and reached back – feeling Fimbulgeir come to her hand. They were close now, close enough to the breached airlock and the shuttle that she could wield the great spear. She activated it and the bladed ends went live. Pure, brilliant, blue-white light rippled along the blades, casting out their illumination in stark contrast to the flickering lights above – the ship's lighting dancing from sodium yellow to emergency crimson.

She thrust forward and the spear opened a screaming horror from groin to crown. It kept coming, with its belly split and a rush of unclean fluids pouring out with the last of its life. She bared her teeth and drew the spear back, turning it to bar the path of any others that would dare.

'Come at me, you vermin,' she spat. 'You are nothing. Figments of false gods. Little horrors vomited from the Underverse. Not even wights, just the leavings and table scraps of your masters. Let them come for me in person, not send their dregs!'

She stood before them, spear readied, burning with the light of the power field, burning with her own wrath and rage, a line in the sand between the darkness and humanity. She laughed in the faces of the monstrous enemy, cutting and slashing at them as they drew near, driving them back with the sheer power and weight of the spear. Clawed hands could not find purchase upon its surface, marked bronze and gold with runes and wards, and she drove them back again and again. It was a dance, now. Back and forth they went. The tide of the enemy surged in and then retreated from her blows, or from Tyra's sword thrusts, or from Calder's desperate fire.

They burst out of the airlock and into the open void, mag-locks clamping their boots to the hull as they lurched forwards towards the shuttle.

The poxtide burst from the aperture like bile, like blood, like pus escaping a wound. They flailed and spasmed in the open void, desperate to reach them, clawing at nothing as they spun away into the darkness or slammed against distant planes of the vessel. The *Flag of Faith* undulated with impossible motion, reactions so immense as to be tectonic. Like the writhing skin of an alien world, the ship spasmed and shook. Even aboard the shuttle, with its steady hydraulics planted to the hull, every-thing was rocking, the floor tilting. Thrusters engaged with a thunderous roar and they were already moving, the doors not yet closed. For a moment Katla felt the pull of the void and the scrape of talons of steel and bone against her neck, and then they were away, heading out and towards home.

The shuttle touched down, ailing and wheezing, its systems so ravaged they seemed to have aged a millennium, in one of the *Queen*'s main hangars. A crowd had gathered to greet the return: armsmen bearing axes and swords, a row of Terran Naval troopers wielding lascarbines, and at its centre, as gilded as the keystone of a ceremonial arch, stood Augustus. His spear was drawn, tip down against the decking.

'Thank the Throne–' Katla began.

Augustus did not answer. He wasn't looking at her. In that instant his eyes had snapped up and his spear followed less than a heartbeat later. A single round hurtled through the air and impacted in the skull of something that was suddenly scream-ing and in motion.

The body hit the ground in front of her, its entire face holed through. It was still moving, still trying to force itself back up, scythe-limbs flailing, fires gurgling from an internalised reactor.

Augustus strode forward, raised his spear, and brought it down through the monster's torso, impaling it, holding it transfixed by the crackling blade till it stopped its sinuous, desperate motion.

Katla looked up at him, chest heaving, and then removed her helm, finally able to breathe freely once more. 'Thank you,' was all she could manage.

The corner of Augustus' mouth twitched, perhaps as close as he was capable to a smile. 'I am here to do the Emperor's work, captain. If that includes keeping you safe then I will do so. It would help, however, if you took a little more care in your endeavours.'

'I will,' she said, head bowed. She considered, in that moment, that she might have misjudged the Custodian. For all his studied inhumanity, for all his detachment and the golden barriers between him and the rest of the species, he was still a servant of the Emperor. Perhaps the greatest example of His servants that she had encountered, outside of Guilliman himself. 'Thank you, Custodian.'

'I do only what He instructs, captain,' he said, and turned away. 'Everything we do is by His will alone.'

Chapter Eighteen

FEAR'S CORROSION

IRON WILL, IRON ENGINES

HUNTERS IN DARKNESS

'Dead?' Melpomene asked, aghast at the very idea of it.

She had not thought much of Cardinal Erikos, true enough. He was a stunted man, far from the mysteries of the Mechanicus or the iron purity of the Titan Legios, but she had considered that he would at least last beyond these storms. The galaxy was aflame, end to end, with war and calamity. Xenos horrors stalked abroad, held back only by the steely determination of the Imperium's defenders – by walls of winter and war – and yet he had allowed fear's corrosion to worm through his heart and turn his hand against himself.

'Dead,' Irinya confirmed. She shook her head. For a moment Melpomene could see every last year of the canoness' long vigil writ upon her features. Each wrinkle and scar seemed deeper upon the tapestry of her skin and the weave of her life. In many ways she was surprised that the canoness was still wholly flesh. Many other warriors, even some of the vaunted Adeptus Astartes, who had fought alongside the Legio, bore cybernetic replacements – sanctified in the sight of the Omnissiah and blessed by their own Chapter rituals. The Black Templars, for all their flaws and their failings, had been especially apprecia- tive of the glorious works of the Emperor-Omnissiah, as they termed Him.

The shadows of faith hung over their gathering like a mourner's veil. Irinya had not chosen a grand hall or the foot of the cardi- nal's empty throne in which to hold court; instead they found themselves in a tiny chapel of remembrance, an antechamber in the vastness of the shrine city. Angelic statues hid their faces as though in shame, turned away from the countless necrolog which had been inscribed into the walls. The rolls of the dead, from across the local sector and the wider Imperium. An undying, unending testament to the crusades which had gone before.

An inferior method of data storage, she had always felt, but one in keeping with this world's accreted soul.

Give me the purity of noospheric communion, rather than the cold and dead recitations of the priests. Carve words in iron that they might live forever, where stone will only weather and wear.

She did not speak her thoughts aloud, just let them coil up through her mind, as she watched the canoness' frustrated grief.

'What do we do now, then?' Melpomene asked. Only she had thus far deigned to speak. The others, Rugrenz of the Savlar and Yitrov of the Hoplites, were yet silent. Rugrenz was placid, patient, waiting until all the revelations had unspooled, where Yitrov fretted and fussed, toying with his gloved hands like a scolded child.

'We must keep this information secret,' said the canoness. 'Obfuscate as much as possible. Morale will not survive news of his passing, especially not the manner of it.'

'Desertions...' Yitrov began, and then swallowed hard. 'Defections, even, in some cases, are up. The commissars have been busy, but even then there are others who slip through the cracks. They cannot be everywhere.' He looked over at Rugrenz. 'No offence.'

'None taken,' Rugrenz said lightly. He seemed unbothered by the unfolding calamity. Not simply stoicism, Melpomene reckoned, but an acceptance born of having seen so very much. As a commissar of a penal legion, especially one as notorious as the Savlar, he would have broad experience in that arena.

She wondered, not for the first time, why the Savlar had even been included in this detachment. Desperation? A desire to have them learn by holy example? Or simply to have a spiteful arrow in the quiver, one that would wound the enemy over and over again in their own depravity.

'We've had losses,' Rugrenz allowed, 'but we are accustomed to such things. The men understand that there is redemption to be earned through sacrifice.' He tilted his head one way and then the other. 'Some fear our guns more than the enemy... Some fear being sent back into the dark beneath Savlar. Some just want the loot. Threads of a common rope, in the end.'

And that, in its way, is its own faith, Melpomene thought, suppressing a chuckle.

'Our war,' Irinya said carefully, 'has always been one of two fronts. The physical and the spiritual. We defend the body of this great institution, the rule of the Emperor upon this world, and we safeguard the souls of its people. Even the most faithful...' She paused. 'Especially the most faithful, will be wounded by the cardinal's passing. Despair will become endemic. We cannot allow that.'

'You have command now,' Melpomene put in quickly, sensing her window. 'Let my engines walk again now. Let us stand as a symbol for others to rally around. That is what the old Templar does now, isn't it?'

The old Templar. That was what they called Toron. The last remaining vestige of their crusade strength. He had involved himself extensively in the defence, striding forth along the walls or out beyond them, bellowing his wrath and his conviction in equal measure. When Melpomene looked upon him she saw the sacred melding of flesh and machine, the embodiment of the Mechanicus creed, and her own communion with the god-engine writ small.

'I have command,' Irinya repeated, almost to herself. Melpomene watched the realisation dawn across the other woman's face, as though it had only just occurred to her.

'Let us range beyond the walls and burn them from their nests. They are as vermin and we should treat them as such. Let my hounds run free and the wild hunt commence.'

Irinya was silent for a long moment. Melpomene watched her as she constantly moved her hand back to the hilt of her sword, and then to her side, as though seeking guidance from elsewhere.

'Very well,' the canoness said. 'Force their hand. Find their siege weapons and bring them to battle. If they will not fight you directly then drive them from our walls. Give us the breathing space we need to endure until Marshal Urtrix can return and relieve our positions.'

'There has still been no word?' Melpomene asked.

'None,' Irinya sighed. 'The astropaths try, and suffer in the attempt, but no message can yet leave this world. Shrouded in psychic miasma, drowning in the darkness of despair. Even those minds sanctified and soul-bound to the Throne cannot penetrate the murk which descends upon us.'

'An ill omen,' Yitrov put in. 'If the Emperor has forsaken us...'

'He has not,' Irinya said firmly, whirling about and stalking forwards towards the other man. For a moment Melpomene was convinced that she would strike him, either with gauntleted hand or with her blade. 'The God-Emperor stands in all holy places, burning beyond time, sacred beyond measure. He does not abandon even an inch of blessed ground, and nor shall we.'

'Then we shall walk,' Melpomene said, smiling. She looked from the canoness to the Militarum men, and then back. 'For the sake of honour and duty. For vengeance, and for hope. Our engines shall march with the dawn's light and bring the illumination these heathens so richly desire and deserve.'

Lesser men, those not sworn to the Martian mysteries, had dubbed the Legio's mustering area as the *god-yards*.

She had never warmed to it, neither the name nor the space itself. The many maintenance yards, forge-hangars and muster spaces that she had occupied over the years had always felt like transient environs. Where her engine was tended and rearmed scarcely mattered next to the crucible of combat, when the vastness of *Vengeance* moved through the world like a sliver of sacred Mars given form. It carried in its heart all the rage and fury that had drowned Sareme in dust and blood; a hate for the heretek that would never truly die, until the great engine did.

Now it was all bustle as crews and attendants flooded through it. Servitors trundled past with pallets laden high with materiel; enginseers and adepts canted binharic prayers and anointed passing machines with sacred oils and potent unguents. Everything stank of incense and burning oil, of gouting promethium vapours and the subtle spice of quiescent weapons.

The prelude to battle, to war, was always to be savoured. A last chance for true clarity and meditation, to scour the mind clean of doubt and to recommit once more to the service of the Omnissiah. When the Legio marched to war it was with fire in their hearts and war-lust burning away at the back of their minds, where the potency of the machine spirit waited and coiled, a dragon made of storm-cloud and volcanic wrath. Even away from it she felt the after-effects, the iron-and-spite memory of the god-machine's talons as they scoured down her spine.

She could still taste the caged lightning of communion, dancing between her teeth like building static. It lingered in its hunger, as the dreams of war bled into her psyche, reshaping her mind to crave the adrenaline of battle. She was not a swift thing like the Warhounds. To stand as a Warlord Titan was to embody death in its most absolute form – it was to be transmuted from mortal flesh to the iron and steel of a god of war. Only the strongest could walk the balance that came with such a duty; to pare away their own humanity enough to commune with the caged divinity, and still remain whole. Countless souls faltered at that hurdle, or succumbed in the heat of the moment.

Melpomene had never given in, and had sworn that she never would.

Now she stood before her peers, example and exemplar, shrugging off the red uniform jacket and letting it pool unceremoniously upon the floor. Bertolt and Lares had both left their jackets to one side, the yard's heat stripping the layers from them bit by bit. Bertolt was constantly in motion, stalking in agitation while his cortical implants twitched and realigned, firing synapses in his brain to keep his mind agile. A hunter's wile. Lares remained placid, patient and focused. They were two sides of the same coin, and time and again they had proven their worth and weight.

'Well?' Bertolt grumbled. She could sense the desperate energy that pulsed through him, the relentless passion that coloured everything the *Dune Hound* did. 'What word from our Imperial hosts?'

'We walk,' Melpomene said simply. Bertolt whooped and Lares bowed her head. The woman looked up at Melpomene with tears brimming in her eyes.

'The moment shall be marked and sanctified.'

'Leave ritual to the priests,' Bertolt said, and laughed. 'Our place is at the fore. We've hidden behind these walls, grovelling for opportunities for too long.' He drew up his fist and held it out before him. 'The time for prayer is over. Let war be our sermon and the battlefield our church.'

Melpomene looked up at the crooked columns which surrounded the yard, like the bars of a cage or the ribs of some colossal beast – as though something had died here long ago.

Perhaps that is to be the fate of us all, she mused. *Our engines have endured the longest of wars, some date back to the Imperium's birth, but time claims all things. Even the iron will of iron engines.*

'We break them, throw wide their defences, and then allow the defenders the chance to sally forth and reclaim. We will risk all our strength in this. Three Titans, no matter how mighty, cannot pacify a world. We forget infantry and artillery at our peril.' She paused. 'The last active auspex had their forces gathering at the ruins of Shrinehold Invicta.'

Melpomene scowled. Once there had been as many minor shrineholds and temples of worship across the surface of Velua as there had been stars in the skies. Since war had come they had been ground down to dust, one by one, the enemy's rapacious advance corrupting or destroying all that the Imperial forces held dear. Reliquaries desecrated. Memorials carved away. Sometimes the enemy would parade the corpses of heroes and saints, martyrs and priests, before their advance. Gouges carved down the cheeks in imitation of tears.

No more. When the Legio walked to war it would be to roll back the tide of blasphemy and reassert the light of logic. The chance they had never had for their own home world.

Her hands tightened into fists at her side at the thought of it. Too far away to march in its defence. Too embroiled in other battles. She could barely remember those early engagements. Had it been the orks and their makeshift god-engines? Or the necrons as they slunk from their tombs, their war machines crowned in emerald flame? Then the skies had wept fire and the daemons had come, conjuring ephemeral giants born of nightmare to challenge the Legio Arconis. The great things, the abomination-engines, had laughed as they killed and they had screamed as they died. She had felt the burning ichor upon her engine's skin as though it scalded and writhed upon her own flesh. Melpomene had shared in the savage joy that came with ending such things – removing a stain from the skin of reality.

Was that the last time war felt truly righteous? Before it turned to ashes in our mouths?

'Ready the hunt,' she breathed. 'We will expunge the stains upon our honour. One battle at a time. As the Legio always has.' She looked up at the banners, at the crowned cog, in green, grey and gold. 'We will fight till only dust bleeds from our engines.'

The great systems sang, ringing with the choir of sacred communion. Every facet of the engine vibrated with the thunder of its reactor heart. Every plate of the vast engine was alive with light, either cast from within itself, bleeding from its great weapons and the lenses of its eyes, or caught upon it by the dying twilight. It moved, slowly and ponderously, out from the god-yards and towards the great gates of the Martyr's Way. The Warhounds followed at the Warlord's heels, loping in pursuit, savouring the thought of the battles to come.

They passed from light into shadow, but that suited them. The Legio Arconis had ever been hunters in darkness, striking from out of the umbra with fire riming their fangs. Plasma crackled along weapon mounts as the great machines strode forth. Their clamorous tread resounded off the walls. The columns shook. As their first horns began to sound, like hunting clarions, the great doors of the Martyr's Way ground open. The Imperial forces upon the walls – Hoplites, Savlar and Sisters – stared out at the god-engines as they walked. A ragged cheer went up from the defenders, faith and defiance melded with relief and hope.

Melpomene, enthroned in iron, her mind burning in communion with the immensity of the *Vengeance*, saw all this through its uncounted auspexes and sensor arrays. She heard their hollow joy enhanced and reverberated until it was a roar, a howl, a storm of worthy voices.

She held those voices tight as she carried them out, beyond the walls, into the face of the enemy.

Chapter Nineteen

OLD GODS AND NEW MASTERS

DESTROYER

THE GIFT OF FIRE

'They are coming,' Weryn whispered, yet the vox-amplifiers turned his whisper into a shout.

Before him the assembled might of the cult had gathered once more, perhaps for the last time. There were new devotees and veterans alike, men with new wounds and brands or old injuries. Whether the scars were fresh or aged, they had all begun to weep. Pus, blood and other fluids oozed down tunics and through armour plates. It congealed upon limbs, dripping from twitching fingers where it hadn't already hardened to a glistening crust.

The city was a distant target, so far away that Weryn could not hear the war-horns of the Titans. Even his psychic sight struggled to grasp any details from this distance. Instead he looked to his soldiers. He was proud to see them, arrayed in their ranks of seven upon seven upon seven. The remaining luminors stood before the line troops, bearing their own weeping wounds and the badges of office which disease had etched into their very flesh. They were giving more and more of themselves to the god, to the power of contagion and corruption. It boiled through their blood, just as it pulsed through Weryn's soul.

The power. The darkness conveyed by the god's glory. The world, remade in rot and gristle.

Had he dreamed of it, as a child? Yearning to see the old order torn down? His resentment had grown and spread, mutating in the shadows of his soul, until it was finally coaxed out by the Pilgrim's voice. He had understood in that moment the absolute power that danced at his fingertips.

Now the appointed moment was close, so near he could taste it. Like copper and bile on his tongue. The acid sting of it was reassuring even when it sought to drown his words. He could feel sickly sweat along the back of his scalp and down his spine and shoulders.

'They are coming,' he repeated, and then continued to the rapt attention of his brethren. The Children were restless now. 'From out of the heavens there shall come angels of ague and anguish. Angels of atrophy and atrocity. They will bear wounds upon their flesh that put ours to shame, for they shall be the true sons of the god. The Guard of Death. Those who have fought through wars longer than mortal lifetimes. Who have striven and toiled for this moment, when the galaxy itself is aflame and inflamed!'

His voice rose with growing surety and confidence. Above them the heavens stirred and curdled. Rain began to fall, the droplets fat and heavy with grease and oil. Flies rose in their multitudes from the plague pits and corpse carts, coiling up into the smoke- and cloud-choked skies. Everything was suddenly alight with static and bursting rainfall. Everything was slick and glistening, glimmering with unclean light. Weryn felt his gifts bite at the base of his brainstem, rising up like the swarms and the smoke and the stench. His teeth clenched.

High above there was tumult. The skies were tortured as, for a moment, it seemed as though new stars had been kindled overhead. It was battle or ship-death, or both. The majority of the orbital strength had belonged to the False Angels, and now they were gone. Replaced by the true. Vessels dived and swarmed above them, like giant insects, their livery black and glossy – previous marks and colour schemes seared away as surely as the oaths they had forsaken, to one god or another – moving through the skies with inky grace.

Weryn began to laugh. The others joined him, punching the air or thrusting their weapons skywards.

From the heavens, glorious in their ruin, terrible in their broken majesty, came old gods and new masters both.

Weryn shuffled forwards to meet the emissaries of the god, his entire body trembling with vindication.

The first ship to make landfall was a squat vessel, still vast beyond Weryn's limited appreciation. Its hull was pitted and worn, burn-scarred and rust-pocked. It was a thing both ancient and newborn to Weryn; he had never before seen its like. Even the blunt attack craft of the black Angels had been weak-blooded and false when compared to this fragment of truth. Its holy surface crawled with organic growths like deep-sea coral, whorls and curves which teemed with strange void-fungus and feeler-fronds. It was a thing of the deep abyss, carved off and cast landwards.

The ramp lowered with a clatter and the hiss of failing hydraulics. Beyond that aperture darkness held dominion, an almost liquid presence that swallowed all light. It was only when the first of the warriors began to descend that the shadows momentarily parted and the angels were revealed in all their horror.

They were hideously heterogeneous, each one of them a being of concentrated ruin. Armour had long since warped or split, while the flesh beneath had transformed – blossoming like strange flowers or stranger fruit. The skin was distended and distorted, ballooned by rot, coloured through with the weird patterns of decay. In places the outer tissue and underlying flesh had rotted so intensely that the white of bones showed through, transhuman and strong where the skeletal remains which decorated the warriors and shrines of the Children were feeble and mortal.

At their head came a warrior shrouded in a pall of background radiation and old death; his armour crawled with weird lambency, as though the taint of the weapons he wielded, weapons far beyond the ken of Weryn, had sunk into his very soul, bleeding through his flesh as it struggled to break free. That flesh had withered and atrophied over time, rendering him sunken and shrivelled within his war plate. Though he was marked by the god and consumed by the Powers Beyond, he was not who Weryn had expected to see.

The prophet blinked as he looked up at the winnowed warrior, and finally found his voice.

'You... You are not the Pilgrim who was promised.'

The warrior laughed bitterly and shook his shrunken head. 'The will of the god is as fickle as contagion, little prophet. He is called by greater hands than yours to do his duty...' He paused as though realising something. He laughed again, this time with genuine amusement, as if enjoying an unintended jest. 'Hands indeed...'

He drew himself up to his full height and Weryn was suddenly aware that, even reduced, the strange warrior dwarfed the prophet and all others who had gathered behind him.

'I am Ulgrath,' the warrior announced with a sneer. The motion of his mouth made the nest of scars and rashes twist in strange ways, making his expression yet more cruel and broken. 'I am the red right hand of Tuul, as he is the hand of greater powers, sent in his name and the name of the god we share to shepherd this world to its end. That finality shall be carried out by you, borne aloft upon your strong shoulders, until every corner of this planet burns with the sacred light of unmaking.' Ulgrath stank of dust and ashes, the movement of his armour echoed with the rad-counter click of a failing reactor. To have his attention focused upon you was like bearing the enmity of a dying star, an angry universe's sharpened spite.

'We...' Weryn paused, collecting himself. 'We are humbled by your attentions, lord. We shall serve you as we would have served him.'

'I expected nothing less,' Ulgrath grumbled. 'He will be made aware of your good and loyal service. He will be pleased, I am sure. When he returns then you shall feast upon the flesh of angels in the halls of your betters, their false thrones cast down, their gold reduced to embers.'

'You spoil us, lord,' Weryn said, swallowing back his disappointment. The tingling was back along his shoulders and neck, sharp with psychic apprehension. This was not how it was supposed to be. The Pilgrim had promised that he would deliver them from their slavery personally. This rad-twisted thing, this shard of apocalypse, was not the guiding hand which had been promised. He was just another servant. It felt like an unworthy gesture.

'We have not even begun to spoil you,' Ulgrath said. 'A siege is a paltry thing. Their walls are weak, their shields flawed,' he snorted. 'Both may have stood for ten thousand years, or near enough, but we will bring them down just as we laid low all the other worlds of their precious Chain.' He gestured behind him with one great blackened hand. 'Dakren,' he called. 'Pustrus, attend.'

Two figures moved forward from the line of godly warriors. Even now, behind them, other craft were landing and disgorging their own twisted occupants, while bulk landers descended and the cult troops began to flood out. Other Children from other worlds and other conquests. Others were unleashing great and corroded machines of war, their squat barrels pointed heavenwards with dire purpose.

The two figures moved before the throng of disembarking warriors and war machines. The first was hung with phials and philtres, each one glimmering with internal light, light which writhed and danced within its prisons of glass. Brass chains bound them to the warrior's ancient and rusted plate, alongside grenades and row upon row of injector vials. One hand held an ornate pistol, augmented and modified to bear the poison fruit of those vials. The other toyed with one of the many jagged knives sheathed at his belt. Dakren, Weryn assumed, nodded with a jangling clatter and then knelt beside the burn-scarred warrior.

The second figure was altogether stranger. Looking upon him Weryn understood, in a heartbeat, that this being – Pustrus – was the apotheosis of everything Weryn was or could ever be. He was clad in filthy robes which were so matted to his armour that they seemed to have extruded from it, like creeping vines or lichen. Life in all its wondrous variety scuttled and crawled through it, squirming over him and through him. Weryn's eyes traced a many-legged centipede as it burrowed its way back through a gaping wound in robe and armour, eliciting a fluttering of Pustrus' cataracted eyes.

He was crowned in broken antlers. They glistened with a pale light, tipped with blood where they had gouged the warrior's scalp. At his temples were the stubs from whence the horns had been snapped before being reworked into a crown of shattered ambitions and spurned gifts. Weryn had thought of how he could rid himself of his own *talents* many times before, as a child, and yet to look upon this god-sworn warrior was to see an entirely other level of shame.

Weryn scarcely understood, seeing the world with his new eyes, how onc could spurn such power – and Pustrus was powerful, it bled from him in an inky toxic light, warping reality simply by existing. He wondered what judgement could have burdened the warrior so. What punishment could have been handed down from on high to make him despise his own gifts, god-granted and sanctified?

'Brother,' Pustrus gurgled, and Weryn was not certain whether he was addressing the prophet himself or Ulgrath. 'You have need of my curse?' Pustrus raised one hand and thick worms of light began to dance around his digits, writhing in the air as they burrowed through the world's skin.

Ulgrath laughed consumptively. 'Quiet, sorcerer. Gift or curse, it serves at my will. I have been given command here. See to the rituals, bind their little warp-speakers to your choirs, and call forth the daemons. Then, we shall show them the true glory of the god.'

'As you wish,' Pustrus murmured, and then spat to one side. Something slithered away, maggot-white and undulating, from the gobbet of mucus, crawling into the shadows. Pustrus turned and followed in its wake, out amongst the mortal cult auxiliaries.

Weryn looked back to Ulgrath and swallowed hard. 'What do I call you, lord? You are not a sorcerer and not a pilgrim, not an alchymist. Are you a siegesmith? A worker of ruin?'

Ulgrath grumbled with laughter again and knelt before Weryn, bringing his scarred features level with the smaller man. 'I am as I have always been, little prophet. I am a warrior of the old Legion. A forbidden weapon in the arsenal of the god. I burn with the fires of Old Night, the weapons of Strife itself. I am as a I have always been – I am a Destroyer.'

Ulgrath led Weryn through the rows of descending drop-ships and troop landers, ducking under wings and waving away dust as though to protect the mortal. Weryn felt nothing except the crawling terror of proximity to the Angel. He was not sure if he would have felt the same in the Pilgrim's presence. Tuul had always reassured him with his words; Ulgrath shared none of that bitter joy.

Ulgrath was a presence diminished by his past deeds – a hollow and shrunken being consumed by his own past atrocities. The power he exuded was not even borrowed, it had simply seeped into his bones until he himself was a walking avatar of radioactive contagion, a living blight upon the world. His brothers, much as they showed him deference, clearly shunned his presence. Even now they were moving away from him, out through the throng of mortals – arriving and native – choosing favourites, gathering small knots around them as they bestowed blessings. Gauntleted fingers brushed over foreheads, the skin smoking where they were touched with holy grace. Contagions boiled through the multitudes, dancing from soul to soul, carried in every touch and breath. Some collapsed to the ground, convulsing in sacred fugue, limbs twisting to the point of breaking. Cracks and snaps echoed across the landing fields as some were transmuted, never to rise again save as the pox-sanctified, or to gambol through the war as bestial spawn.

Weryn saw all this as he was led towards one of the great landing craft. Slab-sided, larger than any vehicle he had seen, it was a bulbous thing, its belly swollen almost to bursting. Tubes threaded through the hull, sloshing with a profusion of viscous, hissing liquids.

'I bring you the end and the beginning you desire,' Ulgrath said, throwing his arms wide. 'I bring you the flame of the apocalypse.' He paused, leaning forward to open a compartment. Wan, sickly light blossomed from within. Weryn leant forward, close enough to feel the rancid heat of the illumination. The shell that lay before him, ancient beyond imagining, glimmered

with internal light, writhing like something deep-sea, flickering
like the tendrils of an anemone. Yet it was crafted of flame;
made of crawling, hungry, impossible fire.

   'You see, my little friend?' Ulgrath asked again, laughing now.
'I bring you the very fire of the gods.'

Chapter Twenty

THE COUNSEL OF WITCHES

GREY AND GOLD

THE AVENGING SON

Of all the places within the great vessel, it was the gothi's chambers which Katla feared the most – despite, or perhaps due to, their similarities to the home world.

Here, nestled in the heart of the ship, near the medicae decks and close to Katla's own chambers, the gothi's sanctum waited like a promise. Like a portent. Its walls were hung with pelts and etched with runes, the script crawling across every available surface, while totems and talismans adorned its sparse shelves or hung from hooks and nails. Things carved from old bone and void ivory, slivers of metal from the crew's old weapons, and even the dried skins, flesh and the bottled blood of creatures that the *Queen*'s crew had slain in their time amongst the stars. The chamber was cold: the void's chill had wormed its way into its heart, and the walls glistened with hoar-frost.

It was a shrine to the Helvintr Dynasty and the battles which had carried them ever forward through the void, in the All-father's name. A piece of Fenris carved off to sail the stars.

'Come in, come in,' a voice croaked. 'Do not wait upon the threshold like a maiden freshly wed. You have nothing to fear from me. I am old, now. My bite is far less than it once was.'

'It's lost none of its potency,' Katla remarked. 'Merely added venom.'

'Ah, my queen,' Bodil replied. She sat at the chamber's centre, upon another ancient pelt, dwarfed by the immensity of the fur. The old woman's hands clapped together with a bony rattle, as much from her ageing frame as from the tiles which she passed between her fingers. Over and over the tokens danced along her knuckles, dipping between, vanishing from one hand into the other. Like a charlatan's tricks. She smiled her broken smile, and her wrinkled features creased with genuine mirth, contorting old and new scars and tattoos. 'You honour me with your presence. How fares the hunt?'

'Not well,' Katla said, and scowled. 'We traverse the void, hunting for shadows – chasing rumours of stable pathways and bearing the hopes of an empire.' She laughed bitterly. 'When the Compact set forth on the same endeavour, there was at least a sense of true unity. That we could accomplish something – not for profit, or for self-advancement. We were seizing the future by its throat. Now, though...' She paused. 'Now we command a fleet that does not belong to us, at the head of a crew we do not know, and aboard a ship that has barely recovered from its wounds. I would know what else fate has in store for us. I would have your guidance.'

'Always you come seeking guidance,' Bodil said, fussing with her robes and her runic tiles. 'Never simply to visit, never to entertain an old friend. Forever seeking to spite the fates and bind them to your will. Hubris has been the end of so many, across all our history, and yet still... onwards come the seekers.'

'Your worth to me is more than simply your gifts. You are my oldest, my truest companion. Astrid is of my blood, and lost to me. Her father fell years ago and I raised her alone. Others have come and gone, down the years, to warm bed or heart, but those men and women were only ever passing presences. I am not cold, Bodil. I have loved, I love still, I will continue to love...' She paused. 'Yet of all those who have come and gone in my life, family or friend, you have been the stalwart. You have served me best and cared for me the truest. You know that.'

'Of course I do, my queen.' Bodil laughed. 'Katla... Of all your line, you have been marked for greatness and tragedy both.' She sighed. 'You were born to live, and to die, in an age of upheaval. The Season of Fire has reached out from Fenris and now all the sea of stars knows tumult. Worlds burn with war, and are winnowed by winter. Yet the great jarls of the Sky Warriors have bowed to the Avenging Son, just as you have. They have welcomed the gifts of plenty which shore up the walls upon countless worlds. They accept the new blood that flows from the Allfather's chosen – from the iron priests of Mars and from the old tithes. The lineage of Fenris is as coiled as the kraken, seething beneath the surface, and the old ice is never as solid as we might think... Not in a time of change.'

'Does that mean all must be cast to the wind?' Katla asked softly. All around them the fire of the braziers was stirring, making the shadows coil and move. If she looked closely enough, Katla fancied she could see serpents striving heavenwards, twining in the darkness, waiting to strike. 'Lost to the whims of a new galaxy? A new order?'

'Oaths are only as strong as the blood we pour into them.' Bodil reached out to a nearby bowl and snatched up a sliver of dried meat, chewing it thoughtfully. 'We have bled for Fenris and for the Imperium. That is what it means to have been born of that world, and to bear the Warrant as you do. A promise, sworn by your ancestors, when they were raised up from the ice.'

'Is it enough?' Katla asked quietly.

'It must be. You doubt, and that is normal. All who live doubt, at one time or another. Russ, Guilliman, any of the others... Surely they, too, doubted? They were greater than men, remarkable, but doubt must have touched them? We cannot know, perhaps. We can only guess.' She looked at Katla. 'You met the Primarch Reborn, after all. You have looked into his eyes and seen what lay behind them. Think upon that, if it would be a comfort.'

'Perhaps it would.' Katla finally sank down, sitting upon a fur opposite Bodil. Between them was a polished slab of stone, dark and smooth, drinking in the inconstant firelight. 'Shall we?'

'Aye, my queen,' Bodil said. The old woman stretched out her hand and snatched up a leathern sack, drawing it close to her birdlike chest. 'We shall read your fate and see what course you should be set upon.'

'The Custodian...' Katla chuckled. 'He will not approve of this. He already thinks you a witch. A heathen superstition.'

'He has stood near enough to the Throne long enough to know how leaders must act,' Bodil said, with a tilt of her head and a faint laugh. 'He has watched from the walls of the great Palace, out across the Throneworld, for so long that he must have seen how the High Lords play their games. All great rulers, in their time, must consider the counsel of witches.'

When Katla finally emerged, Augustus was waiting for her.

'I thought I would find you here,' he said shortly. 'I do not know why I am surprised.'

'Sorry as ever to disappoint,' Katla said. 'Much of this duty must be underwhelming to you. Forced to coddle an expedition that you don't truly believe in, with a leader you don't trust, towards an uncertain end. Such things would not vex you if you were still on Terra.'

'It is not for me to question,' Augustus replied. 'It was the will of the captain-general, and so the will of the Emperor Himself. I am an instrument. I go where I am required. Where He requires me to be.'

'Admirable,' she said. 'As do I. No longer do I roam free, my only limits that of the Warrant's authority. I am bound to the regent's will, and so, like you, to that of the Allfather.'

'Yet I do not require the wiles of witches, nor their flawed prognostication.'

The words hung between them in the chill corridor. They were contrasts, him and her, a hunter's grey against sacred gold. She wore her mortal flaws and failings plainly, where in Augustus they had been bled and pruned away, rendering him inhuman in his perfection. Even their weapons were reflections of each other – her own spear a weak imitation of his own sacred armament. If it ever came to violence, she knew there would be no contest between them. She would die, as would any who opposed his actions. When judgement fell from the Throne, it was absolute.

'Bodil serves her purpose, as we all do. She serves my dynasty, my lineage, and my person. She is not for you to judge or to harm.' Katla stepped forward, closing the distance between them. It was madness to provoke him, and yet she had always survived, and thrived, by force of will and strength. 'She is a faithful soul, and a true servant of the Throne. The same as you. The same as I.'

'Perhaps.' He tilted his head again and stepped forward. Looking up at him Katla could see his face in all of its pale, pristine glory, devoid of helm. His short-cropped hair, the precise angles of his skull, the pale agate of his eyes. Bloodless, and at once vital. 'Time will tell in that regard, captain. In times such as these very few loyalties are beyond question.'

'If she falters, and she shall not, then it will be my blade that ends her – am I understood?' Katla gritted her teeth. 'She is the only reason I am still alive and able to serve. She saved me and my remaining crew from death. It is to her that I owe everything.'

'Be careful that such dependency does not limit your ability to lead,' Augustus said. 'It is a poor leader who finds herself constrained by emotion.'

'Is there so little human care left in you?' she asked.

'Our duty is to the species and its master,' he said. 'Anything else is secondary.'

She scoffed. 'I pity you, Custodian. In any other being such traits would be nothing short of monstrous. Even certain xenos-breeds are capable of caring for their fellows.'

'Careful, captain,' he breathed. 'Even my patience is not without limit.' He paused for a moment, as though processing all that had transpired. 'You were unable to retrieve the ship's logs. Based upon the warp-saturation of the vessel they would have been unreliable anyway. Has your communion with your witch drawn forth any new wisdom?'

She held her silence and then breathed out. 'No,' she went on. 'I will bring my concerns to the magos again and we shall alter our trajectory. Given the fate of the pilgrim fleet, there is clearly a hostile intelligence acting against us.'

'Or it is simply the predations of the warp, cast against their fleet as they are against all the galaxy. Unless you think that our mission is of such import and significance as to be known by the Archenemy?'

'I have long been a hunter, Augustus. I know when a trap has been baited.'

'Yet it need not have been for us specifically. It is pride that compels you to see the hand of providence in these matters. As though only you could succeed. You feel worthy of the trust placed in you by the regent, and yet it is more than that. You

Why?'

Katla hesitated. 'I do only what is asked of me by the regent–'

'No,' he said. 'Do not hide behind Guilliman, as so many do in these times. I have asked you why. I deserve an answer.'

'Your record is nothing if not impressive,' the demigod rumbled.

Katla could not look away as he spoke. Every movement the primarch made was singular, as though he were the first being to ever make it, or to be worthy of making it. In his presence Katla felt insignificant: not a queen or a leader amongst base mortals, merely one of trillions beneath the Imperium's uncaring eye. The room was a standard briefing chamber, buried away at the heart of the Citraxes Naval yard. Everything was burnished steel and concealed machinery. Everything was slaved to the will of the being who now addressed her.

Roboute Guilliman looked at her with absolute detachment, stripping her apart molecule by molecule and rebuilding her beneath his careful scrutiny. There was nothing that could be hidden from the noble gaze of such a being. She was aware of every movement of her body, of the cadence of her breathing and the beating of her heart.

'And yet,' he continued, unaware or uncaring of her distraction, 'you come to us wounded, near to broken. You tell me your allies are dead, lost, or turned traitor.' He paused as he read a data-slate. 'That is how you were found, your ship near to death, burning hard for Bakka.' The demigod sighed. 'I had hoped for better results from as august a body as the Davamir Compact.'

'We could not have known,' she hissed, as much from pain as from insult. She had not truly enjoyed the time needed to heal. 'I have told them, again and again. We had no way of knowing!'

'And those lessons will be learned well,' Guilliman nodded. 'Genic screening will be undertaken wherever possible to ensure

that future infiltration is blunted.' He paused, considering. 'The crusade is a threat to many powers and polities. It is not only the Archenemy who reels from our advance. Xenos gather in numbers not seen since the Great Crusade. Drukhari piracy approaches desperate levels, greenskins gather on our eastward flanks, and on dozens of worlds those infected by the genestealer curse rise up to challenge our advance. They expect a rapture or a revelation, and we bring them only discovery and death.'

'And have they been found and destroyed?' she asked plaintively.

The primarch looked away – just for a moment – and some of her faint hope died behind her eyes. 'They have not,' he said. 'Yet that is a problem for another time.' The primarch scooped up a quill and began to tap again at a data-slate. 'When you were dispatched it was to expedite matters. Now, as the crusade gains momentum, we are forced to consider other options. I am loath to discard useful tools, especially when they have suffered in the attempt to do their duty.'

'I am...' She paused, swallowed hard, and stepped forward. The desk that lay between them was ancient, old and dark wood in the chamber of steel and stone. It was something from another time, transplanted to the here and now. She wanted to place her hands upon it, knuckles down, ground into it, but she kept them knotted behind her back. 'I am not a thing to be pitied, lord.'

'No,' he agreed, 'you are not.' The primarch moved, rising and striding around the desk. In motion he was even more unnerving, terrifying in his impossibility. The armour, she realised, was not the worst of it. Massive powered plate, its every motion a thing of precise mechanical certainty, glimmered in the artificial light and yet blazed like a sun. The primarch, Roboute Guilliman, the Avenging Son and Lord of Ultramar, the Imperial Regent... was like nothing she had ever seen, or perhaps ever would again.

'If there is a chance for me to prove myself anew then I will take it,' she managed. It hurt to look at him. She found herself focusing

on tiny, insignificant details, threatening to become lost in the spectacle of the being's existence.

He was an inferno caged in human skin, a star bound into the
shape of a man, and as he moved through the cosmos he reminded
all who looked upon him that he was too large and too glorious
for this fallen age, for this sundered Imperium.

'You do not know what I will ask,' Guilliman said. 'Yet perhaps
that is for the best. I have considered your previous findings and I
concur with your assessments. Of the many routes possible only the
Nachmund Gauntlet is known to be stable, though treacherous.
The Draedes Gap is lost to us, compromised by enemy action and
unreliable at best. Other crossings are similarly fraught, suited for
only the most desperate of transits – such as the Straits of Epona.
What I require are stable routes. Those capable of ensuring the
mass-movement of men and materiel.'

'You must have some notion,' she began. 'Some sense of where
to start. You cannot expect me alone to map the entire Rift and
find your stable routes! If they even exist!'

He chuckled, like the rumble of a landslip, like the cracking of
sea ice. 'I do not expect that, no.' He gestured and a hololithic
map sprang up from the desk, rotating gently, a study in brilliant
emerald and hateful scarlet. 'You will be but one of many – crusade elements, retasked torchbearer fleets, and those individuals
whom I have deemed worthy of personal service.' He smiled gently.
'Agents from amongst my historitors shall be compiling records of
previous warp anomalies and immaterial dead-zones. Where we
can map the skin and muscle of the galaxy-as-it-was, then we can
judge to what extent the galaxy's bones have shifted.'

'I have other resources in mind to exploit,' she murmured. There
were nests of astrocartographers and warp-transit experts that she
could rely upon, or else press into service. As a rogue trader she
was not without means and ways of her own. 'And if I complete
this good and loyal service, lord? What then?'

'Then I will give you the opportunity to find your daughter.' He paused, reaching out with his gauntleted fingers as though to caress the hovering map. Pain flickered through his impassive gaze as he drank in the galaxy's sorrow. A man such as that, a being of such power and reach, and yet even he would struggle to undo what had been done. She felt, for a fleeting moment, pity for him. Then the moment passed for both of them. 'I have read the reports.' He looked at her again. 'She was taken from you. Lost to the storm at Draedes.'

'Lost to the storm,' she agreed.

'If there is a chance that she is alive beyond the Rift then I would give you the opportunity to find her once again. Find me my stable route and I will attach you to whichever elements are first to cross it. I will give you the freedom of the void in Imperium Nihilus that waits beyond.

Ah, there it is. The lure. The leverage that he does not need, but provides anyway. She wanted to laugh, so transparent was it. And yet, for all its lack of subtlety she could respect it. The primarch knew her worth, he knew her motivations, and he would yoke one to the other to claim what he required.

'A worthy offer, lord. Though, in truth, I would trade any promise of glory or advancement for the chance to see my Astrid once again.'

'That is why I am certain that you will serve to the best of your ability, with the fullness of your skill,' Guilliman said. His hand cut across the air above the desk and the image was suddenly dismissed. 'You fight for more than profit or glory, just as I do. You fight for the safeguarding of that which you hold dear. For you, as with myself, this is a matter of familial responsibility.'

The memory died as she opened her eyes and took another deep breath. Katla returned her gaze to the flawless features of the Custodian, so similar to and yet so different from the primarch of her memory.

The primarch had been post-human in a way she could scarcely comprehend, and yet for all the visceral majesty of his being he had remained utterly human – defined by his faith in the species. A being such as that would do anything, no matter how terrible, in the service of humanity. The Custodian, though, she knew, would do anything in pursuit of his all-consuming duty to his master.

She stepped forward again and looked Augustus in the eye. 'Everything I have done has been for the service of the Imperium and the protection of my family. That is all. I will do my duty, play my part, yet I will look to my family and my crew, and see them through the struggles. It is a poor pack that forsakes its members.'

'How quaint,' he said, but she was already pushing on and past him, out into the ship, up and towards the bridge.

It was only when she was out of sight and around a corner that the first alarms began to sound.

Chapter Twenty-One

DESPERATE MEASURES

SACRED TORMENT

WALLS OF STEEL AND SPITE

The skies were alive with attack craft, blotting out the sun's dying light in a swarm of black iron and glossy exoskeleton. Each ship seemed to have transmuted, changed by the long millennia into something alien and inhuman, more grown or exuded than shaped by the hands of craftsmen.

Above Velua the enemy gathered in strength. Irinya could see, even from the battlements of the outer walls, the new and false stars that graced the heavens. When the first auspex returns had come through she had almost allowed herself to hope that the Black Templars had returned, that Gaheris' certainty had shifted or faded, and that Angels would once more descend to liberate them.

Such hopes had swiftly become falsehood.

Every vox-channel and means of communication was swamped now, drowning in the low droning of insects and the half-hissed hymns of an abominable creed. They spoke of the hand that would shred the galaxy and the times of mankind's ending. The ascendancy of death was come, and the world would suffer and bleed for its petty defiance. They proclaimed that the False Emperor could not protect them from the coming of the dark illumination promised by the galaxy's one true godhead.

Irinya had ordered all transmissions to be blocked, where possible, and for all public vox-links to be severed. A number of secure vox-networks remained within the walls of the great shrine, sanctified by the Adeptus Mechanicus, and kept pure by the constant broadcasting – via laud-hailer – of the Sisters' own songs.

Agata and Josefine stood with her upon the walls, newly returned from their own prayer vigil, their voices hoarse from hours of singing.

'It's time, then,' Agata rumbled. 'Time for the last and most desperate of measures.'

'Aye,' Irinya said with a slight tilt of her head. 'It comes to it at last. I had hoped we would not have to release the sinners, but without their sacred suffering there will be no chance of stymie-ing the enemy advance. They come with False Angels of their own now. With aerial superiority. They will have artillery, fresh men and materiel, and things less than men that wallow in their service. When the enemy strikes it shall be with all the fury of their false god and all the wiles and deceptions of the warp.' She swallowed and let her hand drift to her sword, seeking clarity. 'We must use every weapon available to us, else we are lost.'

'Against the temptations of the enemy, faith builds the strong-est walls,' Josefine said softly, her head bowed.

'Yet heresy erodes even the sturdiest foundation and compro-mises the works of man,' Irinya countered. Josefine blushed slightly at having forgotten. 'I may not have been the keenest of students in my youth, Josefine, but I did not become can-oness without the skills to justify it.' She laughed gingerly at that, and turned back towards the darkening skies.

Swarming with enemy machines, alight with anti-aircraft fire, the sky had turned a bruised and angry purple, streaked with red. The heavens themselves were wounded, bleeding, burning, and as she looked up Irinya understood that only by giving their all would there be any hope of survival.

'Throne preserve us,' she whispered. 'God-Emperor protect us from the predations of the enemy.'

There was only darkness this deep beneath the earth. He knew that much, that they were buried deep in the world's skin, below the crypts and tombs, far beneath the walls and the tumult above. Here light was a distant memory, an idea he barely understood any more. Time had likewise fled, stolen from him like his freedom.

There was only darkness here. And pain.

The man who had once been Colonel Draszen, who could only remember that in fleeting moments of panicked realisation in the darkness, woke again to the flaring of sudden agony, dancing like black fire through his spine, coiling through his body and mind to penetrate his very soul.

There was light now, sudden and foreign, cast by the ignition of spot-lumens and braziers. Details resolved themselves out of the shadows, his light-starved eyes struggling to recognise them. It hurt to look at the shapes as they grew from grey smears and bright points of reflection into clearly recognisable patterns.

A metal table, laden with knives and needles. Red-robed figures moving around it, picking at the tools like fishwives picking at the wares at a market. Bright silver edges glistened under the artificial gazes of the figures. *Tech-priests*, some part of him remembered. They were of the Mechanicus. Buried in their enclaves, deep below the city, deep below the war, keeping their secrets and their strange creed.

He felt more pain, burrowing and buzzing at his lower back. The whine of saw and needle as they incised into the bones of his vertebrae. His teeth clenched, grinding against the iron bar which had been set between his jaws as a makeshift gag. Now, as sensation returned in all its hateful glory, he could feel the restraints set about his limbs and the wires which were pinning open his eyelids. He screamed, teeth locked around the bar so tightly he thought they might break. Drool pooled over it and dribbled down his chin, onto the emaciated ruin of his chest.

One of the figures stepped closer, its red robes trimmed with gold thread, its augmetics of a subtly ostentatious make. It tilted its head one way and then the other, weighing his worth, before it spoke in a machine's rasp.

'Be thankful, for we shall deliver you. The mercy of the machine is the redemption of the flesh. They have given you to us to be remade, to be stripped of your weakness, to be bound to the glory of the eternal machine. Even though you may die, the machine shall endure. It shall outlast all weak and meagre flesh.'

Then the blades descended, and the needles pierced his skin to flood him with chemicals which burned in his blood and made his heart hammer. His eyes were wide, straining, as though they might burst from his skull. The drills continued their progress, searing the wound closed around them, layering them with liquid metal and rubber, forming ports in his spine. He wanted to scream, but he couldn't. There was only the strangled gurgling that rose from his throat, drowned out by the sacred torment he was undergoing and the prayers of the machine-devoted.

Other voices rose from around him, shrill with their own pain, their own worlds collapsing around them to knots of individual suffering. Encompassed by darkness and stone, steel and fire.

'Know that your woes have purpose. You are being remade, fit for sacrifice. You shall serve, till the very last, and expurgate your sins in blood and fire. You shall serve your Emperor and you shall be made pure in the many-sense sight of the Omnissiah. Be at peace, for your deaths shall buy life for others. You shall serve as the fuel for the holiest of duties.'

The walls came alive with light and fury. Lumens stretched out into the darkness, seeking the enemy in the seconds before the auspexes and the gunsights would find them. Soldiers moved in haste, scampering about the walls like startled children. Only the Sisters held firm against the darkness. Unmoving, unyielding, their vigils unbroken.

The skies were alive with crackling arcs of lightning, worming across the heavens like the pale green progression of an infection. Their flare caught on everything, glistening on the surface of the void shields, on the edges of weapons or of armour, on the hulking darkness of the wall guns. The enemy's hellish light touched every part of the defence, crawling across every plane until there was no shadow – no place in which to hide, only the infernal illumination. Faces were more drawn under its baleful radiance, the promise of sickness and death leering out from behind their yellowed eyes.

Upon the walls the defenders wrestled with despair, felt doubt claw at their hearts with talons of ice, and fought against the sudden fear of the turbulent dark. Even with the walls cleared of bodies, even with the marks of battle expunged, the lingering taint of the daemonic assault was everywhere. Wounds in the battlements, gouges that wept with strange fluids that neither Mechanicus tending nor flame could truly purge.

Still the walls held. Without, they were crafted of stone and plasteel, and within of steel and spite. Each and every last defender upon the walls – Savlar, Veluan, or Sister – felt in their very souls the urge to defend the God-Emperor's holy places. Even as the skies burned and trembled, as the lightning cracked the heavens, and the first of the thick, greasy rains began to fall.

Even as the first war-horns echoed out from the plains, and the Titans found their prey.

Chapter Twenty-Two

PLAGUE FLEET

LAST ORDERS

MARKED BY THE CROSS

'Cease that racket, Allfather damn you!' Katla called as she strode onto the bridge.

The great circular chamber rang with tocsins and shone with crimson light. The crew were already at their stations, each with a weapon near to hand: axes and swords, laspistols and autoguns. She watched a gunnery officer, a Terran by birth, stroke her fingers along the haft of an axe borrowed from the armouries. She almost laughed to see the fusion of their ways. An omen, certainly.

The alarms finally ceased and Katla took her place in her throne, aware of Augustus' looming presence to the rear of the bridge. All the crew stiffened that little bit more under the Custodian's gaze, even as it passed over them. It was focused upon her.

'What do we have?' she asked.

'Auspex returns, jarl!' Ana called. Katla warmed to see that she had taken up the Fenrisian title, and wore blades sheathed at her hips. A good omen indeed. 'They came out of the storm, right on top of us, but are holding at safe distance. Waiting.'

'Aye, but for what?' Katla murmured. 'Have we resolved their ident-codes?'

'Taking some time,' Ana said, fussing over her console. Runic patterns flickered down the screen, casting their reflected light over her pale features. She chewed at her lip as she worked, and then huffed out a sigh. 'Older codes, jarl. Sophisticated presentation. I would say they were Adeptus Astartes, only...' She trailed off. Her eyes widened. 'No. *Legiones Astartes*,' she breathed. 'The *Song of Sickness*. The *Balelight*. The battle-barge *Pilgrim's Promise*. Others. More. Throne of Terra! The codes are all ancient, ten thousand years dead, and marked over with new titles.'

'Traitors who renounced their vows to mankind's master,' Augustus intoned weightily. All eyes turned upon him. He barely noticed. Instead he strode forward to stand at the side of Katla's throne. 'These are the enemy of all life, captain. They are the hate and the fire that we are arrayed against. When the primarch crosses the Rift and opposes the lawless void, this is the foe that shall be staring back at him.'

A chorus of small prayers and oaths rippled through the bridge. Some in Fenrisian cant, others in plain Gothic. Men and women made the sign of the aquila or the eye of aversion.

'We should burn them from the void, same as we did the pilgrim fleet,' Katla whispered. 'What is their disposition?'

'They outgun us,' Ana said, brow furrowed. 'Every last ship is of a mightier tonnage than those we possess. It would be hard-fought, and they can take more punishment than we can. We would lose most of the support vessels in the opening volleys. We have heavy hitters, and we have the *Queen*, but beyond that...'

'Then what are they waiting for?' Katla wondered aloud.

'Perhaps they want us to see them and to turn and try to run? They enjoy the chase before they take us between their teeth, the same as any beast born of cruelty.'

'What do we do?' Ana asked quietly.

A hush descended over the bridge as all eyes turned from the viewscreens and the auspex back to their captain, their jarl, their queen. Katla felt her fingers tighten on the arms of the throne as she leant forward, teeth gritted.

'All we can do is fight or run,' she hissed. 'There are no other options. I would rather *die*' – her hand cut across the air – 'than flee from battle. They think to bring us to heel like dogs! They'll know our bite, before the end.'

She looked around at Augustus, but the Custodian remained as impassive as ever. Only the merest nod of his head was his answer.

'They're trying to establish a vox-link!' someone called.

The lights flickered and died. For a moment Katla was back in the dead and churning hell of the pilgrim ship, or trapped in the frozen tomb that the *Queen* had become around Endymica. She felt fear, raw animal panic, surge up inside her.

Whispers came, oozing from the vox-horns, burbling up into sick laughter. It filled the chamber in thick syrupy tones as the screens flickered and crackled with static, their light turned sick and bilious.

'You should not be here,' it rasped.

'Yet here we are,' Katla replied. All she had done was follow the path laid before her. Whether the auguries flowed from Yazran and his calculations, Bodil and her rune-reading, or Katla's own voidcraft, it had set them inexorably upon this path. It felt like the competing whims of rival gods had cast them to this point.

The transmission broke apart in a susurrus of hissed laughter in too many voices. It was the sound of maleficarum. The sort of hateful lie that would slither up from beneath the ice and drag the unsuspecting down. Like all the deceits of the Underverse made real.

'Oh, little rogue trader... The galaxy burns around your ears and here you are, defying the darkness in your own little way. There is so little to admire in you Imperials, but your defiance... That always makes this a joy.'

'I will not listen to your mockery, daemon,' she replied. 'Kill us and have done with it.'

The ship's sacred systems convulsed again. Binharic wailing drifted from hidden alcoves and maintenance naves as the tech-priests recoiled. A hololithic generator flickered to life before the throne, displaying a figure of hideous ruin.

Swollen and distorted by rot, its ancient armour pitted and timeworn, the figure sneered with broken teeth while madness glimmered in its eyes.

'I am no daemon, captain. Look upon me and see your death. See Grommulus Tuul. Barbarus-born. Son of the Fourteenth Legion and proud Mortarion. Servant of the Grandfather of all life and sworn implement of his chosen.'

The generator began to weep oil and billow with gentle smoke. The air around Tuul's rendition was greasy. Infernal. Around her the crew were struggling to sever the link, wrestling with the compromised machine spirits of the great vessel, and finally resorting to cutting through cables.

Tuul burbled with laughter, as though finding the whole affair eminently amusing. 'Oh, there will be time enough for pleasantries later. For now, you are a thread which requires pruning. So desperately, in fact, that you have led me upon a merry chase as the fates shift. The omens spoke true, though, and wisely I thought to range ahead and prepare such gifts for you. Yet you spurn them, as so many spurn the Grandfather's love. All for an absent Emperor. Who does not love you. Does not care if you live or die, no matter what His little lapdogs might say.'

Augustus moved forward at those words, finally roused to action by the relentless blasphemy. A flash of silver passed through the air in front of her eyes before golden flame roared heavenwards. The sickly light died and darkness returned to the chamber for a moment before the systems kicked in again. The crew were in motion at once as stations began to respond.

Beyond the viewscreen they could see the enemy fleet. Each ship was an island of corrupt metal within the void, miasma coiled about them in a putrid, writhing nebula. Katla was reminded of the hive fleets of the tyranids, numerous beyond imagining in their roiling void-shoals, a nest of insects writ god-scale. The plague fleet coiled and spasmed with unclean life, similar but different to the Devourer's multitudes.

She could still hear the laughter, its oily presence lingering in the air. She rose on suddenly unsteady feet and reached for her spear. She wound her fingers around the rune-etched shaft, taking comfort in the patterns there. Oaths and promises. Invocations of the spirits of home. Bound up in Fimbulgeir were hopes; her past, and her future. It was more than a weapon; it was a legacy.

Katla pointed the spear out and across the bridge's expanse, its tip angled at the lead ship in the plague fleet. If she gestured but a little it was as though the pustule of a vessel could be punctured and drained. If it was within her power she would cut it from the firmament.

'Orders, jarl?' Ana asked. The ship thrummed behind her words as the reactor fully engaged. Already the great bulk of the *Queen* was readying itself for war. Somewhere far below the guns were being run out, shells slid into place by the efforts of the sweating, desperate multitudes. Lance batteries were gathering power and the mighty void-harpoons were ratcheting into place.

The *Wyrmslayer Queen* was a hunter, and when pushed she would fight.

'Bring us about,' Katla said. 'Show them our teeth. If they want a piece of us then they can fight us. We'll make every last step of it bloody. Fight, bleed them, and we escape or we die.'

These might be the last orders I ever give. The thought gave her no comfort, but nor did it stir her fear. Katla was not afraid to die. All she feared was that it would not have been enough. To die with her duty undone, without seeing her child again. To fail, not just the primarch but the Imperium...

'They're moving into range,' Ana observed. Secondary hololithic projectors reorientated and cast forth their representation of the battlefield. A sphere of pale blue light, speckled with green and red icons. The enemy icons bled sigils as they moved, tracking across the battlespace in a slow slog of crimson.

Engines fired and the *Queen* began to move to respond. Sirens wailed once more and the light became a dull red throb. Armsmen were moving to their stations in a rattle of chainmail and plate. Horns blew, summoning their warriors to battle.

Against Heretic Astartes, against the plague-ridden horrors set before them, it would make little difference, but they would fight until finally slain – called up to feast at the Allfather's side in the sight of Russ.

'I offer you an honour only the Sky Warriors are privy to!' she called. 'We've come far together, my friends. From separate roots, yes, but with common cause! You have come to me from the ice of Fenris and the grey and gold of Terra. You have been called from across Imperium Sanctus, to serve the Allfather of Man! Our God-Emperor and our regent have put their faith in us, to bring light to the darkness. These things...' She gestured again with her spear. 'These monsters that were once men would seek to stop us. They have numbers, they have the blessings of their false gods, but they will never be a match for you, my friends. With steel in your hands and courage in your hearts, any foe can be bested!'

Vox-embeds would carry her words throughout the ship, but on the bridge there was an immediate reaction – fists punched the air, cheers and roars joined her own defiance.

Augustus turned to her. 'A fine sentiment, captain, yet we remain outgunned. I would gladly bring these curs to battle, the same as you, but the mission must have priority.' Something flickered in his gaze, beyond duty and concern. 'We must–'

'Warp translations detected, jarl!' A new set of alarms undercut the words. The hololith spasmed and new signals began to translate through.

'An ambush?' she asked. 'Have they outflanked us already? Damn these bastards and their sorcerous ways.'

'No, jarl... it's...' Ana trailed off. 'A miracle.'

The ships that tore their way free of the immaterium were not disfigured by plague or the devotions of the Dark Gods. Instead they wore their purity like a torch in the darkness. They burned with captive fire, evincing strength and determination in their every movement.

Great slab-sided ships of war, mottled with old scars and glimmering with gilt. Black. Black against the infinite void, so as almost to blend with that eternal night. At first, from the viewscreens and viewports of the other vessels it seemed that space itself had come alive, to move amidst the heavens at the God-Emperor's decree, for the darkness that moved was dappled with stars.

No, Katla realised, looking upon them. They were not stars, they were marked with crosses. Small and large, white against the black. Templar crosses, the symbol of the longest-serving and most dedicated of crusades.

Vox-alarms rang out and were replaced by hale and healthy signals. The bridge was filled with sudden sound, with the deep-bass hymns of transhuman voices. Singing His praises, invoking His name. The words rolled over the bridge crew and for a moment they knew hope, contentment, and the surety of victory.

A voice cut through the singing, strong and stern, alive with authority.

'*Hail, daughter of the wolf.*'

Katla's brows creased in confusion, but it continued on.

'*I am Gaheris of the Black Templars. I am the Emperor's Champion, and I have been seeking you for some time. Praise be unto the God-Emperor for delivering us to you at your hour of need. The holy sight of the Navigators and the sacred communing of the astropaths has brought us here. To stand against the unholy. To drive back the corrupt.*'

She blinked. *Why in the name of all the hells would a Champion of the Emperor be looking for me?* She looked sideways to try and gauge Augustus' reaction, but the Custodian remained impassive. *Though... do I not stand with one of His own guardians? Should I be so surprised at the nest of luminaries that Guilliman has cast me into?*

'Did the regent send you?' she asked, speaking directly into the vox-horn. 'We've had no word since first setting out, let alone reinforcements.'

'*We are guided by the God-Emperor's grace. His visions led me to you and your quest.*' Gaheris paused. '*We have sacrificed much to be here at your side. Do not spurn His hand, offered in friendship, nor His mercy in the face of damnation.*'

'We are not in the habit of turning away friends,' Katla said. 'Not with red snow on the horizon.'

Gaheris' rich laughter filled the bridge. '*We are His blade, captain. The enemy cannot stand against the faithful.*'

'Black Templars fleet dispositions are falling into formation, jarl. We have the *Sword of Sigismund*. The *Oath Adamant* and the *Sacred Wrath*. The *Torch of Testament* and the battle-barge *Seventh Vengeance*.'

Katla smirked. It evened the odds, and then some. Even if the plague-ridden hulks and bastard-vessels could take more than their share of hits, they would die bloody under the guns of the loyalists.

'You're making yourself at home, Champion,' she quipped. 'Feel free to set about the enemy.'

'We but await the opportunity, captain. In due course I shall join you with my retinue, and then,' Gaheris said, *'all the enemies of mankind shall suffer beneath my sight.'*

Chapter Twenty-Three

THE WALK TO WAR

KINGS AND GHOSTS

ENGINE KILL

Beyond the walls the storms raged and Melpomene urged the great engine into the very heart of it. Through the blasted land that had once been shrines and sacred gardens, grinding broken columns to dust beneath her iron tread, they walked. The greatest of all marches. The only one that mattered.

The walk to war.

Vengeance strode forth, the Titan's pace increasing as they forged onwards into the new wastes. The blight and taint of the enemy was everywhere, increasing by the day. Since the landers had come down from the heavens and the ships had appeared in orbit it was as though the corruption of the enemy had reached a new height.

'Environmental contamination reaching critical levels,' Tovrel commented. 'Soon the outside will be unliveable for the unaugmented. The Ecclesiarchy might never reclaim their pretty little world.'

'War makes desolation of all things in the pursuit of peace,'

Melpomene said. 'Those who cannot accept a little devastation will lose everything, trying to preserve their normality.'

She had seen it herself, on the home world. Sareme had been a world in flux, drowning in the relentless tide of industry which had endured since the Age of Strife and Old Night. That suffering had forged the Legio. It had made them the Iron Kings.

'Maximum motive power attained, princeps!' Skell called. 'The Warhounds are ranging ahead.'

'Confirmation from the other princeps,' Tovrel added. 'The enemy outriders are within engagement range.'

'Disposition?'

'Heretic Astartes and cult troops. Armoured detachments. Advancing en masse. Headed for the walls. More than any previous push. The armour...' Tovrel shook her head. 'Old make. Patterns corrupted. Siege-class artillery. They get within range and the walls will fall. The shields won't hold. They are city-breakers.'

'Then we burn them from the earth as we did before. Their cultists were toy soldiers, their armour borrowed finery. Now that their masters have appeared, we will drive the lesson home.'

'This far out we will be vulnerable to orbital and aerial counter-barrage, my princeps.' Moderatus Valtin spoke now.

'If we are swift and sure then we will buy the city all the time they require. Even if it costs us our lives. Sacrifice and suffering. That is the lot of the Legio Arconis. That is the legacy of Sareme. That is what we live and fight to uphold.' Melpomene closed her eyes. When she opened them she could feel the serpent-storm of the great machine's consciousness twined about her own. Promising the final reckoning.

<That is what we are Vengeance *for.>*

'*Nightbeast* and *Dune Hound* report engagement,' Tovrel stated. The returns were becoming harder to read. Static and scrapcode feedback whined across the sensorium. 'Reporting minimal resistance...'

'Take us in, Steersman Skell,' Melpomene hissed as she regained herself. 'Full stride.'

The engine shook with motion as it stalked onwards. The thrill was in her now. The blood-keenness of the hunt and the yearning to make war and join battle. Soon they would be within range themselves, close enough for the volcano cannons to reap their tally. She would reduce the enemy's siege weapons to slag and ruin. Then she would stride through the wrecks and grind the cultists and their masters beneath her tread.

'It will be a sacred thing,' she whispered, 'to see them dead and destroyed. As we should have done upon Sareme. As we will one day return to do.'

The air sparked with static and every system within the Titan's cockpit began to scream. Feedback whined through the air and flickered across the sensorium and the manifold. Melpomene gritted her teeth and felt phantom pain lancing through her nerves in waves of heat and electricity. She shuddered upon her throne as the engine's stride faltered until it slowed and stopped.

'What in the name of the Omnissiah was that?' she bellowed. 'I need tactical awareness!'

'Sensors are disrupted, princeps!' Tovrel called. 'Massive immaterial feedback! I have active transmissions from Bertolt and Lares.'

'What do they say?'

'They say...' Tovrel swallowed. 'They say the enemy are summoning gods of their own.'

The world was crowned in sudden fire.

Unnatural flame screamed from the heavens in a deluge, caustic greens and vibrant scarlet warring with black fire and glowing white ghost light. It flowed from the tormented skies like unclean water spilling, like a blade scything through flesh. It cut and bit into the world with all the hateful fury of the warp. Reality bowed outwards and undulated with impossible movement, writhing with the motion of grave worms too big for the mortal world. The earth and sky sloughed away as the unreal shed the material caul and birthed forth its immense horrors.

The two figures were as large as the Warlord itself, each a monster unique in scale and disfigurement. Once they might have been war engines of the Collegia Titanicus, but if they had shared those origins then they had long since lost any connection to them. They were forged of flesh and bone rather than steel and adamantium, all of it diseased and rotted through. Spurs of osseous matter had shaped themselves into claws and fangs, dripping with venom.

Lightning crackled between their jaws like active power fields. Eyes opened in the wet and gangrenous flesh, staring out with yellow sclera stained with blood clots. Rheum and ichor oozed from too many wounds and cavities in the great machines of rancid flesh. When they moved it was with an unnatural swiftness. They lurched and lumbered across the broken earth, casting up clouds of dust and atomised bone. A haze of vaporised bodies hung about them, stinking of charnel houses and teeming with flies.

The murk swallowed *Dune Hound* before the daemon-beast reached it. Ensconced within the cockpit of *Vengeance* Melpomene felt Bertolt's rage bleed across the manifold, before the first lashings of sympathetic pain reached her.

He screamed and raged, even till the end. As the thing's massive jaws closed around the Warhound's head and the tendrils closed about its body, Bertolt coaxed the god-machine's weapons to full activation. Mega-bolter rounds hewed into the daemon engine, carving a great chasm of weeping flesh and black blood. The beast pulled back and the Warhound's head came free in a welter of sparks and debris. The murk cleared for a moment, as though to let her see the tiny bodies tumbling out as the monster reared up and swallowed the Titan's iron skull whole.

Melpomene fired.

The volcano cannon dispelled the darkness in a roar of cleansing illumination. The daemon engine turned ponderously, silhouetted in the glare of the weapon's discharge. Mountainous boils, ulcers and cysts burst in a rain of blood and pus – a cataclysmic release of tainted fluid staining the dusty ground beneath it as the blast found its mark. The beast turned in its agony, bellowing from spit-flecked mouths, and staggered onwards in pursuit of *Nightbeast*. She couldn't see the second creature, lost in the smoke and dust, biding its time.

The smaller engine sprinted away, desperate to evade the twisted hunter that pursued them.

'Bring us about and ready missiles. I want them immobile when we unleash our wrath,' Melpomene snapped.

The crew assented with a chorus of ayes and went about their business. They were well disciplined and committed to the moment. There were none she would rather have at her side.

'Lares,' she whispered. 'Rejoin the line. We will kill them together. He will be avenged.'

'*Melpomene,*' Lares hissed. Her voice was streaked through with grief and pain. '*I will kill them myself if needs be. The unholy bastards.*' Her utterance was punctuated by new thunder. Explosions rose around *Nightbeast*'s desperate flight as the enemy tanks found their range and gained confidence. '*They're pushing forward. Brigade strength. Kill them. Kill them, by the Omnissiah, before they–*'

Nightbeast shook and its war-horns bellowed as great lances of bone lashed out from the innards of the wounded daemon engine. The monstrosity brayed goatishly and lowered its head, hurling itself forward in pursuit, closing the distance with the Warhound. *Nightbeast* strained forward, weeping smoke and oil from its wounds. Lares' voice came through the manifold accompanied by a rush of sensory bleed-through. *Vengeance* knew in its machine-core the agony of its sibling and the war-horns blared unbidden.

The damage was severe, nigh terminal. Melpomene allowed the engine's agony to envelop her. She surrendered to the kill-urges boiling through her blood, forced by a reactor heart that was not truly her own.

She fired again.

The monster vanished. Obliterated. Unmade. Flesh turned to ashes and blood was reduced to smoke, all of it becoming immaterial as the thing discorporated. It screamed as it died and the world was lashed with foetid lightning as the warp reclaimed its own. She watched it flail out across the enemy lines and she knew that somewhere their sorcerers were suffering with the feedback.

'Into them!' Melpomene roared. 'Support *Nightbeast*!'

Lares' engine was limping, dragging itself forwards with every step. Melpomene was certain it would collapse and that its last moments would be spent casting up dust with its final fitful exertions. Dying, drowned beneath the sands.

Missiles sang from *Vengeance*'s pods, bursting around *Nightbeast* in a cordon of flame and smoke. The advancing ranks of cultists, Heretic Astartes and tanks faded from view as the fires burned amidst the dust and smog.

There is a chance here. We can salvage this. The Omnissiah is with us. If we embrace sacred stratagem and logic then we cannot falter. We are as iron.

The second impossible beast hurled itself through the flames, trailing burning warp-matter and false flesh as it latched on to *Nightbeast*. Nests of snapping beaks and sucking tentacles coiled around the noble war engine, incising into it with a thousand cuts. Acid vomited in through the wounds in *Nightbeast's* hull and screams echoed through the Titans' shared sensoria. Melpomene gritted her teeth through the aftershocks of Lares' death agonies – to say nothing of the howling, screaming death of the venerable engine – and pushed forward.

'How long until we can fire again?' she growled.

'Still charging, princeps! We will have a firing solution in...'

But it didn't matter. The warp-thing was already up and moving, oil and metal dribbling from between its malformed jaws. Something crunched wetly, *organically*, and then fell away from its mouth in merciful silence.

Lares. The thought itself was agony.

Melpomene was still waiting to fire when the daemon enveloped them. Tendrils flailed across the viewports of the Titan's eyes and burrowed for its belly. She pushed back hard and the engine mirrored her movements, flinching away from the enemy contact. She tried to raise her cannon but the monstrous form batted it away, pinning it to one side as its tentacles scored across the green and grey plates of the great war engine.

Sympathetic pain lanced through her belly and she felt the wetness of blood from the psychosomatic wounds. Missiles fired in futility, arcing over the beast and impacting behind it. Sensor arrays responded to the detonations and for a moment she was hyper-focused upon the impact sites. She could see the enemy's advance clearly, now. Trudging through the fire and enduring all wounds that were rained down upon them. Even as the cultist chaff flailed and burned, even as they died in their droves, their masters forged through the conflagration, unbothered and unbroken.

Melpomene reared her arm back and *Vengeance* responded in kind. She slammed the cannon's length against the thing's stunted skull. Again and again she hammered at the beast, trying in desperation to drive it back. Warning sirens began to sound and the lumens around them flickered and turned suddenly red. She could smell smoke and burning metal, the acid reek of bile, and the sickly sweetness of rot. It was oozing its way inside, cutting through systems and connections with its caustic bulk alone. She felt her own legs go limp as the Titan's motive force ebbed away.

The beast yanked its whole mass sideways and the Titan followed with it. The fall felt stretched out, viewed in slow motion, as they tumbled groundwards. She felt the impact shudder through her bones – through the iron skeleton of the Titan. War-horns screamed in desperation.

'We...' Moderatus Valtin gasped. 'We have weapon readiness!'

She fired.

The volcano cannon jerked up as it discharged and the beam hewed through the creature's grip. Tree-thick tentacles dissolved like melting ice, blown away by the sheer intensity of the blast. As the weapon fired she directed the beam, carving a great chasm through the tormented earth and catching the very edge of the enemy advance. Men caught fire and blew to ash in the face of it. Tanks and their munitions exploded, blowing skywards in great toxic mushroom detonations. Even the Astartes faltered in the face of such an onslaught.

They had already scented blood, though. Now the enemy came; once again pushing on through the hellfire and the toxin clouds. They advanced with greater relish, knowing that they would, in their multitudes, finally kill the god-machine that lay before them.

The Titan would not, could not, right itself.

Melpomene was sprawled half out of the throne, MIU links straining. She could taste blood and metal. The air had grown thin in the compartment, dirty with dust and smoke and spreading mud. If she didn't move then the impact alone would ensure she died here, entombed and enthroned, sharing in the machine's agony.

Valtin and Tovrel were moving to help her. Skell was dead, slumped at his station. Melpomene made a small noise, an animal whimper of pain and fear, and hated herself for it. It was a sound that should not have come from her. A pathetic, keening thing.

'We need to move,' she whispered as she finally disengaged. Part of her mind was screaming and bellowing in pain and rage – enmeshed with the great machine spirit of the engine. Part of her was dying as she sacrificed the link. 'We move or we die here.'

Chapter Twenty-Four

THE DEAD'S DUE

GIFTS FROM THE GOD

AS THE HEAVENS BURN

Weryn watched another of the prophets, his brethren, collapse face down into the stinking mud and be trod underfoot. Seven had died now. Seven holy souls offered up to the hunger of the masters in the long march towards the walls. Even as the Titans had fought and died he had been there, watching, observing the losses forced upon the Children by the hateful enemy. Yet now the machines were dead and little lay between the cult and their prize.

He had not imagined that it would be like this – never once in his most fevered of dreams. It was to have been a joyous thing to be liberated; they would be spared the predations of uncaring institutions. They would reign at the right hand of the Grandfather. Looking down at the husk which had once been his friend and colleague, Weryn could scarcely visualise that promised paradise now. He reached down with a pale trembling hand and turned her body over.

Weryn gasped. The prophet had been reduced to a twisted

husk – her skin blackened and shrunken, her eyes gone. Her limbs were broken, twisted at impossible angles by pure psychic spite. He looked up, through the ranks of advancing cultists and Astartes, and beheld the architect of woe.

Pustrus hung suspended in the air, thin strands of lightning connecting him to the ground. His pale and drawn skin writhed with internal motion as worms and maggots squirmed out of his wounds and dappled down his ruined armour and the robes of human skin which swaddled him. When the sorcerer turned his gaze towards Weryn it was hollow and hungry. He grinned emptily, tongue lolling around broken and stunted teeth.

'You feel it, don't you, little prophet? The pull of the Grand-father's love?'

'I feel...' Weryn said breathily. 'I feel weak.'

'Because you *are*,' Pustrus laughed. 'You are all weak little things. Playthings to be used and discarded as we see fit. And you accept it because the god wills it, and because the Pilgrim has promised you salvation. So you grovel and beg, you plead and you expire. More mulch for the Garden. By your sacrifice is the veil weakened, by their deaths are the instruments of the god summoned, and by your labour shall the False Emperor's temples of lies topple down to rubble.'

'We're just men,' Weryn whimpered. His skin was crawling with the by-blow energy of Pustrus' great working. He could feel his bones weakening beneath the sorcerer's gaze as something coiled and uncoiled within his guts. If he looked away he would die, but if he continued to gaze upon the numinous being of rot and ruin then he knew he would vomit.

'Just men...' Pustrus tilted his head as he weighed the words. 'Yes, yes you are. But in an age long lost to memory and myth the primarch came to us. He took those who were just men and he gave them purpose. He led them, but it was men who toppled the fortresses of the Overlords and gave hope to their fellows. With the right motivation men can topple mountains and reshape the world.' He bowed his crowned head and gurgled with laughter. 'Do you have the will to do the same?'

Weryn thought of all that had been done in the name of the Pilgrim and the god they shared. He had fought and bled, killed and corrupted. He had allowed his mind and his gifts to soar. Weryn had become a leader amongst men, a symbol of rebellion and revelation. Now he felt like an unhelpful servant or perhaps an unruly pet – slaved to a master content to spend his life as easily as coin. The love and respect which had once flowed from the Pilgrim's promises were long gone, so absent as to have never existed. He might die without ever seeing Tuul or the final victory his arrival presaged.

'I have the will. I can serve. I shall endure.'

Pustrus nodded. Something throbbed wetly at his neck and he turned away to cough up a writhing gobbet of maggots and mucus. 'Then that is enough. Keep your choir of lesser lights close – I will need their power again before the final temple falls.' He looked heavenwards, momentarily distracted. 'It hurts just to look at it,' he murmured.

'What does?'

Pustrus' gaze snapped back to Weryn and he sneered. 'The light!' he snapped. 'Can't you see it?'

Weryn looked up. The clouds above were grey and white and streaked with green. Fire flickered across the skies where the orbital elements were establishing superiority or hunting for sport. There was light and fire, but it did not seem hateful to his eyes.

'No?' he said meekly. Again that spasm of self-revulsion shook through him.

'Such weak gifts. Give thanks to the Pilgrim that he entertained your low efforts for so long. There is a war to be won now, the light to be finally put out.' He gestured with one gnarled gauntlet towards the walls. 'We must take their hope from them – one and all – or else the cycle will only ever continue. Half of their bitter Imperium burns beyond their reach and it galls them, every single day. They know their time is short. The hour of the reaper is upon them and the scythe falls.'

'I believe you, lord,' Weryn said and nodded eagerly, like an obedient canid. Perhaps he was at the lowest ebb of his pride now or perhaps he had remembered at last how to love the lash – no matter the hand that wielded it.

Pustrus snuffled appreciatively and turned away from him. He had lowered to the ground now, the power within him earthed back into the warp. 'Do not dawdle, little witch,' he said. 'The Destroyer has need of you at the front. He wishes to give you a gift.'

'A–' Weryn swallowed and looked down at the ravaged corpse of his fellow prophet. One of many, for death was never singular but sevenfold. 'Is there not time to see to them? They fell in service of the faith. Do we not have a duty to the dead?'

Pustrus scoffed. 'They are *dead*, little witch,' he explained, as though to a small child. 'We can mourn for them when the war is done. Let pox take their bones and raise them up for the Grandfather-God. Else it is all for nothing. You are young, yet perhaps one day it will be you who pronounces judgement upon worlds.'

'I understand, lord. You honour me.'

'I educate you,' Pustrus huffed. 'There is a difference. Go now. The Destroyer will share with you the newest gift of the Plaguefather.'

The advance seemed to have slowed as Weryn made his way haltingly to the front.

Here the Titans' ravages were more evident. Tanks had been reduced to burning ruins, still sputtering and smouldering, metal edged red and white in the devastation. Bodies lay about them – the seared and broken bones of the cult auxiliaries alongside the shattered armour of the Death Guard. One of the Astartes had been hewn clean in half, and clawed impotently at the fused glass of the ground. Black blood trickled from between its lips as it tried to speak and the entrails which hung from its rent armour wormed and squirmed with unnatural endurance.

Weryn looked up from the ruined warrior and saw Ulgrath staring at him. The Destroyer's features were inscrutable, too worn and warped to truly gauge his reaction. He reached out with one black gauntlet and gestured for Weryn to join him at his side.

'The Pilgrim wished for you to see this, before the end,' Ulgrath crooned. 'He wanted you to see the god's gift, and a world made free.'

'He did?' Weryn's brow creased with confusion and suspicion. Till now the Death Guard had treated him as an annoyance, as a pet, a reminder of the world's failure to revolt. Now Ulgrath extended his confidences, as though Weryn had proven himself in some indeterminate way and was now worthy.

'Of course he did!' Ulgrath rasped enthusiastically. 'He is very fond of your efforts upon Velua. Very pleased at your progress unaided. He sends us along to hasten the work now that the False Angels have fled.'

'Then by all means, lord, show me.'

Ulgrath chuckled and swept his arm about. The tanks that had survived were idling, squat barrels angled towards the enemy's holy walls. 'I showed you before, my friend, the fire of the god. Now see it directed and unleashed by my order. In the name of Grommulus Tuul and the dark master he serves. By the guidance of dread Mortarion. For the Plague God and his glory. I give you victory!'

The armoured divisions of the Astartes began to clank and

ring with thunder. They braced, stabilised, and began to fire. First in small numbers and then with growing confidence. Weryn watched, dumbstruck, until he was forced to cover his ears. The prophet hunkered down on his haunches and rocked as the relentless barrage began.

The world began to burn in the fires of the apocalypse.

The first indication of the defenders' doom was the low rumble of distant thunder. Men and women rose to the firing stoops upon the walls and gazed out. The horizon was shrouded in fog and smoke where the battle had been joined. No word had come from the Legio and now the world shook.

The air began to scream. First as the shells hurtled from the heavens, then again as they detonated. The void shields above the primary walls flared hot and white then rippled into a refracted rainbow of light. The shells which hit vanished in a flash, disappearing as they were shunted into the warp. More came, and this time they detonated just above the shuddering barrier.

The shields joined the air in screaming. Where the shells burst they bled fire. Green-white and eternally in motion, the fire flickered and spun across the voids. The interplay between the ancient, tainted fire and the active shields sent migraine-bright pulses across the dome of the voids, keening and wailing. The fire moved as though aware, with a wilful and questing *need* to consume. In the days when it had been forged that had been an almost superstitious supposition. Now it was entirely true. It burn-crawled across the skies and the void shields shivered beneath its probing advance.

The shields broke. They shattered with a burst of ozone odour and a shockwave of displaced air. The sentient flame rained down from above in great sheets, crackling with malice. Laughter whispered in the midst of it, daemonic and inhuman, mocking the defiance of the defenders who now found themselves trapped beneath its hungry gaze.

The fire found the first of the soldiers quickly. Savlar, their armour ramshackle and badly maintained, caught alight as it coiled about them. The phosphex bit and burrowed. Flesh ran like tallow, stone ceased to be. Metal flowed molten and the guns creaked and shuddered as their mechanisms fused and burned and broke. Everything was alight.

The Savlar were not alone in their suffering. Whether soldiers wore the bronze armour of the Hoplites or the sacred plate of the Sisterhood, they burned. Men and women hurled themselves from the walls rather than endure the agony. Some fell to their knees, blindly trying to end their own lives with their weapons. Yet their guns were useless slag and their blades had turned to liquid in their sheaths. All that was left for them to do was die, their ruptured eyes weeping blood and vitreous humour down their burn-scarred cheeks.

The second volley hit moments later. The shells no longer had to fight the turgid shields and instead glided, near gracefully, to impact the lower structure of the walls and the gate. Metal and stone buckled and burst apart before the phosphex began to crawl from the impact craters. The walls groaned as gravity finally asserted itself. The third bombardment was almost unnecessary but it struck home regardless. More thunder. More fire. The walls were melting as the phophex moved within it, the fire of the god, the flame of unmaking let loose. All the horrors of Old Night and the blackest moments of the Heresy slid forth. The flame laughed as it killed, as it reshaped the defence in mere moments, as it drove more from the walls and cast the pall of despair out across the ailing city.

Weryn watched from a distance through magnoculars. Even though it was happening to the enemy, a foe he had hated all his life, it was horrific to observe as it unfolded. He had seen daemons walk and summoned them by his own hand, and yet to watch the fire as it coiled and rose – alive and animate – was something strangely unnerving. The wind whipped up as the artillery fired once more. Ashes drifted down from the walls with the stink of human fat cooking and the screams were carried on the sudden zephyrs of hot air and dust.

'We never knew,' Weryn whispered. 'How could we have known? We thought we could tear this world down with our hands but we were children, playing at war.' He shook his head and slumped down onto his knees in the muck of the murdered world. He felt the filth seep into the fabric, rendering it yet more profaned. 'We knew nothing about the necessary evils for victory. I understand that now... Now as I watch the world begin to die at last.'

There were tears of awe and terror upon his cheeks, burning and rancid as Prophet Weryn knew revelation at last.

Chapter Twenty-Five

THE SHIELD OF ANGELS

KNIGHTS AND WOLVES

BREAKOUT

'Say nothing unless I address you,' Gaheris said as they walked.

Aneirin nodded and struggled to keep pace. Ever since their arrival the Champion had become implacable. Nothing would keep him from their objective now nor dissuade him from his course. *Not that it had been any different during the transit,* Aneirin thought grimly. The Champion had kept his own counsel in the long marches since Velua. When he was not training or praying he spent his time communing with the Navigators and waiting, fevered in his desperation, for astropathic word.

Nothing had come. No crusade missives. No word from the sainted primarch or from Marshal Urtrix. And no word from Velua, the world they had defended and abandoned. The world they had betrayed. All the astropaths had heard from that world was screaming and suffering.

'As you will, Champion,' Aneirin said at last. The young warrior was still unsure as to why he had been chosen. Gaheris had swept into the embarkation decks with fire in his eyes and had gestured across at the warriors of Crusader Squad Fidelitas.

'You will be my honour guard,' Gaheris had growled before his gauntleted hand had swept around to point at Aneirin. 'This one will be my equerry.'

That had been that. They had joined him upon the Overlord gunship which bore the name *Shield of Angels*. None had commented upon the irony inherent in such a choice, and the Champion had not seen fit to give it voice himself.

The stalemate yet held between loyalists and traitors as fleet elements gathered themselves together and exchanged tactical information. Already the ships of the Black Templars were blazing their way to the fore where their strength could best be used – like the chosen warriors of an ancient army, preparing to face their opposite numbers.

None held the advantage, not truly. The Death Guard's stance had shifted from overconfidence to a wise caution. The plague fleet seemed content to idle and exude its malice out into the universe. It waited like a pustule upon creation's face as fat craft hurried between the hulks with insectoid industry.

'It would not do to force battle,' the Champion had declared. 'Not yet. Not without making sure that we are where we must be.'

Looking around the interior of the *Wyrmslayer Queen* Aneirin was more and more convinced that the Champion's vision had shone true. It was a ship of war that brimmed with the trappings of distant Fenris. Others amidst the crusade detachment had spoken of the Space Wolves in tones variously approving and judgemental. Fine warriors, true enough, but rumour-shrouded and strange. Their cults were not those of the Imperial Creed. They burned older and stranger – replete with old gods and secrets. They revered the God-Emperor, true enough, as the Allfather of Man and lord of their pantheon, but it was not a wholesome worship.

'Is the God-Emperor not one of the gods of Fenris? Just as He is the Walking Sun of my home world?' Aneirin had asked, overeager.

'Perhaps He is the chief of their gods,' Barisan had allowed carefully, 'but a son of Fenris would never tell you that plain.'

Aneirin wondered if the daughters of the winter world would be more forthcoming.

They marched through the great vessel, up from the landing decks, through corridors etched with runes and hung with trophies and talismans. The signs of old battle had been repaired and smoothed over, but the disparity in the metalwork still shone through to the trained eye. The marks of claws and blades which would never entirely fade sat alongside the signs of bio-acid scarring. It was fine work, if hurried, but as they advanced upon the bridge Aneirin noted more and more of it. Atrocity had befallen this ship at some point in its past. Dire enough to etch its way into its bones and humble its proud soul.

They came armed and armoured, the Champion at their head. The Armour of Faith was immaculate – freshly treated by the Chapter's Techmarines with the rites of the Emperor-Omnissiah, and blessed by the Chaplains. He smelled of machine oils, sacred unguents and incense. As he strode the corridors of the vessel, mighty though it was, they seemed smaller. The Champion was too massive for the world. To look upon him was to see the Chapter's faith carved from the firmament and given a place at the fore.

He had been chosen by the God-Emperor, Aneirin thought. The Champion had been *chosen* through the holy visions and given his sacred task – and such a warrior had selected Aneirin to be his personal equerry. Even if he was forbidden from speaking, it was still a singular honour.

He looked back at his brothers and Barisan met his gaze with his own cold scrutiny. The old warrior had been subdued since the flight from Velua. Aneirin was not sure he could blame him.

They arrived before the great bronze doors of the bridge, gazing up at the inscribed history of the vessel and the line Helvintr. These too were marked with battle damage.

'Into the lair, then,' Gaheris grumbled. His hand went to the Black Sword, as though seeking guidance or comfort. 'Let us see what fangs this she-wolf possesses.'

The bridge of the *Wyrmslayer Queen* was ancient and proud, well manned and orderly, and yet it was utterly lacking by every metric Aneirin had assimilated during his brief time as a warrior of the Chapter. It was not made for his transhuman bulk. It felt cramped and limiting even though it dwarfed the humans who attended it. Still, it was impressive enough for the dominion of a rogue trader. There had been little enough reason for Aneirin to associate with such fringe elements of the Imperium during their own crusade. He considered them, in execution, more similar to the Savlar than to any of the other forces he had fought alongside.

The crew were a mix of Imperial Navy order and finery and Fenrisian hauberks and leather. All of them were looking at the knot of black-armoured warriors who had suddenly graced their sanctum. The command throne faced away from them, and Aneirin watched as a lone figure rose from it and turned to behold them.

She was striking for a mortal. Half her face was inked with winding knotwork tattoos in the rictus of a wolf's skull. Her scalp was half shaved, surmounted by a shock of auburn hair. Like fire upon snow. She smiled when she saw them; not in welcome, but a wry acknowledgement.

'To what do we owe the pleasure of an Emperor's Champion?' she barked with a laugh. 'You are not the first warriors of your clans to set foot upon my deck, but I dare say you have the advantage of rank.' She tilted her head towards the viewscreens. 'There's something to be said for the Allfather's timing as well, eh?'

Armour clattered behind them and the squad turned as one. Even the Champion seemed awestruck for a moment.

Before them stood a warrior of the God-Emperor's own Custodian Guard.

Every warrior went to their knees. Even the Champion knelt to honour the Custodian. He looked up, tears in his eyes.

'Praise be. He guided me true. He led me to where I was needed most.'

'Rise,' the Custodian said, as though he was unsurprised by their presence and annoyed by the intrusion. 'What are you doing here?'

'We bring much-needed salvation,' Gaheris said.

'Yes, Augustus,' the warrior-woman said as she interposed herself between the Custodian and the Champion. 'They bring much-needed salvation.' Her eyes flickered back to the view-screen. 'We're all friends here, Augustus, unless you would have us face the enemy with fewer friends and guns?'

The Custodian looked from the captain to the Champion and then back again. Such beings as he, Aneirin imagined, were beyond mortal pettiness, but he still fancied that the Custodian's lip curled with distaste.

'It remains, as ever, your ship of mongrels, captain,' he said. 'I only ask that you keep them to their place.'

'Does our presence offend you?' Gaheris asked. The Champion rose and stepped forward to look up at the Custodian's pale and perfect features. 'We serve His will, just as you do.'

'Just as I do...' Augustus shook his head and stepped closer to the Champion. 'It is bold for any warrior of the Astartes to claim as such.'

'We are His most faithful, sons of the Eternal Crusade. I will suffer insult from no one, Custodian, least of all you.'

Augustus laughed. The sound was of such surpassing rarity that even the wolf-queen paused.

'As you say, Champion. So long as you do not keep me from my duty we shall have no quarrel.'

'How magnanimous,' Gaheris rumbled. 'We are all joined here in common purpose.' He pointed out beyond the viewscreen. 'To see our enemies driven before us and the God-Emperor's way made clear.' He turned to the captain. 'What auguries do you pursue? Why have you found this course above others?'

'We have a magos astrocartographic sifting the tides of the warp, and my own meagre talents,' she said. Her eyes sparkled as she downplayed her own gifts. 'We know we are close to finding it, the Gate, but even before the enemy appeared the warp's tides fluctuated to some hellish design. As inconstant as war.'

'We will have our Navigators collate their findings with yours,' Gaheris affirmed.

Aneirin watched on, dumbstruck while the others stood silent behind him. Beyond the screens the plague fleet loomed, still and silent as deep-ocean predators.

'That is well,' said the captain. 'First, though, we must deal with the enemy that bars our path.'

'What path do you speak of?' Gaheris asked. 'Why are you here, alone?'

'We seek a new path across the Great Rift,' the captain said. 'We have been dispatched by the regent himself and we know that we are close. If I did not know it before then I do now. Look what stands against us.'

'What can you tell me of your enemy?'

'He calls himself Grommulus Tuul,' the captain said. 'A plague-ridden monster who claims to be of the blood of the old Legions.'

Gaheris scoffed aloud. 'It is a sickness of the times that we are confronted by such horrors in force. Yet still you stand against it, bearing only your oaths to the Emperor and the authority of your Warrant. It is admirable.'

'I will do my part, Champion,' the captain said and spared a look to the Custodian, Augustus. 'We all will.'

'Then the way is clear,' Gaheris said and spread his arms. 'We fight our way free of the predations of the wicked.'

Aneirin watched the Champion and thought that he understood. Gaheris had come here to find the measure of the captain and understand her place in his vision. The enemy's presence was like a sign from the heavens. Here was the woman he had sought. Here was a mission from the regent himself. It had the touch of destiny about it, even to Aneirin's limited experience. The Imperial fleet had grown and merged, enough to give the enemy pause. Now all that remained was to take advantage of that passing caution.

The fleet began to move in a great sweeping arc, out from the translation point and towards the plague fleet. The hulking behemoths of the Archenemy hung, unbothered by their opposite numbers as they moved into place. Craft still drifted lazily from ship to ship like flies around corpses.

This close the Imperial ships could see the changes wrought upon the once proud vessels, their ancient patterns twisted. They had grown strange and unreal in their long sojourns through the warp. Whether they came from the Eye or the Maelstrom or stranger seas besides, the ships sworn to Grommulus Tuul were dead hulks filled with unnatural life.

They should not be void-worthy. Holes gaped in the flanks of the immense ships, glistening wetly where fluids had congealed or vomited forth into frozen belts of debris around them. Boarding craft and skiffs forced their way out of great pore-like apertures in the surface of the vessels. Where the plate had been flayed back, by accident or injury, flesh undulated with constant peristaltic motion.

By comparison the Imperial profiles were strong and proud – rambunctiously martial and declaring to all who would look upon them mankind's forthright mastery of the galaxy. Whether cross-marked or rune-etched, all bore the Imperial aquila proudly. It glowed beneath the weak light of the distant stars alongside great golden inscriptions of prayer tracts and perched above marks of aversion and eyes of warding. The great ships of the line, of the crusade and of Task Force Saturnine, slid forward and turned, speaking with a single voice. Thunder cut the void as the great guns committed themselves. Macrocannon shells hurtled across the distance between the fleets even as lance fire cut through the abyss in moments. All became fire and wrath. Across all the ships of the Imperial fleet the Black Templars began to sing, their rough hymns rising above the tumult, hurled forth in defiance of the darkness.

From the fleet of Grommulus Tuul there came only laughter, before their cyclopean vessels began their own ponderous manoeuvres and joined the battle in earnest.

Chapter Twenty-Six

FROM THE WALLS

IN HIS SHADOW

THE HIDDEN BLADE

The enemy drove them back from the walls with fire and hate.

Irinya cursed the foe and their twisted gods for the daemonic flame they had brought against them. She had seen the sacred stones crack, metal run like water, and the bodies of the slain burst apart into ashes and entrails. The stink of it was still hot and urgent about them – caught on the never-ending winds, spiralling through the streets like the promise of contagion. Cultists surged into the breach in great living waves, banners swaying in the caustic breeze. They scrambled over the baked rocks and fired as they ran straight into the lines of Imperial fire.

Well-disciplined shots found them. The Sisters, the Hoplites and even the Savlar claiming their own tally of enemy dead. Swollen bodies burst in meaty showers of flesh, bone and pus. As one fell another took its place in the line. Irinya lost count of the twisted faces she had put down. Her bolter rounds found target after target and reduced them to slurry and mulched flesh.

Few of the cultists wore armour now. Robes trailed from them in tattered streamers of filthy fabric and armour had been cast aside. They fought with rifles so rusted, their machine spirits so abused, that they jammed more often than they fired. Men and women stalked ahead of the firing line with machetes and other blades. Some stumbled and fell or took las-bolt, bolter shell or bullet to the chest or head and tumbled into the dirt. Their comrades trod them beneath their feet, forcing them down into the muck and rubble. On they came as the sound of bells tolling echoed all around, catching upon the broken masonry and ringing strangely through the shattered cloisters.

'Fall back!' someone was screaming. 'Fall back! Rank discipline! Fall back and fire!'

The Savlar's rate of fire hitched and focused. Irinya turned through the smoke to see Commissar Rugrenz striding forward. He raised his bolt pistol and fired, turned and fired again. He gestured with his free hand and the Savlar obeyed. Grenades hurtled over his head and detonated in the ranks of the cultists. Bodies flew, limbs hurtled skywards. Bursts of gore sent crimson rain over the heretics. They gloried in their baptism, rejoicing as they were anointed in the infected lifeblood of their brethren.

The hail of loyalist fire and the narrow confines of the breached gates funnelled the enemy towards them into perfectly constructed kill-zones. Soldiers fed shells into entrenched weapons positions where ornamental fountains had once sat. Statues had been toppled and reinforced to form barricades. The defenders had not been idle – Irinya's hand had crafted defence in depth for the enemy to break upon.

The Sisters stood like the displaced statues amidst the multitudes, singing as they fought. Bolt-shells streaked across the battlefield to brutalise the enemy. Not a single cultist had managed to get into melee range, but it was only a matter of time.

Soon the Sisters would feel the blades of the enemy against their armour.

Irinya could almost feel it already; the inevitability of death. Las-impacts found her armour and deflected harmlessly. Bullets were turned aside. She felt the plate burr and whine as she moved back, firing as she went. They fought their way back across mosaic floors stained with blood and mud and ichor; back behind row after row of rockcrete barriers. The main devotional roads to the walls were littered with bodies as the Sisters and their allies retreated.

Missiles streaked the sky as, to the east, in the shadow of the great reservoirs, Sister Eloise roused the Exorcist launchers once more. The enemy's barrage had lessened beneath the counter-assault, but it still came. Behind the Sisters a bell-tower detonated in a shower of metal and stone, the bells themselves screaming as they were mangled.

As if in response to their death cries, Irinya heard the sound of other bells tolling in the distance. Somewhere beyond the walls and drawing ever closer, they rang on. Irinya felt her head pulse and ache at the sound. An unnatural thing, oily upon the air and upon the mind. She gritted her teeth as she hurled herself over one of the barricades, taking cover alongside her Sisters.

'All forces have withdrawn from the wall sectors, canoness,' Josefine said. The woman was helmed, rendering her impassive and cold despite the eagerness in her voice. Her whole squad, indeed the entire preceptory, trembled with nervous agitation. This was what they had been waiting for. This moment, when battle was finally joined.

'Good,' Irinya said with a nod. 'We will continue the retreat to the central shrines. No matter the losses, we shall make them pay for every inch of ground.'

'Aye, canoness,' Agata put in from the other side of Irinya. She hefted her flamer approvingly. 'Finally they come close enough to burn again. I will send every last one of the bastards to meet their gods in person.'

'Praise be unto the Emperor for delivering the enemy to us,' Irinya finished. 'Though our walls are broken, we hold true to our faith.' She holstered her bolter and drew Truth's Kiss. The blade ignited with a crackle of caged lightning, like the God-Emperor's own radiance. 'Send word to the Mechanicus contingent. Enact protocol Omega.' She paused, hesitating. 'Send word to Eloise that Lethe should be held in reserve.'

'As you will,' Josefine said and turned to find a vox-caster.

All was flux as the artillery duelled overhead and the warriors clashed in the streets below, the sacred against the unholy. Still the lesser walls held. The barricades rose higher as the Sisters moved through the defensive lines. The first were merely waist height, but the lines further along the highways were six feet tall, with platforms behind them from which the defenders could fire. Each had become a bastion in miniature, manned by the faithful.

Cultists hurled themselves at the barriers, emboldened by the ringing of the bells. They scrambled up, fingers clawing at the stonework, weapons sheathed or left forgotten. Irinya stepped up onto the makeshift firing step and swung the blade about. A head tumbled free in a gush of foetid blood. Flies fountained out of the wound with such intensity that the corpse crumpled, empty and used up.

'This is His world!' Irinya shouted. 'We are His people!' Her voice boomed out over the conflagration, stilling the sound of battle for but a moment. Soldiers looked up at her, haloed in the sword's light, spattered with the blood of the enemy. 'No traitor or monster can stand against that! An army bearing His faith cannot be undone. Stand with me, brothers and sisters! Fight and die in His name!'

She swept the blade around again and carved open the chittering face of a cultist, breaking chitinous growths and driving him into the dust.

'His world! His people!'

'His world!' voices clamoured. 'His people!'

Agata was beside her and her flamer spoke at last. Bodies and living enemies were caught in the fire, rendered into silhouettes before they were reduced to ashes. Bolter fire peppered the ranks, bursting amidst the malignant throng. Irinya saw one cultist with a vestigial head growing from the side of her neck scythed down, the gut-shot spilling her entrails and bowels out in a near-liquid tide. Yet Veluans also fell, clawed down by the enemy, brass armour sundered. Savlar fought with their bare hands or with crude trench clubs; they wielded knives and bayonets as the enemy continued to rush in, unceasing.

Everything was reduced to a smear of grey and black and red. The combat had become constant. Electric. Men and women fought for their lives, for the barest strips of land, for the salvation or damnation of their very souls. Behind the defenders the cliff-face magnificence of the shrines was burning. Impacts marred the white marble and gold relief like blisters. Black smoke and fire damage ran rampant along the frescoes and murals. Millennia of history was being reduced to dust before her eyes. The broken statues of saints and heroes stared up at her pleadingly, their faces shattered. The ruined visage of Macharius lay beside the cleaved bust of Sebastian Thor.

Irinya would have wept but there was no more time for tears. Every atrocity served to harden her heart – to ensure that they would give the enemy nothing. Other worlds had broken in the face of this foe.

I shall not be found wanting, she thought. *I shall do my duty, even unto death.*

A hush fell over the battle as though all present sensed a

change in the world. Behind the massed cultists and their countless dead came the true masters. A pall of silence drifted from the unholy warriors as they finally made their presence known, striding through the broken gates and over the ruined walls as though already entitled to them.

Bile rose in her throat to look at them. The Black Templars had been paragons of martial zealotry yet these Heretic Astartes were bitter and twisted reflections. Trophies hung from their armour – some fresh and some dried by time – in grisly displays of power. Runes in no human tongue wept pus and acid down the front of their armour and horns jutted from their helms or from ruptured bare skin. Some carried swords and axes, their handles chased in human bone, and others carried strange weapons – great gurgling chem-sprayers like unlit flamers, weapons that bulged with organic sacs or writhed with internal motion. Even their bolters were bizarrely overgrown with rust, verdigris and whorls of bone. They were all caught in some cycle of becoming – life to death and death to life, forever.

At their feet trundled a horde of tiny Neverborn, jabbering and clambering up the warriors' legs as they cooed and burbled. One blew a bubble of mucus, giggling as it burst with a rancid pop.

Seven warriors formed the first rank and behind them came another seven. Seven upon sevenfold seven, as though in mockery of the sacred worlds of the Golden Chain. Faces twisted with cruel glee, whether they were shrunken and pinched or bloated and obscene. The Traitor Space Marines stalked forwards, presiding over the slaughter like Knight house nobles at court.

Where the Plague Marines walked, hope died and despair took root. The sacred stones cracked beneath their tread. Vermin and insects wriggled out from between holes in the flagstones and abased themselves before the advance, before

being crushed underfoot or snapped up by the giggling daemonic carpet of bodies.

'Shrinesworn!'

A voice rose above the clamour and Irinya turned to find its
source. Colonel Yitrov stood tall, plasma pistol raised, as he
fired at the approaching demigods.

'With me, sons of Velua! For the God-Emperor! In the name
of the saints whom we protect – stand firm and fire! Our reward
lies beyond!'

The Veluans cheered moments before they drowned their
agreement with fire. Entrenched heavy-weapons teams opened
up with heavy bolters and plasma cannons. Light and fury
lanced across the courtyards before the walls. The cultists
disappeared, atomised in the opening volleys. All that remained
were ashes and gobbets of flesh, scraps and smears where men
had once stood.

The Death Guard strode through the hail of fire, unbroken.
At the centre of the line of seven stood a warrior whose armour
was blackened by taint and time. He smirked as he raised his
own weapon and took aim. The pistol glimmered green as it
charged and then unleashed a searing bolt of unctuous light
directly into Yitrov's torso. The colonel flew backwards, his
flesh already sloughing away, burning and blackening in the
blast of intense radiation.

'Bastards!' someone screamed from the Veluan ranks. More
fire found the Death Guard and they strode into it, through
it, with utter contempt. The rad-scarred killer who had ended
Yitrov turned with a grin and saw Irinya at last. She saw him
point and the first line of Traitor Astartes pivoted towards her
squad.

'We need to move,' Irinya hissed. She swept Truth's Kiss
around and pointed back towards the central shrines. Even
burning they would offer greater protection than the open

courtyard. 'Phased tactical retreat,' she instructed. 'Spread the word. I want all elements mobile and fighting. Savlar to the rearguard.' She cursed under her breath. 'Prime all delaying methods and give the order. Omega is authorised.'

She swallowed and began to move. Her Sisters came with her, pausing only to turn and fire.

'We will seek our salvation in His shadow.'

Ulgrath forged on through the mud and blood as he always had. War was many things, yet above all it was unchanging. The grind and toil was the same as it had ever been. Barbarus, Galaspar, Terra, Velua. World after world, all blighted with the same sickness. Humanity's desire for war was insatiable and absolute. It had carried the species to the stars and placed the galaxy in its palm. Yet what had come of that? The Emperor's ambitions had been still-born and Horus' own dreams had died. Those who remained had embraced ignorance or exile and all that had been gained tumbled into the abyss.

Tuul would turn it into a moral lesson. He would dissect philosophies as easily as he did bodies, deconstruct theorems as readily as the sacred sites he integrated into his ship. Ulgrath didn't care enough to envy his brother. Both of them had followed the primarch to war, once, and now they fought other wars for a new master. In such a changed galaxy, Tuul remained a thinker and Ulgrath was as he had ever been – a breaker of things. A Destroyer.

Ulgrath sneered as he strode the avenues of power and watched the dreams of self-proclaimed holy men die around them. He paused only to unmake the edifices of Imperial rule. One shot from his pistol and statues melted to so much useless slag; he lashed out with his hand and the skull of a preacher-militant was crushed.

'They are nothing, Dakren,' he said with a laugh. 'Weak little men hiding behind their walls of marble and gold. Just like their false god, eh?'

Dakren's helm clicked and realigned, making his phials shake and jangle. The Biologus Putrifier's beaked proboscis tilted one way and then the other before he responded. His voice was a tortured whisper, warped by centuries of self-experimentation and chemical exposure.

'Perhaps the Pilgrim overestimated this particular knot of resistance. It would not be the first time he has allowed his... sense of whimsy to interfere.'

'Ah, but now, he has a higher purpose,' Ulgrath scoffed. 'And all of us are bound to follow his lead.'

Autogun and las-fire pattered off their armour like soft rains and they strolled onwards through it. Dakren reached up and pulled a glass orb from one of the chains adorning his armour. He twisted it, shook it once, and cast it in a smooth arc up and over a nearby balcony. It detonated with a wet *crump* and the sound of breaking glass. Greenish gas drifted up in a miniature mushroom cloud a second before the screams started. A man in the bronze of the shrine world's defenders hurled himself over the edge and impacted the ground in a spray of blood and vomit. Dakren chuckled again.

'Our purpose is as it always was. We exist to dispel the lies of unworthy lords. Whether they sit on their thrones amidst the toxin-clouds of Barbarus or within the heart of Terra, their lies must be repaid with blood.'

And He is a lie, Ulgrath thought. *He always was. There is no truth but the Grandfather and no way but in the footsteps of his ascendant servant.*

Ulgrath had tired of the Long War, content only to surrender himself to its apathy and drawn-out spite. He had followed Tuul precisely because he ranged widely and often, almost never returning to the Plague Planet – but now there was new purpose and vigour in the galaxy. The Rift had opened and the entire pathetic nest-hill of the Imperium had boiled over with their petty soldiery.

They call it a crusade. As though any of them truly understand the undertaking. Even Guilliman has forgotten what it means. Weakling wars for a lesser age, devoid of the purity of the Long War. We have split the galaxy and Guilliman's weak-blooded crusade will never mend it again.

'Still,' Ulgrath allowed, 'there is yet sport to be had. They cower behind their walls and we rain fire upon them. They dig trenches and raise barricades and we stride through them. Against us they are nothing. Will their faith protect them, come the end?'

'Did it protect us?' Dakren laughed. 'All faith in Him is doomed to failure.' He hefted up another grenade and threw it ahead of them, reducing an Imperial firing position to molten flesh. The Guardsmen screeched as their skin boiled away and their muscles ran together like wax, till they were a mere ball of mewling meat wrapped around their heavy bolter. 'Their belief is simply...' Dakren waved his hand in the air, seeking the words. 'A failed hypothesis. A flawed experiment.'

'Yet the seers would argue that He moves in the firmament, alight and alive once again – that the fire we have kindled in the galaxy moves with Him and through Him.' Ulgrath chuckled bleakly. 'The self-denying godhead shining like a star to remake the galaxy entire.'

'Stranger things have happened,' Dakren muttered with a jangling shrug. 'The sooner we burn places like this to kindling the better. Ten thousand years the mind-sickness of their faith has ravaged the body of the Imperium while *true* divinity waits in the wings. I wonder sometimes why they have allowed it when the Word Bearers suffered so for their faith.' He had drawn his injector pistol and began to take idle pot-shots at the enemy as they retreated. There was little sport in shooting men in the back, but Ulgrath was sure that Dakren only regretted that he couldn't see their expressions as the toxins took them. There was a delight to be had in the strychnine grins of the dying and the last gasps of the hypoxic. He had savoured so many of the ways in which men could die, down the millennia, and he never truly tired of it.

'I would have liked to have fought the Black Templars here,' Ulgrath enthused. 'There is at least joy to be had in fighting them, I've found. They are not as ossified in their faith as the sons of Lorgar proved to be. It burns in them, raw and vital, so intensely that it puts fear into their fellows.' Ulgrath snorted with laughter. 'Can you imagine? That other brotherhoods of their dilute bloodlines actually turn away from them for being too devoted to what they imagine He might have willed? Eternal crusaders, they claim to be. Proud sons of a stone-hearted father. Yet their faith is anathema to so many who claim to be His champions!'

The two warriors advanced in lockstep as they conversed. The monotony of their stroll was broken only when their arms snapped up to take a shot or to throw a grenade. Death followed with them – not just in the presence of their brothers in arms but as a consequence of their tainted being. The ornamental gardens which bordered the winding thoroughfares between the great shrines wilted and died at their very presence. Fragrant blossoms crumbled in on themselves as the concentrated plague-essence and radiation bled from the pair.

They advanced out and into a square that dominated the space before the central basilica. It was, from a certain point of view, a truly beautiful space – dominated by artful ornamental fountains which curved around a central statue of the Emperor. It rose, carved from pale marble, crowned in laurels and with a flaming sword held high. Looking upon it Ulgrath wasn't sure whether it matched his memories. The Emperor, on the rare occasions that the Destroyer had seen Him, had been a numinous thing of deceits and falsehoods. The image raised upon a million worlds was dubiously true to a being who had never known sincerity.

Before the central statue a small congregation had gathered. Grey-robed figures knelt before the statue as though offering obeisance, even in the heart of war. As everything closed in about them and threatened to overturn their world in fire, the figures knelt – placid and uncaring as the conflict drew ever nearer.

Perhaps, Ulgrath imagined, it was the woman who held their attention.

At the base of the statue, black-armoured and with a whip in her hand, the Sister of Battle stalked before the grey-robed figures. Occasionally the whip would snap up, tasting the air like a serpent's tongue, before it dropped to kiss the ground once more. Lightning crackled and danced along the length of the whip, betraying it as a power weapon.

Ulgrath and Dakren closed the distance even as other brothers of the Legion gathered behind them, their weapons already raised. Braziers burned behind the Sister, hiding the lesser statues that sat alongside the hateful visage of the Emperor from view. Ulgrath chortled to himself as he drew near to the backs of the kneeling figures, following their gaze to the armoured warrior who presided over the circus of faith.

'You will die here,' Ulgrath said. 'My brothers and I will unleash such horrors upon you and your flock. Yet you could be spared our wrath if you forsake your false god.' He gestured with one corroded gauntlet towards the statue. It stood towering above them, haloed in the fire of the shrine's ravishment, as though it burned with its own internal light. 'Renounce Him. Throw yourself at our mercy and perhaps, just perhaps, you might be spared long enough to embrace the Grandfather's consumptive love.'

The woman laughed. The sound was so low that Ulgrath almost thought he had imagined it. He leant forward, eyes fixed upon the warrior woman. She met his gaze without fear and the whip tasted the air again. No one moved. No one fired. They would not end her without Ulgrath's say-so, and he knew it. Part of him wanted to milk the moment until she finally broke and begged. Till there was nothing left but the same banal acceptance which had been theirs these last millennia.

Yet defiance burned in her eyes – ripe with the hate that had been bred into her – and Ulgrath laughed again to see it. Her hate was a tarnished mirror of his own: lesser, but still worthy of consideration.

'I will not bow to your daemon god,' she hissed. 'I am here to fulfil a single purpose.'

'And what purpose is that?'

'I am here to give the word, and nothing more,' she said. He could see the fear in her. Quivering and wretched. She shook before them and yet she endured, motivated by fear and faith in equal measure. 'The word...'

She paused, hesitating, and then drew one deep, shuddering breath and pressed on.

'The word is Purgatus.'

And at that word the figures before her jerked and spasmed, suddenly ramrod-straight, as *things* moved beneath their robes and they began to screech.

Behind her, the statues that were not statues were suddenly in motion and the night was cut by the scream of saws and the bursts of flamers as the sacred damned of Velua were finally roused to the fight.

Chapter Twenty-Seven

THE WAY OF PAIN

THROUGH THE FIRE

WALLS OF FAITH

There was only pain.

The man who had once been Colonel Maxim Draszen knew absolute agony as it pulsed through him, down the ruin of his spine and through his tormented flesh. He could feel every plug and implant site which had been wired down his back as they wormed their way through his flesh to mesh with the branches of his nerves. There was fire in them now, burning and burning and consuming him whole. Endorphins and hyper-adrenals hammered along his bloodstream, fed in a never-ending deluge from tanks nestled at the base of his back. He was swathed in armour so that he was denied a release; protected so that his torment could continue. So that his punishment could be absolute.

He tried to scream but he couldn't. They had taken his tongue and his vocal cords so that he could speak no more heresy. The iron bar was still between his teeth, his jaw locked around it as the steroids tensed every single muscle. His hands were

shackled and a spike had been forced through his palms –
holding him in place. Transfixed, transformed, he knew only
what the helm-displays told him.

PENANCE THROUGH PAIN.

The words seared across his visual centres, weighted with
hypno-suggestive intent. His entire nervous system was in
turmoil, bombarded by overwhelming sensations and the
oppressive surety of his instructions. The words faded and he
could see the battlefield before him. Before, he had hidden
behind walls and directed the fire of great guns; now he was
the weapon. There was only the front line, rearing up to meet
him as the great engine to which he had been wed surged forward. One arm moved, barely directed by his conscious mind,
and found its target. The great saw-blade bit into ancient corroded ceramite and forced its way through. He felt the weight
of the Penitent Engine shift, forcing the Heretic Astartes down
and onto the pristine marble of the courtyard. He heard the
whine as the blade cut into the stonework, felt the shudder as
the enemy scrabbled and spasmed upon the weapon's edge.
Bolt-rounds pinged from the armoured cliff-face of the engine,
right next to his head. He felt a balm of peace spread across
his mind as he killed. There was peace here. True and lasting
peace if he just surrendered to the kill-urges of the machine
spirit and the sacred task that had been set for him.

KILL IN HIS NAME. DIE IN HIS NAME.

Then the words crashed back into his psyche like a brand and
spasmed silently around the iron bar lodged in his mouth. He
pulled back and the blade slid free in a rush of unnatural fluids.
He felt the engine turn, felt fire coil up the arteries of his arm
and then vomit forth as the flamer spoke in wrath and ruin.

He was dimly aware of other presences. There was another
great engine stalking through the ranks of the enemy. And
another. Another. Four in total. Around their feet gambolled

strange things that had once, he knew, been men. Not twisted by plague or warpcraft but shaped by the hands of the Mechanicus for the purpose of killing, slaved to cypher-words and kill-commands. The arco-flagellants hurled themselves into the fray with less control and less choice than he had. Everything that had been done to him was external, but their changes were hammered directly into the meat of their minds and the flesh of their bodies. Arms lashed out, tipped with cybernetic flails, their barbs tearing across the Heretic Astartes' armour and flesh. Cultists were shredded or hammered into the ground by pneu-mattocks. Cleavers split faces and claws tore heads apart as the psycho-indoctrinated killers waded through the enemy, streaked in gore. Their mouths moved constantly in a babble of non-sound, their minds ablaze with neurally inflicted hymns of castigation.

They boiled outwards from the statue's base and around the feet of the Penitent Engines. The flails swept like the motion of a scythe and the arco-flagellants followed through in great swinging arcs. Yet even they stalled against the mottled wall of the Death Guard. The Plague Marines held, locked together like a shield-wall, and began to push back.

Arco-flagellants tumbled like thrown dolls. Pneu-mattocks cracked the stone floor as they sprawled across it, and then pistoned them back up. One spun, flailing for the face of a Plague Marine hung with glass phials, only to be caught by the forearm. He watched as the Plague Marine *twisted* and the arco-flagellant's limb tore free in a welter of gore, the air suddenly spiced by the chemical tang of adrenalised blood. Atonal binharic screeches rose above the fray, eliciting another burst of agony through the Penitent Engine and the body it bore.

SALVATION IN SERVICE. A MARTYR'S DEATH.

Bodies tumbled away from the Plague Marines and the engine crushed them underfoot as it stalked into range. Weeping blades scraped against its armoured legs only to be driven back by the whirring saw-blades and the gouting flames. He barely felt the first impacts of bolt-shells as they blew away his legs. Another took him in the gut. He felt blood and viscera spatter against the engine's armoured back. He ignored it. There was only the joyous peace that came with killing.

Alarms sounded in his helmet, stinging the wounds that had once been his ears. His eyes tried in vain to blink as the screen flashed its near-incessant messages, but he no longer had eyelids. The mutilations were a gift. A sacred offering. His redemption...

REDEMPTION IN BLOOD. REDEMPTION IN SUFFERING. THIS IS THE WAY OF PAIN.

Something broke below him. Machine systems sirened as hydraulic fluid rushed from a severed tube. The man, the victim, the offering, felt the sudden simulacrum of the engine's agony scissor through him and his jaw clenched. His teeth broke around the bar. Blood and drool threatened to choke him as he raged and gurgled before the engine lurched forward and the co-mingled fluids were hurled forth.

It sank to its knees slowly: blade still slashing, flamer still seeking targets. Cultists crawled up and across the engine's shoulders. Pipes and clubs hammered at the armour. Blades finally found his supplicant flesh.

SURRENDER IS FAILURE. ONLY IN DEATH DOES – ONLY IN DEATH DOES

Someone was prising open the armoured plates of the engine. More shots burst around his head and hewed away more of his body. One arm exploded in an eruption of bone-shards and pulped flesh and he tried desperately to raise the other. Promethium gurgled impotently as the flamer failed to fire. His eyes locked wide as he watched the Plague Marines gather around him.

Rough gauntleted hands took hold of his shaven scalp and pulled his head back. His breath caught in his throat as he struggled. A blade was at his neck as one of the disfigured killers glowered down at him.

'An amusing diversion,' the bloated warrior slurred. 'Now at an end.'

He couldn't respond, even if he'd wanted to. He could only watch as the blade began to move.

The chassis shook with sudden impacts. Precision shots ripped open the promethium tanks and detonated a moment later. There was no time to scream, only the sudden release of fire and pain.

The last thing that the man who had once been Maxim Draszen saw was Canoness Irinya and her warriors as they strode through the flames, weapons raised.

They came through the fire like angels: bolters howling, flamers roaring, melta singing.

The Sisterhood had withdrawn and consolidated, gathering all their strength for one single moment. The others – the Savlar and the Veluans – had bought them that time. Even the criminals and the deserters had played their part once rendered into instruments of vengeance and penance.

Irinya didn't think of Draszen or the others as she bestrode their burning bones. They had performed as well as could be expected. No more and no less. She spared a glance across the square where one of the Penitent Engines still lumbered and fought as smoke gouted from the fluted exhausts at its back. Countless bodies littered the field, numerous cultists lying alongside the less common bodies of the Plague Marines. At least six, perhaps more, of the monsters lay dead. The ghoulish puppets of the arco-flagellants were breaking – reduced to smears of blood and bodily fluids, broken bones and shattered cybernetics. They had done their part. Sacrificial lambs to blood the enemy for the true battle.

She hurled herself forwards, no longer relying on her bolter, and Truth's Kiss bit through armour and corrupted flesh. Black blood thundered from between the rent plates and the Plague Marine staggered back, still aflame, before Oxanna's meltagun carved him in twain.

The lines met in earnest. Sisters were thrown aside or beaten down. Bolt-shells detonated against armour or punched through to explode within flesh. Irinya watched women pulped within their plate, blood hissing under pressure from between the interlocked segments. Eye-lenses burst outwards in a crimson rain, like tears of blood.

Still they fought on, each warrior knowing this might be their last stand, each consigned to eventual death in service. They stood in the shadows of saints and martyrs. How could they do less in His name? Behind them the great statue of the God-Emperor loomed. Haloed in fire, He was rendered vital and glorious, an icon carved of flame and gold.

He watches us, she thought, dazed. *He is with us!*

'The God-Emperor is with us!' she bellowed. 'Every step forward serves Him! Every death is an offering before His altar! Return these bastards to the earth! Back to the gutter which birthed them!'

'In His name!' her Sisters cried as one. They fought harder at her words. The air was thick with shells and shot, so that the clouds of enormous biting flies seemed drowned in the rush of sound and smoke.

Above, artillery scraped the sky as Sister Eloise's martial choir fired again. The Exorcist missiles burst above the traitor lines or impacted the already riven marble of the square. All was confusion and turmoil. Yet at the centre of it the Death Guard remained resolute. Unbothered. Unmoving. They held. They fought. They killed, letting the Sisters come to them and expend energy and ammunition against their indomitable forms.

Irinya's grip tightened on her blade hilt. The Heretic Astartes had overcommitted but she knew that they could soak up more damage, more losses, than her Sisters could. The Traitor Space Marines led the charge now, adapting to their circumstances, drawing the fire of the Sisters and the Militarum while their cultists ran rampant behind them.

She had planned for this eventuality.

The preceptory had drawn the enemy's ire but the Savlar and the Veluans were spread throughout the city – fighting their own isolated wars. Temples and shrines had become makeshift bastions. Fire lanced down from high balconies and out from between columns, keeping the cultists at bay, preserving islands of calm amidst the maelstrom. The fighting was desperate but the men knew their purpose. They had trained for this. Drilled in the holy places that they had turned into fortresses.

Columns fell. Statues broke. The enemy vented their spite and their bile against the holy places and the sacred icons with increasing venom. Chains were lashed around decorative aquilas, yanking them from the walls even as the chainbearers became a focus for the fire of the defenders. One of them was transfixed by weapons fire, pulling at the chain even as he slumped to the ground, bleeding from multiple wounds.

'They fight like bastards,' Agata growled, 'but they die like dogs.'

'Not enough of them,' Irinya hissed. 'At this rate we'll have to invoke Lethe.' Their conversations were clipped and curt as they fought. All around them the anarchy of war swirled and moved. Shapes flitted in the smoke and fog, things made of whispers and stinking of old rot, not yet able to attain physical form.

In other places they had seized those forms as their own. Things loped amidst the cultists, their bodies distended and misshapen. Eyes glowed in the ruin of chests or extruded from distorted limbs. Faces so gnarled and horrific as to seem draconic leered and snapped at the air as the monsters stalked forwards, bearing their torment proudly.

Irinya pointed her blade at one of the monstrosities. It turned and lowered its scaled head, growling as it began to bound towards her on its twisted limbs. Marble cracked and crunched as it threw itself forward, scrabbling towards her as her Sisters hammered it with fire. Claws scraped across her armour, driving her back before she brought the sword up. A grasping limb flew free and she drove in, weaving under its flailing talons.

The blood sizzled and boiled against her armour, crawling across the plates as though alive. Even in its death-agonies the thing, every part of it, wanted to kill her. She swung again, catching it in its throat. Black blood surged up from the wound, writhing in the air, assuming a daemonic shape – like black smoke and madness coiling from the corpse.

Agata's flamer reduced it to burning meat.

'We cannot hold for long,' Agata said. Irinya nodded.

'Then we pull back.' She gestured with her blade and the Sisters moved. There was no time to gather their dead, only the moment in which to respond. 'We fall back and we build walls of faith. Walls of our bodies and our will. Signal Eloise. I want this square bombarded flat. The enemy will come for her. Then she is to enact Lethe and commend her soul to the God-Emperor's mercy.'

'As you will, canoness.'

The line contracted away from the Death Guard. They were still firing as they went. Even as the heavens began to burn once more and the shells of the righteous rained down behind them.

Chapter Twenty-Eight

THROUGH THE STORM

BOARDING ACTIONS

SWORD SERMON

They gathered to find their way through the storm; through both the storm of the enemy's wrath and the wiles of the immaterium. The Rift was set against them as surely as the foe was, taunting them with the fluctuating certainty of the Gate.

Magos Yazran chirruped in binharic irritation as he was led into the bridge by armsmen, his own skitarii following a few paces behind. His stride faltered a moment later as he realised just what sort of gathering he had been summoned to.

Within the bridge, beneath its vaulted ceilings of old wood, stone and bronze, a motley court had formed. The ship's Navigator pored over astronavigational charts alongside the captain's gothi. Katla herself hovered nearby – occasionally interjecting her own wisdom – but was caught in the orbit of another gathering. The black-armoured figure of an immense Space Marine stood near to the command throne, locked in deep conversation with the Custodian, Augustus.

He watched the interplay of black and gold, momentarily

transfixed. Behind them the viewscreen yawned. The void was alive with movement. The ships of the enemy drew nearer like hungry leviathans. They reminded him of the great habitat modules of Vandium, above which he had built his observatory. Great tunnels and compounds of plasteel, ceramite and rockcrete had sprawled out across the barren, pockmarked face of Vandium. These ships were like the great spires that rose from the low-habs: huge beyond imagining, as immeasurable as the stars themselves. Given engines, given fire and will to sail the stars.

Yet, they were pale reflections. Ruined simulacra. Unfaithful renditions. Yazran looked upon them and saw only the perversion of the machine's purity and mankind's manifest destiny.

'You sent for me, captain?' he asked, using his flesh voice as a courtesy to those around him. Those... not of the Cult Mechanicus.

Katla spun about as though suddenly realising he was there. She moved away from the duelling circles of attention and placed a hand upon his robed shoulder. Yazran felt it distantly, through the medium of sensory simulation and nerve-bundle approximation. Pain and pleasure were both muted philosophical concepts to him now. Mortal affection scarcely seemed real.

As though I were ever such a limited being, he mused.

'We must be swift,' she stated urgently. 'There's no point in fighting our way free if we have no clue where to go. The enemy bar our path with their blockades. They want to keep us from our goal, for they know that we draw near. As much as we have read the signs and auguries, so too does Tuul possess scrying of his own.' She growled and shook her head. 'No more running. No more confusion. I want answers. You will give me answers. Gather your learning and share it with them. Find me that path. Honour the primarch's will. Even an inkling is enough. Better that than waiting to die.'

'I have notions, captain, but no accurate results. Not yet. The data-omens are not in ideal alignment.'

'Then we will force them.' Her tone brooked no disagreement. Katla Helvintr stood armed and armoured, not as imposing as the Champion or the Custodian but equally as driven and fierce. Ready for war, she looked unconquerable. She carried her spear, its surface gleaming gold and bronze in the low light of the lumens and braziers.

The ship shook. Yazran looked around sharply, eye-lenses dilating with sudden fear.

'Entering into range of the enemy guns!' one of the bridge crew called.

Katla turned on her heel and cursed. She moved back to the Champion and the Custodian. Hololiths of the impending battle flickered into being before them and immediately they were moving about the projections, scrutinising and pointing out vulnerabilities.

'They will strike for the flank,' the Champion said. 'We have prepared for that eventuality. They cannot face us directly – the flagships would turn them aside. Instead they will drive for weaker elements and attempt to divide us – to prey upon us, a few vessels at a time. Their overconfidence will be their undoing. We will draw them in and bloody them. Once that is done we will be able to find a path through the storm.' He looked back at Yazran. 'If you have determined it by then.'

'We will,' Katla insisted. 'The magos is no small talent. That's why I snatched him up.' Her teeth flashed in a feral grin. 'We three, we will coordinate the defence. Bloody them, as you say. Create distance between ourselves and the enemy. Once that is done... Perhaps then we will have our true course.'

'If He wills it,' the Champion agreed.

The hololith flickered and changed as one of the heavy crimson icons of the enemy began to move. Another moved with it and then a third. Yazran's eyes followed the altered disposition. It did not pass unnoticed by the commanders.

'So it begins,' Augustus said with a sigh.

Even compared to the vessels of the Black Templars the three ships which slid towards them were monstrous.

The void around them rippled with motion – not with the bubbles of certain reality enforced by a Geller field or the pulse of active voids, but with great clouds of insects. Warp-swollen and as large as servo-skulls they filled the space around the ships with a milling storm of legs, wings and eyes.

Behind the great sheets of bodies, the ships were running out their guns. They slid from gun-ports with a slick, organic motion, long since fused to the matter of the ship. No gun-crews toiled in their bellies and tugged at vast chains to lever the weapons into place. Such things had ceased to be, long ago. The bodies of those serfs and slaves had flowed and melted, yoked to the chains more viscerally than their Imperial servitude had ever managed. Diseased and corrupted machine spirits burbled into animation, bleeding scrapcode, as the ships began their ponderous advance.

It had always been their way. Right back to the beginning. The way of endurance and attrition. Now more than ever it was needed, while the galaxy burned and the Imperium ground onwards in its doomed defiance. Now Tuul gave the warband new purpose. Fighting for their master to serve a greater goal. Perhaps one day they would stand at the side of the primarch, but for now... there was only the work.

The ships turned and their guns finally spoke. Vast corroded shells cut across the gulf between the fleets, their courses directed by daemonic intelligences and plague-seers. They impacted the void shields of the strike cruiser *Sword of Sigismund* with sluggish, almost wet detonations. Sickly light spilled around the vessel as the shells exploded and wreathed the Black Templars ship in lurid flame.

The *Sword* turned to meet them and its own guns replied. Lance batteries scored lines of flame across the foremost of the Death Guard ships. Metal peeled away like flensed skin, screaming into the void as men and materiel bled outwards from the ravaged vessel.

The lead ship was called the *Balelight*, a name it had always borne with pride – even in rebellion. As it let the *Sword*'s lances rake it, it rolled inwards and towards the enemy ship. Another bombardment snapped out from the gun-decks and a moment later they were followed by a lesser rain. Drop pods and boarding craft streamed from the *Balelight*, each one a hideously twisted mockery of what it had once been. They moved in a swarm as thrusters coughed and wheezed, propelling them across the closing distance between the boarding craft and into the range of the *Sword*'s guns. Point defence weapons lashed out, cleaving dozens of craft from the void. They burst apart in clouds of meat and metal, or tumbled into the looming hull-plates of the Black Templars ship, dashing themselves to splinters.

For every craft that died, countless more forced their way through the fire. Whatever hand or intelligence guided their paths seemed to act at random, and yet they knew that wherever they landed they would achieve their objectives. Even as the rest of the loyalist vessels moved to meet them and the trickle of incoming fire roared up into an inferno.

All that mattered was the work.

The Chapter-serfs and servitors had been busy while Brother Tavric readied himself and the warriors of his Crusader squad for battle. In the God-Emperor's sight they had gathered in one of the *Sword*'s many chapels to offer their final prayers to Him and His glory. None of the warriors expected to survive. Fear of death was anathema to them and they praised Him for His foresight in allowing them to die in glorious service.

'Thank you, O God-Emperor, for the path you set before us,' Tavric intoned. Beneath the light of burning candles his dark skin glistened with sweat and scented oils. The chamber smelled of weapons oil and incense, of raw human exertion and of melting tallow. He ran one armoured hand across his shaven scalp, tracing each and every scar which lay there. 'Yours is the sermon of swords and ours are the blades of the faithful. Never shall they be blunted in your service.'

'Amen.' The other members of the squad bowed their heads in solemn prayer. Around them the ship was shaking with impacts, palsied by violation.

Tavric reached down with his free hand – the one which was not bound by thick black chains to his sword, Heathen's Bane – and smeared his fingers with ashes. He raised his hand and daubed a cross upon the foreheads of his warriors. All knelt, unhelmed, awaiting the sacrament. He was no Chaplain but the imminence of battle rendered men as many things. He still remembered the Champion's words when he had given them their orders.

You and your men are castellans of the moment, my brother. You will light the way with fire and wrath. You will be the metric by which the enemy judge our resistance. Fight well. Die well. Trust in the sword as Sigismund once did.

It was an honour to serve His Champion. From amongst multitudes Tavric's squad and his ship had been chosen by the God-Emperor's own instrument. They would bear the brunt of the enemy's wrath.

He marked the brow of each warrior in turn. Neophyte Eralicus bowed his tonsured head and received the mark with a thankful prayer upon his lips. He looked up at Tavric with wide eyes and Tavric warmed to see the belief that flickered in that gaze. The Initiates were next. Micael with his ruddy complexion and twinned honour scars upon his cheeks. Ranulf knelt, gauntleted fists held against the ground, head bowed so low that Tavric had to tilt it up to administer the sacrament. On and on he went. Each warrior submitted himself without question or complaint until each bore the ashen cross upon their brow.

'I stand as your Sword Brother,' Tavric said, 'yet we are all as equals in this holy undertaking. I stand with you and with the serfs who crew this ship. I stand in defence of the Imperium and the vindication of the Reborn Son's crusade. It is an honour and a privilege to be here at your side.'

'The honour, brother, is ours,' Ranulf said and rose. They were all of the Primaris pattern: inducted into the Chapter in the days since the primarch's return and shaped by Cawl's Gift. They had not been made by the archmagos' own hand as the earlier Neophytes had been. They had been raised up by the Apothecaries of the Chapter and instructed by the holy Chaplaincy.

The ship shook again and broke Tavric from his thoughts. The enemy fleet was moving closer, already committing itself to longer-range salvos. Shells exploded in the void around them or displaced against their void shields.

'The enemy draws near, my brothers. Ready your weapons. The tainted bring corruption as their vanguard and know not the worth of purity.'

He paused and raised his sword. The blade ignited in the close confines of the chapel, illuminating the great double-headed eagle which loomed over them in divine judgement.

'We shall show them the sanctity of sacrifice.'

The Death Guard marched down the corridors of the strike cruiser and all who came before them knew the final gift of the Grandfather.

The Chapter thralls and slaves of the Black Templars were brave, Fedrach had to give them that. He strode through the mortals like the passing of the scythe, his plague sword cleaving them apart and leaving only blood and entrails in his wake. He laughed to see it. He *enjoyed* it. There were few pleasures left to him now since their long-ago transfiguration. He drew the weeping edge of the blade along the walls. A line of creeping rust formed where he cut, spreading like a bloodstain, eating away at the inscribed oaths and prayers. Even his footfalls formed burning imprints upon the decking. Fedrach chortled as he marched.

By the Pilgrim's own hand he had been selected for the honour of first blood. He would lead the advance into the enemy's heart and kill them a ship at a time. To kill the weak-blooded cousins who had replaced the Legions of old was a fine thing.

'This,' he slurred, 'is to be savoured.'

These zealots fought with the fire of the Great Crusade, tempered with the stony fortitude of the bloodline of Rogal Dorn. They were a strange blend of the ancient and the newborn. Perhaps when these skirmishes were done and the Pilgrim's will was executed then he would dissect some of them – see what lurked in their marrow and their blood.

Other warriors of the Legion were falling into lockstep behind Fedrach, in respect of his primacy. The Pilgrim had daubed the sigil of a black, clawed hand upon his armour and that darkness had begun to spread like sweet mould. He wore that favour as he strode through the broad corridors of the Black Templars ship and let ruin spread about him. Smoke coiled from his armour as systems shifted and failed, realigned and rebooted again, died and lived in perpetual struggle.

He drew his pistol and fired down the corridor, catching another two of the Chapter thralls in the chest. Vivid crimson blood stained their black-and-white tabards.

'This is beneath us,' grumbled Brother Ertros. The warrior's bulk was so swollen that in places he bulged fully out of his plate. The elephantine growths had buckled armour and wept with pus, crusted with dried blood. 'They do not even show themselves. Where is the sport in that?'

'They have a whole ship to play with, brother. It will come in time. Right now they are likely fortifying choke points and establishing cordons. They will build their little walls even if they will not hide behind them.'

'You expect and allow this?'

Fedrach shrugged jovially. 'Why would I wish for swift victory when it can be enjoyed? We can murder these dogs at our leisure. We can take the bridge and turn the guns upon their own fleet. We can steer into their midst and let the reactors sing with the Grandfather's last song.' He chuckled and tapped the flat of his blade against the side of Ertros' boil-engorged skull. 'Think, my brother, of the joys to be had when their systems are confounded by phage and pox. We will illuminate before we destroy.'

Ertros scoffed and turned away, hefting his plague-sprayer. As they passed the bodies he paused and doused them with a thick coating of slime. He didn't linger to watch the bodies boil away, flesh disintegrating as the thick toxic brew sizzled through their uniforms, flesh, and the decking below.

They turned a corner and Fedrach laughed aloud. As predicted, they waited for him. A laughable diversion, if nothing else.

Before the gathering warriors of the Death Guard, at the end of the central arterial which led to the bridge, stood the Black Templars. The warrior at their head wore the red of a Sword Brother and his dark skin was mottled with scars. Fedrach could almost taste the wars which had inflicted them – the wounds stank of old brushes with death. Behind the warrior, armoured in black, stood the other members of his squad. Fedrach counted fourteen in all. *An auspicious number,* he thought, *for those who cleave to the sacred numerology.* Neophytes and Initiates both.

'You could surrender,' Fedrach called. 'There would be no shame in it. Your Emperor is not here to be disappointed.' He threw wide his arms and decay rippled along the walls and the decking. 'The god sees, though. The Grandfather laughs at your defiance for soon all will be entropy and decay. The stars will burn out and the Rift will swallow all the little lights. You will not be here to see when the warp drowns creation and the throne of the god is set within the galaxy's corpse.' He sneered. 'You will not even be alive when Terra is finally broken and the Warmaster carves your lichyard-lord from His Throne.'

'The words of traitors are but the lies of daemons in a throat of flesh,' said the Sword Brother. He stepped forward and his brothers raised their bolters. He held a glowing power sword, bound to his wrist by black chains. Fedrach laughed again to see the World Eaters' little tradition borne out by this son of Dorn.

The warrior raised his glowing blade and pointed it at Fedrach. 'I do not fear you. For I have heard His word. Listen. Do you hear?'

'I have not heard His word for a very long time,' Fedrach said with a sigh and stepped forwards. His gaze drifted as he did. He finally saw them.

The swords.

Blades had been embedded into the decking at irregular points down the corridor. Hidden behind columns and tucked into alcoves, with a care that approached love. It seemed as though every last blade in the vessel's armouries had been taken and prepared. Here. For this moment.

'It is not His word I heed now,' the Sword Brother said, already in motion. 'It is the sermon of the sword.'

* * *

Tavric hurled himself forward and into the fray.

Bolt-shells burst around his head like bloated flies, impacting with unnaturally wet detonations. He strode onwards as his brothers returned fire. The air was a storm of shot, clouded with munition smoke and alive with sudden flame.

His free hand found the first of the waiting blades and swept it up. They had been prepared, honoured, anointed, and finally placed here where they would do the most good. Blades enough to cut and impale the enemy before moving on to another. Always moving forward. Ever in motion.

In his hand the steel felt righteous and alive. He thumbed the ignition rune and the blade went live with a snap of actinic light.

Warriors in twisted and corroded armour shouldered their way past their leader, their own axes and swords weeping ruinous light. The air was filled with the stink of rot and the screaming of abused machine spirits as the traitors' blades ignited. Ten thousand years of torment and death hung heavy upon weapons as warped and twisted as their wielders.

The first, a hulking, horned thing with a nest of tentacles thrusting from within his distended jaws, lunged from the right. Tavric's bound blade came up and turned aside the edge of an axe. Power fields met with a thunderous roar of duelling energies. Tavric was already moving – ducking under the return blow and driving his other sword up and through the monster's breastplate.

He let go of his borrowed blade. He spun as he did and Heathen's Bane cut the thing's throat. He felt the shudder as the blade scraped across transhuman bone, vertebrae cracking under the impact. He moved on and away, suddenly blade to blade with a bloated Heretic Astartes enormous in its armoured plates. The swollen warrior bared its teeth in a feral sneer and swung for his head with a wickedly curved sword, its edge glittering with poison.

The weapons met in a shower of sparks. Viscous fluids caught fire along the edge of the heretic blade and Tavric pushed forwards, driving his foe back against the opposite wall. The warrior's obscene form rippled with strength and it pushed back hard. Tavric staggered, steadying himself on the hilt of another prepared blade.

He drew it and lit it. Light and fire filled the corridor as they fought. Nothing else mattered but the moment. Not his brothers as they advanced and fired, disciplined shots keeping the Death Guard at bay.

Chapter-serfs flooded in behind the warriors of the crusade, firing with las and autoguns. Cultist wretches matched them in a tide of filthy leather and ragged robes, firing from between the hulking silhouettes of their infernal masters.

Tavric fought. He fulfilled the single function he had been shaped for. First by his ascension to the Eternal Crusade and then by his acceptance of Cawl's Gift. Others had died in their attempts at rebirth – too old, too weak, unblessed by the God-Emperor's mercy – yet he had endured. He endured now. He pushed forward. Through. Ever onwards. There could be no backward steps now. Only forward, to fight and hold, or to die. The blades met the enemy's swords, again and again. The Death Guard were swarming him, the distended brute at their head. It came for Tavric again. Lightning danced from between the competing fields, around metal pure and corrupted.

The leering thing leant forward and its tongue danced over its rotten teeth. Their blades met repeatedly, yet Tavric held. He held the enemy's sword between his own blades for a moment, before it pulled back sharply.

'Weak,' the abomination slurred. It slammed its blade forward.

Tavric's guard broke and he felt the line of pain blossom as the creature followed through. Agony spiralled through him from the wound now open in his chest and he staggered. He sank to one knee, jaw tight, teeth grinding as he pushed it down and swallowed it.

Tavric dropped and slammed the sword through his opponent's greave. The Plague Marine grunted and tried to pull back, but Tavric was already pulling himself up and driving the other blade under its chin. The Plague Marine gurgled piteously and toppled backwards with such force as to rip the still-powered blade through the rest of its leg. The limb remained, transfixed, as the rest of the body slumped to the ground.

Tavric kept moving. He was sluggish now, weakened by his wound, but he still moved with power and purpose. Another blade found his hand. More enemies came forwards to meet him. He stopped being aware of individual details – cognisant only of their proximity, their disposition, their weapons. Two of them rushed him, moving with more speed than their bloated forms would suggest them capable of. Tavric weaved and slashed. Impacts rocked his arms.

'We do not yield!' he roared into their faces. They didn't react. He snarled. His strikes became ragged, desperate things. If he didn't know better he would swear the enemy were toying with him. Letting him exhaust himself. He could feel a dull ache as his transhuman biology struggled desperately to strain the toxins from his blood. 'No pity!' he growled.

Other figures crowded in about him. He heard the roar of chainswords in his ear and turned his head. The others were with him now. Micael, Ranulf and Eralicus forced their way forward, blades readied. He had drawn the enemy out and now they met the Chapter's fury.

'No remorse!' they called as one. The Chapter-serfs and their other brothers were still firing, still fighting for their ship, their Chapter and their Emperor. When they finally responded once more their voices roared louder than the torrent of fire.

'No fear!'

The leader of the Death Guard advanced, bringing his remaining strength with him. He growled under his breath, all his previous mockery lost to his frustrations.

'You cannot win,' he snapped.

Tavric looked up at him and shook his head. He forced himself forward. Each step had become torturous. His swords had become leaden weights in his hands.

'I don't have to,' he managed. 'Our duty is done.'

The *Sword of Sigismund* lit its drives and pushed away from the fleet, haloed by fire from its fellows. The ship turned ponderously before driving forward, hurled like an arrow from the quiver of a god. Enemy fire found it swiftly enough and hewed into its void shields. They flared hot, staining the darkness with colour, before finally bursting.

The ship was already amidst the enemy. Broadsides raked across the flanks of two of the swollen hulks even as the prow drove for the *Balelight*.

The *Sword* impaled the enemy vessel as surely as its namesake. It kept moving, kept shooting. The *Balelight* struggled like a living thing, more beast upon the tip of a spear than a ship of war. The *Sword* continued to fire, weapons committed until the Death Guard interlopers on board reached the gun-decks themselves. It fired until the ships of the enemy closed in around it with their own spiteful volleys. It fought and fired until it had no choice left to it. Until the final manoeuvres were done at last and the final rites of obliteration could be intoned by weeping tech-priests and bridge crew.

It was no small thing to sacrifice a ship such as this. The vessel had to be an appealing target for the enemy and so the *Sword*'s crew had offered it up with all the furious zeal expected of the Black Templars. There was honour in such a death.

The reactor of the *Sword* finally went critical. A new sun was born for a fraction of a second amidst the enemy's ships, obliterating the *Balelight* and all who sailed upon her in a glorious moment of annihilation. The other two ships listed, wounded, their hulls finally shattered by the impacts and reduced to flaming debris and dust.

And as the false sun burned, the rest of the loyalists finally took their chance to move.

Katla directed the fleet from the bridge of the *Wyrmslayer Queen*, gesturing across the martial space with her spear as she shouted orders. She led the ships with her gift. When Katla Helvintr closed her eyes she could *feel* the undulations of the immaterium. She knew them in her bones, the way a seasoned sailor upon Fenris' Worldsea knew the spirit of its tides.

Engines kindled to full burn and cut across the void. The fleet propelled itself forward with weapons fire at its back and the enemy already in pursuit. But the plague fleet was wounded now, distracted by the *Sword*'s sacrifice. Katla offered a silent prayer as her ship shook, engines blazing and void shields alight.

'We run,' she breathed, 'but eventually the wolf shall turn and strike. When the moment is right and the omens speak true.'

Chapter Twenty-Nine

HIS SACRED STONES

SON AND SERVANT

THE WATERS OF LETHE

The battles raged across the city. It felt to Irinya as though every building and street were contested or under threat, despite their best efforts. The inner precinct shuddered with the bombardments of the enemy. The turmoil which the walls had long held at bay now spilled through every boulevard and avenue, lapping at every sacred place like the motion of a hateful sea.

Here they could shelter from the storm. The walls of the inner precincts enclosed the core of the High Sacristy – the Tomb of the Saint, the cardinal's palace and the Great Basilica itself. The great devotional avenues of the outer districts narrowed as they drew near, becoming winding pilgrim's paths for the faithful to march along into the heart of holiness, not as a milling horde but as more presentable groups.

Irinya waited behind the barricades, coordinating the defence. Around her stood innumerable soldiers and Sisters, their looming presences marbled through with the constant stream of grey-robed refugees and civilians being herded into safe zones.

The survivors had been meticulously screened in the outer wards, at other checkpoints and lines of defence, even as the enemy advanced and the lines contracted.

Irinya had not rested. She had not stopped or slept in what felt like days. Even the bitter reprieve offered by the Exorcists' bombardment had only bought them so much time. Enough to pull back and secure yet another line of defence. She could feel the weariness of the relentless retreat clawing at her. Sometimes she was certain only her armour kept her standing.

That and His grace.

Above them the great spires and towers of the shrine city were being reduced to rubble, meticulously demolished by the remaining Death Guard artillery. Dust had infiltrated every facet of the low city, slowly drifting down from the skies like falling ashes, recycled by the ventilation systems and spread throughout the makeshift bunkers and sanctuaries. Irinya brushed it from her armour and shook it from her hair. Every last one of them was tainted with the world's slow death and the city's present suffering.

Agata and Josefine joined her as she oversaw the fortification of a tunnel nexus.

'Canoness,' Josefine began, 'you should–'

'I should do a great many things, Sister, but rest is not one of them.'

'Even the most devoted must tend to their own wellbeing. You must be the best servant you can for Him,' Agata said. 'You are an inspiration, canoness, Throne but there can be no doubt of that. You fight with all the fury of an Angel of Death. Yet you are still mortal. If you will not rest then at least take the time to meditate and pray for His guidance.' She looked out over the crowds of soldiers and civilians. 'We will tend to the flock – lesser shepherds with rougher crooks.' She chuckled to herself.

Irinya sighed. She tried in vain to dislodge the knots of pain and tension which had gathered in her back, making the armour growl with the uneven motions.

'You speak with wisdom, my Sisters, and I thank you.' She put a hand on each of their shoulders. 'I will seek His guidance.'

Irinya wandered through the inner precincts of the great shrine almost at random, seeking salvation and revelation in equal measure. It had taken everything she had not to flee straight for the saint's tomb, to gaze upon her golden martyrdom and to try, as others vainly tried, to wring some sense of solace from Teneu's death. Instead she had allowed her meandering step to lead her here.

Once it had been a minor shrinehold – as minor as any dedicated to one of the Nine Primarchs could be said to be – but in the years since the Miracle upon Macragge it had been revisited and expanded. The walls were pale marble and rich, dark obsidian, inlaid with gold and silver, lined with platinum and lapis. Countless sapphires had been painstakingly set into the walls and ceilings until the entire chamber seemed to glow with a lambent summer sunlight, a clear blue sky trapped and encapsulated within these walls of stone and devotion.

She knelt before the great statue of the Avenging Son, wrought in gold, carrying a quill in one hand and a sword in the other. His was the metric of rule and the calculus of battle. To look upon him was to understand what was required to lead in the name of the God-Emperor.

Irinya closed her eyes and knelt, hands clasped before her. She did not pray or dream.

She remembered.

'This is the one?' the hololith rumbled.

Even as an image the regent lost none of his power. Irinya could not help but look upon him in his glory. The light of the hololith, pale blue threaded with white, seemed to shine brighter with his presence.

She knelt in one of the briefing halls within the Convent Sanctorum upon holy Ophelia. She was clad in simple white robes, lined with gold thread to signify her office by subtle means, gazing up at the armoured form of a true demigod wrought from light and wonder.

'This is she,' spoke another artificially rendered voice. The second hololith was golden. Vital where Irinya was aged. Despite her youth the woman's vigour and skill was undeniable. She did not flinch or falter in the shared hololithic space, despite the presence of the God-Emperor's son. She took it in her stride.

Irinya supposed she could expect nothing less of a High Lord of Terra.

Abbess Sanctorum Morvenn Vahl looked down upon Irinya and gestured with one hand for her to rise. Irinya obeyed, even as her legs shook with her own weight.

'This is Canoness Irinya Sarael. Of the Order of Our Martyred Lady. She has distinguished herself in many campaigns. She stood shoulder to shoulder with Saint Teneu upon the blood-fields of Katrabar. Since then she has ever defined herself by wrathful devotion. There are few finer amongst all the Orders of my Sisterhood.'

Irinya felt herself flush. She felt unworthy of the praise or scrutiny of individuals so very much her betters. Yet here she was.

'You honour me, Abbess Sanctorum. I am unworthy of such praise. Indeed, I am unworthy to stand in the sight of the Reborn Son.'

Guilliman rumbled. She realised a moment later that it was with mirth. A curiously human sound to pass from his lips. He looked at her with eyes that had seen and suffered too much; a gaze which passed through her and, even across galactic distances, took in everything that she was.

The Emperor's Administrator, she had heard him called. A father

*of empires. A being able to judge by holy metric the correct imple-
ment for any task. In the near-mythic history of the Imperium,
Guilliman had ruled over five hundred worlds, each a bastion of
the Emperor's rule – yet he had given up such office for the good of
the Imperium. To rule as the first lord regent and guide the Imperium after the Nine Devils had wounded it so.*

'*You are worthy,' Guilliman stated plainly. 'Rise, please. There
is much to do and little time in which to do it. Even this communion is fraught.' The hololith flickered as he spoke the words.
'The crusade continues apace yet more is required.' He paused.
'More is always required. I have need of stalwart souls to serve
the fleets of the Imperium. Your name has been raised more than
once. You have petitioned for a higher posting for some time and,
if nothing else, I appreciate initiative. The Abbess Sanctorum has
vouched for you.*'

'*Her sentiments echo my own, lord regent,' Morvenn Vahl put in.
She smiled beatifically as she spoke, roused to the moment by her
faith and her pride. 'It is not for us to hide the fire of our wrath,
nor our faith. I have advocated, in these nights of fire and madness, that more of our holy notables ought to lead from the front. I
intend to bear His fury out into the galaxy again and again. Irinya
is of the same cloth, and I commend her for it.*'

'*I have considered your record already, canoness,' Guilliman
said. He turned aside as if consulting a data-slate – though she
imagined he would have no true need to double-check anything.
'Katrabar was a loss for you, I can see. You rose from the ashes of
that engagement with something to prove.*'

'*I–' Irinya began. The primarch continued regardless.*

'*She was dear to you, was she not? The saint.*'

*She swallowed. She could hear the judgement of the title in his
words but ignored it.*

She was dear to you, was she not?

'*She was,' Irinya said softly. 'She was a light and an example.*

We were together from the schola, my lord. We fought and bled together. It was my honour to serve with her until the end.'

'Such devotion is all I can ask of any who fight for my father's Imperium,' Guilliman said with a nod. She found herself fascinated by the little gestures he made, as though the movements themselves were unreal when writ so large.

'To serve you is to serve Him,' Irinya said without hesitation. 'As He burns in the firmament so you are caught in His orbit and we all move to your desire.' She looked to Vahl and the High Lord nodded approvingly. 'High Lords themselves are chosen by your will and the greatest of wars are shaped by your wisdom. Merely speak the words, my lord, and I shall obey. I shall go where He requires – into the dark places with Angels at my side.' She swallowed and bowed her head. 'Let me do His bidding and know again His grace.'

The eagerness and honesty of her confession surprised her. She saw Teneu again, just for a moment, reduced almost to a shadow by the hellish light of the enemy. Her sword raised in simple defiance of the Ruinous Powers. Irinya had failed her Sister when she needed her the most. If the chance existed to redeem herself then Irinya would take it. Even if it led to death.

Irinya opened her eyes and the memory fled.

She looked up again at the golden rendition of the primarch. A good likeness, certainly, but it possessed so little of the fire that made him what he was. She had seen variations of the same image gracing a hundred temples upon a dozen worlds, and still none of them captured how he looked in life. In judgement. She thought again of Teneu. Of the girl she had been and the icon she had been rendered into.

If she sits at His side then He knows the truth of her. Why then is His voice so absent in my prayers?

Tears welled in her eyes and she brushed them away roughly.

She rose and turned to leave even as the vox-bead began to chirrup in her ear.

'Canoness?' Josefine's plaintive tone reached her a moment later. *'The signal is given, canoness. The enemy are in place and, by your order, Lethe is invoked.'*

Sister Superior Eloise watched as the Exorcists turned with a thunder of treads and readied themselves for the sacred undertaking.

She understood artillery. For year upon year she had served as a self-proclaimed mistress of the annihilatory choir. War and battle were all well and good, and righteous undertakings, but she had committed herself to the purest form of warfare. *For does not the wrath of the God-Emperor fall from the heavens wreathed in fire and perdition?*

Eloise stood before the gathered tanks, the flames of burning buildings catching upon the black of her armour, and admired the murals etched and painted onto the tanks' sides. The history of Saint Katherine was engraved upon each – the vehicles rendered into a living memorial to the life and martyrdom of the founder.

'We shall sing a song worthy of you, my lady,' Eloise promised. 'Our voices raised along with our hearts as we do your work.'

The other Sisters lifted their voices in joyous song as Eloise coordinated their movements. Already the great engines of war were primed and loaded for the appointed moment. Their songs had been relentless until now, but each warrior knew that the part they had to play in the symphony to come would be the most important of their lives.

She touched her fingers to a set of bone beads wrapped about her wrist, tapping them for comfort. In times of strife she trusted in the token and knew that, if she prayed fervently, the God-Emperor would hear her invocation. He was a wrathful god, stern and distant, yet proud of His myriad disciples.

The clamour of battle drew nearer. All across the city the battle-lines were drawing inwards. Attack and riposte met defence and counter-assault. Cultists were dying in droves to open the way for their masters. Where once the Black Templars had wrought bloody ruin against the Children of the Sevenfold Revelation, now it was the turn of the Death Guard to brutalise the Astra Militarum regiments and the Sisterhood.

'That it has come to this...' Eloise sighed. The canoness had approved the sanction herself. The city was burning and the enemy was within. Now, more than ever, desperate times required the most desperate of measures. The shrines were closing every entrance and accessway. Each temple was becoming an inviolate unit in the face of the enemy advance. Their lower levels sealed, braced for the storm to come.

Eloise closed her eyes and began to sing, her voice rising and carrying across the firing field. Her Sisters joined her. Each knew the words, had learned them by rote in the Schola Progenia which had raised and shaped them. The Sisters of the last defence had gathered in force. They stood and sang upon the holy stones wielding only bolters, or mounted in the cupolas of their tanks. Others let their voices echo within the iron sanctity of the tanks themselves. Their words drifted and soared and the hearts of those who heard and joined in soared with them. Eloise felt tears upon her cheeks as she continued on through the verses of 'He Is a King Upon Distant Terra'.

She stood with Him. She would fight at their side even as her words guided the Exorcists in this holy duty. She had directed armoured vehicles for so long that the ways of infantry almost felt new again. A fitting symmetry to a life of service.

Bolt-shells exploded around them and she turned, her own weapon raised even as the first shots detonated waiting munitions or *crumped* through an Exorcist's armour. She cursed.

'Not yet, Throne of Terra, not yet.'

Yet the enemy was here. Advancing in their hobbled lock-step, the Death Guard moved along the glass-lined streets of the Via Aqua.

A firing line had formed, almost naturally, encouraged by Eloise, along the far edge of the Square of Succour, their dark tanks hidden beneath the shadow of one of the great reservoirs which slaked the thirsty city's eternal need. The artillery had ceased to fall in the wider city. All that held the enemy at bay were the guns of the basilica. Still, the enemy could not ignore the Exorcists or their strength. Now they came to rob them of their voice.

I do not give this order lightly, the canoness had confided in her. *Invoke it at the correct moment. Hurt and stymie them. Buy us time for the defence. Even at the cost of your own lives.*

The great Prioris-pattern engines thrummed behind her with ignition now. Pintle-mounted storm bolters opened up with a roar of beauteous clarity. Now, more than ever, Eloise was reminded of the trumpets of cherubs and the great clamour that must accompany His movements in the heavens. She smiled as she stood before the tanks and fired.

The enemy did not stop or slow. They forced themselves onwards through the fire of bolter rounds and the bellow of flamers. She heard a Sister scream, saw her slumping in the cupola of a tank, her armour devastated by a well-placed shot.

'Silly children,' one of the plague-ravaged killers said finally. He raised an ornate but rust-worn pistol and fired again. Another Sister died in agony. 'You are facing the wrong way. Were you going to run? Try to find a better firing solution? Strike and fade like some ridiculous child of Corax? It is too late for such things, little ones.' He chortled piggishly. 'You're all going to die. Whether here and now or in the coming days as we hunt you through the ruins like vermin.'

Eloise held up her head and smiled. 'And there were vermin in the gardens and the God-Emperor stretched forth His hand. He said unto the faithful, "Look, and I shall send a deluge to drive away the unclean."'

The Exorcists began to sing. The great fluted launchers angled and fired and the air was filled with the song of artillery and screaming shells. The Death Guard looked up, scarred brows furrowed. They turned their fire against the Exorcists, struggling to stop them, already too late. Eloise was firing too. They all were. Every weapon that could be committed was firing. The common soldiers of the Sisterhood fired at the Death Guard to delay their steady advance.

And the great Exorcist launchers vented their holy wrath at the walls of the great reservoir.

White marble cracked. Plasteel bent and buckled. Gold ran like the tears of a wounded god. The walls bowed outwards and held, for one terrible moment, before the second volley found them. And a third.

There was a thunderous crack, immense beyond reckoning. The world shuddered and shook as though caught in tectonic agony. The water swept down and through the streets. Columns were swept away like logs. Statues were cast beneath the waves. And, as it reached the Sisters and the Death Guard, it began to break bodies and drive them through the city. Tanks were hurled through the facades of buildings or wrecked entirely.

Eloise and her Sisters paid it no mind. As their end crashed down upon them they were still fighting.

They were still singing.

ACT THREE

THE JUDGEMENT OF THRONES

Chapter Thirty

WOLF DREAMS

THE VOID'S CALL

THE WAY AND THE GATE

'Móðir?' the voice whispered through the snows.

Katla blinked and knew in that moment that she walked in the unreality of dreams. How else could the snows of the winter world be falling all about her? She was home... though it had been some time since she had thought of Fenris as home. Her cradle, crucible and cairn, but not truly home. The void had become her home. The ship had become her throne.

'Móðir.' The voice came again. Firmer now. Katla breathed deeply of the mountain air, felt ice and iron earth beneath her feet, and turned to regard the speaker.

Astrid stood before her, her expression sternly set. The girl was just as Katla remembered her last: armoured for war and armed with spear. Her hair spilled down her shoulders in blonde braids and she bore the wounds of recent battle upon her flesh. A new scar here, a graze or bruise there. She wore them with a stoic pride.

'My daughter,' Katla breathed. She moved to rush forward and embrace her and then stopped. 'If this is a dream then is it

a dream of death? Are you cast up from the Underverse to mock me as a wight?'

The younger woman laughed and shook her head. 'The Allfather moves the heavens in strange ways, móðir. Even now there is fire across the skin of the night and the stars hide their faces. Yet we fight. We always fight. You taught me that – to carry the ice and the storm in my heart. If I did that then nothing could conquer me.'

Thunder echoed in the mountains as Astrid spoke. At first Katla thought it was the first rumblings of an avalanche or landslip, but it was different to the memories of her sojourns here. The sound was rhythmic. Almost organic.

'If you are not dead then I will find you. Even if it takes my last breath.'

They stood upon the wintry surface of Fenris itself, the air streaked with snow. Walls of almost sheer rock rose around them, reaching for the frigid heavens. Behind them a pile of rocks stood, each one precisely placed in remembrance.

'There are worse things to lose than your life,' Astrid said. The girl wrung her hands sadly and turned away again. Katla followed her gaze. She knew where they were now. At the place where her father's cairn lay and where her own bones would be laid, one day, when her saga finally ended. 'There is always dishonour. To die is natural. It comes to most. To die with duty undone is to fail. And fall.'

'You don't think I know this?' Katla asked as she stepped forward, her arms outstretched plaintively. 'I have always done what I must, in the Allfather's name.'

'And that is all He asks,' Astrid said.

Golden lightning cracked the dome of the sky, flashing amidst the roiling storm-clouds. The world erupted in sudden revolt. Snow and wind lashed at Katla, threatening to dislodge the stones of the cairns.

She held firm in the face of it. Katla had long since moved beyond fear. Death had passed her over, having held her in its icy grip. She had stared into the face of the enemy and defied them. No dream of storms could match that visceral sensation.

'I will do all He asks,' Katla said at last.

'Will you?' Astrid asked. Her voice was the breath of the storm and the whisper of the forest. Tears glittered in her eyes like meltwater. 'If it meant choosing between your duty and me?'

Katla was silent. She heard the roar of the storm and the rush of the wind down the mountains. She heard the hammering of distant waves and the rumble of thunder. Beneath it all there was another sound, scraping at her mind, so familiar and yet so different. Like the massed migration of a populace or the movement of a pack. Yet stranger, and foreign to Fenris.

'It would never come to that,' Katla began, but Astrid cut her off.

'Wouldn't it? Worlds burn all across the Imperium. The darkness has fallen across fully half of them. On warfronts beyond count, every hour of every day, people must choose between duty and love. How many would stay true and who would falter?'

'I am not most people. I am Katla Helvintr. I bear the Warrant and have stalked the void doing His work. I have hunted and discovered. Conquered and preserved. By my hand has the Imperium prospered and the Allfather's rule been extended. Whether I stood alone or as part of the Compact I have always done my duty. The Compact's king reached out his hand and commanded that we find a way across. I did as I was bid. We were betrayed and I returned to the hearth. The Reborn Son instructs me to complete my duty and here I am! Facing down monsters and madmen at the very skin of the hells!' She swept past Astrid and went to one knee before her father's cairn. Tears graced the rocks and the snows beneath. 'There are none who can say that I have ever done less than my duty.'

Her daughter sighed and placed a hand upon her shoulder. 'And yet... you would cross, given the chance. You seek this way across the Rift to make sure that I live, to find me and to save me if you can.'

'What mother would wish otherwise? But it remains that – merely a wish.'

'Because you believe you will abandon pride or because you do not expect to find it?'

'Careful, daughter,' Katla said as she stood and shook off the dream-image's hand. 'Nothing is beyond my sight or my reach.'

Astrid, the image, the memory, the dream of her, laughed. 'I learned all my lessons of rule at your side. How to lead and command. How to kill. At your word I was taught the ways of the ship. I toiled in the gun-decks. I undertook field medicine and hull repair. I served as a sworn sword. You told me I had to understand what it meant to serve before I could lead. You made me swear that I would temper my ambition with the knowledge of who depended upon me, and who would suffer for my mistakes.'

'Aye, I did that,' Katla muttered. 'And you did well. You exceeded my expectations as you did in all things. I know in my heart that you live.'

The distant rumble came again. The hammering of countless hooves upon the far-off slopes.

'Follow the sound of their passage, móðir,' Astrid said. She embraced her mother. 'When the time comes you will know what must be done. I know that in my heart.'

Katla woke with a start, alone in her chambers. She stirred and rose, holding one of the many furs close about her naked form.

She shivered. The chill of the dream still clung to her, wrapped around her soul like the memory of Fenris. *Perhaps later, when there is time, Bodil can parse the omens.* She shook herself and began to dress.

She had only agreed to rest knowing that Gaheris and Augustus would hold the bridge and guide the crew. Even then she had felt the guilt seeping into her soul. There should be no rest or idleness in such times as these. Even with the enemy behind them, dogging their heels, she could feel no true peace.

The sacrifice of the *Sword* had bought them time, disrupting the enemy's ranks and allowing the fleet to push ahead. Whatever means the Death Guard had used to track them seemed to persist, however. Phantom returns whispered across the auspex whenever they translated to the materium.

They had broken one blockade but the hunt persisted.

'I cannot do nothing,' she said to the empty room. 'I will not do nothing.'

Their flight had been so desperate that there was still not a proper course set. Despite all their best efforts the path to the Gate still eluded them. It taunted her. So near and yet just out of reach, as ephemeral as dreams.

She dressed quickly, arming and armouring herself as though battle were already upon them, and hurried out and into the ship proper. Her chambers lay close to the bridge, the better to expedite her comings and goings. Even the short walk felt like a struggle. Her bones ached with residual fatigue and the effects of lapsed stimulants, the only thing that had kept her standing for so long.

Still she forged on. It was all that was left to her now.

Katla passed under arches of stone, iron and driftwood. She smelt the smoke of burning braziers and the stink of human exertion as she strode through the great doors and into the hallowed space of the bridge. Heads turned as she entered, but she ignored their gazes and salutes. She noted the nods of Gaheris and Augustus and then turned to the group who had gathered again before the throne, fussing over the hololithic map.

'The Straits of Epona, perhaps?' Navigator Arkadys Solvarg leant forwards and scratched at his stubbled chin. He was young and carried his mutant lineage with a peculiar grace. Katla had met many Navigators in her time and most had been warped in some way. Arkadys, with his dark braided hair and lean musculature, seemed almost normal save for the metal plate bound to his forehead with black iron chains.

Yazran made a small tinny sound that might have been a snort of derision. 'A poor choice, save in direst need. That path could burn a hundred years and never grow less perilous.'

Arkadys sighed and shook his head. 'Then we must look to other productive avenues.' He looked up at Katla and then swiftly bowed his head. 'Jarl, we have turned all our talents to this single endeavour but to no avail.' He tapped a ring-bedecked finger against the projector. 'There can be no consensus met here.'

'Your Navigator, captain, is of middling birth and low cunning,' Yazran stated. 'He can sail you from one point to another with no real difficulty, but his grasp of the prevailing astro-empyrean current displacement and realignment is woefully lacking.' He tilted his robed head towards Arkadys. 'No offence intended.'

'Very much taken,' Arkadys groused. 'My family has served at the leisure of the Helvintr jarls for generations. I will not sit here and be insulted by a trumped up mind-blunt dabbler in matters he treats as a mere *hobby* rather than the sacred birthright of the Navis Nobilite.'

'Spare me,' Yazran replied archly. He drew himself up and mechadendrites twitched beneath his robes. 'My peers and I have forgotten more astrocartography than your house has ever known. If there is anyone who will discern the path then it shall be I.'

'Enough,' Katla said. She gripped the bridge of her nose. 'Throne of the Allfather, we do not have time for this nonsense!'

'My apologies, jarl,' Arkadys began, but she cut him off.

'No more apologies and no more excuses,' she grumbled and leaned in close to the hololithic map. She reached out and the

image responded to her manipulations. She expanded a portion of the Ultima Segmentum. Names flickered into being.
Some were solidly represented on the Sanctus side of the Rift
while others were indistinct smears of letters within Nihilus.

Schindelgheist. Cirillo Prime. Corinthe. The Ymga Monolith...
She paused.

'Attila,' she said simply. 'And the thunder of their hooves.'

'Pardon?' Yazran asked.

'Never mind,' Katla said, and sighed. Could she truly explain
the dreams which haunted her and the revelations they carried?
'I want you to study the immaterial translation vectors at the
Rift-edges near to Attila. Everything we have. Past and present.
I want to know how reality's shadow moves under the skin of
the materium. I want to know it all. This is it, Yazran. This is
the Gate. The Attilan Gate. And our chance to seize it.'

'As you will, captain,' Yazran said and bowed. 'Why there,
specifically? Far be it for me to question a rogue trader such as
yourself, but... What guides your eye in this?'

'My...' Katla faltered. All eyes were upon her now. Not just
the little knot of competing experts. She held her head up and
drew in one deep breath. 'He spoke to me. The Allfather com-
muned with me. I have no other explanation.'

'Just as He guided me,' Gaheris said. The Champion had strid-
den across, towering over the assembly. Caught in the light of
the hololith he seemed aflame, an icon brought to life. 'The
God-Emperor stirs upon His Throne and He casts His light out
into the troubled void. Where there is discord, He brings order.
Where there is doubt He brings surety. Those who trust in Him
are delivered from their failings.' He drummed his gauntleted
fist against the projector's housing. 'If you bear His word then
I will follow you, captain. Our faith will burn through the darkness and dispel the warp's hateful tides.'

'There is precedence for such an assertion,' Arkadys began,

toying with his sleeves and shrinking beneath Gaheris' even gaze. 'Records speak of Saint Celestine forcing open the way with the raw faith of the Champion's Chapter brothers. Belief in the Cartomancer's great design has the power to shape reality.'

'Then we stand in good company,' Katla said with a nod to Gaheris. The Champion's men had gathered about him and went to one knee in a single motion.

'You are the Emperor's hand in this endeavour,' Gaheris intoned, 'just as I am His sword. Together we shall hew our way through fire and shadow and restore His realm as it ought to be. Templar bodies shall be the first through the breach. The glorious dead and the victorious living.'

'If it is within my power to deliver it then I will,' Katla said and turned away from Gaheris' penetrating gaze. She gestured to her crew and they snapped to attention: every set of hands and eyes moving to their respective stations. 'Set us a course in agreement with the magos' and Arkadys' evaluations. We sail Riftwards with the hope of finding a route across. If the Allfather is with us then we will find a way. If not, then I swear to you, we will die well.'

A ragged cheer rose from around the edges of the chamber and all immediately began their preparations.

'Allfather guide us,' Katla murmured to herself as she took her throne. 'To whatever end may come.'

Chapter Thirty-One

INTO THE DEPTHS

THE LAST TEMPLAR

IN GLORIOUS SACRIFICE

The enemy attacked again before the flood-waters had even fully receded.

The great wave had slammed through the city, devastating loyalist and traitor alike in its wrath. The Exorcists had been dashed against the rocks and walls of the city, breaking apart to drown their occupants. The infantry had died with placid acceptance upon their features where the cultists had perished in desperate agony. Animal fear had swamped them even as the flood-waters had done so. Hardscrabble ends. Only the Death Guard had endured, largely unperturbed.

The monstrous and distorted forms of the Heretic Astartes lumbered through the waters now, chest-deep in places, until their groping advance finally found the sealed entrances to the central basilica. Slime and mould dogged their steps, sullying the perfect white marble of the great structure and the stairs which led down to the apertures. Gnarled and ancient power fists clawed at the doors and the stone walls. Axes rose and their edges crackled with caged lightning. Mauls and hammers fell and shattered stonework which had endured generations beyond count.

They vented their spite and their malice against the great edifices of the Imperium of Man. Ten thousand years of frustrated bile was purged from them, blow by blow, as they advanced and struck again and again until something at last gave.

Water rushed down and into the confined spaces of the temple – vented, at last, like pus from a lanced boil. Like blood from veins. The Death Guard strode into the aftermath with hateful determination even as their every footfall defiled the holy ground they forced themselves onto. The water pooling about their ankles was filthy as it drained away into the lower levels of the shrines and sanctums. Thick with muck and decayed matter, teeming with vermin and bacteria swept from the dying city, it flowed before them like an omen, like a herald of their tarnished glory. It oozed and coiled about them like the mists of old Barbarus – half forgotten now, even by its children – and like the creeping awareness that characterised the Plague Planet.

Those places were altars in their own right. Greater and more terrible than what the Imperials had carved from the bones of this world. One had shaped the primarch and the other had been made for him.

Ulgrath snarled his frustrations as he thought of it. So many lesser worlds dominated the galaxy. They could not all be dark beacons as Barbarus had been before the Lion's pique, nor swaddled in holy unlight as the Plague Planet yet was. They could not even be hateful in their soured radiance, as Terra remained.

We were raised from cruel cradles and what did we accomplish? A galaxy almost rendered sterile by lies. We fought and bled and died for it. For nothing. We still fight and we still bleed, but we will never die. Not in truth.

He drew his sword and coaxed it to sparking, weeping life. He swept it across the walls in punitive arcs, cutting away the signs of lightning bolts and eagles which adorned them in inlaid gold. He turned his fist about and shattered the looming faces of saints, casting them to the ground in shards.

The enemy were near now. He could almost taste them. Burrowed into the meat of the city like maggots – hiding from his gaze. They would be dragged out into the light. Made to stand before the unholy multitudes and paraded through the broken streets in a triumph. When the Pilgrim finally descended upon Velua he would flense those who remained and reshape them to his whim. Their bones would adorn new spires and their flesh would feed the fecund earth. Everything would change.

Dakren and Pustrus marched with him, ever at his back. He could feel the burning resentment that bled from them at his pre-eminence. The favour that had been placed upon him seared like a brand and the others shunned him for that.

'Soon all shall be as it must be,' he rasped. He tore another icon from the walls and then stepped forwards and out into an open space of columns and murals. Mosaic tiles glimmered in the floor, depicting the galaxy under the dominion of the False Emperor, as though every corner of creation lay at the feet of cowards and weaklings. He swept his sword up and pointed across the chamber. His pistol was heavy and clicking in his other hand. He moved onward. 'We're close. They cower around the light of their little martyr. We shall put it out. We shall–'

Fire and thunder cut across the darkness of the subterranean chamber, staining the air with light, fury and gun-smoke. The brothers to either side of Dakren and Pustrus fell backwards, great wounds carved into their armour. Ulgrath looked about in disbelief, movements leaden, as he fired into the gloom. Shots burst between the pillars in sickly explosions of rad-light, illuminating the foe.

'Heretics!' the voice brayed, vox-amplified and animated by primal fury. The image of the galaxy cracked beneath its feet as it advanced. Servos screamed and hydraulics realigned. The autocannon opened up again and the Death Guard moved to take cover behind the columns.

And the Dreadnought, Brother Toron, the last Black Templar left upon Velua, marched to his final war.

Toron's blade swept round and cleaved one of the Death Guard in half at the waist. He strode past the twitching legs and let one of his massive feet crush the torso as it turned over and tried to crawl away.

Fire broke through the darkness again as he let loose with his autocannon. They were flooding into the chamber now, like extensions of the filthy water. Like a tide coming in. He fired again and again. Bodies burst beneath his wrath. He kept moving. The only way was forward. He could not take a step back. The enemy would not allow it. Duty would not allow it.

'Traitors!' he roared. 'You who turned from His light are abhorred in His sight! The sacred places are denied to you! I deny you!'

Grenades clattered off his iron skin and detonated in clouds of shrapnel and poison. He was proof against them. He had passed through death once before and been reforged, reborn. Wedded flesh to machine, in holy mimicry of the Throne. He pivoted and fired. Turned and fired again. Shells impacted the columns and blew chunks of them to powder, filling the air like snow.

He remembered past victories in a blur. Worlds of icy mountain fastnesses burning as he had stormed them, when he was still flesh. He had fought upon burning rocks of basalt and beneath crushing oceans. Upon every form of world the galaxy could cast up, he had fought in the God-Emperor's name. Though time and injury had reduced him he had never given up. Never stopped fighting.

Internal systems flickered across his vision and clicked as they detected atmospheric toxins and increased radiation. It might have hampered any of his brothers but Toron strode through it without fear. He fought without pity. He killed without remorse. More bodies came at him. Bolt-shells burst like fat black beetles against his chassis. He saw ammunition counters flash empty and spun about. He fought with his blade. The weapon he had demanded.

Bodies came apart in a rush of black gore and other coagulated fluids. Blades scraped his armour and were turned aside. He bludgeoned them away with his body, pushing his armoured bulk into the Death Guard's ranks as his sword scythed through them.

He was the reaper now. The last bulwark and bastion that the enemy must overcome. Here and now he was the Praetorian upon the walls of the Palace. He was Sigismund before them. He was every last warrior of his bloodline who had ever sold their lives dearly in service of the Throne. There was nothing left to him outside of the battle. His life, his second life, had contracted to a solitary engagement. He fought because the fate of thousands, tens of thousands huddled in the shelters and sanctuaries below, depended upon him. They depended not upon victory but upon resistance. Every moment bought was another chance to fortify, to endure, to *survive*.

He fought the war the species had been fighting ever since it crawled from Terra. How many worlds had burned or decayed in the void before He had come forth to rebuild and cleanse?

The Great Crusade.

The Eternal Crusade.

The Indomitus Crusade.

All expressions of the same impulse. The same need to enforce control and sanctity on a galaxy gone mad. Even now, girdled end to end in warpfire, it did not belong to these grubbing traitors and their daemon gods. It belonged to Him.

Swords and axes found purchase now. There were too many of them. Toron swung his sword and knocked three of them flying, their armour rent, and then turned and swept it round just above their heads. A column slid neatly in half, its split bulk weeping vaporised stone dust.

The ceiling groaned. Stones that had sat sentinel for thousands of years were finally being jointed out of place. The debris from higher spires was resting upon them now – pressures they had never been expected to bear – and the supports were being snatched away from under them.

The enemy assault ticked up in response. A final burst of pique. The vox ground and snarled with Toron's laughter.

They bathed him in stinking fire that smouldered with a green flame. They bombarded him with plague and phage, with slime and acid. He fought them every step of the way. He barrelled his armoured bulk through one column and slammed his sword through another. They fought a roaming battle as he vented his wrath upon them with every strike of his blade.

This is what it means, Toron thought, *to stand as a Sword Brother of the Black Templars. Thank the God-Emperor that they gave me my sword. The last line of defiance in the cold dark.*

He could feel the cold seeping into his iron shell. The tomb that had sheltered and protected him was breached. Somewhere in the amniotic tank he felt his teeth grit with phantom pain. Scrapcode flickered across his vision but he ignored it, proof against its corruption.

'I renounce you!' he shouted.

Bolt-rounds and fire found the joints of his sword-arm. He felt something pop, the distanced sensation as fluid spurted from ruptured hydraulics. The great blade dropped, bisecting another traitor in its downward arc. He staggered back, trailing the great sword. Sparks flew from his chassis, smoke billowed from ravaged systems. His consciousness was a guttering candle within the sarcophagus. He held close to that meagre light and coaxed it into an inferno of intent. He sharpened his will into a blade. A sword that no enemy could rob from him.

'I am the God-Emperor's wrath made manifest!' he broadcast. 'None can stand against me and live! None can endure the light He casts forth from Terra!'

'Yet here we are!' a voice cried back. The figure, black-armoured and shrunken, fired with his ornate pistol and Toron felt systems finally buckle and succumb. His gait became faltering. 'Where is your god, Templar?' The warrior threw his arms wide and looked around. 'He cannot stop us because He is weak. Dying. A mere shadow. We saw Him in his primacy and even then He was a desperate and craven thing. He built a temple of lies around Himself and we indulged it. We served at the whim of a self-serving divinity. A false grandsire. Embrace the Grandfather of all things to your breast and you will live forever! Not in this living death but in new and terrible flesh! Resist us and die. Die and be damned forever.'

'I will not bend the knee to false gods, for I have torn them from their temples and their tabernacles,' Toron fumed. 'You are simply more of the deluded and the profane. I will never bow to you or your god. I shall burn with His light and fire before the end.'

'Then you will die,' the warrior said. His visage twisted into a sneer. 'If you so love your Emperor, go to Him.' He raised his gun to fire again. All the gathered Death Guard joined him.

'I go with grace and glory,' Toron said. 'I am His sword and their shield. By my sacrifice shall the faithful prosper and the unclean be driven back. For He has planted seeds in the green places that shall grow as dragon's teeth, and the armies of faith shall rise in light and triumph to drive back the heretic!'

He could feel his control slipping. The connection between his meagre flesh and the iron tomb which shielded him was failing. He drove the blade of his will into the core of the machine, pushed past the safeguards and invoked the rites.

The machine screamed. Joints locked and the chassis angled forwards. Toron heard the whine of the reactor. He could feel the building lightning upon his skin as it flickered through the casket which held him. The fluid around him began to boil to steam. He tried to close his eyes. He tried to focus his mind. It burned. He could feel the weighty hand of judgement finally upon him.

'I die as I have lived. By His will and His want. I shall be risen up and I shall fight forever at His side. Clad in new flesh. Reborn as an angel-in-truth. I shall battle forever at the side of saints and the elect. I shall never die. For I have passed beyond death. Not once but twice. Thricefold I deny you. I am His sword. I am His servant. I...'

He could feel his remaining time ebbing, moment by moment. It was now or it was never.

'I am the flame that cleanses.'

The reactor spoke in fire. The detonation erupted through Toron and out through the violated skin of the Dreadnought's chassis. The flame tore him apart, atomising him, and casting what remained outwards in a wave of light and fury. Columns shattered. The ceiling bowed and broke. Masonry and rubble and ruin crashed down upon the Death Guard and the shattered remnants of Toron in a tide of shattered faith.

Yet the sound was as pleasing as the most sacred of hymns sung in His name.

Chapter Thirty-Two

SACRED WAR
LOVE AND DUTY
AT THE GATES

Irinya lifted her head from prayer when she heard the explosion.

Yet another contingency come to pass. Another wound in their unravelling defence. She did not mourn it for its inevitability. She accepted it as another fact of the world, writ upon creation's skin by circumstance and suffering.

'The Last Templar sold himself dear. As he promised.' Agata nodded respectfully. 'True to the end. Faithful and fearless.'

The old warrior had bought them time. Time to prepare and turn every last corridor against the enemy. They would direct them through tunnels turned into kill-zones. Every moment spared was another opportunity for survival. To hold out until the crusade could send aid.

'As we must be now,' Irinya said. She stood and rolled her shoulders. 'Every shrine must be a fortress. Vox instructions to all surviving Militarum elements and Sisters. They hold until the last man. If they cannot, and our holy places will be defiled, then they are to destroy them with all enemy elements still within.

We hold for as long as we must until we are relieved. That is the hope we give them. Resist until the last.'

Selene caught her breath at that statement and Irinya fixed the girl with a withering stare.

'You might think it blasphemy, Sister, but we do this only in desperation. Better that the sacred places of this world be destroyed by our hand than perverted by the enemy. Would you see the holy places sullied? The relics debased? We fight a sacred war now. The holiest of conflicts. We fight for the survival of this world and our species. We have stood together against the xenos and the heretic, but this? This is the culmination. This is the apotheosis of war.'

The other woman nodded tersely. Irinya sighed. For this to succeed, even as the most desperate of propositions, then they would all have to sing from the same parchment.

The undervaults were cramped and sepulchral. It befitted their station as the pathways through the crofts towards the crypts which ringed the martyr's tomb. The hallowed dead had been entombed, row upon row, around Teneu's final resting place as though their very proximity would ensure a higher place at the Emperor's side. The skulls of the less worthy, the less monied, and those who had simply died in the construction of these tunnels, lined the undervaults and gazed down with hollow sight.

There was a peace here, in the embrace of death. Irinya had often thought it before. She had not sought death or succumbed to the maudlin urge to sell her life for little reason. She had known in her heart that the God-Emperor held out His hand for those who served best.

She thought of Katrabar and the great slaughter there, entire mortal lifetimes ago. She had stood with Teneu, then. She had known her and she had loved her. The adoration of the multitudes could not compare to that knowledge. Hers was an understanding that could not be matched by even the most zealous study of the saint's life.

All saints are broken reflections for the people who knew them best.

She wondered if Teneu could see their desperation, ensconced in some heavenly abode, her eyes downcast and weeping. Did the saints not observe the world, and whisper the prayers of those who had been left behind to the God-Emperor's very ear? Perhaps, she mused, the concerns of saints were so far removed from the mortal realm that the lives they had lived before were functionally meaningless.

The things which must be cleaved from the human that they might approach the divine.

She shook the thoughts away and returned her attention to her Sisters.

'They will be coming soon. We need every corridor and thoroughfare manned. They will find a way or they will make one. The sealed chambers will only hold them for so long. They will not flow as water to the path of least resistance. They will wear at us until we break.'

'Then we will not break,' Josefine declared.

Irinya laughed dryly. 'That would be my preference as well, Sister, but the enemy may have other things to say.'

She shook her head. Around them candles were being lit, offering wan illumination amidst the darkness of the underground warrens. Incense was burning somewhere nearby and its drifting smoke coiled around the servo-skulls and cyber-cherubs that bobbed and weaved in the low rafters. Their normal prayer rotations had been disrupted and now they waited in the darkness like abandoned toys, their prayer parchments drifting lazily in the recycled air.

'We hold here or we fall forever. The God-Emperor will not look kindly on our failure,' Agata put in.

'Then we hold and we fight until we triumph,' Irinya said.

She drew Truth's Kiss again and began to walk through the undervaults.

Her Sisters hurried to follow her and formed an honour guard around their canoness. She strode with purpose so that the soldiery and refugees could look upon her and know that the God-Emperor's light and favour yet walked amongst men.

They moved past barricades formed of stone slabs and statuary, past men checking and double-checking heavy bolter and plasma positions. Power cables wound across the floors to distant conduits, and munitions dumps had been prepared. She watched as soldiers in the mismatched armour of the Savlar worked alongside the bronze-clad fighters of the Hoplites. With them came men and women who still wore their grey robes, though with flak-plate over the top of it. Children scrambled underfoot, darting from place to place, pressed into service as message runners or ammo-jacks. Everyone who remained was doing their part. As the God-Emperor intended. An Imperium made of human bodies, all of them slaved to service. In all the galaxy there remained nothing finer than the determination of thousands of human beings united by one faith and one creed.

Devotion such as that could shatter mountains.

They moved through the throngs of defenders and into the heart of that devotion. The great tomb itself glimmered under the lumens and was lit from below by a sea of votive candles. They had spilled out from the approved stands and now wept wax across the marble plinth of the golden edifice.

'This is the core of our defence,' Irinya declared. 'Where she rests in death and glory. Her mortal bones have lain here for years and known the love and respect of countless pilgrims. She died for Him and for us. We honour her with our sacrifices and protect her with our lives. For those who die in the defence of saints and martyrs shall live forever at His side. Just as she does.' She swallowed and then let out a breath. 'Come,

Sisters. If this is to be the final day then let us kneel and share prayer, as we have before.'

Irinya led them. She stepped forward and took the knee before the tomb. Her head lowered and she let her eyes close. She surrendered herself to thoughts of Him and to the memories of the woman who had become the saint.

'I have been offered command,' Teneu said. The woman's nervous agitation filled the barracks hall, empty save for the two of them. Irinya looked up from sharpening a knife and crooked her eyebrow at the other woman.

'A command?' she asked. She placed the blade down and folded her hands before her. 'Which one?'

'I am to be entrusted with the role of Sister Superior,' Teneu said. She forced a smile. 'An honour, of course. A true honour, and yet–'

'And yet you feel unworthy of it,' Irinya finished with a roll of her eyes. 'Throne, Teneu, how can you think you don't deserve this?'

'Because I have done nothing of note!' she exclaimed.

'Haven't you?' Irinya chuckled. 'Have you not been marked for greatness and favour all your life?'

'No more than any other... I–' Teneu scowled. 'You know as well as I do that I've never sought command nor any special treatment.'

'But you receive it nonetheless,' Irinya said with a shrug. 'By all means question the judgement, but by the God-Emperor's light at least believe that they have seen a worth you truly possess.' She allowed herself a smile.

The women sat in the empty barracks hall, dressed identically in cream robes marked with a crimson fleur-de-lis. The design put her in mind of a bloodstain slowly seeping from a wound to stain the purity of the cloth – a design consideration she was certain was intentional. Trained beneath the stone eyes of saints, martyrdom was never far from their mind, as befitted the Order of Our Martyred Lady.

'You truly believe so?' Teneu asked quietly.

'I know so, you fool.' Irinya laughed. 'Have I not always been there? Steadying your arm?'

'Of course you have,' Teneu said. She looked down and away from Irinya. There was only the quiet now. Only the silence looming between words within the sombre stone space of the barracks. Devoid of any warmth or comfort – the many beds simple hard frames on which to sleep, but never truly rest – the space had all the welcome of a tomb. 'I do not doubt that you would tell me the truth and never steer me wrong.'

'Despite what some of the existing Sisters Superior would say, eh?' Irinya laughed. 'They still think me a bad influence. Unworthy of standing alongside their gifted little prodigy.'

'And I have always told them what to do with such assertions.' Teneu sniffed. 'There are advantages to being so well regarded, I suppose. Ever since–'

The utterance died in her throat and the silence returned.

Ever since the eaglet. That was what she had wanted to say, Irinya knew.

They had been inseparable, even before that moment. Their fates bound up together – so close to one another that the distinctions had long since blurred. Irinya had pondered over the occurrence many times. Sifting her memories and her doubts for clarity. Had she truly healed the eaglet? The long years had made her feel unworthy of such praise. Her light and her love had been bound up in Teneu, caught in the other woman's gravity.

'It is not my place to justify their misconceptions,' Irinya said. 'They made up their minds a long time ago.'

'Yet yours is the counsel I value the most and that I trust,' Teneu replied too quickly. 'And the one I turn to when I need that support.' She paused, collecting herself. 'That is why I want you to remain with me, as my second. If the omens preach some great destiny for me then, by the Emperor, it is a twinned fate.'

Irinya blinked. 'You're serious? More than that – you're certain?'

'More than anything,' Teneu said with a laugh. She nodded and her dark hair moved. Irinya looked at her and felt the smile warming her own face.

'Then of course, I have to say yes.' She reached out and cupped Teneu's cheek. The other woman stilled.

'There is little difference, so we are taught, between love and duty. Duty to Him is love for Him. Duty to each other is bound up in that same love. The veneration and the exaltation of it.'

Irinya nodded softly. 'That is what they tell us. So love must be bound up by duty. Love for the Throne is love for the Imperium and love for the Imperium is love for its people.' She blinked. Her hand still rested on Teneu's cheek. She drew it away softly as though fearing she had been burned.

'Then we will follow that course, that logic.' Teneu sighed. 'Duty. To whatever end.'

Irinya smiled gently and looked away. 'To whatever end.'

Irinya opened her eyes and let the tears stream down her cheeks. Pain decades old bubbled up from within and she pushed it back down again. She reached up and wiped away the tears with the back of a gauntleted hand. Pain stung her cheeks but that pain, at least, she could conquer.

She looked up at the gilded visage that looked down at her with its hollow, soulless gaze. Irinya held it for a moment and then turned away. The tomb's golden surface burned with trapped and reflected light. She couldn't bear to look at it any longer.

Irinya felt a hand on her shoulder, and then another.

She looked around. Agata and Josefine both stood behind her, a hand on each shoulder, bracing her as she stood.

'We are with you, Sister,' Josefine said softly. 'To whatever end.'

Irinya nodded. She turned and embraced them both. 'Thank you, my Sisters.' She bowed her head. 'There are no other souls I would rather face this end with.'

The others had risen from their prayer. A moment later the first cries and alarms began to ring out. She could hear the distant crunching of masonry and the forcing of metal as the first barricades began to fail and the enemy was, finally, at the gates.

Chapter Thirty-Three

THE TALLY

SONS OF DEATH

LAST GASPS

Ulgrath forced his way through the sealed door and opened fire.

A soldier in the bronze of the Hoplites died screaming, cooked within her armour by a single rad-blast. He fired again as he advanced, storming through the melting flesh and bone of his first victim. Another soldier burst, casting the scavenged gear of a Savlar to the winds. Return fire found Ulgrath and skittered off his armour. He grunted with each impact. Accepted them as a sacrament.

'One,' he muttered. 'Two.' He fired again and then brought his sword up. He sheathed the pistol at his belt and stalked forward. He would savour these kills personally, with his blade, in the old way. His sword cut a throat, casting a shower of suddenly rancid blood across the white marble of the walls. 'Three. Four.'

Ulgrath's already rad-burned skin had been warped further by the Dreadnought's sacrifice. He had been luckier than others of his number. Their ranks had thinned once more. Brothers crushed beneath collapsing masonry or ripped apart by the fire and shrapnel of the warrior's death. He spat to one side and growled as he thought of it. Curse them. Curse every last one of them. He almost lost count, so immersed was he in his rage.

There was a blessing in the old numerology. He had never embraced it before but loss upon loss had forced it back into his mind, like an itch he couldn't quite scratch. He thought of all he had suffered and endured. Floods and collapses. The death of brothers. Dakren was dead. A spar of column had crushed him, detonating his remaining munitions and spreading fire and plague throughout the confusion.

So many brothers dead. Gone to the Grandfather, fodder for the Garden of Nurgle.

When they had eventually dug themselves out Ulgrath had begun to count the tally. Now the dead stretched before him in a limitless tide, Militarum and Sisters both. He would gut this world of its defenders. One by one. Seven by seven. Until the end.

'Onwards!' he snarled. Spittle flew from his lips, hissing against the stonework. He lashed out again with his blade, cleaving off an arm from one of the soldiers. Half a point. Maybe a third. He chortled to himself and then finished the man, taking his head in a single stroke. 'Five.'

Other brothers marched with him now. Bolters were raised and firing. Flamers belched their acrid fire. Men died around them in droves. Like cattle. Six. Seven. Eight.

Pustrus stepped forth and conjured lightning that writhed through the air. Marble cracked and fell. Flagstones shattered beneath his step. Fungal blooms squirmed up from the cracks, tasting the air with mycelial tongues.

The tunnels were a maze beneath the earth, delving into the depths. Narrow accessways flared out into audience halls and abandoned shrines. Columns had been felled and broken to create makeshift barricades and to force structural weakness. Collapses had become common. The Death Guard fought through rubble-choked redoubts as often as they strode through vacant holdings, ever mindful for concealed explosives.

The defenders had used their time well. Every inch and mile of the shrines beneath the Great Basilica had become lethal. A poisoned promise.

A brother fell and joined the tally. All were equal in the Grandfather's sight. Knocked back by focused fire, the Plague Marine tried to rise when the plasma cannon found him. Armour cracked and the flesh beneath cooked away in a blast of white-hot light.

Ulgrath cursed and gestured to Pustrus. The sorcerer grinned with his broken smile and twisted his hands in the air. The lightning coiled and spiralled above them and then pivoted, tearing through the plasma gunners in a spray of viscera and broiled meat.

'You think this can stop us?' Ulgrath called. 'We are the sons of death itself! Come to kill your little world! Cleave close to your martyr, for her tomb will soon be yours!'

The enemy fire came at them in a wave so intense that the air itself seemed almost solid. They strode on through it. They had weathered fiercer storms through the millennia of the Long War. What was this battle next to those upon Terra, or that had chased them back to the Eye? Thick runnels of blood seeped from between armoured plates and down onto the floor. In the low light it was black, as though darkness itself wept from their wounds. They were every monster that these anaemic sons of the Imperium feared. Made enormous and twisted by time and torment.

'Do you think they know? That they have no escape?' Pustrus asked with a wheezing laugh.

'How can they? They still fight,' Ulgrath complained. 'They are a desperate and pathetic breed.'

'And yet they still fight, as you say,' Pustrus said, tilting his head. A bolt-round shattered one of the barbed antlers that formed the sorcerer's crown and he scowled. He raised his staff and lurid green flames manifested from the tip. Men died in screaming agony as the fire consumed them, till their bones broke and left only steaming ashes smeared across the marble stones. 'Mongrels,' he spat. 'Look what they've done to me!'

'You will endure, I am sure,' Ulgrath said and chuckled. 'They fight in futility. This is the end. This is their last gasp. A few more strokes and it will be done. We will carve their saint out of her casket and parade her through the streets like a trophy. Perhaps I shall make something from her bones. Scrimshaw it for the Pilgrim to bear when he at last descends. That would be a pleasing thing, I think.'

'Let us not get ahead of ourselves,' Pustrus muttered. 'There is work still to be done. The Sisterhood have stalled us at every turn.'

'No longer,' Ulgrath snapped. 'I will not suffer any more of their puerile resistance.' He gritted his teeth and fired again. A return shot scored a line of blood and muted pain along his cheek and he roared. He reached down and unclipped a grenade from his belt. In one swift motion he bowled it into the midst of another squad as they struggled to reload and select their targets. It detonated in a burst of sudden diffuse light. They died in an instant as the rad-blast took them. Lesions blossomed instantly across skin. Eyes melted and ran down their cheeks. Their wargear caught fire or deformed from the sudden intense heat and radiation.

Still the Death Guard came onwards, implacable. As inevitable as the end. Others followed in their wake. Cultists wearing the sullied regalia of the Children of the Sevenfold Revelation marched alongside shambling Chaos spawn and the flickering presences of daemons.

The advance had carved a glorious wound into the body of the great shrine, like the progress of an apothecary's scalpel. Now that the flesh was punctured, so the infection could begin. Now all the filth of the ruined city was spilling into the shrine, defiling as they went. Relics and statues were cast down and smashed. Artwork was destroyed. The sacred image of the aquila, wherever it was found, began to corrode and weep rust.

On and on they came as Ulgrath and the Death Guard began to lead their men in the unholy chorus. As they raised their voices to sing the songs of the Grandfather, and unmake the world.

Chapter Thirty-Four

TERMINAL CONDITION

FALL BACK

THE MARTYR'S TOMB

'They're coming! They're coming!' a Veluan screamed, and
then went silent. Irinya was too far away to know if the speaker
had died by the enemy's hand or been quieted by his brothers.
Everything was in uproar and upheaval as she strode from the
tomb complex, out past the rows of crypts and into the catacombs once more.

Detonations echoed through the chambers as distant bridges
beneath the earth were collapsed and tunnel roofs brought
down. Centuries of accreted growth, layer upon layer of holy
delving, were returned to ruin. She heard the whisper of binharic
cant as logic engines triggered inlaid electric grids and roused
servitor kill-clades from concealed alcoves.

Throughout the complex, the vox reported, men and women
were fighting and dying in droves. They fought with las and
autogun until their reserves ran dry. Some turned to blades in
the last moments, despite knowing it would do nothing against
the Heretic Astartes. They fought, knowing they would buy

time, certain that they could – at the least – take a few of the cultist acolytes with them.

Others ended their defiance in fire. Grenades were thrown. Hidden explosives were set off. Yet more collapses were triggered. All to lay the way for the coming of the crusade; to earn salvation. A few more deaths and perhaps then the God-Emperor would grace them again with His Angels. So long as they kept fighting and screaming into the void.

Always the same words were upon their lips as they died. As they sacrificed. As they martyred themselves.

For the Emperor. For the Lady of Woes. For the saint.

'For the Emperor,' she whispered. 'For the saint.'

Already the defence felt flawed and failing. A body wracked by illness, forced into terminal condition. Dying by degrees. She shook the thoughts away. As the enemy travelled, so a miasma of despair followed with them. Irinya wouldn't allow herself to falter. Not now.

'To your stations!' she bellowed. 'The God-Emperor stands with us and He demands you protect His holy places! Sacred ground! Hallowed relics! These are nothing to the enemy, but to you they should be everything!'

Voices chorused in agreement. At her side her Sisters began to sing again. They raised their vox-amplified hymns above the thronging violence and screams of pain.

Even this far back from the enemy the air stank with the spice of shed and burning blood, the stink of the cultists and the absolute organic reek of their masters. Fyceline and promethium fumes fogged the air.

Flakboard shook with the pounding of feet as men rushed here and there. Manning positions, sending vox-responses, rearming. They moved with a well-drilled desperation. Irinya was put in mind of an insect's hive, the earth upturned and the masses roused to its defence. All those able to fight were in

motion beneath the earth. Here the ceilings were a little higher,
raised up in reinforced stone arches, surmounted by skulls and
the wings of eagles. Secondary firing positions waited around
the bases of columns like the candles of offerings, merely waiting their true ignition.

Her squad rounded a corner and found Commissar Rugrenz
casually reloading his weapon. He nodded to them and Irinya
returned the gesture.

'Canoness. Sisters,' he said with another nod to her squad.
'Things are certainly proceeding apace.'

'Quite,' Irinya agreed. She looked to his pistol and then back
up to his rugged and unbothered features. 'For the enemy or
your men?'

He chuckled dryly. 'I pray they are purely for the enemy. I've
given the Savlar full dispensation to *indulge* in their chems. They
couldn't be happier. They'll fight like bastards, to the very end,
you can rely upon that.'

Irinya's lip curled but she didn't press the man further upon
it. The ceiling was shaking again. Dust trickled down, staining her armour and the commissar's uniform. 'We shall all
do what we must,' she muttered. She could smell it now.
The crackling frisson of combat drugs on the air. Slaught,
perhaps frenzon.

She continued onwards with her bolter raised. More detonations echoed through the tunnels. Closer now. Close enough
that she could feel the hot breath of the explosions purring
against her armour. She watched cultists stagger from the
tunnels, shell-shocked and ashen-faced, covered in blood and
powdered stone.

Irinya and her Sisters began to fire.

Bolt-rounds hurtled into the smoke and flame. Cultists died
with strangled screams as their chest cavities caved in. Limbs
and heads tumbled free, filling the close spaces with blood and

viscera. Sprays of it lashed up the white marble walls, joining the black smears of soot and smoke.

There was no purity left beneath the earth. Only the dark heart of humanity laid bare.

Half a heretic corpse was crawling towards her from out of the aperture, mouth yawning uselessly. Organs trailed behind it as it moved haltingly along the ground, fingers clawing impotently at the stonework. Irinya put another round between its eyes and the skull detonated with a wet crack. Agata was at her side a moment later and her flamer coughed, spewing its holy promethium to cleanse the corpses – whether they walked or crawled or lay finally unmoving.

Still some of them writhed and thrashed in the flames – like a depiction of eternal torment. Irinya watched faces melt like wax models, sloughing away to reveal the screaming rictus of bone beneath. They cracked and burst in the heat with sprays of boiling marrow.

Even helmed she could smell roasting human meat, the hot stink of illness, the odour of burning hair. The stench of the enemy permeated every seal and filter as though they wanted, *needed*, to be experienced. It was a corrupt, living thing, rendered vital by the unholy attentions of the warp. Whatever daemon god these cultists and their masters bowed to, it delighted in despoliation. Foulness was rendered fair to all who supped of the poison draught it offered.

Face to face with it Irinya knew only disgust.

They will not touch her, she vowed silently. *They shall never defile her rest.*

She mag-locked her bolter and drew Truth's Kiss. The pale light seemed brighter here, in the darkness and the smoke, and she swept it forwards and through the murk. A thing with a bifurcated face lunged to meet her and she took the malformed head in a single stroke. More came. A tide of unholy auxiliaries.

They moved shoulder to shoulder, three men across in the narrow confines, and sought to encircle her. Bolt-rounds and fire drove them back or floored them entirely.

The Sisters forced their way forward. Through the tunnel. Into the enemy.

Irinya could hear vox-calls and replies within her helm. In other tunnels, at other choke points, the Sisters of the preceptory were doing the same. Engaging. Holding. Buoying up the defence where soldiers alone would falter. They were not the Angels of the Adeptus Astartes, not brothers of the sword, but they were mighty, and in this place they were symbols of all He held dear.

'We are His daughters!' she bellowed.

'Raised up by His hand! Shaped in His service!' her Sisters chorused.

'We stand against the faithless and the unclean!'

'Driving back the dark with the fire of our faith!' came the reply.

The rhythm was palpable. Organic. Powerful. It rang through the corridors and out in a wave, crashing against the oncoming rush of cultists. The mortal slaves faltered in their stride as though the despair they had served had turned back upon them. They were screaming even before bolt or blade found them.

The Sisters did not ignore their window of opportunity.

Irinya charged forward and her blade flashed in the close darkness. Truth's Kiss burned the shadows away, illuminating faces sore-marked and bleeding. Irinya felt knives against the second skin of her armour and turned, weaving through the parade of hooked blades. Her sword cut. Her fists pounded. She took hold of a skull and smashed it against the wall. Once. Twice. Three times.

Her Sisters followed suit. The defence was reduced to a primal melee. Armoured limbs staved in heads and crushed throats. Gauntlets drove the enemy to their knees for swift kicks to smash their faces into the ground. Krak grenades burst around them, rendering the subterranean vista yet more hellish. The cultists fell back or died, trampling their own dead beneath their confused pattern of advance and retreat.

The confusion ended with a single shot.

One of the armoured giants moved through the ranks of the cultists and their resolve stiffened around it. Like cowed dogs they turned and gazed up at the Heretic Astartes with curdled, petulant awe.

The bolt-shell tore through Josefine's shoulder and hurled her back in a spray of blood. Agata and Selene dragged her up and back, shouting for support as they went. Irinya gritted her teeth, barely aware of the wounding. She slashed and punched her way through the foe. She drove her armoured helm into the screaming face of another cultist and then cut her across the chest. Flak-plate fell away amidst a rush of fluid and broken ribs.

'Fall back!' The cry rose from behind her and Irinya whirled about, seeking its source. Agata was rallying the defenders, guiding the torrent of fire that now hammered into the first of the looming monsters that were the Death Guard. 'Canoness! We must fall back!'

The line of defence drew back around the tomb of Saint Teneu.

The Savlar left their dead where they lay while the Hoplites and the Sisterhood dragged their wounded away from the enemy advance. Heavy-weapons positions were still firing, filling the corridors with fire, as Irinya moved back towards the tomb. Blood spattered her armour in lunatic patterns of black and red. Like the livery she wore, mimicked in spilled life.

'Do you want to die?' Agata asked her as the canoness drew level with her. Irinya gave her a withering look. Agata shrugged. 'You fight with little regard for whom you leave behind,' she continued and gestured to where Josefine lay, a Sister Hospitaller tending to her wound. The shell had blown a great gouge into the armoured plates at her shoulder, mangling the flesh beneath. The smell of counterseptics overwhelmed the woman as she gasped wordlessly.

Irinya looked away and moved to push past Agata. The other woman slammed Irinya against the wall.

'Don't ignore this!' she snapped. 'We need you. Here. Now. Without you this is all for nothing.'

'Do not tell me the stakes!' Irinya shouted back. 'Everything I do is for the sake of the defence! Look at them!' She swept her arm around and her cloak snapped out. 'How many are left? Spread throughout this complex? A few thousand? A few thousand more in the other shrines? The core of our defence is a few hundred strong. They need to see that we still fight for them. That these monsters can be driven back and beaten! Kill a dozen of their minions, a hundred, a thousand, and it will mean little, but if we take down even one of the bastard Heretic Astartes... then the common man can hope. They can *believe* that we can win!'

'And you don't?'

'I believe that if we do all that we can then we will have done enough. We have made this world into a quagmire. We have dragged them down into the muck. Let them burn themselves out here. Let them spend lives and time digging us from our holes. Perhaps, if we kill enough, and take enough time dying then the crusade will sweep back to us and burn them from orbit. That is my hope. That is my dream. That is perhaps the only victory left to us. One of attrition.'

She breathed hard and swept out and away from Agata.

'Move everyone who can be moved. Wounded first,' Irinya declared. 'I want a fighting rearguard to keep them occupied as long as possible.' She swallowed hard. 'Seal the last tunnels.

I want everything on our side of the barricades to be locked down. Every last man and woman we can muster. There are chambers beneath the tomb – make sure the children and any refugees who cannot fight are secured there.'

She kept moving. Through the rows upon rows of crypts that encircled the central tomb, through the great gold-and-iron double doors which marked one of the tomb complex's entrances.

She passed under the sight of the God-Emperor and His saint, and into the chamber of the martyr's tomb.

Chapter Thirty-Five

HALF-LIVES

PROPHETS AND SAINTS

WAR OF GODS

Weryn tried to keep his footing as the crowd jostled him along.

Even here in the heart of war the surrender brought its own peculiar peace. For the first time since the rebellion had been kindled, he felt as though his agonies had ceased. Even as he moved through halls he had only dreamed of seeing as a child, through cordons his rank had never allowed him to bypass, there was something akin to acceptance.

A homecoming.

Eventually his transit through the thronging multitudes of the Children and the masters brought him to a small gathering of Astartes. They waited in one of the outer tunnel nexuses, directing the flow of soldiers and materiel. Their supply lines had grown increasingly strained as they wound down into the depths, like fat through meat, prone to attack or stymied by collapse.

Now Ulgrath and Pustrus guided the Children in their sacred duty. He bowed his head and then looked up at the sorcerer.

Pustrus' robes were stained with blood, soot and foul matter. His crown of broken antlers had been shattered further by enemy action. The air around him buzzed and writhed with immaterial insectoid motions, mirroring his foul mood.

'My lords,' Weryn murmured as he abased himself.

'Oh, excellent,' Pustrus muttered. 'We were due some amusement.'

'Careful, brother,' Ulgrath laughed. 'Even here and now, as victory dawns, we cannot squander any resource.' He placed one blackened gauntlet on Weryn's shoulder. The prophet could feel the radiation as it bled from his master, etching its way into his bones. All of them, every mortal left upon Velua, had their existence measured in half-lives now. 'I am glad to see you have managed to get this far. The Pilgrim will be pleased, once he joins us.'

If the enemy doesn't kill us then the Gifts will, Weryn thought morbidly. *Will I ever see the Pilgrim? Will the future I was promised come to pass?*

'Thank you, my lord,' he murmured. 'You honour me.'

'It is fitting that a prophet of the Sevenfold Revelation will gaze upon the Imperium's false saint. You will tear her bones from her sepulchre and wear them as the world is reborn anew. From a womb of cold stone and brittle faith we shall bring forth a place of yielding flesh and fertile growth.'

'Pah,' Pustrus muttered. He tapped his staff against the floor and then spat to one side, watching as the maggoty gobbet squirmed away into the shadows. 'It cannot happen soon enough. I despise this little world and its mouldering tombs. There is no joy here – only the weeping of their mewling acolytes. It turns the stomach.'

'Then let us end it,' Ulgrath said with a nod. He lifted his pistol and checked it. The Destroyer's withered features twisted into a sneer and his old scars flexed. 'We will need your strength at the end, prophet. The saint will be warded. We break the wards. We shatter the tomb. We put out His light.'

'And our victory?'

Ulgrath chuckled. 'Oh, not to worry, my little friend.' The pistol clicked and whirred in his hand with an almost living eagerness. Strange lights danced within its complex surface, yearning to be unleashed. 'Soon you will have everything you have dreamed of and fought for, and more.'

Weryn learned he was the last of the prophets who yet lived. The common soldiery of the Children whispered as they marched into the darkness. Beneath the earth, far from the sight of the sun, they unburdened themselves.

The others had been sacrificed, their lives bled away to feed Pustrus' rituals.

Weryn felt no fear or hate when he learned of it. Such things were the Grandfather's will and he subjected himself to them with pride. *This is a war of gods now. Ours against theirs. The Grandfather's great love against the Emperor's atrophied attentions.*

And he knew that as on Velua, so it would rage across the galaxy until time's ending. Their struggle was a microcosm of the wars which had raged for ten millennia. The Long War, his masters called it. The greatest conflict in human history waged by its most favoured sons. A truth hidden by the corpse-worshippers of the Imperium behind lies and slander. Yet still the masters endured. Still they fought. They stood as examples to all who had the will to see it. Despite everything he had suffered Weryn still shared that will.

He fell in with a group of Children in their ragged livery, bowing to him as he hobbled to their head. He looked about, nodding from face to face, and then paused. He almost laughed.

'Ceren?'

The luminor had grown famine-thin with the ravages of time and the pressures of war. Her hair was gone, fallen out or roughly shaved. Her gaze was feral as she looked to him, blinking as though seeing him for the first time.

'Prophet?' she asked.

'The Grandfather must truly love you to see you through the wars,' he said with a laugh. 'I've only survived by his grace and the protection of his chosen warriors.' He brushed his hands down his soiled robes, almost black now, and then took her by the shoulders. 'You look...' He paused. 'You look ready.'

'I...' She swallowed. Her pupils were wide, too wide, delirious and wild. She blinked and focused on him again. 'I feel ready. To fight at their side has been an honour and a blessing. Now all we have hoped for is within reach.' She pointed with her machete blade. Down the tunnel where the war yet waited.

'And we will face it down together,' he said with a sigh. 'If you will guide me to where I am needed.'

She laughed darkly and slashed at the air. 'We are where we must be, prophet. It cannot be any other way. This is not a fate shaped by the gods. It is corroded into the universe's skin. It is wrought of eternity's bones.'

'I had no idea you were of such a poetic bent,' he mused.

'We have all become other than we were,' she whispered. 'Being near the masters puts strange thoughts into my head. Like my mind is on fire.'

'Such is the price of standing too close to divinity,' he said softly. 'The fire of the god burns us, inflames us, and makes us mad.' He raised his arm.

Sickly light coiled about his outstretched liver-spotted hand. He felt his skin tighten around his digits as he invoked the warp.

'When we end this, you can stand with me as we remake the world. We can carve our poetry into the face of creation.'

Chapter Thirty-Six

FAITH'S END

NO REPENTANCE

THE VOICE OF SAINTS

The doors were sealed and the end began.

Beyond the sealed chamber the last explosions sounded through the darkness. Tunnels collapsed. Walkways were caved in. Murals were buried under tons of marble and rockcrete, burying heretics and heroes alike. Within, the Sisterhood led the remaining defenders in prayer. Soldiers ate their last ration packs as though it were the finest feast, huddled around burning candles and braziers for warmth.

Irinya watched them. Something akin to pride stirred in her breast as she observed them – the common flock of humanity united in sacred duty and defiance.

'Here, at faith's end.' She sighed to herself, gazing up at the golden edifice of the tomb. Soaring flames, angelic wings, the false simulacrum face staring back at her. Judging her. *Forgive me,* she thought.

Here in the shadow of the monument the marble seemed to glow with reflected light, with the fire of the candles and the braziers, with the radiance of the remaining plasma weapons, which had been set up on either side of the tomb. It was a space rendered more sacred by battle. Sanctified for the coming moment.

Her Sisters were readying themselves. Checking and recheck-ing their weapons or offering quiet words of encouragement to the defenders. Josefine had been taken below and yet had insisted on keeping her bolter with her. She was propped up, quietly praying, ready to defend the pilgrims with her life. Irinya had been forced to watch her hurt and betrayed expression as they had helped to move her.

Irinya drew Truth's Kiss and laid it before the tomb. She placed her hand on the unpowered blade and gazed up at Teneu's immortalised visage.

'Canoness?'

Irinya turned from her meditations and smiled as she came face to face with a young girl in the grey robes of a novitiate. A girl she recognised. 'Novitiate Angharad,' she said. 'Your vigil continues.'

'It never ended, canoness,' the girl said and sank to her knees beside the older woman. Her hands trembled as she reached out and lit a votive candle, before placing it at the base of the shrine. 'I pray to her every day. I pray for victory and succour. I pray for our world and for all those who suffer upon it. I know in my heart that she hears us and she pleads for us at His right hand.' She bowed her wimpled head and began to weep. 'Yet they're here. They're here now and nothing seems like it can hold back the tide.'

Irinya placed her hand upon the girl's shoulder and smiled softly to herself. 'Thank you, my Sister.'

'Canoness?'

'For being here to remind me of what is most important in life.' Her hand found the girl's shoulder and she patted it before she rose to her full armoured height.

Irinya swept up Truth's Kiss and let it ignite. Light filled the air. The reverberation of the power field vibrated with the harmonics of the chamber and the tomb, till a ringing filled the place. She swept the blade about and the subtle song changed. She replaced it with her voice.

'Hear me! Defenders of the last shrinehold! Sons and daughters of the Imperium. No matter what world you call home, no matter what path brought you to this place, you are welcome here. This is sanctuary. You stand here in the defence of a sacred world and its holy places. You defend the most sacred shrine they have raised. You stand in the shadow of a saint!'

The Sisters went to their knees as one. The Hoplites followed a second later.

'We fight the last war. For the sake of our God-Emperor and His saints, but also for the common people who shelter below. This is their world. These are their relics. We have offered arms to all who will bear them and they are *righteous* in their fury! Those who stand with gun and blade in hand are heroes! They shall be raised up to His side to fight forever! Venerated amongst the elect! Martyr's blood is the seed of the Imperium. By sacrifice are the walls kept standing! By offering our lives and our souls to Him we defend what His glory has built! Cities of sanctity that have endured ten thousand years.' She paused. 'Consider that. Ten thousand years of history and pain. Ten thousand years of veneration and want. Ten millennia of His rule and His guidance. Rejoice!'

Weapons clattered against armour. Against stone. The faithful responded as one body, voices raised in praise.

'Even now He is with us!'

She looked across the chamber and her eyes found Agata. Even her bellicose comrade could only return her gaze for so long.

'She is with us too!'

The sword tasted the air again and a cheer rose around her. The light reflecting from the tomb seemed to shift, burning brighter, co-mingling with the pure light of the blade's power field.

'This is her sword! She fought with it and she died with it! It passed to me and I bear the weight of that responsibility.'

There were tears in her eyes again and she blinked them away. Through the pain and the sorrow, to where the rage burned. Hot and urgent. Pure and good, and terrible.

'She raised this blade in defence of the Imperium she loved! Time and again, across a dozen worlds, she fought with it until the bitter and bloody end. As we fight now! As we fight, surrounded by the enemy. They are many and we are few. That is not weakness. It makes us mighty. It makes us giants in the face of the horde. They will try and tear us down. They may even succeed, but so long as a single one of us stands and raises our banner and spits defiance in their faces – then we will have done His work, just as she did!'

Impacts rang through the chamber. The doors shook and bowed. Everyone was in sudden motion, rushing to fulfil predetermined roles. The defence shifted and moved. More detonations echoed from without as the last mines and improvised explosives went off. Screams filled the air, muted by the doors and walls. Irinya looked around and saw that Angharad was already on her feet, autogun in her hands.

'Fight them, my friends! Resist them and their corruption, brothers and sisters! The God-Emperor is with us! The saint is with us! For the glory of He upon Terra! For His servants! For His warriors! For Teneu!'

'For the saint!' they chorused.

A black blade forced its way through the doors and began to cut with dogged strokes. The masses inside were already responding. The waiting ended. A tide of fire finally broke

free as the doors bowed inwards and the first hulking warrior
appeared in the gap.

Irinya was stepping forth, moving without truly thinking. Responding to a call as instinctive to her as breathing.

The call to war.

Chapter Thirty-Seven

DEATH AND DEFIANCE

THE FINAL STAND

BY HER GRACE

The Death Guard led the final assault from the front.

Where once the teeming multitudes of their slave soldiers had attempted to drown the defence in a rush of filthy bodies, now the elite came in their small numbers. Others would be moving throughout the complexes – killing at their leisure, forcing gaps for their soldiers to exploit. Irinya's defence had drawn them in too many different directions.

Now they fought with a quiet fury. The songs of rot and ruin had stilled. The bells no longer tolled. They fought their Long War in stony, frustrated silence, as though humbled that mortals could put them through such suffering.

The first legionary of the Death Guard through the breach died in a hail of directed heavy fire. Bolt-rounds drove him back against the ruptured doors before Oxanna's melta sheared an arm from his torso. He spun sluggishly, oozing turgid black blood from the wound, when a plasma blast caught him squarely in the horned helm. He died in silence, corrupt and corroded flesh spilling from between the split plates of his helm like vomit.

He was almost instantly replaced. The new warrior stepped over his comrade's body and fired. His bolter barked consumptively in the tight confines of the doorway and a Sister died. Sybele took the round in the chest and fell back without even a moment to cry out. Her lungs were gone, torn away by the mass-reactive shell's detonation. Hoplites and Savlar began to die moments later as the precise marksmanship of the monster swept across the chamber. The heavy-weapons teams adapted and sought their target but the moment they fired, reality warped around the doorway. Vast bubbles of tortured and distended force swept outwards. Irinya could taste the witchery upon the air. She heard the pop and hiss as sacred wards smoked and broke.

Bullets burst in the air around them. Plasma blasts dispersed themselves in sickly pulses of light. The meltagun screeched as its fusion beam bored at the shields and did nothing, the light dying until only a seared after-image remained upon the retinas.

Then there was another Death Guard in the doorway, vast and swollen, hefting a sputtering flamer and firing into the shrine itself. Where the flame landed it burned and crawled, aglow with unholy chemical radiance. The Militarum and the pilgrim auxiliaries fell back. The Sisterhood moved forward, even as men scrambled and panicked at their feet.

Each black-armoured warrior woman was a rock of defiance. Even when they died they went down fighting. They gave nothing to the enemy. Irinya could not have been prouder as she led them, as she fought at their head with her sword raised.

'Bring it down!' she bellowed. 'The price of sorcery is death and damnation!' She slashed out with her blade and the holy steel passed through the boil of unreality. Charnel air surged forth with a corpse's hiss.

The flamer-carrying warrior looked confused for a second and then exploded in a torrent of long-rotted flesh and entrails. Selene's heavy bolter continued to speak – throaty and wild – as it carved through the warrior and up to riddle the high arch of the doorway with fire.

More rocks fell but the Death Guard forced their way under them, over them and through them. Debris was crushed to powder beneath their boots as they fought on. A fourth. A fifth. Behind them two more. Seven warriors had passed, or would soon pass, beneath the sacred stones of the tomb's entrance.

Irinya hurled herself behind a column as the chamber filled again with fire. *If this is to be our last stand then let it be so. I will serve Him unto death, and if I die a martyr's death then I will stand with her again.*

Men and women died around her as she spun out and struck. Her blade cleaved the weapon arm from another warrior before he turned about and drove his other fist into her breastplate. She tumbled back, still holding her sword, as the monstrous thing towered over her.

Autogun fire clattered against its armour. She almost felt she could see the moment when the thing blinked behind its helm, before it turned and looked around. Angharad stood, shaking, yet still firing. The monster's shoulders rolled and its empty hand clenched and unclenched. It began to stalk towards the girl. Her lips moved in constant, desperate prayer and Irinya tried to force herself up. To intercede and save the novitiate.

Fire swept up and enveloped the Plague Marine as Last Light spoke. Agata hurled herself forward through the frenzy of combat. Burning sacred promethium swathed the Death Guard, engulfing the traitor in cleansing flame.

It staggered, stumbled, then fell at last. Irinya forced herself up and stood over the burning corpse. She inverted Truth's Kiss, holding the hilt aloft as she drove it down through the monstrous thing's throat. Blood puffed the air like a burst of spores, sighing from the wound with a hissed resignation.

Irinya...

She turned at the word, but no one had spoken. Agata was already moving and fighting. Angharad was choosing her targets and firing with new determination. Fear had passed over the girl and now when she fought it could not control her. The inevitability of death was liberating. They could all feel it, circling the chamber. The enemy's wiles had brought doom and despair to their sacred halls, the tolling of a bell that presaged their inevitable end.

Yet Irinya felt no fear or doubt claw at her soul. In its place she felt elation. Freedom and peace, for the first time in a long time. She would not lie down and die. She would fight with fire in her heart and raw rage in her marrow. She would spit blood and teeth into the enemy's face and laugh as they tried to end her. They had already won. They fought and bled on the holy stones of the temple.

On the enemy came. Around the rocks of the Death Guard surged the onrushing storm of their cultists. The warriors were fevered now, shuddering with new plagues and palsies as they hurled themselves forwards to die by gun and by sword. Irinya met them blade to blade.

The cultists fought with a savage desperation, motivated by fear and fugue. One swung at her with a rust-weeping spur of iron, shattering it against her sword. She pushed forwards, driving him away, ducking low, cutting at his legs and abdomen. She bowled him back and turned just as a punch dagger cracked against her armour. She felt the ripples of pain and turned to meet her opponents.

They swarmed her in a rush of soiled bodies. Above them banners had caught fire, showering them with ashes and seared fragments of ironweave fabric. Cultists, luminors with hessian hoods and powered blades, threw themselves through the smoke. Irinya's sword snapped up by instinct and the dance began anew.

The enemy's blades found her at last. One of the hooded assassins drove their sword through her side, making her rear back from it in sudden agony. She could feel the heat of her own spilling blood as it slicked armour and skin. Her armour snarled and servos caught with contradictory feedback. Irinya gritted her teeth and struck out. Weapons clashed in a crackle of lightning as the competing power fields met. Sparks stained the air.

They fought in the midst of the storm. Shells and autogun rounds cracked off her plate or were turned aside by the foe's flak-armour. Flamer fire lapped the air about them and Irinya ducked and weaved through it. Her cloak was smouldering as she passed through the flame and swung for the throat of one of the masked attackers.

The assassin's head snapped back, blood pouring from a slit throat. She turned to strike the other and her sword passed through empty air. When she looked about for her enemy, all she saw was a robed figure. The man smiled at her – a gesture so utterly at odds with their surroundings that it gave her pause – and reached up with one gnarled hand.

The air around his outstretched claw curdled and lashed out. Unreality took hold of her and hurled the canoness back. She heard the crack as she hit the golden façade of the tomb, transfixed by the unholy power of the warp.

Irinya.

She heard the voice again. Louder now. Burning in her mind like a brand. Searing into her thoughts with a staccato drumbeat. She blinked away the pain of the sorcerous assault and tried to push up from where she had fallen. Her armour wouldn't respond. Artificial muscles bunched and seized. Her gauntlet was locked around the handle of her sword, preventing it from falling or moving. She struggled to rise. Everything was agony. The pain saturated her body until her interface ports burned and bled. Irinya hissed, her breath forced between her teeth.

The robed figure simpered off to one side as another Heretic Astartes moved to loom over her. His face was a burn-scarred horror of tight, withered flesh and oozing mucus.

Irinya, the voice whispered, more urgently now.

The figure stood and raised his sword. He looked from the blade down to Irinya and his mouth twisted into a grin of triumph.

'At last, an end to this,' he hissed.

Irinya. Listen.

The warrior plunged his blade down, its tip aimed straight for the immobilised canoness' heart.

Time stopped, and in a moment, all was fire as the saint's grace enfolded Irinya.

Chapter Thirty-Eight

FIELDS OF BLOOD

THE BURDEN OF LEADERSHIP

HEARTBLOW

Katrabar was burning.

It had been a verdant world, once. Great plains of golden grass had stretched out around the vast protrusions of the hive cities. Now the plains were blasted ruins, reaved clean of life. No natural growths thrived upon the burning fields of blood and no fauna remained. All was dust and suffering. Madness and pain.

The great cities burned like candles and wept their human tallow. Rivers of blood poured forth from the mighty edifices as they burned. Columns of refugees fled from the undulating warfronts, desperate to find some safety and sanctuary before they could escape from the doomed world.

The Astra Militarum regiments who had been trusted to defend this place had defected or gone mad. Eight million soldiers had turned their knives upon themselves – sacrificing their lives to the hunger of their bloodthirsty demiurge. They were the first. From those dragon's teeth a new army had been born. An army that burned crimson and black in the dying light of the local star and scoured across the land in a butcher's flood. Outposts had burned in the slaughtertide as it clawed its way from city to city. They died in a single night. Set ablaze as the lifeblood of their inhabitants flowed from the high spires and drowned the depths.

Irinya watched from the walls of Port Plenty as the ragged lines of civilians and depleted military elements made their slow way towards the safety of the high adamantine walls. Their passage had worn tracks into the landscape where none had existed before and, looking upon them, Irinya found herself uncomfortably reminded of cracks.

Even now compassion could be the killing blow.

'Irinya,' Teneu said as she stepped up beside her. The Sister Superior was resplendent, a true embodiment of her rank. Authority borne with grace. She stood and gazed out at the unfolding horror with her back straight and her head held high. It seemed nothing could blunt her limitless determination.

It had been the same since the schola. That eagerness to serve to the best of her ability. In a sea of accolades it was one of the traits Irinya found most admirable, and the one she had tried the hardest to mimic.

Futility in itself. There are few others like her, and I am not one of them.

'Sister Superior,' she replied and the other woman laughed.

'Don't stand on such formality,' she said as she returned to the tormented, seething landscape beyond. 'The last relief columns are making good speed.'

'Not good enough.' Irinya pointed out across the plains where, beneath the screaming and sanguine horizon, the legions of the Blood God advanced. Dust clawed at the sky, spurred up into lunatic whorls and patterns that hurt to look at.

It was a wounded world. A dying planet caught in the talons of an immense and terrible force of ruin. Reality was in upheaval. They could all feel it. The febrile sickness upon the skin of the universe as nature itself recoiled from the advance of the corrupt and the profane.

Daemons.

The word lingered upon the mind. To so many they were cautionary tales of what would happen to those who erred, or the whispered peril of void travel. To know of them was to risk profound and terrible moral corruption. Yet it was undeniable. The legions of Chaos advanced upon them. The warp given flesh. Nightmares made real. They came for the blood of this world's children, and for the iron surety that girded the defenders' very souls.

'Against an army of the faithful even the hordes of the Outer Dark cannot find purchase,' Teneu said simply. Irinya scrutinised her placid features for doubt or fear, even for bluster, but there was nothing. Only the acceptance of His will. His word to her hands.

'Yet the numbers of the unrighteous can tear down the temples and salt the fields,' Irinya replied.

'We're debating scripture now?' Teneu laughed and raised an eyebrow. 'Some things truly never change.'

'Ah, I like reminding you of our humble roots,' Irinya teased. 'Especially when we face down such fearful odds.' She gestured out across the smouldering plains. 'A little levity is needed, sometimes, in the face of impossible odds.'

'Impossible?' Teneu smiled. 'Perhaps. But with faith in our hearts and swords in our hands we can stand against any foe. I truly believe that. If we do not put our trust in each other then there can be no victory. Our trust in each other is our faith in Him.'

Out beyond the walls something blew apart and died in fire. Screams echoed with the carrion wind and Teneu's smile died on her lips.

'Here they come.' Irinya sighed. She folded her hands across her breastplate in the sign of the aquila. 'Throne of the God-Emperor protect us.'

Teneu drew her blade. Pale light danced across the iron edges of the walls.

'He is with us, Sister. For we are here in His name.'

The enemy was at the walls before the last of the refugees could find the succour they so desperately sought. A filthy, bloody smear of light and fury rushed at the defences, a swarming storm of bodies, all crimson flesh and glyphs of beaten bronze, and was met by fire. Bolter rounds howled down from the gathered Sisters and the hastily constructed defensive positions, even as Militarum Guardsmen brought their lasrifles and autoguns to bear. Daemons burst apart in clouds of bloody ashes, staining the ground and the walls with every unmaking. Shadows crawled at their passing. Smoke wrought itself into strange shapes and symbols, lingering only long enough to scar the mind, before dissolving into so much ephemera.

Still they came.

Unstoppable. Up, hand over hand, claws and blades cutting into the very fabric of the walls, gouging burning handholds as they scrambled and scampered up. There was something of the canid in their motion – the violent desire of the hunting hound. Vastly deformed skulls tilted upwards to glare with eyes the colour of bruises and spilled blood.

Irinya sighted and fired. Sighted and fired. Others along the line did the same. Ordnance and gunfire hurtled down at the attackers in a hail of punitive spite. More of the daemonic army burst apart, their remains cast to the wind, while others soldiered through the storm of shot and shell. Maws opened wetly. Needle teeth glistened around black tongues, lapping at the air like serpents.

Massed bolter fire greeted the first head to rise above the parapet, reducing its snarling mouth to slurry and bone. The death scream of the thing echoed and reverberated across the wall like a physical wave. More came in its wake. Scrabbling up and onto their feet, blades already swinging as though they were born to battle. Their very existence was limitless and eternal slaughter. Before their rage and their hate, mortals rightly quailed.

Irinya did not buckle or break. She raised her voice in a chant of praise, in a song of victory. Her Sisters joined her. She could hear Teneu's gentle tones, so near to her and yet rendered an eternity away by the growing tumult on the walls. The gates held for now. They were, if anything, ignored by the daemonic horde. The incarnations of the Blood God's wrath yearned for worthy foes. The Sisterhood provided that in abundance.

'Hold this line! Hold these walls!' Irinya bellowed. Her Sisters fired into the surging enemy, driving back one daemon after another. Through the ashes of the first wave came the second, blood clinging to the harsh angles of their snarling faces. Every part of them seemed sharpened to a killing edge, the planes of bones half forced through their red skin like rusted knives.

Black blades flashed in the dying light, cutting across the air and leaving burning after-images as they passed. Flesh parted and blood flowed. Plate was no protection. One by one her Sisters began to fall, staggering back clutching at impossible wounds or trying desperately to stop their entrails from slipping out. Some fell from the wall, their screams echoing up above the killing.

There were so many. Too many. For every one that fell to a bolt-shell another would rear up and take its place. They covered the walls with their relentless numbers. They clawed their way up and over, then the blades were swinging and blood was spiralling into the air.

Irinya holstered her bolter and drew her chainsword, triggering the ignition rune and gunning it into motion. Teeth bit the air and she swung for the first of the daemons. It spun to meet her, eyes flaring bright in the shadows. Its black iron blade met hers in a flare of sparks, teeth grinding against the unnatural surface of the daemonic weapon. She could see herself reflected in its obsidian surface: her eyes wide with fear, despite herself. Raw terror exuded *from the thing, forced through every pore. It bled rage and fear as its very presence scarred the world.*

Irinya's will sharpened into a spear. She pushed forward, defying her tensing muscles, and swung again at the enemy.

'They are nothing! Figments of false gods! Echoes of atrocity! Hollow puppets!'

The daemons howled with fury and threw themselves forwards into the melee. Blades clashed. She was only peripherally aware of the movements on the walls as the Sisters strove to hold. The daemons slammed against them over and over, relentless and insatiable.

Eight million lives. *She could well believe it. The daemons were made of that spilled blood, those despoiled souls. Carved from suffering and hate to drown the world in gore and offal. When the macro-scale candles of the cities had burned out only immense offering-pyres of bone would remain.*

Impacts jarred along her arm. Irinya felt the systems of her armour revolt at the contact. Servos strained. Her ports ached. Blood oozed around the implant spikes. She moved and swayed through the combat, parrying the relentless blade strokes. It was a battle of contradictions. In a moment the daemon fighting her switched from savage and undirected to intense martial focus. Its skull was a gnarled thing, threaded with veins and adorned with a crown of bronze spikes. Its teeth ended in iron points, gnashing continually as it babbled the same phrase over and over.

'Blood for the Blood God, Blood for the Blood God, BLOOD FOR THE BLOOD GOD!'

Crimson spittle flared out across her faceplate, smoking as it etched its way into the armour. She turned aside one blow and spun through another, bringing her chainsword across its bare chest in a whirring arc. Teeth caught and bit. Ichor sprayed the air and the thing brayed in pain and frustration.

'Teneu!' Irinya shouted as she kicked the creature away.

The Sister Superior fought her own solitary battle. Daemons swarmed her and yet she stood undaunted. Fire streaked the air around her as bolt-shells whizzed and spat past her head. Above them the bloodied sky wept fire and crimson rain. Artillery shells hurtled over her from within the confines of the wall and for a moment, for a glorious moment, she seemed winged in fire. An angel of the Emperor, clad in armour and wrought in wrath.

Irinya moved and felt the claws of the crowned daemon rake her armour. She stifled her cries, unwilling to give the monster the satisfaction, and slammed the pommel of her chainsword into the side of its head. It reared back with an animal ululation and she drove in against it. Her blade cut across its torso, across its throat. She slammed the whirring teeth of the weapon into its face and watched its snarling visage shred. Blood gouted, thick and urgent, from the myriad wounds, hissing into the air like a serpent's exhalation. She drew back and struck again. Caving in its enormous horned skull, slamming into it with such intensity that the crown of bronze spikes shattered and tumbled to the wall.

She turned again, sprinting across the wall towards where Teneu fought. She watched the Sister Superior turn aside one desperate attack and cleave another daemon's head from its shoulders with a flick of Truth's Kiss. The sword spun in her hand and brushed aside a counter-assault. She fought like a hero. Like a propaganda mural given form. For a moment there was no other defiance or defence than Teneu. Irinya felt her heart sing at the sight. In that fleeting moment, beneath the burning skies, she blazed with His grace. Irinya felt her own soul rejoicing as she struggled onwards towards her Sister. Others, she knew, would feel the same. Teneu was the example and the inspiration, now. She fought with the strength and the determination of the saints of old.

And she died like one.

The first blade cut low and almost swept her right leg out from under her. Blood poured down her greave and pooled around her *armoured boot, but she forced herself to stand. Her blade swung round and caught the attacker at the shoulder, bowling it off the wall with a rabid wail of hunger.*

Another blood-red creature hurled itself at her from behind and twin blades of volcanic glass punched through her armour, through the breastplate and her stomach. Teneu screamed, thrashing upon the blades like a pinned insect. Irinya was moving to meet it. Too slow. Too far. She drew her bolter and fired.

The thing looked up with its hellfire gaze and laughed. It laughed as it killed her Sister. It was still laughing as the first rounds split its skull and detonated within the meat of its inhuman brain. It spasmed back and shuddered as it came apart in a rain of blood and ashes.

'Teneu,' Irinya whispered as she staggered and limped towards her Sister. She put her hand at the woman's neck seals and reached with the other to disengage them.

There was a hiss of releasing air and her face was finally revealed. Blood stained her chin.

'Iri...' she whimpered piteously. 'Iri, I–'

'Hush,' Irinya whispered. 'Hush. The Sisters Hospitaller will come. They will–'

Everything upon the wall had grown quiet. Silent. The world held its breath in that moment as she tried, desperately, in vain, to save her friend. Despite her own wounds, her heart and soul ached with deeper pain than any physical blow.

'Hold on,' Irinya said. She attempted to stop the bleeding, hands pressed to the wounds. She remembered the eaglet, so many years ago. She remembered every time she had tended to a Sister's injuries and seen them heal beyond expectation. She remembered every reassuring word and the wave of solidarity that exuded from her when she relayed Teneu's commands to her Sisters. She remembered what it meant to bear His grace.

Irinya bowed her head and prayed. She let the words leave her lips in a river of devotion. She clasped her hands and invoked His name again and again.

'Spare her in your mercy, O God-Emperor,' she whispered. 'Bless your servant with your grace. Let your light enfold her. Shield her from the ravages of the enemy. Please. Save her.'

Nothing happened. Irinya looked down at Teneu's face – streaked with blood and warped by pain. Her eyes were wide, staring, unseeing. She tried to speak as more blood poured from her mouth. Her teeth ground together, pink with her own life. Irinya took her hand. Felt the last shudder of life pass through her.

Teneu fell finally still.

Irinya wept, alone upon the walls.

Time had ceased to exist. Around her the daemons had frozen in their rampage. Ashes and droplets of blood hung in the air, suspended in the moment.

Wan crimson light framed them, still locked together as Irinya cradled Teneu's head. Her blood covered Irinya's trembling hands. Tears fell down Irinya's cheeks, dislodged by the shaking which rocked her entire body. Her breathing came in ragged, heaving sobs. There was nothing beyond the pain and the loss, wounds etched into her very soul.

Irinya had known even then what would come next. The tallying of the dead and the evacuation proper. Those refugees who had seen even a fraction of the battle would speak of those who had died for them, and the Lady of Woes who had given all to ensure their survival.

They had gone on to a dozen other worlds, a Saviour Cult in all but name, bearing the word of their exemplar to the masses. So many had come with Irinya back to Velua, to mourn their heroine. To lay their saint to rest. And yet, for Irinya, there had been no light and no peace. Only the bitter mourning for a beloved soul, and the void – the wound – that lingered within her own heart.

Then the timbre of the memory, the vision, shifted and she felt a hand upon her tremorous shoulders.

'Why do you weep?' asked a voice, impossible in its familiarity.

Irinya turned and looked up into the face of Teneu. Her skin shone, burning with an internal light that rendered her near golden – almost the very image of her statues, of her tomb. Irinya's grief halted in its tracks. She blinked away her tears, fighting shock.

'How?' she breathed. 'How is this possible?'

Teneu smiled. 'By His glory and His grace I will live and fight forever, amidst the faithful and the elect. One day that fate shall pass to you.'

'I failed you.'

'No,' Teneu said with a small shake of her head. 'You could never fail me. You serve, you continue to serve. You have done His will across the stars. You have been singled out by His son and by the abbess herself.'

The light behind Teneu was blinding. A pure and clean illumination that dispelled the sullied hell-light which spilled across the tormented sky. Lightning crackled there now: golden and fierce, splitting the toxic twilight. Things moved within it – their shapes indistinct and half-glimpsed. The armoured profile of a warrior became the hooded visage of a scholar. An ancient man was transmuted to the glowing visage of a youth.

When Teneu spoke again it was in two voices. Behind her own dulcet tones another speaker lurked – strong and certain, it spoke with clarity and power. It spoke with words which had once shaped creation itself.

'You are worthy, Irinya Sarael. You have not erred. Now, more than ever, you are where you must be.'

She looked up at the burning figure of Teneu and saw the compassion that shone within those eyes. Love for her. For all of humanity. For the species she had sacrificed herself to defend.

Teneu reached out and took Irinya by the shoulders. Looking up at this burning angel of His will, Irinya could see the fingers of golden gauntlets upon the saint's own.

'I'm not worthy,' she said as her head dropped. 'She died because I wasn't strong enough. Because I wasn't at her side. Because the gifts you bequeathed to me failed her.'

'You acted as you had to, so that you could be here, in this moment, at my tomb,' Teneu said. 'Your gifts did not fail you because you were unworthy in His eyes. A single death can inspire multitudes. Worlds have been saved by my example. Your gifts were always there. Doubt drowned them. Grief smothered your light.'

She leant forward and removed Irinya's helm.

She was young again. A warrior-daughter of the Emperor. The ravages of age and time had no hold on her. Irinya closed her eyes and felt the gentle pressure of Teneu's lips upon her brow. Teneu pulled back and held out her hand.

'Will you stand with me now, my Sister?'

Chapter Thirty-Nine

FILLED WITH HIS FIRE

ARMY OF FAITH

LIGHT OF THE THRONE

She opened her eyes and moved, faster than she had a right to.

It was as though no time had passed and yet she felt she had lived an eternity. Trapped in the cage of her worst memory. Of her once-supposed failure. Irinya rose in one smooth motion and her blade cut through the air, turning aside the Plague Marine's caustic weapon.

Light haloed her as the sword burned with sacred flame, its power field howling as it drew new vigour. She felt her armour's systems purr with fresh strength. She allowed herself to laugh as she swept the sword round and drove the withered warrior back. He no longer felt like a fallen example of the Space Marines. He was only a heretic, standing against the faithful. A rebellious implement whose defiance was finally being punished.

'Parlour tricks,' the warrior snarled. He stalked forward and raised his pistol to fire. There was a grunt and he flinched back, arm raised and ending in a stump. Irinya was already past him, blade turning as she spun around to face him.

'It is the gift of faith, monster. Perhaps you would know that if you had not thrown away His trust in ages past.' She lunged at him. Swords met again. Power fields screamed in opposition. One sacred and the other despoiled. 'I am filled with His fire. What are you against that?' She laughed. 'You are nothing.'

Behind her the tomb was burning. The light that blazed there spread around the room, the air aglow as though it had ignited. It moved and shifted with the defence and the defenders. Every loyalist seemed wreathed in it, swaddled in it, enraptured as the holy light enfolded them. Soldiers and Sisters who had been as good as dead rose to stand with their fellows.

An army of faith, shaped by His will, empowered by His miracles.

Crypts and tombs shone, their marble sparkling as though freshly polished. The light pouring from them became blinding. Everything was surrounded by a nimbus of gold. Beneath it the defenders fought harder. Even the Savlar moved and fired with discipline as Rugrenz shouted his orders.

Truth's Kiss was a blur of grey and gold. In her hands it sang like the holiest of hymns. It thrummed with bound power. Holding the weapon, Irinya saw with His sight and what she saw sickened her. The enemy's corruption was complete. Body and soul. She beheld the ruin in their hearts that had driven them to these ends. The weakness and doubt. The blind faith in their gene-father and the betrayal that had followed.

So many of them were rancid with heresies. Traitors. Blasphemers. Kinslayers. Ten thousand years of sins etched onto their hearts and worn upon their skin. Every twisted form that presented itself mirrored the excesses of their bleak and hateful souls.

She hated them.

Each and every last one of them had turned their backs upon Him and upon the survival of the species. They had always been beyond forgiveness, but now the galaxy burned. Now the enemies of mankind beat at the doors and threatened those places once thought inviolate. Six worlds had fallen to these monsters alone. A handful in the grand scheme of His design, and yet they had been precious. Sacred in His sight. She mourned the losses of those worlds and those who had lived upon them. Even now she felt the weight of their deaths as she fought and bled for the last remaining world.

Velua burned now.

Not with the ravages of war or the excesses of the enemy. It burned with His light. His wrath. His fury. The roof shook with the thunder of distant artillery. Dust and ashes coloured the air. Blood boiled away and swirled amidst the clashing forces. Everything was light and fire. Everything was coming apart.

The one-handed warrior rounded on her, snarling. His black armour was stained with his blood as he lifted his sword again. He swung for her and his blade cut into her shoulder, sawing through her pauldron till it tasted flesh. She drove Truth's Kiss into his side. Fire screamed across his plate and he staggered back.

'Do you see?' she asked. The light around the tomb was as bright as the ring of blazing crypts now. Pulsing out from the centre of the chamber, crawling over every surface.

The robed mortal psyker who had incapacitated her was on his knees at the edge of the conflagration, screaming as his mind buckled and broke beneath the judgement of the God-Emperor. The other cultists fell to their knees around him. Irinya saw a scar-faced woman bludgeoning her face against the stones, tears pouring down acid-etched pathways on her face.

The Heretic Astartes endured, like rocks amidst an onrushing tide, but even they found the etheric resonance weighing upon them. Massed fire found them, humbled them, drove them to their knees and to the ground. Behind each and every defender, behind soldiery and Sisters, shades and echoes moved with martial keenness. Saints and heroes cast their pale reflections into the world. Hands graced shoulders or guided weapons.

Irinya struck again and gouged a great groove into the monster's chest. He spat at her and she heard the hiss as acid sizzled against her faceplate. She turned the burning sword over in her hands and drove it through the thing's breastplate. Something cracked. Brackish, stinking fluid began to trickle from the wound, hissing where it touched the flame-wreathed weapon.

The light flared behind her, harsh and absolute. She screamed with triumph and rage. She howled with the building radiance and the vengeful screams of the dead and the dying.

And the fire spread. It surged forth, out from the tomb, out from the shrine, out to touch every last fastness and holdout on the planet where the Imperium's defenders yet struggled and fought. The world of Velua began to burn and shine.

To sing.

Chapter Forty

GATES OF FIRE

THE EMPEROR'S WILL

DAEMONS FROM THE DARK

The void burned before the great ships: an inferno, rendering them as mere pinpricks of darkness silhouetted in its unholy majesty.

Katla had ordered the great shutters sealed the moment they had entered the system, for the sake of her crew's very souls. Only Navigators could look upon the warp without losing their mind, and the Rift was the warp intruding into the physical realm with wild abandon. Maleficarum mighty enough to split the very stars. If they allowed it, if they were incautious, then it would claim them. Body and soul, it would twist them and break them. She had gazed into the Rift's hellish light once before and survived, but even she dared not risk it again.

The one Black Templar left upon the bridge seemed to approve of her choice.

He was called Aneirin, she had learned. A Neophyte of his Chapter. A warrior yet in training. She did not know how he had gained Gaheris' favour, to stand with the Champion as his equerry, but here he was. The Champion, on arrival in-system, had made his excuses and returned to his ship. Aneirin was to remain as a liaison.

Aneirin had not questioned the Champion's judgement. The duties of the great warrior were surely far beyond the ken of a mere Neophyte, whether they kept him bound to the *Wyrmslayer Queen* or, as they had, drew the Champion back to his own ship. He must have been aware, though, of the responsibility placed upon him. The Champion had placed faith in Aneirin, seeing some potential in the young Astartes.

With the enemy still in pursuit each warrior had to rise to the occasion. Aneirin seemed happy enough to comply, even if it meant watching the rogue trader and serving as the Champion's eyes and ears.

Duty was duty.

'Monstrous, is it not?' she asked with a sly smile.

The young warrior blinked as he looked at her. She had risen from her throne and marched quickly across the bridge, standing at the Black Templar's side where he lingered – his fingers outstretched to touch the heavy shutters.

'Of course,' he said with a simple nod. 'To stare into the hells of the enemy is to court damnation. To embrace it is the loss of your very soul. So the Chapter teaches.'

'And they teach well,' Katla agreed. 'Though I've no doubt that your souls are doughtier than ours. The Allfather raised you up and made you Sky Warriors. Angels, to some.'

'On the world of my birth we were thought of as the Children of the Sun.'

He paused and Katla took the opportunity to study his inhuman features. Warm brown skin that spoke of a childhood lived beneath a hot sun – so different from her own icy death-world pallor – with ritual scars and tattoos peeking from the neck of his armour.

'Dakaram was what I now know to be a death world,' Aneirin continued. 'Jungles of tremendous scale dominated its inhabitable regions and we were shaped by those verdant crucibles.' He paused. 'I understand that Fenris is quite a different world. Wild and deadly, yet caught between fire and ice. A cradle of storms.'

'You have heard correct, Brother Aneirin,' she said with a sigh. 'Fenris is a world of harsh beauty. I haven't returned to it in some time – though, as I understand it, it has suffered much since then.' She forced a sad smile. 'And your world? Does it endure?'

'To the best of my knowledge it does, captain,' he said. He closed his iron fist and drew it back from the shielding. 'Do you truly believe there is a way across?' He turned his gaze upon her and stepped forward. The young warrior towered over her. In a heartbeat he could end her life in a hundred ways.

Thank the Throne we are on the same side.

The thought skittered across her mind. The Black Templars were not the base monsters that Tuul and his servants were. They had fought in her defence, as they fought for the defence of all humanity. The Astartes were the backbone of the primarch's new crusade.

'I believe there are ways across the Rift, yes,' Katla said. 'I almost risked one before. The Draedes Gap, we called it. A trap, but an enticing one.' She looked away from him. 'It claimed my daughter. I hope against hope that she endures beyond... But even if I could cross, would I be able to find her?'

'The God-Emperor places these trials before us for a reason,' Aneirin mused. 'If you had not lost then you would not be here. Whether or not your daughter lives it is the hope that drives you to do His will. Just as I was raised from my world to serve Him as the Walking Sun, so you have been called to serve Him as pathfinder and herald.'

* * *

Aneirin admired the woman's determination. She spoke of her past and the adversity she had risen from to serve the regent, and she yearned for a path to her daughter in some idealised future of triumph over impossibility. That was faith, he had realised, as they fled across the stars, their jumps ever more erratic. She honoured the God-Emperor in her actions, in her unceasing pursuit. She carried all the primal energy of her home world close to her soul and forced the universe to bend to her will, and so to *His* will.

Guided by dreams, she now led them true. All could feel it in their hearts. The journey, the crusade and pilgrimage, were almost at their end.

'Perhaps...' she allowed. The captain turned away from him and strode back to the throne, letting her fingers dance along the back of it. They closed for a moment about the haft of her great spear, before she moved away from where it hung above her. 'This ship has always been more of a home to me than Fenris ever was. I was raised here, amidst cogitator-stack forests and mountains made of engines. I knew the ways of the ship before I was even a woman grown. I never knew the kiss of a sun. I had the lumens for my stars. I was not born upon a home world to be stolen away from. Nor was my father, or his fore-bears. Not for generations.' She paused. 'And yet it is in my blood. I sail these stars as though they were the wild World-sea of Fenris.'

'I can respect that,' Aneirin replied as he moved to join her. He reached out, his fingers halting just short of touching the spear. 'A fine weapon,' he said. 'A hunter's weapon. I know the allure of such a thing. I was raised up to run the Forever Hunt in His name. Forever Hunt. Eternal Crusade. I think I realised that they were mere semantics. I have always been fighting His war.'

'Don't we all?' the captain whispered. She closed her eyes. 'His wars and His will. These things hold the galaxy together.

It is wounded now, but we will mend it in time. These ways across – they are but the first stitches in restoring His domain to order. There will come a time when Nihilus will need to be saved and redeemed. Inch by bloody inch.'

'I relish the opportunity,' Aneirin growled, and Katla looked back at the young warrior.

She laughed. 'I have no doubt that you do.'

She lifted the spear from its mount and turned it in the air, casually. If Aneirin felt threatened he didn't allow it to show. She doubted he did.

'I will relish it too, come the day.' She smiled to herself. 'Not because it is an opportunity to be seized, as other rogue traders would have it. Nor because there will be glory to be won – though it will be a thing of glory to reclaim what has been lost. I will fight and liberate because it is a right and just thing.'

'Admirable,' Aneirin agreed. 'We fight because it is right or we do not fight. Those without the ambition to serve are lost. They die, their dreams unfulfilled and empty.'

'A risk we all take when we walk in His service,' Katla said. She let the spear rest at her side, tip pressing against the decking. Around them there was only the purr of cogitators, the dull thrumming of the lights, and the subdued clatter of keys and levers as the crew worked diligently and in silence to enact her will.

Katla was about to continue when a siren cut across the subdued atmosphere.

'Throne damn it,' she muttered. 'What now?'

Aboard the *Seventh Vengeance* Gaheris knelt within the central chapel, bowed his head to the deck, and prayed.

The flight from the void battle grated on him. They had offered up the death of a vessel and the lives of brothers to secure their escape, the better to preserve their strength for the true objective, yet it still sat ill. He was a warrior born and an Astartes forged. To flee from a confrontation, even when cloaked in wisdom, chafed upon his very soul. Yet it had been the Emperor's will.

The Emperor's will...

Gaheris had served His will in his every deed for so long now. The weight of it would have broken lesser men – even lesser examples of the Astartes brotherhoods – and yet he bore it with what he considered to be grace. It was as much a part of him now as his armour or his blade. Though, he remembered bitterly, the Armour of Faith and the Black Sword were transient blessings.

Even without them he would still be a Black Templar. Still a scion of Sigismund.

'I have always been His champion,' Gaheris whispered. 'We all are. We do not have to bear the sword or wear the armour to be His chosen instruments.'

He cast his gaze upwards to where the impassive features of the God-Emperor gazed down at him, rendered as a warrior of the void, bearing a sword in one hand and a compass in the other. Gaheris rejoiced in the likeness of His divinity.

'Give me guidance if you wish it, O Master of Mankind,' he said, and bowed his head again. 'If you would guide me then speak your words in your tongue of fire. I am ready, God-Emperor, for your glory to embrace me. This is the eve and the time of testing.'

He could taste blood, hot and coppery as it filled his mouth. He looked up again and the statue was cracked and broken, molten where weapons fire had ravaged it. The sound of battle was all around him. The world shook – not with the motion of a ship under fire but with the apocalyptic thunder that spelled the end of things – and he moved to steady himself.

He turned and the world was black stone, rimed with fire. The cavernous chamber burned with strange light, witchfire crackling along the great prongs of black crystal that forced their way through the walls.

Gaheris stalked through the vision of the dying place and stopped. Across the black gulf he saw a figure fighting for its life.

The figure was his mirror in every way. It wore the holy armour and wielded the Black Sword of Sigismund with an almost contemptuous ease. Whatever he fought was obscured by shadows yet it lashed at the warrior with lightning and fire, stinking of the foul sorcery of the warp. Gaheris wanted to charge into battle and save this Champion. To fight and die at the side of a sworn brother.

He did not. He could not. The dream would not allow him.

He could only watch as the darkness swarmed about the lone warrior and forced him to his knees. Lightning crackled in the darkness and Gaheris could see where the Champion fought. Around him were gathered eight thrones, one of them already broken, forged from the same black stone as the rest of the chamber.

The darkness hooked under the Champion's chin and yanked. The warrior's helmet flew into the air, clattering to the ground at Gaheris' feet. For a moment it was as though he looked down into the impassive eye-lenses of his own helm.

Gaheris tore his gaze away and looked up. He saw the Champion as he was. He saw *who* he was.

'Praise be,' he whispered.

Sirens sounded. They cut across the impossibility of the dream and when he blinked he was back in the close confines of the chapel, beneath the untouched gaze of the God-Emperor. Gaheris rose unsteadily to his feet and placed his hand upon his sheathed sword.

There was work yet to be done.

* * *

The void screamed.

Pustules of unlight forced their way through the skin of the universe and asserted their hateful dominance over reality. Light writhed from them like worms, to coil and twist through the darkness as though questing for sustenance. Reality recoiled. Warp translation was always an onerous undertaking but this passage seemed especially fraught.

Auspex systems detected the ships as they slammed their way into realspace and the great vessels of the Imperial fleet were already turning ponderously to face down their foes. The newly arrived flotilla had almost anticipated such a response, as though they had foreseen not only where the Imperial fleet would be but how they would react. They came from the warp with their weapons primed, readying even as they swam back into realspace with murderous eagerness.

The plague fleet had scented blood before and been denied. They had no intention of being thwarted a second time. Other ships had been summoned to join them, called from whatever cruel rapine they had been engaged in, lured with promises of power and influence. Tuul had honeyed words and trinkets aplenty with which to cajole others to his service. Ships of the line that had served in the glory days of the Great Crusade paraded themselves forth, bearing names of infamy such as the *Barbaran King*, the *Throne of Apotheosis* and the *Reaper's Light*.

One by one, ship by ship, the fleet of Grommulus Tuul assembled itself for battle, slipping into the void like daemons from the dark.

Ready to slake their monstrous hunger for the last time.

Chapter Forty-One

MASTERS OF DEATH
BY HIS HAND
THE STORM

Grommulus Tuul stood upon the open space of the bridge and basked in the light of the Rift as it cascaded in through stolen glassaic.

Others would have lost their minds to gaze at its untrammelled splendour, but Tuul had long since grown beyond such things, his soul slowly ossifying beneath the Grandfather's sight and the patronage of his master. One had to have an unshakeable will to defy the ruptured heavens, to orchestrate the chase across system after system. He had tired of traps and blockades, in truth. The pilgrim vessels left to moulder, the brash shows of intimidation. Before the arrival of the Black Templars perhaps that would have sufficed, but now the old bloodlust had risen anew.

To slay cousins was always a delight. Too many of his joys had curdled down history's long march. Now he could indulge and serve his master in the same stroke. He let his fingers beat against his armoured flank in their sevenfold rhythm and continued to observe.

The glassaic panels had long since absorbed the strange radiances of the immaterium, casting them out in mad patterns, scintillating with the sunlights of other worlds and other times. Souls screamed from their depths before vanishing into the ether, swallowed by whichever daemons lingered at any given moment, leaving only the echo of their gibbering laughter.

The ship was a graveyard of the holy. Relics, Tuul enthused, came here to die. To be forgotten – appreciated only by a son who disbelieved their sacred prominence. Tucked away from the wider galaxy like a shameful secret. Appropriated for a collection that few would ever understand.

Even amongst his own brothers he was considered an oddity. *The Pilgrim* they called him, and he relished the title. There was beauty in it and there was truth, both of which had been lacking before he had dedicated himself to the path. He had fought the Long War, but the conquests had always rung hollow.

After Terra, what is there? he had often asked. *What are these little wars and tawdry victories when the greater triumph still eludes us?*

Yet when he had plucked his first spur of saintly bone from the embrace of a reliquary he had known the most sublime joy – blossoming within him with hepatic certainty, a pulse and a pain, like the birth of something new inside. Soon he was transplanting the entire bodies of saints and martyrs into the ship, then the crypts which held them, and then finally entire sections of cathedrals, tomb complexes and chapels.

Bit by bit, brick by brick, he had colonised his ship with it. He had rendered the vessel a profaned marvel that sailed the stars in stalwart service to the masters of death. Warriors without peer, who drank the wine of heroes when it had been sweetened by the offerings of the carrion-bees. Death was their draught and their elixir. It held no fear for them now that they had taken it into themselves. Consumed and become it.

'And so we come to it at last. A beautiful reckoning. If only our friends had the wit and will to see it, eh?'

None answered. His brothers were readying themselves for battle and the things which had once been crew could no longer answer. Men and women long since fused to their stations, preserved in the awkward glory of living death. Extensions and excretions of the ship, growing from between the borrowed flagstones like obscene weeds. He had made sure to plant them well and to tend to them when he had reworked the bridge. Heaving, wheezing things, their minds meshed to cogitator hubs and command matrices, looked ahead with milky blind eyes, tears of rheum dried upon their cheeks.

Tuul snorted at their silence and stalked forward, his axe whirring and clicking as it tasted the air, as though it knew murder was near.

'Time has blackened my armour – almost as badly as poor absent Ulgrath's,' he said with a sigh. 'He would have loved to be here, standing shoulder to shoulder as we readied to end them. Still, he will be well occupied in the absence of these little zealots.'

He raised his free hand and ran it across his armour. Five black gouges had once been cut across the plate, as though by the actions of an immense claw. He had repaired the markings, of course, but they had been left unpainted as a testament to his sacrifice and his devotion.

'By his hand am I raised up and made his instrument,' he breathed. 'And I shall have my reward when the galaxy breaks and burns, and the Path cuts the Imperium's throat. Until then we put out the lights... and then put out the lights.' He chortled to himself at the half-remembered verse.

Tuul sighed and then finally engaged the vox.

'Rouse yourselves, my brothers! Call your cult echelons to attention and prepare the boarding craft!'

A chorus of voices greeted his pronouncement with maudlin glee and resignation.

'You can do better than that!' he burbled with barely contained delight. 'This night we avenge ourselves on our lesser cousins. Bastards of Dorn, eternally seeking an enlightenment that never comes! We shall give them the illumination they so crave! Ten thousand years we have fought and struggled in the Long War while generations of them prosecuted their Eternal Crusade! Ten millennia of being poor reflections. Now we come to the test.' He grinned. 'We will break the Astartes defenders and prise the little pathfinder from her ship. Cut her throat and their dreams die – regardless of whether Velua burns or not.'

It had been some time since Ulgrath had spoken to him through the corpse ministries. No matter; he was certain. The Destroyer would simply be enjoying his defilement. And if not... well, Tuul would simply finish it himself.

'Now, my brothers, we honour our fallen and our missing. Once, long ago, we would strike from the darkness of the dusk. Now, let us call down the storm upon them.'

Every hangar bay and launch berth unleashed its charges in one motion, flooding from the ships in an almost liquid surge.

They swarmed out and into the void even as the great weapons of the Death Guard fleet opened up behind them. Light and flame crossed the void in questing fingers of lance-fire or the howl of macro-munitions. In many of them the powder had long since dampened and gone rotten and yet the vast ship-killing shells still flew and burst against the enemy's void shields, or buried themselves in iron hulls like ticks into flesh. Corrosion wept from every facet of the war fleet, the vessels a cursed approximation of an Imperial detachment. Each boarding craft and drop pod was ancient and rusted, encrusted with void-lichen and strange barnacles, or rendered glossy and black like an insect's carapace.

They crossed the void and the Imperials met them with fire of their own. It blazed in the holy darkness as though their weapons discharge alone could dispel the horrors of the void or the madness of the Rift. The Astartes vessels were the first to commit themselves.

In his sanctum Tuul waited. He held his axe close to his breastplate and he began to whisper to himself, counting the myriad wars he had fought, trophies he had taken, and men he had killed. His fingers tapped against the haft of the axe. Seven taps and then silence. Seven taps. Silence. Beating out the future's metre.

He could have weathered these storms from behind the stronghold walls, gathered with the others of the Hand, but he could not bring himself to miss what was to come. He would blind and break them, one by one, till their sevenfold dead clogged the very abyss. Then he would know that it was done, and his master would be pleased.

He mused to himself that he had not thought to scry this engagement. No organ had graced his hands to bind the future into place. There was a savage joy there, one he had not felt in quite some time. The Grandfather had brought him to this place. The Grandfather had appointed this moment.

Here and now, he would carve his own fate into creation's skin and see his favour rise in reality's shadow.

Chapter Forty-Two

WOLVES AND KNIGHTS

WALLS OF IRON AND GOLD

QUEEN AT WAR

The ship shook as it turned into the storm of enemy fire, void shields flaring in the darkness and lighting with a cascade of impossible colour. Enemy ordnance and boarding craft were burning and dying against the shields, their mass and energy shunted sideways into the roiling maw of the warp.

Behind them the Rift roared and spat, too mighty for the mind to hold. The laws of physics ceased to have any true meaning this close to it. The ruins of what had once been worlds turned, half-devoured like an abandoned meal, in the clutches of the Rift's infernal energies. Shades and hues which had no place in the material universe oozed across the cosmos as surely as oil across water.

A polluted sea. A hateful tide.

Katla did not look back at it. She forbade her crew to look back either. Crimson light filled the bridge, bleeding from the emergency lumens as the waves of corruption flowed out behind them. All focus was turned upon the looming horror of the plague fleet and the swarms disgorging endlessly from their puckered iron flesh.

Their own formation kept moving in response. The ships of the fleet turned and let their broadsides sing back at the plague fleet. Where the Imperial vessels demonstrated a unity of purpose in their active voids, the plague fleet was ragged in its disarray. Oily fields sputtered at the impacts or crushed the incoming projectiles against bubbles of stolid energy, where others simply took the punishment. Detonations rippled through their bloated bellies with muted thunder and dull light. They endured. The great hell-ships swallowed down pain and injury as though it were nothing and cast it back with spiteful glee.

'Get me a vox-link to the magos in his observatory,' she snapped. Katla turned her spear over and over in her hands as she paced before the command throne, ignoring the mad light of the shifting hololith.

'*I am here, captain,*' Yazran's tinny voice said, crackling over the bridge's vox-horns. '*Is this truly necessary? I have calculations to perform. The data we are gleaning from the empyreal-spacial overlaps at play is truly remarkable.*' He paused and static rushed in to fill the silence. '*My requirements are simple, captain. You brought me here for a purpose. Allow me to fulfil it.*'

'You have my leave to do just that,' Katla said evenly. She ran her free hand through her hair and sighed to herself. 'But you may not have noticed that we are under attack.'

'*I could hardly ignore it, captain. Immaterial translation vectors are rather obvious to my equipment and my specialised cerebral processes. The enemy have found us again. We shall fight and prevail or we shall fail and die. Perhaps at the very end I shall miss the sterile spires of Vandium and its Navigators, though I doubt it.*'

'All I ask is that you keep working while we deal with these matters,' Katla said. 'Seal yourself in and prime your skitarii. Open the chamber to none but myself. Is that understood?'

'Don't make me come up there and kill you myself, magos,' she barked. 'Allfather watch over you, you cantankerous little priest of iron.'

'Omnissiah protect your physiological integrity, captain.'

The line went dead. There was only the sounds of the bridge as it readied for war. The crew were animated now, their discipline twinned with passion.

She spared a glance to the hololith. All across the battlesphere the fleet was aligning. The vessels of Task Force Saturnine moved into formation alongside the ships of the Black Templars. An alliance of wolves and knights. Katla tapped the tip of the spear against the hololith's plasteel casing and closed her eyes.

Without looking at the viewports, without recourse to Yazran's machines or to the auspex, she could *feel* the rhythm of the battle as it changed. Ebbing and flowing with the swiftness of the seas. Machines could scry the heavens and Navigators could set their course by their stations of passage and the Astronomican's glorious light, but she... Her gift was a raw and wonderful thing. An instinct. A hunter's knack – as much a part of her as the world of Winter and War which had informed her lineage. Even now she could feel the shifting of reality's skin as it grated against her mind. The enemy ships like arrows as they tore into the materium, as they trailed their witch-light ephemera in a cloak of screaming souls.

Gooseflesh prickled along her arms and back. She could feel sweat pooling along her spine, slicking the inside of her armour.

'Whatever comes,' she said, loud enough for her crew to hear, 'we will be ready for it.'

The basic principle of defence was an awareness of what you protected and what was arrayed against you. Such things had been taught to Augustus since he had become a Custodian. So long ago, it seemed, by any mortal metric. Years growing into decades, slowly becoming centuries. In that time he had not faltered or failed, and he had yet to feel the creeping touch of weakness. Dedicating himself to the Eyes of the Emperor was a distant prospect, and one which the doomscryers had yet to foresee.

You must roam beyond these walls and taste the galaxy. You shall carry a gift until it becomes a burden. You will light the way and guide the seeker. You shall be a bulwark when the hour grows dark.

'And here we are,' he intoned to himself. 'The walls without are iron. The walls within must be gold.'

The Palace was a distant dream and yet a memory held close no matter where he roamed. He had set it pre-eminent in his thoughts as he served Task Force Saturnine and delivered the Primaris miracle to the Lion Warriors. He had thought of it as he guided the fleet to unite with Helvintr. He did not know if he would survive to return to it, to walk its walls and serve its one true master. He had not yet borne the honour of serving as a Companion.

It mattered not. What came next was *His* will.

Augustus knelt in the central corridor which led to the bridge, his spear before him. He checked the weapon and then checked it again. The sirens and flickering lumens did not disturb him, could not break his absolute focus. There was only the weapon. Only duty. Only the walls without and within. Only the woman.

Augustus could feel the graven names upon the inside of his armour, pressed against his flesh, reminding him who he had become. Who he had been shaped into. Each name a gift.

His vigil had become his world, his moment, and his Palace. All that remained was to wait for the true test to begin – like a final Blood Game playing out.

* * *

Katla watched as the first boarding craft finally penetrated the voids.

Like the bursting of a dam, they flooded inwards – a rush of storm-tossed detritus thrown through the shields. Metal and air vomited into the void, screaming from the impact sites, bleeding out as ancient systems engaged and bit. Melta-cutters and plasma-drills tore at the *Queen*'s hull. The boarding craft were of ancient and ill-trusted patterns. The hulking menace of the Kharybdis and the spiked horror of the Dreadclaw vied for prominence along the spine of the flagship. The wilful and long-since-insane machine spirits delighted as they drilled home.

Alarms began to sound. The crew readied for the true test. Runes flickered amber and crimson across myriad consoles as the venerable ship responded to the violation. Her guns fired, speaking in sweeping arcs of ordnance as they sought vainly to keep the enemy at a remove. Whole flocks of the boarding craft were atomised in the crossfire. Point defence turrets swept others from the stars, letting them clatter in flames against the hull.

For every boarding craft that died there were countless other things that waited to replace them. Fighter craft that swooped on smoking thrusters and enormous, horrific flies, some with Neverborn clinging to their backs. They dived for the *Queen*, weaving between arcs of fire, burrowing deep. Further swarms of boarding craft were sweeping out towards the other ships, especially the *Seventh Vengeance*. Relishing the promise of the battle to come.

'Focus fire upon the *Pilgrim's Promise*!' Katla snarled. The enemy flagship loomed large in dire reflection of the *Seventh*. Other ships were moving to protect it. The *Song of Sickness* and the *Throne of Apotheosis* interspersed themselves, turning to soak the maximum volume of fire, even as their guns coughed throatily and hurled their own vast shells.

The *Oath Adamant* was the first ship to die. Caught in the crossfire of too many enemy vessels, its shields burned away and burst. It listed, still firing, still fighting, as the enemy carved it apart.

Katla watched it die. To see a ship die, to see the entire world it represented snuffed out, thousands upon thousands of souls consigned to death, to burn or to freeze in the void. To die screaming, scrabbling for air, was a hideous way for a life to be ended. An infinity of bad deaths: disaster, war-atrocity, environmental collapse. All bound up into one. Void war held a million different ends, an eternity of red snow stretching out forever.

Katla blinked away the thought and turned to regard Aneirin. 'You are with me,' she ordered. 'To the end.'

He drew his chainsword and knelt, pressing the tip of it to the deck. He looked up at her.

'As you will it, captain. To the end.'

Chapter Forty-Three

SEEDS OF RUIN

CHAMPIONS OF FAITH

CONJUNCTION

The *Seventh Vengeance* rang with the sound of bells and crawled with a pungent miasma that spread and scuttled through the ventilation systems.

The ship was a mighty thing – forged in ages past by master shipwrights. A battle-barge was not an easy ship to murder and the *Seventh* was amongst the sturdiest of vessels: made to fight and endure, to slay mankind's foes and to carry on until the next battle. The next war. The Eternal Crusade tolerated no laxity or weakness. The only way was forward, until death finally ended duty.

Gaheris strode through the ailing ship and let his sword speak for him.

The Champion split the skull of the first Plague Marine and kept moving. The Black Sword rose almost of its own volition, called to violence, incensed by the enemy's very presence. With the blade in his hands he felt righteous. He knew, in some small sense, how Sigismund himself must have felt as he fought before the walls of the Palace.

Terra was so far away now. Humanity had clawed their way forth, back across the stars, out from the Solar System again and again. Mankind had striven for the heavens in a Dark Age, and it had risen from the ashes of Strife. Then, when Horus' madness had at last been ended, humanity had once again surged forth from its birth world.

He turned aside another strike, ducked under the sweep of a weeping mace, and hewed the Plague Marine apart at the knees like firewood. He turned the blade, and drew it upwards, parting the breastplate. He watched it peel away, taking the lion's share of the warrior's skin and muscle with it. Armour and warrior came apart in a rush of black gore.

He did not fight alone. His brothers, the majority of their strength, were with him aboard the battle-barge. Around him the brothers of Squad Fidelitas battled. Barisan fought his way to Gaheris' side, his sword sweeping around to protect the Champion's flank. The Sword Brother grunted as a plague-ridden blade glanced off his armour, but uttered no complaint.

Already the seeds of ruin had embedded themselves in the fabric of the ship, pumping their poison into its veins. Chapter-serfs fought valiantly with cultists or were cut down by the relentless advance of the Heretic Astartes.

Hulking figures advanced, swinging censers that puffed and hissed with stinking incense. Brother Arvin charged them, his pyreblaster singing as it bathed them in sacred burning promethium. The Plague Marines paused in their ministrations, glaring at him as though they could rend him apart with their hate alone, before they collapsed into ashes and ruptured war plate.

Havdan fought his way forward and let his bolter speak. More of the enemy turned as he came at them, soaking up his fire before they raised their own corroded weapons and returned it with gleeful interest.

Havdan faltered. The Initiate went to one knee, struggling to raise his bolter, not realising the arm that held it was already gone. A bolt-shell impacted his helm and his head snapped back, before a second shot detonated within his skull.

'Avenge him!' Gaheris bellowed. 'The enemy are weak! Let them die for their betrayal!'

They were dying by degrees. Gaheris knew it. The enemy seemed without limit, crawling through the guts of the ship like maggots, seeking to overwhelm the Black Templars with numbers alone.

'Champion!' Barisan called. 'We are outnumbered! What are your orders?'

'We fight to the embarkation decks!' Gaheris shouted back. 'Give the order to as many brothers as we can muster. All squad detachments. We are to make our way to the *Pilgrim's Promise.* Once aboard we shall disable the vessel and take their leader's head!'

'Praise be,' Barisan said and bowed his head. 'It is an honour to fight at your side, Champion. I only wish that Neophyte Aneirin were here to share in our glory.'

Aneirin.

'The order extends to the Neophyte,' Gaheris said bluntly. 'The rogue trader will have, I am certain, some decisive means of delivering him to the enemy's flagship.' He chuckled dryly. 'Once aboard we will do all we can to ensure his transit is successful. It *must* be successful.'

They kept fighting, never stopping as they advanced towards the embarkation decks. Cultists died in droves, carved apart and left like so much offal at their feet. Heretic Astartes tried to bar their way and were cut down. They fought as a unit, now, the Champion at their head. Blades and bolters operated in perfect, glorious harmony. They battled like champions of the faith. No saint or martyr could equal their devotion, their dedication or their zeal. They fought as the ship died around them, as the crew bled and fell so that they might live. Entire sections of the *Seventh* were vented, killing fire in its cradle, flushing the foe from its decks like so much waste.

They forced the final door and stalked out onto the embarkation deck, past the burning ruins of crashed enemy drop-craft. The Overlords and Thunderhawks remained almost miraculously untouched.

Other battle-brothers came after them. Their markings belonged to different squads. The dour warriors of Iram stood alongside the glory-hounds of Squad Excelsis. With them came the crusade's few Techmarines.

'Brother Hargus,' Gaheris said. He strode forwards and placed his hand upon the warrior's crimson shoulder. 'The Emperor-Omnissiah calls for your expertise, and that of your brothers. Will you bear us forth with fire and fury, alongside our battle-brothers?'

'It would be my honour, Champion,' Hargus growled. The servo-arm attached to his armour pivoted and whirred, clamping at the empty air as though with animal hunger.

The enemy had been dispelled for now, their first assaults blunted. Now the initiative lay with the Black Templars.

'Send word to all other squads,' Gaheris said. 'Have our ships enact aegis primary interdiction patterns. Protect the rest of the fleet and converge upon the enemy. Bring us about them like a mailed fist, while we slip beneath the Death Guard's notice and kill their master.'

'It will be done, Champion,' Hargus said, with a nod and vox-click.

'This is to be our moment of glory. Sacrifice and death in His name. No one can ask for more,' Gaheris said. 'Let our lives be our offering.'

Chapter Forty-Four

AQUILAN SHIELD

FOR THE THROAT

THE FACE OF DEATH

Augustus fought his way through the ship as it descended into madness.

The *Queen* was a doughty vessel, strong and ancient, its hull so recently reinforced by the Imperium's finest artisans. Shielded by the strength of other mighty vessels, by the Black Templars and the war-might of Saturnine, it alone had the chance to endure. Perhaps the realisation was new: that the entire endeavour had been sacrificial, to shield a single ship – and indeed a single soul – at the expense of all others. Even his own.

Now he ranged ahead of the defenders, outpacing leather-clad Fenrisians and flak-armoured Terrans as he sought the enemy. Out and away from the bridge, into the compromised areas of the ship. He had memorised the layout, mapped out the potential avenues of attack and already determined where he would be best placed to aid. The ship was a warren of chambers, levels one atop another. There were transit nexuses throughout, where major thoroughfares met. The ship's schematics had contained melodramatic designations such as the *Wolfway* and the *Halls of Steel and Fire*. Augustus ignored them, rendering everything down to pure tactical acquisition.

He stood at a confluence of passageways that would bring the enemy either directly to the bridge or on a path to secondary fire-control infrastructure abutting the gunnery decks. He thought of his creed.

Find them before ever they threaten the Palace.

That was the only creed which still mattered. Ten millennia they had served, generation upon generation, as the Ten Thousand had slowly regained their strength. His order had fought and bled for the Emperor – as was their solemn right and duty. He had stood sentinel upon the walls for so long before ever he had been called out to open warfare. Others had borne that honour, moving in secret amidst the multitudes of humanity. Addressing distant threats and sombre eventualities. All before the galaxy had split and the Edict of Restraint had loosened its bite.

Now he did the will of the regent and the will of the Emperor in one stroke.

Augustus passed through the smoke of a burning cogitator bank and straight into the path of seven traitor warriors, stopping them in their tracks. All were helmed and yet Augustus was certain he could sense their bemusement.

'What do we have here?'

'One of His little pets? A golden guard, all alone.'

'Like a little lion,' another chortled. It raised an ornately rusted bolter and tilted its head. 'Far from your walls, are you not?'

'Be silent,' Augustus said at last. He raised his spear. 'You will not speak your hollow treacheries in my presence.'

'You always were a brood of arrogant bastards,' snarled the

first. Augustus marked it as the leader by its girth and the great horns which protruded wetly from its helm.

Augustus moved, faster than they could follow, already firing. Bolt-shells caught the leader high in the chest, staggering it even as the Custodian swept his guardian spear round to rake the other traitors with fire. Armour distorted and broke. Flesh burst apart in a wet rush of unclean fluids.

Bolt-shells whistled past his head and detonated against the walls of the corridor. He swept his spear up and cut the head from one of his attackers, letting its bolter clatter to the ground beside its shorn helm. Spinning, his blade cut the throat of another, before he ducked low and drove the powered blade of the spear up and through the breastplate of a third. He drew back and then thrust once more, ensuring that he punctured both of its hearts.

Augustus felt a blade scrape down his back, skittering off his armour as it failed to find purchase. Fat bolt-shells pummelled his armour and hammered him into the wall before he pushed back, whirling about and repeatedly slamming his spear into the shooter's face until the helm caved in. Blood fountained from the wounds. He kept striking. Driving it into the deck, forcing his boot against its chest and kicking it back.

The remaining three traitors were retreating now, stumbling back and away, firing as they went. Augustus raised his spear and stood in the midst of the maelstrom of fire.

'Do you see His judgement? Do you see His will incarnate?' Augustus said, without joy and without true anger. 'I am Augustus. Sworn in this moment to the Aquilan Shield.' He lunged forwards and the spear's flawless tip gouged into the leader's chest. Augustus pulled back and the traitor was yanked towards him in one swift motion. Blood trickled from its faceplate.

'And I will not fail in the mission He has set for me.'

* * *

'Bring us about,' Katla snarled.

She had finally allowed herself to sit in her throne again. Her armsmen were gone – out and holding the line beyond the great doors. Aneirin was gone, summoned to the ship's depths by a call only he had been privy to. Even Augustus was elsewhere, fighting his own war.

Katla sat enthroned in bronze. Her fingers danced across the knotwork patterns etched into the seat, chasing wolves and eagles and serpents along their paths. There was an agitation that came with battle – one that warred with the perfect peace that could be found in surrender to combat. This was the true balance of life and death. Where she burned the brightest. She was a huntress queen. A jarl of Fenris. She had hunted the void-kraken and the great stellar whales. She had led her crew against the Devourer's spoor time and again. She had survived the ravages of the genestealer and their cults. All for this. All to be here at this moment. Fire at their back and the enemy before them.

She considered the galaxy's relentless symmetry. She might die here, as she had almost died before.

The void shuddered around them as more ships died. The Death Guard had numbers and unholy endurance: for every ship the Imperial volleys claimed, two more died in retaliation.

'We have launches from the Black Templars fleet, jarl!' Ana called. The Master of Auspex seemed incredulous. 'At least a dozen gunships under cover of bombardment.'

'I want our guns to lend their strength to the Black Templars' endeavour,' Katla said, hunching forwards. 'Every weapon we have should be committed. All save the spears.'

'Aye, jarl!' the crew chorused as one.

'We will sweep in on them and do what we do best,' Katla growled. 'We will go for the throat.'

* * *

The words filled Yazran's artificial mind like a mantra, prayer wheels of code and cognition turning over and over within his head. So much of his mind was cybernetic now that he found it a task to lower his processing ability in order to commune with *base life*.

Standing upon the bridge, in the presence of two genetic masterworks of the Omnissiah's own design, he had found himself only ever deeply unimpressed. Yes, the Astartes and the Custodes showed that it was not the tip of the spear that would conquer the galaxy but the point of the needle – yet all that they were depended upon sacred knowledge: cast out into an uncaring and unforgiving universe by the Machine God in His Golden Age.

It was not enough to chart the heavens. Not if there was no will to claim them.

That was the fascination with Imperium Nihilus. Lurking, primal and terrible in the reptilian meat of his flesh brain. It was impossible to truly know what transpired beyond that wall of fire and madness. Stable routes across the Rift were vital, as vital as any war of the crusade that was yet raging. Remaining trapped above Vandium, gazing at the stars, would never have truly been enough. It was only now he stood in the heart of a warzone that he understood that.

Katla, for all her flaws, had liberated him.

Visualise. Interpret. Analyse.

In an isolated substrate of his cognitive matrix he could see the Rift. Its hateful eccentricities. The patterns emerging from the rampant and untrammelled chaos of it. This route – this, as he now thought of it, *Attilan Gate* that Katla was so convinced existed – was a marvellous and terrible thing. Not stable by any stretch of the imagination and yet... poised upon the brink of something transcendent.

His eye-lenses clicked and rotated as he watched the abstract approximation rotate and shift as an ocular overlay. He reached up and his iron fingers stroked the empty air, making fractal constellations of pure data shift and congeal into truth. The chamber was sealed. He could barely even feel the shaking of the ship as it moved under power and fired into the darkness, driving back the enemy. He was only tangentially aware of his skitarii outside the chamber, holding their vigil. There was only the mathematics of the moment.

Stability here was a fitful concept. The current route, the Gate, as Helvintr insisted on referring to it, had, by his estimation, been in flux for the entirety of the period since the Rift's opening, sometimes yawning wide and other times contracting until the way was obscured entirely. It was, he thought, as though an external force were acting upon it. As pernicious and uncertain as the flow of a battle.

Perhaps the Omnissiah fights for the sanctity of His dominions and the forges lost beyond the veil?

A reassuring thought, and yet an unlikely one. Yazran, whatever else his failings, was a being of logic. Enough of his mind had been excised and replaced, reworked and expanded, that mortal emotions and doubts held little sway. He aspired to the uncaring purity of the machine.

When this was done perhaps he would be granted the honour of more alterations. There would be time then to consider these things. Free of onerous obligations, fatted with new wisdom, and with the influence and resources to dedicate himself anew to his fixations. There would be much need of maps and their makers once the galaxy was open to the Imperium once more. From out of the ashes of a dying empire he would craft the Astrocartographica Yazran Imperialis. All would know his glory then.

Something changed in the interpretation.

His eyes stalled, stuttering in their motion the way a man of flesh would blink. There had been something there, for just a moment. A creeping error, expanding into an anomaly. Black against the roiling colour. He sought it again and found nothing.

Fleeting. Unstable. As he had surmised. Yet if it were a sign to steer by, another station of passage or landmark of note, then there would be use for it.

Yazran let his hand drop and took up the info-quill, idly taking notes upon a data-slate. They were simplifications of what he processed but they would have their uses.

It happened again. A momentary flash of something dark and vast. Hidden in the warp's shadow. Yazran felt fatigue creep into his circuits just from having glimpsed it. He felt it deep in his iron bones. He reached up with his free hand and expanded the image once more, staring intently and waiting with bated respiration. All that mattered was this moment. There was nothing else in all of creation as important as–

He saw it this time. By the Omnissiah he saw it!

It was a false divinity cast in noctilith and cruel metal. It stared at him with the features of death itself, immense and enthroned, its surface studded and barnacled with monolithic constructs. A flawed colossus that had held the fabric of the universe itself together in brighter days. Now it struggled, ailing and flawed, as the galaxy trembled and broke and burned.

He stared into the abyss of its eyes and it stared back. He watched, powerless, unable even to move as emerald fire kindled in those sockets. As it truly *saw* him and understood his purpose. An imperfect machine and lesser form of life, trying in vain to interface with something potent beyond his ken. A gnat trying to understand the workings of a god-engine.

Yazran's fingers clenched into fists. His entire body seized and spasmed. He could feel himself rising off the ground, connected to the floor only by the static streamers of green lightning. He could smell cooking meat and burning machine parts. It held him in its gaze. A gaze older and vaster than worlds, more ancient and potent than the entire history of the human species. When man had first crawled from the muck, this edifice had been there. A pillar of creation, labouring even as all around it burned.

It saw him, perceived him with an intelligence that was not truly alive nor dead. It did not dream. It simply waited.

Yazran felt something pop in his head. He tasted metal. Smoke was drifting around him as his systems overloaded, as his mind cooked in his skull and his remaining organs ruptured.

If there is a path through then this is the ferryman. The taker of tolls.

His fingers spasmed against the data-slate, driving the quill against its surface hard enough to snap it between his metal digits. Yazran screamed. An atonal screech of machine pain forced its way out of his vox-emitters. Binharic agony saturated the close space of the observatory. Around him the lights began to die, the great mechanisms he had transplanted and nurtured began to fail.

The last thing Magos Yazran was aware of was the sensation of a great hand of black smoke and flickering lightning closing around his meagre, mortal consciousness and snuffing it like a candle.

Chapter Forty-Five

THE LAST CRUSADE

DUTY'S TORCH

MIRACLES AND MEN

A dozen craft weaved their way through the burning void, crossing from the *Seventh Vengeance* to the *Pilgrim's Promise* upon wings of fire. Stocky Overlords shared the skies with the reliable profiles of Thunderhawks. They dived between immense detonations, swerving around deployed munitions, and fired as they passed the enemy boarding craft. Fat black-armoured Dreadclaws burst apart, casting a rain of flailing bodies out and into tremulous space.

Gaheris watched each kill with muted pride. The Champion sat apart from his warriors and checked the chains binding him to the Black Sword. Now more than ever those links were a promise, as true as oaths. He had been chosen: set to burn with the God-Emperor's fire. Even now there was a nimbus of light around his helm, catching on the angles of his armour. The Armour of Faith had dents and scratches upon its holy plate, smeared with blood and ashes, and yet it had never looked more noble.

He was just another link in the chain, bound to generations past by purity of purpose and surety of duty. To bear His wrath, as Sigismund had in the days of the Siege. To pursue the lords of the enemy host even to the gates of the warp itself. That was their glorious purpose, etched into their very heart and soul by tradition, carved upon their being by the sacred gene-seed itself. Every brother of the Eternal Crusade, be they High Marshal or Neophyte, was shaped by the warriors who had gone before. Names that would live forever in the annals of the Chapter.

Helbrecht. Grimaldus. Kordhel. Bohemond. Sigismund.

And yet, above all of those mighty names, beyond any of those luminaries there was Rogal Dorn himself. The Emperor's Praetorian. Lost to them these dark millennia. Gaheris remembered pilgrimaging to the *Phalanx* as a member of the Chaplaincy and gazing upon the preserved bones of Dorn's own hand. It had been a wonder in a galaxy of miracles. Each bone of the sacred relic had been scrimshawed with the names of the Chapter Masters of the Imperial Fists – the very Chapter from which Gaheris' own gene-line flowed – and Gaheris' heart rejoiced to look upon it. Yet behind that savage joy there had been doubt.

Would that it was his body entire, preserved for our reverence.

The galaxy was a cruel place. Hope was so often blunted by harsh realities. Yet even in the face of such odds there was a place for faith. They had learned with awe of the rebirth of Roboute Guilliman, after all. The successors of the Ultramarines had exulted and yet, to Gaheris' eyes, it had been a hollow celebration. Too many of their number fought with their heads and not their hearts – devoid of soul.

Perhaps it had always been so. Sons of too-different fathers, their common cause frayed by circumstance. Gaheris knew the reputation his Chapter courted and the distaste that other Space Marine brotherhoods held for them. Belief in His sacred divinity was rare among the Adeptus Astartes but Gaheris felt no shame in his beliefs. It had carried them this far, and the God-Emperor had guided their endeavour with His own hand.

'Champion?' a voice asked, and Gaheris shook away his thoughts. He looked up at Barisan. The old warrior held tight to a support strap and rested his other hand upon his sword. He stood unmoving even as the ship shook and moved, gazing down at the Champion with restrained admiration.

'Speak your mind, Brother Barisan,' Gaheris said with a sigh. He leant his head back against the ship's hull and waited, measuring his breathing.

'It is an honour to stand at your side, Champion,' Barisan said with a nod of his head. 'Even if this is our final stand, our last crusade, we shall not fail you. You have led us true thus far.'

'Though you had your doubts,' Gaheris said.

Barisan looked away. 'I did, Champion, and it shames me that I was wrong.'

'You were not wrong, Barisan,' Gaheris stated evenly. 'Much has transpired in these last years of battle and madness. We have crossed the void in true and noble service to the Indomitus Crusade, to Battle Group Thor and Fleet Sextus. But we are Black Templars first, by the God-Emperor's grace.'

Gaheris stood as he spoke. The ship shuddered again. Beyond its walls, ships were still dying. Not all of the transports would make the crossing – some were already reported as lost. Warships died in fire, their hulls coming apart in flame-edged shards like the debris of tectonic world-death.

'We are all bound by the blood and will of Rogal Dorn, through the martial example of Sigismund.' He placed a gauntleted hand upon Barisan's shoulder. 'There will come a time when we are gone and those who remain will stride forth into the darkness, to bear the God-Emperor's light into Imperium Nihilus. New leaders and Champions, set upon new crusades.' He sighed softly. 'This may indeed be our last, but the crusade itself is eternal. We shall never stop. Never cease. Not while a son of Dorn yet draws breath in this galaxy.'

'Praise be,' Barisan said and then turned to regard the other members of the squad. 'Praise be unto the God-Emperor, who sets our Champion in our midst!'

'Praise be!' the remainder chorused. Blades and bolters were readied with abandon now. Arvin's pyreblaster ignited, bathing the interior of the Overlord in flickering crimson light.

New thunder sounded as the Overlord's heavy bolters opened up, joined immediately afterwards by the scream of the nose-mounted melta cannon. Return fire burst around them and the gunship veered, before turning again to fire. There was resistance, but against their numbers and their zeal, it did not matter.

The gunship shook with the unleashed assault and then banked hard, swinging itself round before finally hitting the embarkation deck of the enemy vessel with a thud. The weapons were still firing, relentless in their fury. Alarms began to sound and Gaheris was up and on his feet, moving towards the ramps that were already falling.

'With me, my brothers! We end this!'

The Overlord's ramp hit the deck with a squelch and the warriors rushed down it in one swift motion, out and into the hangar bay of the *Pilgrim's Promise*. The vessel's baroque design was truly ancient, a pattern lost to the ravages of the Heresy War which had killed the dreams of the Great Crusade just as they had been about to achieve fruition. Now the decks were furred by ferric mosses and distended by growths like iron wasps' nests. Things scuttled and crunched beneath their footfalls as they spread out across the hangar bay, weapons raised and seeking targets.

The enemy lacked the numbers of the Black Templars but replied with impressive commitment. Fourteen Plague Marines stalked along the upper observation platforms, firing down at

the Black Templars and their transports with an almost lei-
surely disdain.

The Black Templars returned fire. More than half of the
fleet's Space Marine contingent had come with Gaheris, to fight
and die at the will of their Champion and the God-Emperor.
Bolter fire and plasma hammered the upper reaches, driving
the Death Guard into cover, slamming them back against the
walls, or bowling them over entirely. Ancient armour cracked
and melted. Blood and pus oozed from wounds in plate which
had long since become a true living component of its wear-
ers. Some of the warriors came apart in clouds of screaming
insects, their voices rising on the air like the howls of dying
children.

The Overlords continued to fire from their landing sites, their
heavy weapons hewing through sealed bulkheads and compart-
ments. Misshapen things that might once have been servitors
burst like buboes, staining the ground with yet more bloody discharge. Where shells struck the walls they too began to bleed,
weeping rusted trails of sanguine fluid as though the ship itself
was alive. Gaheris didn't doubt that it was possible. The ways
of the Archenemy were corruption and horror.

He surged off the ramp, across the wide space of the burning
hangar, and up one of the flights of stairs onto the observation
levels. The Black Sword was already kindled, its edge aglow
with killing fire. One of the Plague Marines turned, bolter lowering, raising his sword – but slow, too slow. The Black Sword
struck the powered blade with a thunderous clang and drove
it back. Gaheris turned the blade and swung again. The traitor's blade snapped back and Gaheris heard the satisfying pop
as something broke in the Plague Marine's arm.

Rusted and rotted armour seized. Joints and gears stuttered.
Gaheris spun about and drove the sword through the thing's
bloated chest, bearing it to the ground and then pushing back

up. The sword trailed behind him, burning blood hissing from its edge.

He advanced upon the remaining Plague Marines. Bolt-shells burst around him and against his armour. Still he came, undaunted and unbowed. Something broke within his plate and yet he pushed onwards and raised his blade.

Weapons fire transfixed his foes, soaked into their bloated forms as they lumbered forwards to meet him. Three remained. Two continued to return fire, arcs of hissing bolt-shells pounding down at the ranks of the Black Templars. Brothers died screaming, hurled to the decking by the impacts. They writhed and spasmed in agony before finally falling silent.

Gaheris snarled and lunged forward, hewing one of the Plague Marines clean in half. The other two turned to fire. He engaged the vox in his helm.

'Now.'

The ship shuddered a moment later as massed fire found its shields, collapsing them.

A second after that it shook again as it came under sustained assault. Boarding torpedoes hammered into its metal skin, meltas and drills cutting through the rusting hull and biting deep. A number of them tore through the embarkation deck's ceiling, slamming into the ground as the shock assault found its mark. Doors exploded free and smashed down.

Behind the Black Templars another ship skidded its way onto the deck, wreathed in fire. It was not as doughty as the Overlords or the Thunderhawks, nor as swift as a boarding torpedo, yet the armoured shuttle had done its part.

Aneirin threw himself from the ship's lowering ramp, his blade already singing for the enemy's throats.

One of the Plague Marines burst apart in a fresh volley of shells as the other Black Templars joined the fray, and Gaheris swept high for the remaining warrior. His blade found the neck seal of the enemy helm and sent the head flying, off and away into the midst of his brothers. A cheer rose, greeting him as he stood before them, surrounded by bodies.

Gaheris looked down at the assembling ranks, yet only one of the warriors truly caught his eye. Of all the brothers who had made the crossing – through the fires of combat or the travails of the warp – it was Aneirin whom he fixed upon, bound as though in the aftermath of a dream.

'Brothers!' Gaheris called. 'We stand upon the cusp of victory or death. We fight as the primarch himself fought, so long ago. Aboard an enemy vessel, bearing only our weapons and our wits. Serving His will.' A cheer went up as Gaheris descended once more, boots clanking on the metal steps. 'Neophyte Aneirin, step forward.'

Aneirin obeyed, going to one knee before the Champion.

'Aneirin,' he said. 'You have fought and bled for your brothers. You have followed the God-Emperor's will. The crusade waits for no one. It is rapacious.' He deactivated the Black Sword and placed it upon the young warrior's shoulder. 'On this day I bequeath upon you the title of Initiate and all the honour that encompasses.'

Aneirin was silent. He looked up at the Champion agape, as though not believing what he was hearing, before looking down once more.

'When we are returned to the fleet than you shall be granted your full armour and all the responsibilities of an Initiate. There will be much to discuss in the days to come.'

'You honour me, Champion,' Aneirin began.

'No,' Gaheris interrupted. 'You honour yourself, in word and deed.' The Champion smiled. 'Duty is a torch. It burns bright and weighs heavily, and from time to time it must be passed on anew.'

'And I shall bear it gladly,' Aneirin said. He rose and looked the Champion in the eye. 'I shall not fail you, Champion. Nor the Chapter.'

Gaheris felt the familiar pressure building within his skull and turned from Aneirin, gazing up into the looming bulk of the vessel. Beyond the sundered doors, through the wet and corroded meat-metal of the ship, lay corridors of stone lit by low braziers and ancient sputtering lumens.

'Now we go onwards, to face the enemy in his lair. The God-Emperor's light shows us the way.' He swept the Black Sword around and pointed it through the smoke and miasma of the ship. 'We will take his head, or die in the attempt.'

Aneirin fell into lockstep with his squad brothers, elated and perturbed in equal measure.

He hadn't expected his elevation to come so soon, much less at the hand of the Champion and in the midst of pitched battle. None of the others said anything. Even Arvin, his humour usually ascendant, seemed subdued and distracted.

The atmosphere within the ship was oppressive, the air thick with strange vapours and buzzing insects. The creatures scuttled over the stonework, fluttering from statue to statue and perch to perch. Other things moved in the shadow, made of the shadow, their bloated forms burbling as they scampered out of the Space Marines' sight. Ephemeral things, waddling around like lords of all they surveyed. Merely another symptom of corruption.

Upon Dakaram there had been castes of Aneirin's tribe who had wallowed in the plague pits and carrion grounds, their minds so broken that foulness seemed utterly fair. Whatever sickness had lurked within the rotting flesh had addled their minds and left them as palsied and twisted things. Wars had been fought to drive them out, but the infection always reared its head again.

Now Aneirin understood why, when vectors such as these

roamed the stars, resisting the cleansing fire of the Walking Sun. He thanked the God-Emperor every day that he had been raised up to embody the Eternal Crusade. He had passed through the trials which would have humbled lesser applicants: spirited away to vast ships of steel and fire, forced to undertake leaps of faith into hidden grav-traps in the darkness of the deep engine holds. To starve. To fight his fellows. All while his mind and soul were put to the question, to see if his faith burned true.

Beneath the eyes of the Chaplaincy he had become a Neophyte of the Black Templars and now, in the sight of the holy Champion, he had been elevated again to stand as a true Initiate.

'Stand tall, brother,' a voice barked from beside him and Aneirin turned. Barisan looked back at him, and Aneirin could almost hear the smile in his voice. 'You doubt, and that is natural after a sea-change, but you are worthy of this honour. Do not forget it.'

'Thank you, brother,' Aneirin said, his head lifting. He felt his fingers close about the activation rune of his chainsword, spurring the weapon to another furious snarl. 'I had expected the elevation to come at your hand, not that of the Champion. A rare gift, and one I shall not neglect.'

'These are strange times,' Barisan grunted. The Sword Brother had kindled his blade and shield, hoisting both up before him as they advanced into the belly of the leviathan. 'In an unending war we take what small rejoicing we can. No matter what else comes to pass, you have earned this. It has been a privilege to watch you adapt to our ways and to surmount every challenge presented to you.'

The squad continued to advance, weapons rising at every shifting shadow and vaporous discharge. The interior of the ship was an ever-shifting thing, warped by the touch of the Dread Powers and yet, fundamentally, a thing of Imperial familiarity. The decking had changed and the layout had been altered, yet the ship had once sailed under the Emperor's colours and fought His wars. More than that, every surface had been laid over with stone and statuary pilfered from a hundred, perhaps even many hundreds of worlds. Imperial saints gazed out from alcoves and places of bleak reverence, their stony eyes impassive and uncaring of who walked beneath their sight.

'This place feels more like a tomb or a museum than a ship of war,' Arvin muttered. Even he couldn't bring himself to burn the idols that rose around them, monolithic and apathetic. 'Where the past comes to die.'

The statement hung over them like a shroud as they passed under stolen arches and the leering skulls of long-dead martyrs and heroes. Banners had been nailed to the walls while others displayed full-length glassaic panels, taller even than the Space Marines who stalked beneath them. Stylised Astartes warriors fought alongside gilded renditions of the Adepta Sororitas, frozen forever in the glassaic tableaux, their presence almost mocking.

There was a resounding pulse behind their advance, a heartbeat in the metal which was soon joined by the tolling of bells. Stinking incense puffed from opening doors and the first of the enemy began to move into these mockeries of sacred spaces, just as they were mockeries of the holy warriors of the Black Templars.

Where the others had been bloated and distorted, these warriors were truly immense. They wore ancient, heaving Terminator plate of the Cataphractii pattern. Moving like stuttering pict-images they lumbered into view, and they raised immense weapons. Rotor-cannons whirred and clicked like insectoid mandibles. None of them wore helms. Each displayed the grotesquery of their flesh with a strange pride. Rot and rash were worn as badges of honour.

Some chuckled or babbled and others whispered prayers

to their obscene god. Seven warriors in all – and by the God-Emperor Aneirin despised the hateful repetition of it – advanced into the corridor.

They began to fire in the same moment. And the warriors of Squad Fidelitas began to die.

Chapter Forty-Six

A QUEEN'S CHOICE

BLOOD OF WOLVES

THE WINGS OF SAINTS

Beyond the viewports all was fire and death.

The great war galleons of the plague fleet were unnatural in their endurance, soaking up damage that would have slain vessels which still obeyed the laws of physics. Explosions burst within them and the hull plating distended and bowed outwards, or spewed forth macro-volumes of artificial blood and pus into the waiting void. Katla had watched the bio-ships of the hive fleets at war in the past, and these vessels mimicked that hatefully organic presentation, through the warped lens of distorted human technology. No matter how much ordnance they poured at them, or how many lance beams found the enemy's hulls, the vast ships refused to die, as if reducing all the struggle to just another game, a pleasant diversion from more important matters.

Men and women rushed about the space of the bridge now. Consoles had begun to burn and smoulder. Cogitators had blown out with the strain. The vox had grown unreliable, rife with artefacts and the daemonic laughter of the enemy. Yazran was silent and she cursed the magos for his laxity or his weakness. There were no bodies to spare to check on him. Not now.

Tyra and Calder had joined her within the sanctum of the bridge, alongside other members of her honour guard. Bodil lurked about the edges, checking runic wards and muttering to herself.

Everything beyond the viewports was lit by fire or the Rift. The enemy ships loomed through the flame like giants, wearing their wounds and their spiteful existence in a cloak of damnation. Katla pointed here and there with her spear, identifying targets. Lesser ships fit for their guns. Few assaults reached the swollen majesty of the *Pilgrim's Promise*.

'Has there been any word from Gaheris or his men?' Katla asked.

'Nothing, jarl!' someone called. Katla cursed under her breath and tapped the spear against the ground.

'Throne take these bastards,' she snapped. 'We hold until the Champion sends word.'

And yet... In her heart Katla knew that to do so would mean their death. She had the Rift behind her and the enemy before her – like an echo of past pain. She remembered Draedes and the wounds which bit from there, scars which would never heal, losses she could never recover from.

Móðir.

The word cut across her thoughts and her fingers tightened around the spear's haft.

Why shouldn't I risk it? Here and now we have our chance.

'Get me Arkadys on internal vox,' she called.

A moment later the connection was made. Katla heard the weariness in the man's voice, pained by his undertaking.

'Jarl,' he breathed through gritted teeth. *'This is unsustainable, jarl. The Gate is screaming, waxing and waning. It will not hold. We cannot hold.'*

'If there is a way through, you could lead us?' Katla asked. She heard the man laugh bitterly. She envied him – not his gifts and his suffering, but to be apart from it all. Ensconced in his eyrie, safe and warded.

'*If I try then we will likely die, jarl!*' Arkadys called. His words filled the air, stilling even the din of battle. '*There is a narrow passage and a narrower window. Some of the magos' observations might help to extend our chances, but I reckon them to be low. Everyone on this ship will die and they will die screaming.*' He paused. '*There are* things *nearby, jarl, waiting in the warp, hanging like dreaming planets ready to wake and feed. Entities of such horrific might that they would end us. They linger like patrons for the battle to come, watching their own champions as they ready for the kill.*'

'Lay in the course,' she said bluntly, and cut the link.

No one spoke or responded. She turned to looked at them all.

'I will turn from no option available to us,' she said. 'If we are forced to flee then we will do it. If we can find the primarch a way into Nihilus, we will find it. And if we can survive to seek my daughter, then by the Allfather we will do it!'

'We are with you, jarl,' Tyra called. Others took up the chant. Katla girded herself, her jaw set grimly.

'It is not inevitable. Not yet. I will turn aside no chance for us to survive and do what is required of us.' She turned and gestured to her honour guard. Her huscarls fell in about her with practised ease. 'Now. Let us cleanse our ship.'

The enemy had brought multitudes, a swarm of bodies, a tide of filthy and scrabbling cultists, to flood the *Wyrmslayer Queen* like a plague through veins.

They were poison. Hunger-sharpened and pale, their skin bruised and puckered by blisters and buboes. They wore flak armour and boiled leather, wielding lasguns and autoguns with a hateful intensity. They were a grey and green surge as they thundered through the ship's corridors, inexorably borne towards the major organs of rule. Bulk landers had brought them here. Some still wore void suits from where they had been forced to march across the exposed hull of vented sections of the *Queen*. Others had likely plunged into the void with no such protection, their lives offered as a sacrifice to their god.

Katla's armsmen met them head-on.

As the cultists rounded corners they slammed into readied shield-walls and knew the bite of sword and axe. Others fired from between the swordsmen, drilling precise holes through the skulls of the cultists. There were so many. Too many. Yet the narrow tunnels and passageways worked against the unholy tide. The warriors of the *Wyrmslayer Queen* knew their ship and their craft of war. Equally monstrous invaders had been repelled and the ship taken back. It had happened before. It would happen again.

Men fought against cultists, hand to hand, battering them back with the rune-etched edges of their shields, carving them apart with precise bladework.

Katla was amongst them, waiting for her chance. Whenever it came she would lash out with axe or spear and stave in a skull or impale a body. She felt the line hold, then bulge, and then bow outwards again as her men slammed back against the cultists. Her men dug in their heels as the enemy met them again and again, the cultists' bodies making a wet rapid staccato as they hit the shields over and over. Then they fell. Heads smashed or cut free, throats opened, bodies split or pinned by spearwork.

Death stalked the ship with all its myriad faces and all its horrors, come to cut threads; to spill the blood of the wolf and make red snow here amongst the stars. No true earth beneath their feet. Only the sea of stars and the broiling hunger of the Underverse.

When the xenos came for them it was with a rapacious desire to destroy human perfection, to drive it out in the foolish hope that this could again be *their* galaxy, yet when the traitor raised arms against them it was a keener struggle. This was a battle for humanity's very soul, for the sake of every last loyal son aboard the ship, and for the ship's sanctity itself.

Katla relished it.

Blood coloured the air again and again. Cultists dropped in droves, felled like firewood. Hooked blades and rusted machetes slammed against shields and yanked them down, allowing other filthy robed figures to strike at her men.

A screaming cultist hurled itself at the shield-wall, scrabbling up and flailing at the armsmen with hands knotted into mouldering claws. Flesh sloughed away as it fought and screamed, thrashing and dashing itself against the wood and metal. The claws found a skull and squeezed, clenching until the armsman's eyes burst and ran down his cheeks. His body tumbled back, his shield clattering to the ground as the ghoulish thing bore him down. Teeth flashed in the darkness as the cultist began to gnaw at the man's neck.

Katla's spear impaled it. Driving it back, forcing it into the midst of its kin. Wide eyes stared at her from dirt- and rot-smeared milk-pale faces. She slammed the cultist into the deck and pulled back her spear. Blood sizzled upon its edge, burning away to powder.

'Forward!' she roared. 'For the Allfather!'

More cultists died in a hail of blows and bullets. Galvanised by their jarl, the crew rallied. Ranks closed. Weapons drummed against shields. Their resolve tightened as they watched their leader, their jarl, their queen, stalk forward, her blade already bloodied.

The cultists shrank from them, outmatched and outgunned. They backed away along the blood-slicked deck, staggering and stumbling until their backs hit something solid. Not the walls. The cultists turned, scrambling on their knees before they looked up and their faces broke into grins.

Through the throng came their masters.

Katla had yet to see one of the monsters in the flesh and now that they were before her she found she almost couldn't look away. Vast beyond imagining, larger than Gaheris or one of his warriors and even more terrible. Rendered strange and twisted and cruel by the attentions of dark gods. Katla had seen what the ravages of Chaos could do to a world – there were few now, since the opening of the Rift, who had not – and yet, to see these warriors before her was to be confronted with the inevitability of ruin. Even the mightiest could fall. They could falter and succumb.

Giants in corroded plate, warped and overgrown like coral, strode through the ranks of their acolytes like heathen idols brought to life. Crooning, verminous obeisance followed after them as the cultists rallied and simpered at their feet. As they moved Katla could feel dread coil in her heart, writhing like a serpent through a great tree's roots. Nothing so corroded and broken should move as they did. Their entire existence had been reduced to a mockery of their former purpose – a cracked reflection that showed only the cost of turning from the Emperor's light.

The giants raised their immense weapons and fired.

Shields broke. Men burst as bolt-shells found them and detonated within them. Blood painted the walls and covered their fellows, streaming down their armour, gumming against shields and blades. Some of her troops threatened to break and desert their posts. She could see the wild animal fear flaring in their eyes, the sweat sheening their faces as they turned and looked for any way out.

Katla stepped forwards. She buried her spear in the decking

then drew and raised Wrathspitter. The volkite weapon whined and kicked as it fired, as a beam of crimson energy hurtled out and into the midst of the enemy. Cultists who had interspersed themselves between the jarl and her prey were atomised, reduced to clouds of ashes. When it hit the first of the Plague Marines it seemed as though the armour would hold, just for a moment, before it began to slough away and melt. The warrior staggered backwards, his entire form juddering as the volkite blast cored him out. Blood and fluids cooked off in a disgusting mist, rising from the body in plumes of charnel steam.

The other Death Guard halted in their advance, pausing only long enough to laugh. Bolters fired with renewed vigour and other Heretic Astartes produced sputtering flamers or gurgling chem-throwers.

The line began to fall back, to fragment and break. Katla readied to fire again but too many were already dead. Bodies lay spread out across the deck and smeared up the walls. Pale, tattooed faces stared up at her with accusatory eyes.

'Fall back!' Katla called. She fired another searing blast over the heads of the retreating men. It went wide, the giants side-stepping it with contemptuous ease, as though she had only succeeded in slaying one because they had allowed it. Laughter burbled down the corridor as they advanced.

Bells were tolling again. Ringing in sudden alarm.

Not them. Katla blinked at the thought as they fell back, sealing another door behind them. The sound of the Death Guard's laughter faded, replaced moments later by the clatter as they began to force the door. All of it drowning beneath the ringing, the ceaseless siren.

'By the Throne,' she whispered.

'Jarl?' Tyra asked, her weapon raised, awaiting the inevitable.

'Mass immaterial transit alarms. Something is coming.'

* * *

Beyond the battle reality undulated once more, rippling with the psychic bow-wave of many vessels. They forced their way back into the material realm like knives, rimed in warpfire and burning with unnatural light. They blazed as they tore out of the sea of souls, as their Geller fields died and void shields crackled into life. The tumult of their passing washed over the gathered fleets and then fell away as the first vox-broadcasts began to ring out through the murdered system.

They were singing.

Voices were raised in hymns, praising the God-Emperor with rapturous fervour. They came like lightning from the clear sky, a sign from the heavens burning across the stars. An impossibility. They sang of the death of worlds and of their salvation, and of the burning tomb of the saint. They spoke of His grace and her glory, entwined and risen up. They spoke with the voices of Velua and the Golden Chain, of the living and the dead.

The fleet that emerged was ramshackle. Every last vessel bore scars of battle. Hulls were split, transmuted by fire or by the touch of the warp. The very universe had rallied against them in a vain attempt to delay their progress. They were the war-wounded of a besieged shrine world and they were the dying embers of a crusade fleet, bound together by faith and fire.

The flagship of Marshal Urtrix, the *Terra Eterna*, wore its wounds upon its iron skin with bellicose pride and roared ahead of the co-mingled fleet, loudly broadcasting its furious intent. It barrelled onwards towards the *Pilgrim's Promise* and lit its primary guns. Its weapons had burned in anger across the vastness of humanity's beleaguered realm, expending their ammunition in a hundred battles. They had chased the spoor of the plague fleets and their cults in a dozen engagements, each one a diversion, drawing them away from their true targets.

Yet Velua had burned. Not in the fires of the enemy but with a glorious light, a flame of faith which had flared – momentarily – brighter than the distant light of the Astronomican. The fleets had turned at that signal, returning to a world at war, a world resurgent, a world *blessed*.

Now the great ship fired. New thunder split the void. Shields blazed and burst under its fury. Behind it came other ships which had kept their bellicose vigils, the remnants of Battle Group Thor. At their sides were pilgrim barques, mass-conveyers and prayer-arks from the Veluan orbit. They bore no weapons and no shields, minimal armour plating save what Imperial belligerence provided. An army of desperate men and women, in the mould of the ancient and fabled Proletarian Crusade, cast forth into the void to spit blood and teeth into the face of a spiteful universe.

The bridge of the great vessel rang with confusion and discord as Chapter-serfs and Astartes warriors rushed to respond to immediate threats. The war was amongst them now and they rose to the challenge with typical zeal.

A figure stood alone before the great viewports of the *Eterna*, their arches marked by the Templar cross clenched in the talons of Imperial aquilae. The dirt and grime of the war had yet to be scraped from her flesh or washed from her armour and yet she evinced only strength. She did not, or perhaps could not, stand still. Her hands clenched and unclenched with fevered motion. She watched the fleets clash and re-form, shift and move like flotsam upon the wave.

Her entire body moved as though aflame, held in a fist of fire, burning with His light and His love.

Irinya Sarael looked out at the world with eyes of golden flame, her armour battered and broken, her sword held before her. Tears flowed down her cheeks only to evaporate to steam mere moments later. Laughter threatened to break free from her lips but she swallowed it back. There was a time and a place for her joy – this was not it.

'He led us true. All of us,' Irinya breathed, unheard. 'Glory be unto Him.'

And at her utterance the great ship lurched onwards into the fray, guns sounding through the tumult like the call to prayer, hymns sung on every channel by the voices of mortal men and women, and the throats of transhuman warriors.

Into the battle and unto the fire.

Chapter Forty-Seven

DEATH OF FAITH

BY HIS VISION

CHAINS BROKEN

They died.

Aneirin staggered back from the tumult. The solid plane of bone which had once been his ribs was broken, fragments of it biting into his flesh as he swayed like a drunkard. Larraman cells flooded his bloodstream, desperate to arrest the bleeding. He could feel the warm heat burning through his extremities, building in his chest. Toxins danced within vein and artery, making his oolitic kidney ache.

Every advantage the God-Emperor had handed down to His Angels through sacred bioengineering was failing him, struggling to compete with the ancient and ossified fury of the Plague Marines.

They strode forwards undaunted. Their leader was a warp-swollen thing: his helm ram-horned, his faceplate weeping pus and old blood. Fangs curled up from the gorget, rendering his visage that of an animal's skull. In the inconstant light of the cursed vessel it seemed almost mocking. He rejoiced in the killing, as he had savoured it down ten millennia of unholy warfare. Oaths forgotten and purity surrendered.

Aneirin breathed blood and bit back agony. *What could drive a warrior of the Adeptus Astartes to spit upon his vows? What could make him such as this?*

If his squad brothers had answers then they had neither the will nor ability to speak them.

Arvin had been among the first to die. The enemy's fire had found his pyreblaster. Heavy shells burst against its housing before they penetrated, hitting its fuel tanks and igniting the volatile promethium within. Arvin died screaming, cooking within his armour before the second volley detonated his helm and skull in a shower of shards and fragments.

Fenek and Partus fought as one unit, throwing themselves forwards, bolters singing. Grenades had arced through the air to detonate in futility amidst the enemy. Fire and shrapnel could not touch the Terminators. It barely even slowed their stride. The hulking monsters passed through the flames and the dust of ruined stonework. Glassaic shattered and fell in a lurid rain of shards, revealing the rotted bulkheads beyond. Battle peeled the veneer from the vessel, bit by bloody bit. Not a temple, not even a heathen fane; simply a mask for atrocity and evil. Disgust flooded through Aneirin with the surety of pain.

The Death Guard laughed while they killed. The lead Terminator reached out with one crackling power claw and slammed Fenek's head against the wall. The warrior barely had time to strike, his chainsword chewing against the armour impotently before falling away. The traitor hooked its claws under Fenek's chin and flicked them. Blood rushed from the sudden wound and Fenek dropped to the ground, drowning in his own spilled life.

Partus howled in anger and threw himself forward, heedless of danger. His blade rose and fell, tearing at the plate, scouring

growths and barnacles from it in a wet rush. A sound rumbled
up from the monstrous figure and Aneirin realised a moment
later that it was a sigh.

'How disappointing,' the monster burbled, before a melta-
beam carved Partus in half.

Aneirin forced his chainsword down against the decking and
pushed himself up, standing as tall as he was able. He could
feel the building pressure in his chest, the Furnace readying to
burn hot within him and bear him forwards in a final fugue of
glorious battle. A last stand worthy of the primarch. One even
Sigismund would have relished.

Barisan hurtled past Aneirin and brought his blade up, slamming it through the Terminator's breastplate. Servos snarled as
he pushed forward, forcing the blade onwards through ruined
plate and rotted flesh. The Terminator chuckled and stepped
forward, pushing the blade deeper.

'That's better,' the Plague Marine said, his voice a breathy
whisper, like a corpse's exhalation. 'Still some spirit in you.'

'More soul and spirit than you, daemon!' Barisan spat.

The Plague Marine laughed in his face again, holding his
arms wide, shielding Barisan from the bullets of his fellows.
'Oh, child,' he said. 'If you cannot tell the difference between
daemons and disciples then it surprises me that you have lasted
this long fighting His wars.'

He raised his clawed hand, digits flexing, and drove them
down. The claws dug into Barisan's helm, clenching and flexing as they bit through the ceramite. The monster tore it away
and hurled it to one side, savouring the bloodied face of its prey.

Aneirin fired his bolt pistol. Shells clattered against the plate,
detonating and skittering aside. The Death Guard turned labo-
riously and regarded him with cold detachment.

'There's that youthful spirit!' the monster chortled.

He was about to strike down and end Barisan when he

paused. His entire form began to shake. The other Plague Marines faltered around him. An atonal gurgle flowed from the Terminator's helm, threatening to break into a scream.

'Can't you hear it?' he hissed.

Aneirin couldn't hear anything. Even the most rudimentary of squad-to-squad vox had failed in the embrace of the enemy. He looked around and blinked.

Light was filling the chamber in a wash of ephemeral gold. He could almost reach out and touch it, hold it between his fingers.

'Initiate!' Barisan called. Aneirin's reverie broke. The golden light retreated. He rushed forwards, still firing, lending his own strength to the Sword Brother's.

Yet when the first of the Death Guard began to die, it was not by Aneirin's hand.

Gaheris had become a ghost within the ship, a black smear of light and fury, bringing the God-Emperor's wrath to the impure.

He had fought through the vistas of a hundred temples, beneath the eyes of saints and heroes. Broken thrones had sat over many of the chambers and yet they were not the edifices of his vision. The future called. It beckoned with golden promise and he was the puppet that moved to the will of those hands. *His* will.

Crawling things made of rotting flesh and perverted will died under his blade. Cultists were carved apart in his relentless advance. When he crossed the path of the Traitor Astartes, he fought them blade to blade. None were his match. The God-Emperor had chosen him to bring wrath to the unholy, to the greatest of their number. He sought Tuul. By the God-Emperor's guidance he knew the champion of the Death Guard was near. It spoke in the very marrow of his bones.

Yet the Emperor's wisdom was absolute, and he could feel the pull of the vision flowing and changing. He remembered the figure, fighting the final battle, tearing down the cloaked shadow with blade and bolter. Limned in fire and lightning.

He knew who lurked beneath the Armour of Faith and had been chosen to bear the Black Sword.

Gaheris fought on until the horrific sounds of the ship finally faded away and were replaced by the purity of combat. He rounded the corner at a run, suddenly confronted by the backs of a number of massive figures. Terminator clad, overgrown with corruption and madness, the sins of their souls plain upon their flesh. Gaheris did not hesitate. The Black Sword came up and a foe died in a rush of unclean gore. It slammed through the thing's spine, twisting to be sure, and then he swept it sideways. The traitor slumped in its armour – already dead, and he was already moving.

The sword swept round and cleaved through a gorget, down and round, severing an arm. In such close quarters only melee weapons counted for anything. The blade was sharp, expertly honed. His foes wielded great power mattocks and scythes, like agricultural workers rather than warriors. They struggled to bring them to bear, snarling and growling as he weaved amongst them.

He could see his brothers now. Barisan and Aneirin yet lived. He muttered a blessing under his breath. Barisan pulled his blade back and swung again for a horned monster which was already moving, too fast for its bulk, to slam its claws down.

Bullets impacted the monster as Aneirin fought to save his mentor. Gaheris gritted his teeth and surrendered to the ebb and flow of battle. He surrendered to the sword.

He hammered against ancient servos, slamming and slashing until they seized or shattered. He hurled a grenade from his belt and watched it detonate. He hurled himself through the fire, trailing it from burning purity seals, coated in soot and ash. He spun the pommel into the side of a warrior's exposed skull and then slammed himself right against the wall. He turned and drove the tip of the blade through the thing's open mouth. Up and into its brain.

He heard Barisan cry out as the Death Guard's claw cut low to bury itself in his chest. The old warrior spat blood into the Death Guard's face and pushed forward with all his weight. Gaheris watched as the tip of the Sword Brother's blade pushed through the Terminator's back and he moved in that moment, slamming the Black Sword through from the opposite side and out in a spray of rancid blood.

It turned, ponderously, like a Titan or a Knight might turn, like a starship reorienting itself, and backhanded Gaheris. The power-fielded digits sizzled against his sacred armour, etching their passage across his faceplate. He growled and yanked the sword back. The air was filled with the stench of burning flesh.

'Insect,' the Terminator spat. 'Unworthy even to play at being Champion. You are not as he was, not even a fragment, not even an echo, and you–'

Gaheris bellowed with hate as he threw himself at the enemy. The sword swept in and turned. Rose and fell. Barisan had fallen, his hands slipping away from his own sword.

New hands took hold of Barisan's blade and *pulled*. The Death Guard growled as the blade slid from its fleshy scabbard and then swung around. Transfixed again between two blades, the remaining Terminator looked around at his slayer in disbelief – suspended between the swords of Gaheris and Aneirin. The younger warrior was panting, crawling with sweat. Gaheris could detect the macro-adrenal stink of the Belisarian Furnace's activation.

The Death Guard hung, quivering, before both blades completed their arcs. The thing's torso slid apart in three still-spasming sections, drenching the floor in a myriad of stinking fluids.

The enemy were dead and a brief moment of respite fell.

Gaheris turned to aid their brother, but Aneirin was ahead of him, already kneeling at Barisan's side.

'Brother,' Barisan gurgled through a throat filling with blood.

Gaheris was no Apothecary but he could tell, from the wound placement alone, that the Death Guard had known exactly where to strike to puncture Barisan's secondary heart, multi-lung, and the primary lungs. Even had there been an Apothecary present, there would have been little that could be done.

'My brother... you fought well. You fought as an Initiate ought. I–' Barisan paused, fighting the pain. 'I am proud.'

'I only wish I could have done more,' Aneirin whispered, head bowed.

Barisan looked up and past him, finding Gaheris' eyes. Gaheris nodded slowly, softly.

'You will,' Barisan said. He reached up, his hand quaking, and took Aneirin's hand. 'You fight with zeal and fury. Fire and faith burn in you. I know that the Chapter will endure with young blood such as you coursing in its veins.' He coughed and the air was coloured crimson once again. 'Champion?'

'Aye, Sword Brother?' Gaheris said and stepped forwards. He remembered his vision. The valiant warrior locked in their final stand. The helmet torn free. The face beneath it.

Aneirin.

'The boy must live,' Barisan whispered.

'And he shall, Sword Brother. I shall ensure it with my life. His work is not yet done, but yours is at an end. You have served well and you have died well.'

Barisan's lips creased into a smile and he fell finally silent and still. Aneirin reached down and closed his eyes, gently, with the tips of his gauntlets.

'He died for me,' Aneirin said uncertainly.

'He died for all of us,' Gaheris corrected. 'He died for the God-Emperor's dream.' He reached out and took Barisan's sword from Aneirin, weighing it in his hand. 'A fine blade. It will suffice.'

'I don't understand,' Aneirin said.

Gaheris let the sword's tip bury itself in the decking and turned the Black Sword over. Slowly, with his free hand, he unwound the chains which bound him to the holy blade.

'I will not survive this,' Gaheris said. 'Perhaps I was never intended to survive it. I have fought and bled for the dream. It is not my place to see it realised.' He laughed. 'The future is the province of the young. You shall be that future, Aneirin. Already I have seen His hand upon you.'

He handed the sword to Aneirin, watched him test the weight of it – wrestle with the perfection of it – and then hold it too low to his side. Gaheris knelt and scooped up Aneirin's abandoned chainsword and Barisan's longblade, holding one in each hand.

'Go,' he said. 'My chains are broken. My oath fulfilled. The sword cannot end here with me. Bear it back to the Chapter's bosom. Tell them I have seen you armoured in faith and bearing Sigismund's sword. You shall break the enemy's black hand, before ever it finds our throat.'

He revved the chainblade and turned from the young warrior. The golden light had returned. The God-Emperor was guiding his arm one last time.

'Go in His light, Aneirin.'

Chapter Forty-Eight

AEGIS OF GOLD
WITH HIS VOICE
THE CHOICE

They were being hunted through the ship like vermin.

For every doorway Calder's talents sealed they were granted mere moments of time before the enemy smashed through them. The line drew back, bit by bit, step by step, chamber by chamber, back towards the bridge. It galled Katla, the necessity of retreat, yet all other courses were denied to her. Even the volkite's fire had done little to stay the Death Guard's stolid and lumbering advance.

Neverborn things capered and gambolled at the feet of the Heretic Astartes, their every step leaving little hissing footprints or snail-like trails of slime. They cooed and burbled from between needle teeth, pausing only to chew at the corpses left behind, tiny jaws ripping at the dead flesh and swallowing it down in greedy gulps. The Death Guard stepped over their tiny charges with exaggerated care, even as they trod through the corpses of the slain defenders. Bones snapped beneath their boots and they chortled in time with the parasite things which now clung to their greaves, gurgling and hooting with their own tinny laughter.

She fired Wrathspitter, cutting a line of crimson down the corridor towards the advancing warriors. The shot winged one of the trudging Plague Marines, blowing an arm apart in a burst of ashes and fire. It looked down at the severed limb, almost glumly, and then continued on its path, muttering blackly to itself.

More bolt-shells exploded around them and Katla ducked through another closing door. Calder looked up from his efforts as the door began to seal, in time for a round to reduce his skull to a burst of crimson slurry. Katla felt the hot spray of blood on her face and staggered backwards, almost falling to the ground. Someone, Tyra she thought, began to scream.

Katla blinked. She reached out for Calder, blood staining her hands, and then pushed back up.

'We need to move.'

'Where?' Tyra looked up at her captain with wide, wet eyes, swallowing back her sorrow. 'He was sealing the gates and there's nowhere else to go. We're almost at–'

'The bridge,' Katla finished. 'We gather all we can there and we defend it.'

Tyra looked nervously from side to side, paralysed by fear and indecision, her eyes wild, before Katla seized the other woman by the back of the neck, pulling her close.

'Up,' Katla said firmly.

The defenders moved without discipline now, driven only by fear. The line fragmented as the huscarls began their desperate retreat, tripping over each other and the fallen as they hurried towards the bridge. Katla joined them, moving at a run. Walls passed her by in blurs of grey and gold, the flickering of runic markings whispering across her vision. They hurried under black iron arches and carved spars of driftwood.

These halls had been violated before – too recently in the memory. Old wounds were being reopened. She remembered *hordes that had worn human faces and yet bore the spoor of the genestealer etched into their very souls, the masters of those multitudes scrambling through the flesh of her ship with their great claws and wicked tongues, talons puncturing her flesh.*

Katla Helvintr had been left for dead once before. Never again.

The lumens were flickering and dying around them as they drew near to the bridge. Darkness fell. The only light was the sparks rising from the doors behind them as they were slowly forced by the enemy.

'Skitja,' Katla cursed. The great portal of the bridge had stalled, wedged half-open, a black abyss opening between the brazen doors.

Something moved in the darkness. Katla raised her weapon and then paused as a blade kindled. Light bled out into the space, catching on the carved doors, picking out the details upon the wielder's form.

Augustus' beautiful armour was a ruined aegis of gold, marked and scored by enemy action. He was panting, his form heaving with the effort.

'Captain,' he offered, his voice even and calm, in contrast with his wounded state. 'The bridge is yours.'

'Augustus... Throne, you look as though you gave a good account of yourself.' She looked behind her. 'More are coming.'

Augustus moved forward and brought his spear up, letting the glittering edge illuminate the shadows. 'Then they must be vanquished utterly.'

'You cannot mean to fight them all,' she breathed, bracing herself against the wall.

'If that is His will,' Augustus said simply.

She could not look away from the weapon he wielded, like a

bolt cast from the heavens. It might as well have been the Spear of Russ, or the Allfather's own great weapon, forged to carve the very firmament.

'I will hold this ship as though it is the Palace itself, captain. That is why I was made. It is why I am here.'

She was silent and then sighed and shook her head. 'It is madness for one such as you to die for this endeavour.'

'I do not die for this crusade, captain,' he said. He did not smile, nor was there despair or sorrow beaten into his features. He remained statuesque. Impassive. 'If I end here then it is in His service. The auguries brought me to this moment – to ensure that the choice is presented. That you live to make it.'

'All this? For me?'

'The fate of billions may depend upon the actions of a single life, for the choices of a single Guardsman upon the line can change the course of a war. The correct preacher in the right place, their lips dripping with inspiration, can set a thousand upon the proper path. Destiny is not the great sweeps of High Lords and inquisitors. It is the flesh and blood of the Imperium, yearning to do as they are bid. We serve Him. We protect Him. We shelter His Imperium and His Palace from the storm.'

Augustus stepped forward and she followed him with her eye. Ahead of him the doors were breaking. He hefted his spear up and sighted along its length. Then he knelt and readied himself.

'If we do not meet again, captain, then I ask only that you commend me to my order.'

'I shall,' she whispered. She turned and hurried into the bridge. 'Get the doors moving!' she called. 'Rouse the machine spirits! Force them closed if you must. We move!'

Men struggled and toiled, pushing and pulling at the immense slabs of metal. Hydraulics squealed in protest, their mechanisms silenced, as slowly they began to move.

The last thing she saw as the doors ground closed was the

shower of shrapnel and sparks at the corridor's end, as the enemy broke through and Augustus began to fire.

'Do you hear?' The voice whispered from the vox-speakers mounted into the throne as Katla took her place. *'We speak with many tongues upon the ether. Do you hear us?'*

'I hear you,' Katla said. She still held her spear. Sat upon her command throne she looked like an ancient depiction of justice, weighing life and death in her hands. 'Who speaks?'

'I was Irinya once. I am still Irinya. I remember being her.' The signal distorted and for a moment Katla was certain that this was the voice of the enemy. A mockery. A trap. *'We bear His light and the light of Velua. We walk with the saints and speak with His voice. From out of the darkness we are come to offer light.'*

'This is your fleet?'

'It is His *fleet, my sister.'* Behind the woman's words someone was singing. The signal crackled again and when she spoke it was as though Irinya, or whoever she was, spoke in more than one voice. *'Even if we die it is done in service. The elect shall be raised up to His right hand. They shall endure even these trials and horrors.'*

'To what end?'

'The only end that matters.' The voice laughed. *'We watched our world burn until we decided that we would burn with it. He gave us His fire and before it the enemy were as nothing. Swept away in the deluge.'*

It was a stream of zealot babble, every word alive with symbolism and madness. Katla was about to question Irinya when she spoke again.

'I have seen you, Katla Helvintr. Wolf of the stars. Queen and conqueror both. I have seen what you will do and what you must do. That is why we are here.' She laughed again. The raw mirth of a warrior. The tinkling laughter of a child. *'Velua and the other*

worlds of the Chain were candles in the cruel dark, yet we made them lighthouses. Faith, and faith alone, can shape the universe. Bring the pilgrims here in their multitudes and have them pray before the Rift, and watch the way open. Bring forth the Mechanicus with their machine-dreams, and watch the door be held. All that shall be done because you have dared.'

'Because it was so fated,' Katla breathed. 'Because it was promised to me.'

The battlescape beyond the viewports was limned in fire. Weapons committed themselves across the vastness of the void and ships dashed themselves to debris against greater foes. They burned brightly, sacrificial offerings before the greater inferno behind them. The radiance of faith warred with the power of the warp. Bit by bit the Rift was changing, shaped by titanic forces beyond her ken.

For a moment Katla was certain she could *see* the light that the woman had spoken of. Cast by the distant surviving world of the Golden Chain, blazing with the Allfather's will. This *was* the Gate she had sought, the Attilan Gate, and blood and faith were its keys.

'And yet you think you know the nature of that promise. That this is your hour.' Katla could almost hear the shaking of the other woman's head. *'That is not to be.'*

'I will not be denied–'

'Who denies you? You deny Him. You yield to pride and self-interest where you ought to think of Him and His dominion. The galaxy is burning. Here and now, before your eyes, it burns. We stare down the outer hell itself, teeming with its devils. Do you think it is an easy thing to bear? If we are not true in this moment then we will fall. There is always a choice. The choice is between Him and damnation. I will not say that it is between the easy path and the hard path. All roads are stony now – paved with the bones of the loyal and the damned, the living and the dead.

If we falter now then all is lost. I have come, we *have come, to ensure that those who are worthy are spared.'*

'I am not worthy,' Katla whispered with a shake of her head.

'In this moment, you are,' Irinya continued. *'One of His golden chosen stands in your defence. Perhaps he bleeds and dies for you. How is that unworthy? Because you have failed before? Your daughter is lost, yes, but what is lost can be found once more. If you have faith. If you believe.'*

Katla held her peace and closed her eyes. The ship shook again. The sounds of battle were right outside, echoing through the vaulted chamber of the bridge, calling her. Calling her home, or down and into the Underverse. The wights were scratching again at the sea ice of reality.

She could follow her heart or her duty, but Katla knew she could not do both. The dream came to her again. Astrid as she had been. Vital and strong. The sum of her joy. She knew what her daughter would have done, were she here.

She opened her eyes. Katla Helvintr made her choice.

Chapter Forty-Nine

THE SANCTUM

ARMOURED IN FAITH

HAND OF JUDGEMENT

Gaheris fought through the bowels of the *Pilgrim's Promise*, through a hundred different shrines, following the God-Emperor's golden light. It burned in his sight: catching upon relics stolen from dozens of worlds, glinting from the wings and talons of Imperial aquilae, blazing through glassaic and glimmering upon the surfaces of bas-reliefs. Faces of legends gazed at him sombrely, half lit by the burnished light of the vision.

Under the light of the God-Emperor's grace the ancient features of Malcador the Hero seemed to bear a passing flush of vitality. The enemy had not defaced the statues but instead preserved them amongst the rotten bones of the ship, locked in a terrible and hateful symbiosis. It was sickening to look at, the defilement. So much of what was rightly the Emperor's domain, stolen away into the darkness to be hoarded out of sight, now just the playthings of traitors and monsters.

Gaheris forced himself onwards, alone, up a flight of stone

steps from another time, around the base of immense marble columns carved with the likenesses of lords militant. He gazed up at them as he passed by, his eyes following the lines of their downturned swords – tips larger than Deathstrike missiles.

Above him a huge dome stretched up, as though the dimensions of the ship had been distorted to fit it there. Constellations scarred the skin of it, picked out in silver and lapis. Behind the stylised stars, in sweeps of gold, spread the wings of the eagle, out from the gilded orb of Terra. His breath caught and the vision-light spiralled across it till the dome was rendered as a blazing sky.

It was beautiful. Truly and profoundly beautiful.

'It has a certain appeal, doesn't it?' a voice grated. 'Trust me when I tell you that it fades with time.'

Gaheris raised his blades as the figure stepped out of the shadows. He was immense, corpulent with borrowed power and aglow with baleful radiance. About him shone the golden light of his vision, singling him out as a true champion of the enemy. The plates of his armour glistened with a sheen of mucus as though freshly anointed. Five black scars broke the green-white monotony of his ruined breastplate and in his hands he bore a massive axe, its edge crackling, with a maw of chain-teeth nestled at the centre.

'Tuul,' Gaheris said at last.

The Death Guard evinced a bow with a growl of grinding servos and then laughed. 'I have that honour, yes,' he said and looked the Champion up and down. 'And you are the Emperor's Champion. I don't see your fancy sword. I had hoped to add it to my collection.' He gestured about him. 'So many holy things find their way to me. Plucked from their doomed bearers so that they might live on as an inspiration.'

'Your blasphemies no longer hold weight here,' Gaheris spat.

'Oh, they have weight,' Tuul said with an indulgent tilt of his

head. 'Especially here. This is where I have raised my temple.
The Plaguefather speaks to me, just as your Emperor speaks
to you.'

'His name is unworthy of your lips. You betrayed Him!'

'That could be argued, but if you had seen what I had seen
then you would not think it a betrayal.' Tuul hefted the axe
and stalked forward. 'No Black Sword... Such a pity... But I
will make a fine display of your armour.'

Above them fleshy sacks rattled around thin bones in the
toxic air, swaying like censers. Stubby insectoid forms crawled
and buzzed from the sacks, from the misshapen remains of what
had once been human beings. Some of the carrion-swollen
bees drifted down and alighted upon Tuul's armour, spreading their oil-on-water-patterned wings before burrowing into
the Plague Marine's flesh. He grunted dully, with resignation
and familiarity.

'One day soon, cousin, you will understand. All these games –
the moves and counter-moves – shall count for nothing.
Primarchs walk the galaxy once more and they will leave only
ashes in their wake.' He slapped the haft of his axe against his
gauntlet repetitively, the sound oddly wet and meaty. 'There
is only the dream of the black hand that will choke the stars
and the Crimson Path it will bleed homewards. That is what
you should put your faith in.' Tuul sighed with sudden weariness. 'One day all of this will end. Perhaps it will be today? I
have no intention of dying here and failing my master, yet the
universe is full of surprises.' The axe purred in his hands. 'Shall
we put it to the test?'

Gaheris hurled himself forwards, already swinging his blades
for Tuul's throat. The warrior turned the axe in one fluid
motion. The weapons ground together, sparks flaring from
their edges as teeth bit and power fields crackled against each
other, venting their caged lightning.

Tuul pushed and Gaheris staggered back. The Terminator-clad giant laughed and turned the weapon over and over in one massive hand.

'Sigismund would be ashamed of you,' Tuul goaded. 'Such anaemic simulacra you all prove to be. Children playing at being their idols.' He stalked forward and slammed the iron ferrule of the axe against Gaheris' chest, staggering the Champion.

Gaheris' grip upon both weapons tightened and he spun about. He felt the chainsword's teeth skitter across the Death Guard's accursed plate, before the power sword swept low. There was less resistance there as the blade hewed into the leg joint of Tuul's armour.

The Plague Marine laughed again, free of fear and devoid of pain.

'Is this all you have? The vaunted fury of the Black Templars? I was at Terra, you know. I was there when your forebear truly began to understand what he was made for. Your milk-blooded generations have lost that surety of purpose. It is no wonder that you need Guilliman to play king in order to restore your domains.' He laughed and swung the axe down. Pain flared in Gaheris' shoulder as he jerked back too slowly. 'The galaxy burns, *child*, and you are too weak to rise from the ashes.'

'I am His strength,' Gaheris whispered and pushed himself forwards. The chainsword snarled in his hand as he spun it in his grip and arced it downwards, unbalancing the other warrior's axe. He continued to fight and parry, moving and dodging, swaying between the Terminator's heavy-handed swipes. Pillars burst apart under the Death Guard's fury, shattering in a shower of debris and bleeding dust from their hissing wounds. Where one was gouged open a reliquary slid free and shattered in a burst of old bones and congealed unguents.

It became a dance, halting steps throughout the immensity of the sanctum. Creatures capered in the heights, giggling and hooting as they watched the eternal combat, the timeless conflict of man against man, each armoured in their own faith. One of the cooing things swung from a fleshy sack, stuffing a handful of bees into its ravenous maw.

Gaheris surrendered himself to the rhythm of combat. He embraced the moment, trusting to gene-forged instinct and the God-Emperor's guidance. Even without the reassuring weight of the Black Sword it felt right to fight as he fought now. It felt righteous.

Tuul, by contrast, continued to fight shaking with his own caustic mirth. Joy blossomed across his features as surely as any rash. Every cut into his armour or flesh provoked fresh humour, suppurating from his sore-ridden lips in a tide of hilarity.

They fought across the smooth marble floors, gouging great crevices into the stonework as they moved and swayed, blades clashing, weapons biting into plate. They fought as though they were the last paragons of Legion and Chapter, down through the relentless march of time, set against each other for the tawdry games of competing godheads.

Gaheris wondered how many of the weaknesses of base humanity had been bled from Tuul down the years to make him as he was, first erased by gifts from the God-Emperor's sacred science and then by the fell blessings of the Dark Gods who had replaced Him.

'I won't lie,' Tuul called. 'I expected better from an heir of Sigismund. Perhaps he would weep to see you so reduced. Weakness is anathema to great men, after all. So many of you must despise this Imperium you defend, an Imperium that my brothers and I built. Built upon mortal failings. Nothing more than a factory for sin and suffering. The prayer wheels turn and the gods laugh and grow fat – even your god.'

'He is mighty for we are weak. He is glorious as we are base. He is the light where we grub in darkness.'

'Such pretty words, each one hollow,' Tuul sneered. He swept the axe round and it slammed against Gaheris' chest in a jarring impact which sent the Champion staggering back, almost dropping his weapons.

This is what it means to be alive. Unbound. Readied for the purity of the moment.

He pushed forward, weapons battering against the immensity of Tuul. The powered blade hewed chasms into the monster's plate as the chainsword snagged and snarled alongside it. Tuul grunted and swung the flat of the axe's blade against Gaheris' head. An almighty crack resounded through the great space and the Champion stumbled, falling to his knees. Blood flowed across his vision and Gaheris shook it aside. He pushed down with his blades, trying to force his way back to his feet.

Tuul seized the Champion by the helm and hoisted him up, squeezing until the broken ceramite began to yield. He prised it apart, his rusted fingers pressing against Gaheris' head. Gaheris thrashed in his grip and Tuul laughed, before slamming him back against a column. Stone cracked along with his armour. Along with his skull. Gaheris tasted blood and blinked through pain.

'You should have stayed down,' Tuul mused.

Gaheris writhed, desperately trying to free himself. His weapons threatened to slip from his grasp as he flailed them against the Death Guard's legs and body, scraping and scoring the plate but failing to penetrate.

'Perhaps then I would have let you die with a little dignity, eh?'

The ship shook and dust drifted down upon Tuul's broad shoulders, like a shroud. The axe was resting at Gaheris' throat and he tried once more to rise. To die fighting.

'Consider this a mercy,' Tuul laughed and moved to cut the Black Templar's throat.

The ship shuddered again, wracked by fire, and Tuul spared a momentary glance upwards.

The dome cracked. The sound was like a thunderclap, turning the confines of the chamber suddenly close and intimate. Great shards of the dome began to tumble from above, their gold and silver designs shattered. An immense spear, like the hand of judgement itself, like the wrath of an angry god, had forced its way into the very meat of the ship. Thrown with a hunter's precision to pierce the *Promise*.

One of Katla's great void-harpoons.

Tuul's features knotted with confused fury. Gaheris threw himself up and drove the axe blade back and away from his throat. The entire ship was lurching, holed through and bleeding, and Gaheris forced Tuul back across the tilting deck. Columns toppled. Vast spans of the roof had caved in, impacting around them in showers of shattered masonry, trailing electromagnetic discharge from the enormous spear.

Tuul grunted as stone broke to powder against his armour, as the Champion's blades cut and gouged at him. He swung his axe around and caught Gaheris in the side, then grinned as the blades bit. Blood burned to dust and yet the Champion fought on. Rage and pain fuelled him, channelled into every strike. Gaheris slammed the chainsword into Tuul's side and felt it finally catch. He pushed it harder against the new wound and then drove the power sword up and into Tuul's breastplate.

Fluids gushed down the Death Guard's swollen chest. He growled and slammed his face against Gaheris'. The Champion let go of his chainsword and fell back. Tuul's fingers flexed and quivered as he reached for the blade that transfixed him.

'Some...' Tuul slurred. 'Some sport in you after all.'

'If I die here, monster, then you will die with me.' Gaheris reached to his belt with his free hand and drew a grenade. The Champion threw himself forwards.

His sword pierced the Plague Marine's gut and Gaheris' weight and momentum finally managed to bear him down. Gaheris let go of the blade and pulled himself up, jamming the grenade against the monster's throat. He felt the pin between his fingers and pulled. Tuul's grotesquely swollen hand reached for him. It clawed at his armour, massive digits tapping, seven times, against Gaheris' sacred plate.

Amidst the collapse and the scouring fire of the battle, a glorious sacrifice was born in the explosion.

Chapter Fifty

FINAL FLIGHT

SALVATION'S WINGS

FIRE AND GLORY

The *Wyrmslayer Queen*'s sweeping arc through the weapons fire and madness was arrested, for but a moment, when the harpoons finally found their mark. The great spears crossed the void in a rush of gleaming, crackling metal and immense chain and embedded themselves in the flank of the *Pilgrim's Promise*.

She watched air and bodies rush from the ship in a blood-like gout, momentarily pleased by the sight. The hunt was eternal. She had walked this galaxy for longer than most mortals had right to, her life drawn out by the poison promise of Idunni rejuvenat work, and in her time she had seen much – yet that truth was inescapable. The hunt was eternal. Whether they stalked the leviathans of the void-whale pods or the creatures of the hive fleets, or set out across the stars in search of stranger prey and places... this was the undertaking of eternity.

Katla sat enthroned and allowed herself a smile.

'Full burn!' she ordered and the ship lurched forwards, engines straining as it began to ponderously drag the enemy flagship out of its held position. The *Promise*'s engines lit with equal fury, blazing with strange colours and smoking heavily as the ancient engines burned their eldritch fuels. It was an ugly and ailing thing. By all rights it should be incapable of plying the void – yet here it was.

The chains began to wind back and the *Promise* struggled harder, thrashing like a living thing.

'Ah, but we are no strangers to unruly prey,' Katla laughed. 'Let them wriggle!' Cheers went up around her at her words. The crew's fear was a primal thing, ebbing and flowing like distant tides, but even the greatest of fears could be ridden out. Overcome.

The *Queen*'s desperate plunge through the battle had slowed, weighed down by the enemy ship, yet still the proud huntress clawed its way onwards, its prey pinned and ailing. The *Pilgrim's Promise*, wheezing and aflame, was dragged in the *Queen*'s wake despite its strongest efforts. Out from the ships and defensive fire it had sheltered behind, where now all could see it in its corroded majesty. The plague ship screamed in infective binharic, a scrapcode howl that caused systems to falter. Cogitators roared in their alcoves, chained and caged against the walls of the bridge, every surface covered in fresh wards; hololiths flickered madly and cast their insane light around the tight space. The smoke from the braziers was momentarily turned lurid with strange shapes and immaterial laughter.

Katla watched through the viewports as the battle shifted about them, contracting with the intrusion of the new vessels. Ragged warships of the crusade fleet brawled with the stolid mass of the enemy, even as pilgrim ships and transport hulks laboured to get close enough to disgorge their cargoes. Each one unloaded swarms of landers and lifters, each one likely rammed full of makeshift fighters.

Katla had seen void war before, many times. She had

commanded it with grace and as an ugly brawl of savage vessels.
Yet to hcr eye this was something different. The ships of the
makeshift fleet, forged from faith and cast upon the storm's tides,
fought with no regard for their own safety. They were fearless,
driven not by the uncaring fury of berserkers but with a determination that would shame even the Black Templars. Mortal
hands turned to sacred purpose.

Through the tumult, blazing with singular determination,
powered the *Terra Eterna*. Its guns did not cease or falter in the
conflagration but burned hotter and raged harder. Fire clung to
its shields and to the wound-scarred expanses of its hull, yet it
did not slow. It speared towards the *Pilgrim's Promise* like the
sweep of a god's sword, lances and macro-munitions scything
from it towards expertly picked targets. Nothing could touch
it, not truly. Every wound dealt to it was fleeting. Every pain
illusory. There was no hesitation in its progress, no doubt, no
pity or remorse. There was only righteousness.

The armoured prow of the great ship slammed into the
Pilgrim's Promise, catching it amidships and spinning it on its
axis. Explosions and great bursts of flame rocked the ship's
length. Casements and battlements slid away with all the fury
of a tectonic landslip. Yet, like its masters, the vessel refused
to die.

The *Eterna* soldiered on, guns still firing. For a moment it was
shrouded in fire, and then the flame unfurled like the snapping
of a banner in the wind. Drop-craft peeled away from the *Eterna*
in a wave, spreading out like the motions of vast wings, as they
swung away from the ship and then swept back in towards the
reeling immensity of the *Promise*. As one the hundreds of craft
descended upon the warped skin of the *Promise* and disgorged
their faithful cargo.

'Jarl!' someone called. 'We have a priority transmission. Overlord incoming.'

'The Champion?'

'No, jarl,' they countered. 'It's the Neophyte.'

Aneirin ran as the ship shook and tried to die around him, his hands locked around the Black Sword's handle with furious intensity.

Everything was reduced to fire and smoke – billowing up from the depths of the ship like the exhalation of a consumptive lung. Things moved in the smoke, flailing and screaming now, as though some guiding animus had been cut free. Bloated mutant things, their corpse-flesh rippling with furious internal motion, dashed themselves against the walls until tentacles snapped free and cysts burst, disgorging maggots and rivers of pus.

He ignored them and pressed on through the smoke. The route unspooled in his mind as he forged on, down through winding corridors and stone stairways from another time and place. Muralled walls passed by in a blur, their surfaces reduced to smears as he rushed onwards. The Black Sword was a reassuring weight in his hands. Time and again he found it rising, almost unbidden, yearning to be wielded with a martial fervour he almost felt he didn't possess.

Aneirin rounded a corner and came face to face with two of the Death Guard. One was already raising a bolter while the other hefted a rusted axe-rake. Aneirin moved almost by instinct. The Black Sword was singing in his hands, rising to meet the foe. It turned aside the first bolter and the shot went wide. Aneirin ducked under the axe-rake's swipe and spun, cleaving through armour and flesh, moving past and through them. He turned and drove the powered tip of the blade through the mucus-drooling faceplate of the gunman, hammering it through with such force that it impacted the stonework behind its head, pinning it in place.

Aneirin grunted with the sudden effort. He felt momentarily

overwhelmed. To bear the blade was a great honour and yet to kindle its power field, to use it in combat... it felt almost akin to blasphemy. As though he had erred.

He watched the impure blood cooking from the blade's energy field. Golden light pulsed along the blade's edge and flickered upwards, drifting with the ashen blood, coiling about the steam and smoke that rose from the blade. His eyes caught on each individual mote of light, seeing the suggestion of glorious eternity within them.

A burning Throne, wreathed in chains.

Eight terrible shadows, their long skeletal hands reaching out to crush the holy light of the God-Emperor.

Golden eyes opening in the face of a child, filled with ancient knowledge.

He blinked away the visions, even as the acrid after-images seared across his retinas. Reality returned and the light retreated with the sigh of grace being withdrawn, a gift rescinded. The grey stone-clad walls of the ship with their subtle veins of encrusted jewels and inlaid silver were before him again and he willed himself onwards through the vessel's innards.

The ship was in turmoil. Moment by moment, inch by inch, it was dying and yet burning with resurgent life. Aneirin wanted to stand and fight. Every part of his being screamed with the need to serve His will.

The sword in his hand, though. It spoke of the duty to come. It was a relic of the Chapter. The inheritance of Sigismund. Above all other things it had to be preserved. Gaheris had willed it so. As a Champion, and as a brother.

Nothing could stop him. The Black Sword burned like a beacon in his hands as it split skulls and shattered armour. Plague Marines fell back, opened from crown to pelvis. Cultists were split in half or decapitated, with barely a grunt of effort. The sword turned aside bullets and blunted other blades. He fought with only a single care – to survive and bear the weapon to where it belonged.

Aneirin burst out into the hangar deck through a storm of loyalist bolt-shells. The Overlord's guns burned incessantly, firing madly to repel the near-ceaseless tide of filthy and rotting bodies that threw themselves forwards. He barrelled through the ranks of the enemy and the Black Sword flashed out, its edge blazing with disruptor field energy. A twitching thing of dried flesh and bird-thin bones burst apart, practically vaporised by the impact.

He rushed through the dust of the dead cultist and up the ramp of the Overlord.

'Hargus!' he yelled. 'Techmarine Hargus!'

'Quiet, boy,' a voice growled in response. 'We are about the God-Emperor's business here. This cordon must be held until the Champion and the others can–'

'The Champion is dead,' Aneirin stated bluntly and held up the sword. 'His last order was that I return the sword to the Chapter and tell them what has come to pass here. I take that instruction as holy writ, Techmarine. Will you honour the Emperor-Omnissiah and bear that message back to the fleet? Back out and to the crusade and the Chapter?'

Hargus was silent for a moment before the Overlord's engines began to cycle up. The craft shuddered and rose into the air, firing again into the throng out of nothing more than spite, before it swivelled on its axis and burned out into the void.

Aneirin let himself fall to his knees, the tip of the blade pressed to the decking and his forehead pressed against the crossguard of the sword.

'By His will am I made whole. By His guidance am I led to battle. By His glory am I made pure.'

* * *

'In His wrath are we armed! With His hate are we shielded! By His judgement do we end the enemies of humanity! Stand firm, brothers and sisters! Sons and daughters of the Emperor!'

Irinya's words echoed through the belly of the great ship, ringing like the tolling of an almighty bell, as she hammered down the stone corridors. Her passage had changed the very fabric of the place and now the stolid, long-dead relics of the past were aglow and ablaze. Every surface crawled with fire and faces snapped and leered from the flame, the long dead momentarily recalled to the places they had fallen and been defiled. She carried the light and the revelation. The fire of Velua clung to her and sang within her blood. Suspended between life and death she had known His truth.

They spoke with *His* words of fire and glory. They chanted, over and over again, their oaths to the Throne. The dead whispered and prayed and begged for vengeance. Beatrice was there with them, demanding her own vindication, and Teneu spoke with her. The dead of a world, of worlds beyond count, of an empire, howled in the walls of the ship, spilling forth their own chronicles of ashes and pain.

Her blade was constantly in motion, aflame and caged in light. Where it touched the enemy faltered and withered. Rusted blades found her but she no longer felt pain. She was above it. Beyond it. Her wounds bled only fire. She could see everything. Understand everything. An entire life sacrificed to the altar of this moment, to be reborn through an offering in flame.

Agata was with her, and Josefine. Angharad was there and even Rugrenz had come, his black coat snapping about him like the shroud of some grotesquely risen corpse. Around them swarmed the makeshift warriors of Velua, the pilgrims and civilians who had taken up arms alongside the soldiers.

All spared their appointed hour to fight now, and die at last in His name.

The God-Emperor had set this task before her. Sanctified it with the death and life of Velua. He spoke in many voices, and yet still they had come to the same moment as the Black Templars. Where each was needed most. She could see it now. A great tapestry of lives woven together by an awareness greater than worlds. By His hand and His will was the cosmos ordered and all things made right. A singular purpose, shining throughout the galaxy, burning all the way from Holy Terra to the galaxy's edge. One day the Halo Stars would burn with His light, and shadow and flame would be dispelled.

She had faith. She believed, with all the certainty of her heart, that it would be so. Irinya did not have to live to see it. None of them did. There was only this moment, played out across the fleet, in battle after battle. The faithful set against the impure.

Men and women fought around her with everything at their disposal. Bolter and blade. Las and autogun. Knives and grenades. Melta-charges and hand flamers. Some beat against the enemy with their bare hands before being cut down.

'The blood of martyrs is the seed of the Imperium!' she bellowed. 'By your sacrifice is His will done!'

Voices chorused around her, united in sacred purpose, ringing off the walls of stone and corroded metal. There were fewer and fewer of the trappings of stolen shrines as they moved on, the looted iconography replaced by the ruined districts of the enginarium.

The things set against them ceased to be identifiably Astartes or cultists – monsters of waxy, running flesh and warped iron. Stilt-legged things with grasping manipulator limbs, mecha-dendrites writhing as though tasting the air. Irinya's blade clattered against great rusted hooks, driving back a screaming horror, its binharic agonies broadcast freely for all to hear.

The enginarium crawled with nightmares, an insectoid hive of terrible industry – now disturbed.

Zealous warriors fell. Rugrenz came apart in a flash of melta-beams and a rush of sudden gore. He barely even had the chance to cry out as he died. Others took his place. There was no time to mourn, no chance to retrieve the bodies of the fallen. Agata stepped into the breach, over the commissar's remains, and began to fire. Sacred promethium climbed the walls and caught at the ragged black robes of the enemy. Things roared and howled with too many mouths as they burned, staggering back before they fell and were silent.

Irinya cleaved another limb from the hook-handed monster, forcing it down before she slammed her blade through its neck. The head tumbled free with a screech of scrapcode and a spurt of tainted oil. Pain blossomed in her shoulder as something else clawed at her. She shrugged it off, pushing on under gantries hung with withered bodies, a gallows offering for the gods of the machine.

The narrow corridors had opened up into expansive spaces, cathedrals of iron built in ages past to honour their monumental occupants. The ages had been cruel, though, and the great machines had become the strange hearts of the ancient vessel. Great swathes of flesh undulated in cages of steel, beating around cores of entrapped plasma. The transformed engines squirmed and writhed with continual motion, like enormous, pulsing organs. Eyes rippled along their surfaces. Eyes and wheels and fire, turning and blazing in the plague-ridden dark like the stories of ancient angels.

Irinya threw herself forward, blade up and ready.

Metal parted and yet it was the flesh beneath that offered more resistance. The daemonic form of the ship's engines lashed out with pseudopods of rotting meat, clawing at Irinya's armour. She felt the echo of pain, the distant suggestion of it as her armour and flesh parted just as she was gouging apart the daemon engine. Last Light spoke again and the tendril burned away, spasming in the toxic air as the fire consumed it.

Gunfire poured into the gaps she was carving. Her warriors hurled their bodies into the engine with nothing but blades, as they affixed their melta-charges in place and let them detonate.

Around her all was fire and death, wreathed in the God-Emperor's golden light. She felt the reassuring hand at her shoulder and heard, in that last moment, Teneu's words at her ear.

'*By your sacrifice shall the way be lit and the wounds avenged.*'

Irinya began to laugh. Even as the engines began to die around her and fire swelled up to consume the mockery of the holy worlds, Irinya Sarael died laughing in the face of the enemy with joy in her heart.

She burned with holy fire as she embraced her fate and hacked and carved out her place in the God-Emperor's great design. As she, with sword and song, prepared her final resting place.

Her martyr's tomb.

Epilogue

No one had looked back. No one had dared to.

Behind them, in the nameless scrap of what had once been a system, ships continued to fight and die in futility. They did not see the immense detonation which roared from the belly of the *Promise*, nor the explosions which caught the *Terra Eterna* and crippled its bridge, sending it yawing out and into the wider conflagration.

The *Wyrmslayer Queen* and her crew understood well enough what was coming to pass: others died so that they might live, might carry the message of the place's import back to those who demanded to know it. The regent called and against all odds, Katla would answer.

Behind the great ship they left a trail of bodies – the odious dead of the enemy cast out into the void without rite or ceremony. Death clung to the vessel like a curse, wreathing it in a charnel air.

Within it was little better.

They had found Yazran, his optics fused and staring into the infinite, his systems and records defiled by what could only have been enemy action. Katla had sent the body to the medicae decks for preservation. Cold and marked with silver, rune-etched with wards of healing and aversion, swaddled in the pale and chill light of a distant place of winter and war.

She had come to the medicae decks alone, to where she had faced down death before, and paid her respects to Augustus. A keener loss than Yazran, though she found herself loath to admit it. Augustus had lain there, his armour rent and stained with precious blood, his noble features pale from exsanguination. They had found him surrounded by the bodies of countless foes – dozens upon dozens of cultists and Heretic Astartes, none left alive before his wrath. He had sold his life dearly so that Katla could live.

'Too much of that abounds,' she had whispered to herself, and reached out. Her hand had paused, trembling mere inches from his corpse. She couldn't bring herself to touch him and instead had turned and left the chamber.

Now Katla stood upon the bridge and allowed herself, at last, to look at their prize. Behind the battle, dwarfing it utterly, the Gate loomed. Sheer walls of immaterial fire had peeled back, opening a gaping wound in the fabric of the Rift. Lightning bolts larger than orbital plates lashed out from one side to the other in arcing discharges which could shred battlefleets. Dead and dying ships had lodged in the flames, slowly succumbing to ruin as the infernal conflagration consumed them.

The horror of the Rift still fluctuated and shuddered across the surface of the materium, but now something else shone through. The golden light that kindled there made hope swell within her heart as she looked upon it.

'He would have been proud,' a voice cut in. 'Augustus. To know that he died with his duty done. Few can ask for more.'

She turned and smiled gently.

Aneirin stood before her, divested of his armour, wearing only the white robes of an Initiate. His wounds had been tended and his armour repaired to the best of her crew's ability, but he had eschewed it with an almost penitent intensity.

He still carried the Black Sword, she noticed, as though he would not, or could not, bear to be parted from it.

'The chains are cut,' she said. 'The enemy lies behind us and others have given their lives to ensure that we survive. You to bear your blade, and I to bear ill news to the regent. A way exists – unstable and compromised, lit only by faith, and known to the enemy. Perhaps we have striven only in futility.'

'I do not believe it is folly and futility, captain,' Aneirin said simply. 'He has put these trials in our way for a reason. Champions rise fleetingly and another rises to replace them – as surely as a Warrant of Trade is passed on. Duty is a chain, made of mortal servants, binding us inexorably to Him. The links can be decades old, centuries even, or they can stretch back millennia to the very dawn of our Imperium.'

'You speak with wisdom that belies your youth, Initiate,' she said with a sad smile.

'War makes philosophers of us all, eventually,' he mused. 'That or corpses.'

'Where does that leave us then?' Katla asked.

Aneirin held the Black Sword up for a moment, turning it in the bridge's pale light, before he knelt and held it tip down against the stone floor before the viewport.

'All we have is our duty, captain. All we have are our oaths. Beyond these storms and trials my Chapter waits, to receive the Sword and Gaheris' judgement upon me.' He paused and swallowed. 'If it is within my power to do so I shall defend you upon your journey. Wherever you must go to deliver your message to the regent in person. If I must stand before the primarch and my Chapter to give my account then I shall do so.' He looked up at Katla. 'Augustus was your shield. I shall now bear that mantle until such time as you no longer require me.'

'You have my thanks, Aneirin,' Katla said and reached out, placing her hand upon his robed shoulder. 'The Allfather of Man is wise beyond measure. He has brought us here for a reason. And we shall seek that purpose together. No matter where it leads us, or at what cost.'

Appendix: Notes on the Crusade

As the Indomitus Crusade approached the conclusion of its first decade, war continued to rage across the Imperium. When launched, Guilliman's grand reconquest was comparable in size to the mythical Great Crusade of the Emperor Himself. As the years drew on and outright victory proved elusive, optimism waned in all but the most fanatical, and some in high command feared that the Indomitus Crusade might one day exceed the centuries-long duration of the Great Crusade, if it ever ended at all.

A HUNDRED THOUSAND WARS

Worlds burned as the forces of the Great Enemy attacked everywhere and xenos races proliferated. We have previously examined some of the major warzones that engulfed whole sectors of the Imperial segmenta, but in truth the violence spread far beyond these readily identifiable areas of conflict.

A case in point are the seven sacred shine worlds of the Golden Chain. Spread across a cluster of closely placed star systems in the north of the Cirillo Sector, near where the Great Rift cut the Ultima Segmentum in two, despite their relative strategic insignificance, the planets of the Golden Chain were exactly the kind of prize the Great Enemy delighted in taking. As previously discussed, the shrine worlds of the Segmentum Solar were a prime target for the blasphemous Word Bearers, whose lord Kor Phaeron wished to deal the Imperium a metaphysical blow by turning their populations from the light of the God-Emperor. Kor Phaeron was far from the only iconoclast among the Chaos forces; each of the worshippers of the false gods had their own habits of desecration.

Yet it was not only the most famous or the most sacred of such planets that drew in the followers of Chaos like corpse flies to a battlefield. Though the worlds of the Chain were not ranked among the most important of the Adeptus Ministorum's holdings, to the followers of the Plague God, the seven planets that comprised this Ecclesiarchical demesne were far too tempting a target. Similar in character and culture, Nema, Tandria, Asininia, St Jowet, Beneficia, Palrec and Velua were each home to the relics of innumerable Imperial saints. Their cities were soaring loci of worship, full of cathedra and mausolea. Outside the walls of their holy cities they were somewhat diverse, three of them agri worlds, two industrial, one classified as an ocean planet, and only Velua, the last to fall, seeing the majority of its surface covered in religio-urban sprawl – but in their devotion to the Emperor and the holiness of the artefacts they guarded, they were the same.

The Death Guard arrived at these planets in force, and commenced besieging and reducing them one by one. As each world fell, it was transformed into one of the foetid hellscapes the Plague God delights in. The holy places of the Emperor, the remains of His servants and the relics they left behind were systematically defiled. Strategically, this approach made little sense. Historitors examining the campaign surmise that the Death Guard could have taken most of the worlds in one blow, but as always when trying to divine purpose in the actions of the Great Enemy, it pays well to see these events not as acts of war, but of worship.

A SHIELD OF FAITH

Once more, the forces of the Adepta Sororitas and the Adeptus Astartes Black Templars rallied to the defence of the Emperor's most holy planets. Both these organisations played a major role in the Indomitus Crusade, not because of their numbers, which lacked the overpowering force of the Imperial Regent's massed armies of Primaris Space Marines, but because of something not even Roboute Guilliman could have foreseen.

Miraculous events appeared to take place. Visions guided the Emperor's warriors to the places they could do the most good, a crucial and often overlooked factor in the salvation of a number of worlds while the galaxy was still reeling from the after-effects of the Rift's opening.

Rare stories of divine intervention were reported from battle-fields. Battle Sisters, Black Templars, even the lowliest Astra Militarum trooper or cowering civilian might serve as His vessel to work His wrath upon His enemies. There were those in the Ecclesiarchy who proclaimed this was an era of saints, and of amazing deeds. Even the Imperial Regent himself came to ruminate upon these strange events.

Some scholars among the Adeptus Astra Telepathica and the more esoterically inclined sects of the Adeptus Mechanicus saw only raw psykana at work, and framed their warnings accordingly. After all, the incidence of psykers was rising rapidly across the worlds of the Imperium, the galaxy was flooded with raw warp power, and the base deceptions of the Dark Powers knew no limit in their insidiousness.

However, the manifestation of apparent miraculous occurrences, even in places where psykers were otherwise unable to function, hinted to some that something else was at work. Those same aesthetes suggested that the presence of His servants allowed a conduit of sorts to be formed, allowing psykana to function where otherwise it would not. But to the Emperor's more ardent worshippers the answer was far simpler, and indeed self-explanatory – the belief of the faithful allowed His hand to touch the world of mortals. To them, He was working to preserve His people. And so amid the despair and the endless war, a little hope was born, even as more cynical heads warned against hope's facile comforts, for in a universe forever in conflict, and bedevilled by malevolent gods, nothing is ever so pure or so simple as it can first appear.

THE SEARCH FOR A PASSAGE THROUGH THE STORM

As the Days of Darkness abated and the scattered possessions of mankind in Imperium Sanctus found ways to regain contact with Terra, Imperium Nihilus remained dark. The fate of a full half of the Imperium was unknown. When a brief contact was made, the truth of the situation was revealed – Imperium Nihilus persisted. Although still denied the light of the Astronomican, some Imperial worlds on the far side of the Cicatrix Maledictum survived, albeit in terrible straits. Many others, it seemed, had not.

Only one known stable passage across the Rift existed, at the Nachmund Gauntlet. From early on in the Era Indomitus, a great war raged between Imperial, Chaos, and xenos forces around the Nachmund System, which anchored the far end of the conduit, and this would continue for decades. Guilliman could not cross there.

Instead, Guilliman decided to seek out an alternative route. This would allow him to bring aid to the beleaguered system in the galactic north, establish centres of resistance, and return worlds to Imperial governance where the situation was less parlous. But his ultimate goal became to circle around behind the Chaos armadas at Nachmund, attack them from both sides of the Rift simultaneously, and put them to flight.

The regent spent many hours examining astropathic missives and cartographic data gathered by his agents, most of a sort those advisors not involved in the plan thought beneath him. Alongside his own efforts, he quietly despatched numerous rogue traders, many of whom were formerly part of the crucial torchbearer fleets that brought Primaris technology to beleaguered Space Marine Chapters in need of reinforcements, to travel the length of the Cicatrix Maledictum. These adventurous captains uncovered some small gaps, some more permanent than others, but nearly all were perilous, and none could accommodate the size of force Guilliman wished to deploy. As more information came from Imperium Nihilus, and the desperate messages of faraway astropaths became more numerous, Guilliman's resolve only strengthened. He must at least force a stalemate in the galactic south.

Finally, a suitable route was found by the rogue trader Katla Helvintr. Named the Attilan Gate for a world nearby, it was far from stable, gradually expanding, then collapsing violently. Yet this cycle was stable, and early exploration proved the gate not only navigable, but large enough to allow many ships passage. Even so, its instability meant crossing it would require something from the primarch that was at odds with his character.

Guilliman would have to make a leap of faith.

But first, before this grand endeavour could be undertaken, new threats would arise...

ABOUT THE AUTHOR

Marc Collins is a speculative fiction author living and working in Glasgow, Scotland. He is the writer of the Warhammer Crime novel *Grim Repast*, as well as the short story 'Cold Cases', which featured in the anthology *No Good Men*. For Warhammer 40,000 he has written the novels *Void King*, *Helbrecht: Knight of the Throne* and a number of short stories. When not dreaming of the far future he works in Pathology with the NHS.

YOUR
NEXT READ

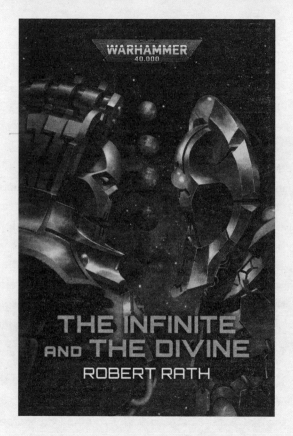

THE INFINITE AND THE DIVINE
by Robert Rath

Trazyn the Infinite and Orikan the Diviner are opposites. Each is obsessed with
their own speciality, and their rivalry spans millennia. Yet together, they may hold
the secret to saving the necron race…

An extract from
The Infinite and the Divine
by Robert Rath

Ancient stories, passed from the lips of spirit-singer to spirit-singer, held that anyone who touched the stone would burn.

Thy hand shall curl and turn black
Thy back-teeth glow white-hot
Thy bones crack like fire-logs
For I have drunk from elder suns

The songs held that the gemstone was a meteorite. Wandering, semi-sentient. Absorbing the energy of each star it passed. During the War in Heaven, it was said that warriors had used it to channel the gods themselves.

Trazyn, however, had learned long ago not to believe the absurdities of aeldari folklore. Ancient though their race was, they were still given to the follies of an organic brain.

Trazyn had travelled the galaxy for so long he'd forgotten what year he'd started. Collecting. Studying. Ordering the cultures of the cosmos.

And one thing he'd learned was that every society thought their mountain was special. That it was more sacred than the mountain worshipped by their neighbouring tribe. That it was the one true axis of the universe.

Even when informed that their sacred ridge was merely the random connection of tectonic plates, or their blessed sword a very old but relatively common alien relic – a revelation they universally did not appreciate, he found – they clung to their stories.

Which is not to say there were not gods in the firmament, of course. Trazyn knew there were, because he had helped kill them. But he'd also found that most of what societies took to be gods were inventions of their own, charmingly fanciful, imaginations.

But though he did not believe the gem channelled ancient gods, that did not mean it wasn't worth having – or worth the aeldari protecting.

Indeed, the sounds of a siege echoed through the bone halls.

Trazyn allowed a portion of his consciousness to stray, if only to monitor the situation. Part of his mind worked the problem at hand, the other looked through the oculars of his lychguard captain.

Through the being's eyes, Trazyn saw that his lychguard phalanx still held the gates of the temple. Those in the front rank had locked their dispersion shields in a wall, each raising their hyperphase sword like the hammer of a cocked pistol. Behind them, those in the second rank held their warscythes as spears, thrusting them over the shoulders of their comrades so the entire formation bristled with humming blades.

Perfectly uniform, Trazyn noticed. And perfectly still.

Exodite bodies littered the steps before them – feather-adorned mesh armour split with surgical-straight lines, limbs and heads detached. His olfactory sensors identified particles of cooked muscle in the air.

Another attack was massing. In the garden plaza before the temple, where five dirt streets converged, aeldari Exodites flitted between decorative plants and idols carved from massive bones.

In the distance, he could see the lumbering form of a great

lizard, long necked and powerful, with twin prism cannons slung on its humped back. Trazyn marked it as a target for the two Doom Scythes flying a support pattern overhead.

Shuriken rounds swept in, rattling the necron shields like sleet on a windowpane. One disc sailed into the ocular cavity of a lychguard and lodged there, bisecting the grim fire of his eye. The warrior did not react. Did not break formation. With a shriek of protesting metal, the living alloy of his skull forced the monomolecular disc free and it fluttered to the steps like a falling leaf.

Trazyn looked at the pattern of it through the captain's vision. Circular, with double spiral channels. A common aeldari design, not worth acquiring.

He sensed a change in the air and looked up to see the first Doom Scythe streaking down in an attack run. At the last moment the great lizard heard it, rotating around its serpentine head to stare at the incoming comet.

A beam of white-hot energy lanced from the Doom Scythe's fuselage, tracing a line of flame through the lush undergrowth. It passed through the creature's long neck and the top third of it fell like a cut tree branch. The great body staggered, heeled, stayed upright. Then the next Doom Scythe lanced it through the midsection and set off the payload on its prism cannons. Cascading detonations tore the creature apart, the purple energy blast throwing the weapons crew hundreds of cubits away.

Pity, Trazyn thought as he watched the carcass burn. *I wanted one of those.*

But he had no time for such side projects. Conch shell horns sounded across the rainforest-girdled spires of the city, and already he could see more great lizards lumbering towards the temple. One rotated a twin-barrelled shuriken cannon towards the sky and began spitting fire at the retreating Scythes.

Though they were primitive, once the Exodites marshalled their numbers his small acquisition force would be overwhelmed.

Cepharil was awakening to defend its World Spirit.

Trazyn left the lychguard captain's body, rejoined his consciousness, and focused on the task at hand.

Before him stretched a long wraithbone corridor, likely salvaged from whatever craftworld these fundamentalists had used to begin their self-imposed exile. Bas-relief carvings depicting the society's exodus, fashioned from the bones of the great lizards, decorated the walls.

Trazyn had been scrying for traps, detecting pressure plates and a huge mechanical fulcrum hidden in the masonry. Beyond that waited the cyclopean gates of the inner chamber.

He finished his calculations and saw the way through.

Trazyn picked up his empathic obliterator and strode into the corridor.

Eyeholes in the bas-reliefs coughed, sending clouds of bone darts clattering off his necrodermis. Trazyn snatched one out of the air and analysed the tip: an exotic poison derived from a local marine invertebrate, unique to this world.

He slipped it into a dimensional pocket and continued forward, sensing a stone shift and sink beneath him.

A piece of masonry, hammer-shaped and weighing six tons, swept down at him like a pendulum. Trazyn waved at it without stopping, the stasis projection from his palm emitter halting its progress mid-swing. He passed it without a glance, its surface vibrating with potential energy.

Finally, the gate. Tall as a monolith, it was decorated with exquisite carvings of aeldari gods. A vertical strip of runes laid out a poem-riddle so fiendish, it would stop even the wisest if they did not know the obscure lore of the–

'*Tailliac sawein numm*,' intoned Trazyn, turning sideways so he could slip through the gates as they ground open.

Normally, he would have put some effort into it. Solved it by thought, then performed a textual analysis. Trazyn enjoyed riddles. They revealed so much about the cultures that shaped them. But a noemic notice from his lychguards suggested that the Exodites were pressing harder than anticipated. No time for amusing diversions.

He hadn't paused to process the meaning of the runes, just fed them through his lexigraphic database and cross-referenced double meanings, inferences and mythological connotations. Even now, he could not have explained what the answer to the riddle was, or what it meant. It was merely a linguistic equation, a problem with an answer.

An answer that had brought him into the presence of the World Spirit.

The chamber swept up around him like a cavernous grotto, its upper reaches lost in the echoing vaults of the ceiling. His metal feet sounded off a causeway, its wraithbone marbled with veins of gold. Filigreed balustrades on either side mimicked the corals of the ocean depths, for Cepharil was a world of warm seas and lush archipelagos. On either side of the walkway, pools of liquid platinum cast watery light across the walls.

'Now,' he muttered to himself. 'Where are you, my lovely?'

Before him rose the World Spirit.

It curved ahead, inlayed into the vaulted surface of the far wall. It too was made of bone, but rather than the old, inert wraithbone of the walls and ceiling this sprouted alive from the floor, branching like a fan of tree roots that had grown up instead of down.

No, Trazyn corrected, that was not quite accurate. His oculars stripped away the outer layers of the World Spirit, refocusing on the veins of energy that ran through the psychoactive material. Arcane power pulsed to and fro in a circulatory system, racing through arteries and nerves as it travelled to the highest forks of the network and back to the floor. Not roots, then – antlers. Yes, that was it, a great set of antlers, large as a mountain, the points of its forks curving away from the wall. Here and there it sprouted buds, fuzzy with new growth.

Exquisite.

Stepping closer, Trazyn appraised the object. The substance was not wraithbone, he noted, at least not entirely. This was a hybrid, a substitute, grown from the skeletons of the great lizards and interwoven with the psycho-plastic wraithbone salvaged from their crashed ship. A gene-sequence scry failed to find where one substance began and the other ended, no points where the ancient craftsman had fused or grafted the two materials together. This was a seamless blend, nurtured and shaped over millions of years, wraithbone woven between the molecules of reactive, but lower quality, dinosaurid remains. A masterwork by one of the finest bonesingers in the galaxy, an act of artistry and devotion that was at once temple, mausoleum and metropolis. A place for the souls of his slain aeldari ancestors to be at rest, united and safeguarded from the hungry gods of the aether.

Trazyn carried towards it on tireless legs, craning his hunched neck to see where the highest forks disappeared in the darkness of the vault. Once, his own kind had been able to accomplish works such as this. But the process of biotransference, the blighted gift that had moved their consciousness to deathless metal bodies, had also burned away nearly all artistry. His kind were no longer artisans or poets. Those few that retained the knack found their powers diminished. Now they forged rather than created. A work that took this much care, this much love, was beyond them.

Such a shame he could not take the whole thing.

Given time he could extract it, perhaps even lock the entire temple in a stasis field and transplant it whole to his historical gallery on Solemnace. To have the gemstone in its original context would be a rare coup. But somehow these primitives had sensed the coming of his acquisition phalanx, and there was no time. In truth, he had broken protocol by waking even thirty of the lychguard before their time. Doing so had damaged their neural matrices, making them little more than automatons that followed tactical programs and explicit commands.

But if they could not remember this expedition, so much the better – Trazyn was not supposed to be here anyway.

He approached the base of the World Spirit – the chamber was a full league across – and beheld the true genius of its creation.

The structure sprouted from the skull of a predator lizard twice Trazyn's height, its lower jaw removed and sickle-like upper teeth buried in the wraithbone floor. A glow, like the orange light cast by wind-stoked embers, emanated from the cavities of the creature's eye sockets.

Trazyn's vision stripped away layers of bone and he saw the gemstone embedded in the predator's fist-sized brain cavity.

'A carnosaur. Astonishing.'

He brushed a metal hand over the skull's cranium, an emitter in the palm casting electromagnetic radiation through its core.

It was old. Older than he had thought possible. Indeed, perhaps Trazyn should have tempered his dismissal of the aeldari tales, for it was indeed a meteorite, and one of extreme antiquity and unknown make-up. He reviewed the spectromantic divination results manually, to confirm its findings. Given the age of the components, their degradation, and the style on the beam-cut faces of the gem, it was entirely possible that it dated from the War in Heaven.

A delicious shiver passed through Trazyn's circuitry.

'Well met, my dear,' he said, his cooing tone offset by the hollow echo of his vocal emitter. 'It is not so often that I meet a thing as old as I am.'

He was so entranced, in fact, that he did not see the dragon riders coming.

Deep focus tended to dim his circumspection protocols, and the beasts' footfalls had been masked via training and sorcery.

And for all his inputs, scryers, protocols and diviners, the movements of the empyrean were muffled in his senses. When it came to warp sorcery, he was like a deaf man at a dinner table, able to make out words through dampened sounds and lip-reading, but unable to even notice the voices behind his back.

An interstitial alert flashed in his vision and he wheeled, dialling back his chronosense to slow the world and give himself time to calculate a microsecond decision.

Scales, claws and sawtooth fangs were about to break down on him like a wave – twenty cavalry riding knee to knee in tight formation, wraithbone lances braced, tattooed swirls on arrowhead-sharp faces. Scrimshawed charms dangled from the halters of their raptor mounts, each leather harness crisscrossing a scaled snout that ended in flared nostrils and hooked teeth. The raptors – underwater slow in Trazyn's enhanced vision – swung their avian frames low, shifting weight to their bunched haunches in preparation for a final lunge.

One lance came at him so directly, its tip looked like a circle in his vision.

Minimal options, none attractive. But his proximity to the World Spirit had at least given him a moment to act as they pulled their charge, afraid of smashing into their venerated ancestral tomb.

Trazyn slid left, past the first lance tip.

Before the warrior could swing the long weapon around, Trazyn gripped the haft and tore the tattooed Aspect Warrior from his saddle. He watched the rider's face twist as he fell from the mount, long hair flying free and hands sheltering his face as he tumbled to the bone floor.

Trazyn, who is called Infinite, a voice said. It was not audible speech. Nor was it telepathy, to which he was immune. Instead, it was a wavelength of psychic pulses pushing on his auditory transducer to mimic language. One of these riders must be a farseer.

He ignored it.

The riderless raptor struck at him, jaws closing on the place where his ribcage met his hooded neck. Trazyn had overcommitted himself and could not dodge.

You will not keep what you seek.

Hooked teeth met the cold surface of his necrodermis – and shattered.

Trazyn channelled kinetic force into his fist and punched the dinosaur in the throat.

Vertebrae popped, cartilage tore. The raptor went down with the noise of a bugle player experiencing sudden and unbearable agony.

Listen to the song. This world sings for the blood of Trazyn.

And it was true – even through the syrupy haze of slowed time he could hear the keening chants of the knights. That he did not have blood was no matter, these aeldari wanted it anyway.

But their formation was not optimised to deal with a single opponent. It was jumbling, folding as the knights tried to get to him. And he had just created a gap.

As the unit tried to wheel on itself, Trazyn slipped through the hole in the line – making sure to step on the fallen warrior on his way through.

Behind him, riders collided and mixed.

'Aeldari,' he scoffed. 'So old and wise. You are children to us.'

This World Spirit is our ancestry, Trazyn. Our culture. Our dead. And it will wither without the Solar Gem.

That's when Trazyn saw the carnosaur. He'd missed it before

now, his focus overwhelmed by the charging raptor riders and senses clouded by witchery. It reared above him, its well-muscled chest protected by a breastplate shaped from dinosaurid bone, twin-linked shuriken cannons emerging like tusks from its chin. Serrated blades fashioned from the teeth of aquatic predators studded the armour plates clamped to its feet and spine. A calcium scythe capped its lashing tail.

And on its back, the farseer – her willow-thin face half-covered by the mask of an unfamiliar god, graceful frame armoured in mother-of-pearl, and pink hair gathered into a topknot.

We have long known that you desire it, but if you take it, the World Spirit will die.

'If you knew I was coming,' Trazyn said. 'You should have made a contingency plan.'